FOTUS

A NOVEL

★ ★ ★

Kevin Kunundrum

bancroft press

Cover and Interior design: Tracy Copes
Published by Bancroft Press
"Books that Enlighten"
410-358-0658
P.O. Box 65360, Baltimore,
MD 21209 410-764-1967 (fax)
www.
Bancroftpress.
Com
Printed in the United States of America

ISBN 978-1-61088-489-1 Hardcover
ISBN 978-1-61088-490-7 Paperback

bancroft
press

"The people will not revolt.

They will not look up from their screens

long enough to notice what's happening."

—George Orwell, *1984*

Sometime in the very near future...

PART ONE

THE RISE

"Cerebro inane gaudium impleatur."
—Alexander Jackson Rett

1

I saw how it is out there. Out there it's a mess, a nightmare, a disaster.

But in here, inside, it's safe. It's the safest place on Earth.

2

Of course I didn't *see*, not at first. It's not like the womb is well-lit. Okay, some backtracking is in order. Consider this my memoir, from me to you via the minuscule keyboard display on my minusculer (is that a word?) smartphone. I thought about getting a laptop, but being a fetus in the womb, I don't have much of a lap. And since I'm not going to exit this personal Nirvana anytime soon, the smartphone is just fine. And not surprisingly, having tiny prenatal hands with even tinier prenatal fingers, I can race over the keyboard like an Olympian, like Usain Freakin' Bolt, my fingers a veritable blur! So I guess we've reached the point in human evolution where being "all thumbs" is a good thing, and where the most perfect, indisputable, unassailable, infallible leader to ever occupy the once unsullied office of President of the United States has been realized. The fetus. Yours truly.

And yeah, my parents *did* give me a name, although technically it's unofficial, since I'm stubbornly prenatal. And sure, the only reason I got elected was because I'm a fetus. Duh! I played that "fetus card" every chance I got. Wouldn't you? Because Americans *love* the fetus. Hell, they even amended the ol' Constitution on its behalf! Never underestimate Republicans. They'll do whatever it takes. And they knew that a good chunk of God-fearing Americans from that infamous basket of deplorables *hate* Mallory Blitzen, as in passionately detest, and they'd vote for anyone, including a fetus, instead of her. So, lucky me!

And being born is overrated. It's no wonder babies cry their everlovin' heads off once they open their eyes and see what fresh hell they've emerged into. Paradise Lost (no shit!), because allvusudden you have to *do* things, like walk and talk and go to college and get a job and be like everybody else. *Arrgghh!* And for those of you grammar Nazis or whiny liberals who bristled at me ending one of the above sentences in a preposition... well, guess who's the President? *Moi!* That's right, muthafucka! Guess who can publicly *Tweet* yer ass into submission and have the IRS audit you and have Homeland Security deport your family and have a drone send an MX missile up your butt... *Moi* as well. So don't fuck with the Big Cheese. Besides, I'm unstable. I mean, by definition. They say a woman's brain isn't fully developed until her early twenties, and a man's brain, like fifty-seven or something. Me? I'm a freaking fetus! (And a *white male* fetus at that.) So when I'm a bit, how shall I say, impulsive, what do you expect?

[The intercom buzzes...]

"Mr. President..."

It's Gladiola Gaze, my trusty personal secretary.

"Yes Gladdy?"

"Sir, your intern is here."

"Intern?"

"You know, Brayden Carter..."

"Who?"

"You know, that thin young Black fellow..."

"Hmm?"

The next part she whispers: "Tall Skinny Sad-Sack..."

"Oh yes! Send him in."

Tall Skinny Sad-Sack, otherwise known as Brayden Carter, is my pet project. He was first in his class from kindergarten through high school, but he was dirt poor and scholarships only go so far, and anomalously, he possessed no athletic ability whatsoever. But he wrote some op-ed about our educational system from an African-American Millennial's POV and the frickin' *Washington Post* printed it. Of course I never *read* the *Post*. But this Congressman to whom I owed a favor said he thought he'd make a good intern and it would be nice to give the kid a break. So we had all these photo ops and it was great PR and I got on the cover of *Time* or *Newsweek* (I always get them confused) with Tall Skinny Sad-Sack. And now the Black Caucus owes *me* a favor and my approval rating went up four points.

"Mr. President," he says, as he looms above me like a lanky African-American flagpole.

"Um..."

"Brayden, sir."

"Yes, Brayden!" I smile. "What have you got for me today?"

"Well, sir, there's that thing with Todd-Krank."

"Todd who?"

"Todd-Krank, sir. The *banking bill*..."

"Oh yes. Don't worry about that one."

"Oh?" He's momentarily taken aback. "Okay, sir."

"Anything else?"

"Well, sir, as per your request, I've been liaising with the Secretary of Education regarding the proposed cuts in funding, *vis-à-vis* teacher's salaries conflicting with the Dafoe bill."

I *love* this kid!

"Okay. Sounds good," I say.

The Dafoe bill is named for that actor who I appointed Secretary of Education, Willem Dafoe, who I loved in *Platoon* and whose bill is now before Congress. The bill wants to condense the twelve years of first grade through high school into a solid seven-year block of continuous schooling, 52 weeks a year, with no summer vacations, so students will be finished by the time they're 12 or 13. This way they can either apply to college or go directly to work in one of the many factories or "labor camps" that have opened up, thanks to my *"Buy America"* initiative. Either that or the revitalized Coal Industry. The bill has many detractors, but in its defense, it keeps kindergarten intact!

"Anything else, Brandon?"

"Brayden, sir."

"Yes of course."

"Well, um, I guess not."

"Excellent, Brendan. Keep up the good work."

"Yes sir."

I love that kid. So where was I? Oh yes! Speaking of impulsive, I gotta attend some important cabinet meeting or something where the fate of millions of poor bastards rests on my capricious, uninformed decision. But *first*, time for some *Tweets!*

Alexander Jackson Rett @realAlexRett

Mallory Blitzen, you lost fare and square. I got the Electrical College! You stole 3 mill pop votes but I won it anyway! The hole enchillata plus a taco! Eat it! Loser!!!

Alexander Jackson Rett @realAlexRett

The Dafoe Bill will make America grater again by consintrating all the nolledge into all the students brains so we can be competitiv agian on world stage!!!

Alexander Jackson Rett @realAlexRett

Anybody who apposes Dafoe Bill is a dummy who wants to keep America dummer! Dont you care about are children and the futur of America? Dummies!!!

Alexander Jackson Rett @realAlexRett

And Secretary of Education Dafoe is also a grate actor and if you dont like it hell go all Sargent Barns on your a#@ so sapport the Dafoe Bill. Ya big DUMMY!!!

Alexander Jackson Rett @realAlexRett

Speaking of Platoon which is a tremendus movie I recommend it, support my Automatic Weapons in Schools Bill unless your a terorist and you want are kids 2 die!!!

3

Later that day at the televised White House press conference...
[White House Press Secretary Wiley DeSembler stands behind the podium before a throng of journalists as they clamor for his attention...]
Journalists: *[en masse]* Wiley! Wiley! Wiley!

Wiley: *[points to one up front...]*

Lyle: *[stands up...]* Albert Lyle, *USA Tomorrow...*

Wiley: Yes...

Lyle: With the President getting his way today with the destruction of Todd-Krank, isn't this giving a big green light to the same reprehensible practices that brought about the financial collapse of '08 that devastated millions and had worldwide repercussions?

Wiley: One is not related to the other.

Lyle: *[incredulous] What?!* The sole *purpose* of Todd-Krank was to...

Wiley: Listen, Sparky, in the words of that great President, Woodrow Coolidge, *the business of America is business.*

Crowd: Yes! Yes!

Lyle: Don't you mean, *Calvin...*

Wiley: Woodrow *Calvin?* I don't think so. Next... *[points...]*

Raditz: *[stands...]* Richard Raditz, *Guns & Grenades...*

Wiley: Yes, Dick...

Raditz: Isn't it true that Todd-Krank was getting in the way of financial progress by handcuffing the bankers, which severely limited their...

Lyle: *[irate]* They should be *put* in handcuffs!

Crowd: *Boo!*

Wiley: Yes, Todd-Krank was a gross impediment to financial progress. I mean, do you want the Chinese to come over here and buy up our country right out from under our noses?

Raditz: They already are!

Wiley: See what I mean?

Crowd: Yes! Yes!

Wiley: *[points to another...]*

Gossage: *[stands...]* Richard Gossage, *High-Powered Rifle Magazine...*

Wiley: Good to see you, Rich.

Gossage: You too. *[smiles]* So with the dismantling of Todd-Krank... and might I say, *good riddance!*

Crowd: Amen!

Wiley: Yes, Rich...

Gossage: My question is, will this free up the President to focus on his Automatic Weapons in Schools bill?

Wiley: Yes indeed! *[cheers from the crowd...]* And we can get back to the important issues! *[more cheers...]*

Hoffman: Trevor Hoffman, *Breitbart...*

Wiley: Trevor... Nice to see you.

Hoffman: You too, Wiley. So what's the hold-up with the *AWS?*

Wiley: What do you think? The left-wing knuckle-draggers who don't care about the safety of our kids.

Crowd: Yes!

Quisenberry: Preposterous! How can you speak of safety when you want to bring AK-47s into our schools?

Crowd: *[resounding boos...]*

Wiley: Who are you again?

Quisenberry: Dana Quisenberry, *Modern Vegan.*

Wiley: *Modern Vegan?* Ha! I think that answers your own question. *[laughter from the crowd...]*

Quisenberry: But...

Wiley: *[points...]* Next...

McDaniel: Lindsey McDaniel, *Ashram Today...*

Wiley: *[rolls eyes...]* What, is there a full moon out? *[laughter...]*

McDaniel: *[persists...]* I think it's a valid question, what Dana asked. How can we hope to keep our children safe if we're bringing *AK-47s* into the classroom?

Wiley: The preferred weapon these days is the *AR-15. [cheers and whistles...]*

Hoffman: *[nodding...]* That's what I'm talkin' about!

Wiley: Obviously, if there are *AR-15s* in every classroom, then the terrorists will think twice about coming in there and running amok. And isn't it about our kids? Their safety? So they can get an education without worrying about whackjobs?

Crowd: Yes! Yes!

Lyle: So what about the Dafoe bill then? How is that anything but a cynical way to make manual laborers out of the next generation of our children?

McDaniel: Yes! You're bringing back child labor!

Crowd: Sit down! Sit down!

Wiley: What the Dafoe bill does is take away all those wasted years spent on summer vacations. We're Americans! We don't go on vacation until we've *accomplished* something!

Crowd: Yes! Yes!

Wiley: And what do kids accomplish when they're not in school? Not much! With the Dafoe bill, they're brought up to be productive members of a society on the move, into the future!

Crowd: Yes!

Wiley: So either you're with the future or you're with the past. *[resounding chorus of affirmation...]*

Wiley: *[continues...]* That's all for today. Thank you. *[exits stage...]*

[Earlier that same day in the Warren G. Harding Room at the White House...*]*

"Let's get this over with," says the President, not hiding his impatience. "I mean, I was in the middle of something."

"But Mr. President," says Senator Nettles, "this is kinda important."

"More important than what *I* was doing?" the President replies.

"Well, I'm sure it's not, but still..." says Senator Burdock.

"If you can give us just five minutes, Mr. President," says Senator Thorne. "Did you get the flash cards, sir?"

The President lets out an exasperated huff.

"Yes. That thing about the Ben & Jerry's bill."

"Todd-Krank," says Senator Nudnik.

"Yes, I want you to kill it."

"Kill it, sir?"

"The Ben & Jerry's thing."

"But sir..."

"Do you not understand what *'kill it'* means?"

"But..."

"*Kill it! Abort it! Murder it! Kill it!* Jeez!"

"Yes sir!" says Senator Makepeace.

"Good. So anything else?"

"Um..."

"Not really," says Senator Nebbish.

"Good, cuz I got stuff to do," says the President. "I'm a busy guy."

"Yes sir," says Senator Scullion. "Consider Ben & Jerry's killed, aborted, murdered, and killed, sir."

"Good."

"Yes sir!"

"Then that's that then. Hey!" the President says. "That's a tongue-twister!"

4

So that word, "minuscule"... When I first typed it, I spelled it as "miniscule" and the damn Spell-Check cut in line like some Socialist Independent with the Trotskies. But when I look at it now, I kinda get it. Like the word "minus" is in there, right? Which means less and less, like eleven minus seven is... *Sigh.* This math shit, I gotta be honest, I hate it. But ya don't have to be an engineer to be President. Hold on, lemme call up the calculator app on my smartphone... It's four. The answer to eleven minus seven. See, that wasn't so hard. So I was watching this documentary on *The History Channel* on FDR. He was some President who was in a wheelchair. Can you believe it? And apparently back then, people were actually *smart!* Yeah, I didn't believe that either! Like some 24-year-old kid ran this thing called the Marshall Plan, which was some big deal after that war they had when Europe was like in ruins, but now we have 24-year-olds playing *Pokémon.* But that's *good!* I mean, it's amazing how easy it is to brainwash someone whose brain is already washed. It's almost too easy, those Millennials. Just give 'em their video games and a new *Star Wars* once a year.

And regarding my campaign, it was *perfecto.* You *know* I'm 100% ANTI-ABORTION. And those single-issue voters (otherwise known as my base, God bless 'em), they love the right to life like they love *guns* and *NASCAR* and *Chick-fil-A* and *Jesus.* And people wanna believe. They do. They've been disappointed by their leaders. And those Democrats? Don't get me started. Besides, nobody listens to them anyway. They're a necessary evil, and the reason I can't come out and announce my dictatorship. Duh! Hitler and Mussolini had it easy, but the one I *really* admire is Franco. He stayed under the radar compared to the others, and he ruled over Spain for thirty-six years and died well-fed in his bed next to his favorite fat concubine, Esperanza! Thirty-six years! That's like... how many Presidential terms would that be? Let's see, a term is four years, barring impeachment, so thirty-six divided by four... *Back to the calculator...* Nine. Nine freaking terms! Suck it, FDR! Suck it, Grover Cleveland Alexander! It's all about strength and the Strong Man, and in this regard, America is like Russia. We only respond to strength. Like that documentary I saw on the Black Panthers... Hey, what *else* am I gonna do all cooped up inside? And besides, knowin' some knowledge ain't exactly a *bad* thing, except these days when you run for President. Ha! So back to the Black Panthers. DAMN! Everybody started to pay attention when all these badass Negroes in black leather and sunglasses started holding shotguns and appearing everywhere. And for a while, white America was scared shitless. *Lock the doors! Hide the women!* But thankfully Mr. Hoover and his FBI guys put a stop to that pronto. I sure wish I had *him*. The guy I got now, well... let's just say he doesn't possess the instinct for the jugular like ol' J. Edgar. But I digress...

Let me impart upon you a bit of political strategery that should not be misunderestimated. A predecessor of mine (his name rhymes with Tush) had this stroke of genius that things would go much smoother if he appeared to be, well, to the public at least, *dumb*. And it worked like a charm! I mean, when everyone's expectations are so low that *not going on vacation* is praiseworthy... Ha! It's all about being selective. To be "deliberately uninformed" is the official designation in the *IntelCom*—the *Intelligence Community*. This way, there's none of that pressure when people expect you to actually *produce results.* FDR, he worked his ass off 24/7! Fuck that shit! But as the world witnessed with my *immediate* predecessor, it's much easier to plummet to the level of peabrain than to collectively get smarter. When you're dumb, your brain has it easy because so little is demanded of you. And everyone knows that happiness fills up an empty brain! Hey, that would sound *really* smart in Latin! But who knows Latin anymore? I guess I can *Google* it. Be right back... *Cerebro inane gaudium impleatur.* Yeah, that *does* sound smart! But let's keep it between us, okay? *Ixnay on the atin-Lay.* Hold on, I got a text from Tim...

To President Alexander Rett:

Mr. President, check out Mallory's latest Tweet.
Chopper

Tim Chopper's my Chief-of-Staff, my main man, my right hand.

Mallory Rodman Blitzen @realPresidentMalloryBlitzen
So our little president who's never been to school is for a bill to bring machine guns into the classroom. What can go wrong? Sounds safe to me. Idiot!

I *hate* that Mallory Blitzen. Sore loser. Hang on... *[a flurry of fast fingers...]*

Alexander Jackson Rett @realAlexRett
Just like a Libtard to wanna kill all are kids. How many more kids must be killed by Terorists before you see the lite? 100? 1000? A millyen? Your evil!!!

Alexander Jackson Rett @realAlexRett
And dindt your kid Chastity have bodygards like since Kinder-garden? Dubble standerd! Only you're kid safe? Mallory=Hippocrit!!!

And speaking of *The History Channel*, there's this thing on there about *me!* Yeah, you know you've made it when there's a documentary about you on *The History Channel.* Lemme call it up on the ol' smartphone. Gimme a sec... Okay, I know it's pretty small, my phone that is, but I got these tiny hands. Maybe lean in real close...

"Most biographies of famous men and women begin the same way: 'Born in 1492 or 1776 or 1958.' However, today we'll make an exception. The story of Alexander Jackson Rett, the fetus who ran for President of the United States, is indeed a story unlike any other in history..."

There it is. What's that? You wanted to keep watching? Well, watch it on your *own* dime! I'm not gonna sit around all day holding up my phone so you can watch TV. I'm the freaking President! And in case ya haven't noticed, I'm not exactly Arnold Schwarzenegger. I mean, look at these puny little arms. I thought about getting some barbells, but it's not exactly spacious in here.

[The intercom buzzes...]

"What is it, Gladdy?"

"Sir, the President of Russia is on the phone."

"Raz?"

"Yes sir, President Putin."

"Is it the regular phone or the Doomsday phone?"

"The Blue phone, sir."

"The Blue phone is the good one, right?"

"Yes, Mr. President."

Ya see, that's confusing because Blue is for Democrats, who are bad, and Red is for Republicans, who are good, but this Red-Hotline-The-Missiles-Are-Raining-Down-Doomsday-Armageddon Phone is definitely bad, so you understand my confusion.

"Um, tell him I'll call him back."

"Yes, Mr. President."

Anyway, that show... I mean, my mom, rest in peace, used to watch one documentary after the next. That's where I learned a shit-ton, in those formative early months so crucial to proper development. Let me tell you, you hear *everything* inside the womb! Maybe that's what gave me the bug to enter politics, because one of my earliest memories was this show on JFK. I didn't like his voice, all high-pitched *pahk the cah in Havahd Yahd.* But other than that, he was a pretty cool dude (even though he was a Democrat). He was a sharp dresser and he had sex with movie stars. And that's one of my regrets, after I decided to never emerge from the womb, as in, what will I do for sex? (Especially with movie stars!) And when she wasn't watching TV, my mom was listening to music. Nope, no Mozart for me. More like Britney Spears. I heard a good chunk of her oeuvre before I ever saw what a babe she is. And that song, *"Work B**ch"... Whoo-ee!* When she cracks the whip on that video, Lord have mercy!

[Alex calls up the video on his smartphone, then plays it through the Oval Office's pulsating, club-worthy sound system...]

This is so awesome! *"You wanna Lamborghini... Sip martinis..."* Yes I do! *[He cranks it up and sings along...] "You better work, bitch, you better work, bitch! You better work, bitch, you better work, bitch!"* Here comes the whip... *YES!*

There's pounding on the door.

"Now get to work, bitch! Now get to work, bitch!"

More pounding, until finally Gladiola Gaze bursts in. Alex sees her and presses the mute button.

"Are you alright, Mr. President?"

"Yes, I... Do you like Britney Spears?"

Gladdy is nonplussed.

"Shall I... get you anything, sir?"

"No thanks."

There's an awkward moment, and then Gladdy leaves.

Way to ruin my Britney jam. *[Alex sighs, looks at his phone, turns it off...]* So I don't really have many friends. Well, none, to be exact. I mean, when you're a self-aware fetus in the womb, there's not a lot of peers to hang out with. It's not like they have prenatal daycare. And nobody calls me *Little Alex,* except for me. It's what I call myself when I'm feeling most badass. And when you're the President, you're called on to be badass quite often. You'd be surprised. And yeah, it's from that movie, *A Clockwork Orange.* Have you seen it? It's saved somewhere in cyberspace, wherever that is, so I can watch it whenever I want. I especially like the happy ending. I relate to Alex because he's kinda little too. But, when it comes down to it, he's smart and tough and a mean-spirited bastard. And yeah, technically I'm a bastard as well, since my parents never got hitched in the tie-the-knot sense.

My father, Josef Schnitzelgrüber (there's a name for ya!) was some minor civil servant stuck in a stuffy office building with no windows and a handlebar mustache. (*He* had the stash, not the office building.) And as far as stashes go, they haven't been fashionable since the 19th century, and when you wear one today, it's like some '70s porn stash or Freddie Mercury. So my dad was disgruntled with his dead-end job, but when he got home, it was even worse. My mom doted on him like the good wife she hoped to be, but he responded with monosyllabic grunts between gulps of beer and belches. In fact, ol' Joe was so un-emotional, unresponsive, and uninspiring that I think the last time he and my mom had sex was the night of my conception, which I have to believe was less than immaculate. I picture this fat, sweaty, Old World bureaucrat with a receding hairline, a protruding beer-gut, and that Bismarck mustache with drops of lustful perspiration hanging from its droopy ends, hovering above my mom's tortured angelic face with eyes clamped shut thinking of Jesus.

And when you're in the womb, all the sounds from *out there* are amplified. Like that time my mom overdid it at *Mi Rancho*, her favorite Mexican place, and indulged herself in what seemed like a non-stop Flatulent Fiesta, to Old José's *disgusto*. Thankfully, the protective integument of human skin is non-permeable, as far as smells are concerned. But *TOOT TOOT TOOT*, like a trombone convention. So with all this in mind, all you pregos out there should be extra careful regarding your precious unborn's delicate sensibilities. And it's not like we're spies. I mean, we would prefer *not* to be a party to your every repulsive utterance, not to mention those trips to the toilet. For the longest time, I had no idea what was happening. The determined jostling, the hurried gait, the desperate disrobing. But a second after I felt you plop yourself down, there was this ominous rumbling like an earthquake and what sounded like Pelham 123 racing past about to derail. And sometimes this lasted for quite a while, as I waited patiently for that sound I grew to long for, to even love—*FLUSH*—which meant the ordeal was over and I was safe again for a while.

So I mentioned being a bastard...

5

"The story of Alexander Jackson Rett, the fetus who ran for President of the United States, is indeed a story unlike any other in history. Medical Science is still at a loss to explain how a fetus within the womb can become self-aware. How it can achieve motility, the power of speech, thought and reasoning, not to mention the ability to make the decision, contrary to all the laws of physiology, to *remain* in the womb, and then to continue to develop and thrive while maintaining its minuscule size.

"We're speaking with Mary Rett," says *The History Channel* host. "So Alexander was your first child?"

"Oh yes. First and last."

"When did you start to notice that something was different with your unborn baby?"

"Well, obviously being a first-time mom, I didn't know what to expect. I mean, I read all the books of course."

"Of course."

"But *oh my God!*"

"*Mom! Hello!* You *know* I'm right here!" says Alex from within the womb.

"Yes, I know, baby. I'm sorry." She leans over to listen, and Alex speaks in emphatic whispers.

"Good, just so ya don't... I mean, we *talked* about this."

"Yes, I know... Mama loves you!"

[Alex shudders...]

Alexander's mom sits up straight and turns to the host.

"He's worried that I'll be nervous." She offers a light-hearted shrug. "So I was saying that nothing in those books could possibly have prepared me for, well..." She motions down below to the bullet-proof aluminum oxynitride glass.

A team of surgeons from Switzerland was called in to remove the flesh from Mary Rett's belly and put in the glass, so her ever-curious and upwardly-mobile fetus could have a window on the world.

"Yes, how could they?" the host says.

"The books, I mean."

"You know, I've always been a skeptic."

"A skeptic, yes."

"So naturally I was skeptical towards most things, *including* Science. After all, our current President has made many provocative points in this regard."

"He has indeed," says the host.

"If we believe anything too readily."

"Including Science."

"Yes! I mean, I'm not a scientist, I'm... a widow, as you know. Even though technically we never tied the knot, my Joey and me."

"Yes, I'm sorry."

"So I'm a stay-at-home single mom."

("Way ta go, Mom!" Alex says to himself from inside the womb, "That'll get me the Single Mom vote!")

"But of course I wasn't expecting anything... well, this remarkable. That's a good word, yes?" Mary Rett looks at the host.

"Remarkable, to say the least!" says the host. "So when was the first time you knew that... well, that this wasn't going to be an ordinary pregnancy?"

"I think it was the Second Trimester. There was a lot of movement down there. And you know, movement is good!"

"Of course."

"But this was like military maneuvers. Back and forth, *tramp tramp tramp*, for days. I barely slept."

"Hmm."

"And then came this bashing against my belly."

"Bashing? From inside?"

"Like he was trying to break out, you know? Like in *The Great Escape*." [Alex smiles to himself. *The Great Escape* is one of his favorite movies. He always pictures himself as Steve McQueen, with an umbilical cord hanging from beneath his cut-off sweatshirt.]

"Yes, a great movie," says the host.

"Although I'm partial to romantic comedies," says Mary Rett. "And of course, documentaries. I can't get enough of my documentaries! I never went to college, you see."

"But you were saying about your unborn child..."

"Yes, trying to escape. And I had such insomnia."

"Because of the back and forth."

"And the bashing." The host nods.

"But then this one night a few weeks later... I was lying there trying to sleep when I heard a voice."

"A voice?"

"And at first I thought I was, you know, *imagining* it. Because I was so tired, I thought I must be delirious."

"Yes."

"But the voice persisted."

"What did it say?"

"It said, '*It's dark in here.*'"

"It's dark in here?"

"*Yes!* And then I heard it again! And I, you know, I was... what's a good word? Flabbergasted! I was flabbergasted!"

"That *is* a good word," says the host.

"Thank you." Alex's mother smiles. "I used to read a lot, but who reads anymore? Why read when there are such informative things on TV and YouTube."

"So did the voice speak again?"

"Well, after I was flabbergasted, like I said, I listened intently. And a few moments later, I heard the voice again, and this time it said, 'Is anybody out there?'"

"Is anybody out there," echoes the host.

"Like from the Pink Floyd song. I used to *love* that album. You know the one: We don't need no edge-u-kay-shun," she sings off-key. ("Mom! How embarrassing!")

"A classic," says the host.

"Although lately I've been listening more to, you know, *happy* music! Like Britney Spears!"

"Ah yes. So your unborn child spoke to you from inside the womb and asked the question: 'Is anybody out there?'"

"Pretty amazing, huh?"

"Yes. So did he say anything else?"

"Not until a few days later. I thought about getting a glass of lemonade, since it was the summer and it was hot and humid and the air conditioner broke and the fan didn't work."

("Mom...")

"So what happened?"

"The voice spoke again and it said, 'No lemonade. Water.'"

"'*No lemonade. Water.*'"

"But the freaky thing was that I, you know, I just *thought* about the glass of lemonade. I didn't actually, like, *announce* it."

"But your unborn child knew it, as through telepathy."

"Telepathy! Yes!" says Mary Rett" "I mean, they say the connection between a mother and her child is a strong one. Boy, were they right!"

"So what happened next?"

"Well, I started a conversation."

"With your unborn child in the womb."

"Yes," she laughs nervously, "and I said, 'But I was in the mood for lemonade. It's really hot.'"

"And Alex responded?"

"Yes! He said, 'Hot? Are you kidding? It's like a Turkish bath in here!'" She laughs and laughs.

"He likened your womb to a Turkish bath, your unborn fetus?"

"Yes, he was very emphatic."

"So what did you say?"

"I said, 'How are you able to talk?' And he said, 'Talk? Is that what I'm doing?' Which was peculiar, since he seemed to know all about Turkish baths, yet he was unaware that he was talking to me. So I asked him again, 'How are you able to talk?' and he said, 'Beats me. Lemonade's too acidic.'"

"That is indeed amazing."

"Indeed it is! So the only thing I can figure is that somehow he absorbed all those things vicariously through me. Like all the music I listened to and all the shows I watched on TV. Somehow it all went inside that little brain of his. So all you expectant mothers out there..." Mary Rett looks directly into the camera, "Be careful the things you introduce to your prenatal girl or boy. I know *mine* turned out okay. I mean, he's running for President! I'm so proud of you, baby!" she says, addressing her womb.

("Mom!")

"But you can never be too careful," she adds.

"Careful, yes." The host looks at Alex's mom.

"Although Medical Science is still confounded as to the exact scientific reasons behind Alex's... well, his amazing story."

"It was *The Day of the Jackal*," Mary says.

"I'm sorry?"

"It's a movie. It has a Turkish bath in it, in one of the scenes."

"Ah yes. So did you continue to carry on conversations?"

"Hmm?"

"With Alex... in the womb."

"Oh yes! It was so nice to have someone to talk to."

"So what did you talk about?"

"All *sorts* of things. My baby's quite intelligent. Although, technically, he's not my baby."

(Mom!)

"But it's a mouthful to keep saying my unborn talking fetus who confounds Medical Science."

"I can imagine."

"I remember one time he asked me what a DeLorean looked like."

"A DeLorean?"

"From that movie, *Back to the Future*."

"Ah yes!"

"Because at that point... I mean, that was before the glass." She reaches down and gently pats the glass cover where the flesh above her womb used to be. The camera does a close-up, and the audience at home can see the thick black curtains drawn from behind the window.

"He likes his privacy, my baby. It's so difficult for him. And for me too, with this running for President thing. I mean, it's all been a whirlwind."

"A whirlwind," echoes the host.

"Most mothers I'd imagine just want their child to come out, you know, in one piece, everything where it's supposed to be, fingers and toes. But my baby, he fast-forwarded right to running for President! It all seems like a dream."

"Yes."

"And he's already smarter than me, my Alex."

"Is he?"

"Oh yes. In fact, there *have* been some smart Presidents. I saw this documentary on FDR. And JFK too, although I don't like his womanizing. Not that I'm a Feminist."

("Mom...")

"Although I *am* glad for my rights. None o' this barefoot an' pregnant stuff for me! *See...*" She raises her legs to show off her high heels.

("Mom!")

"Very fashionable," says the host. "Like the right to vote."

"Hmm?"

"That women have that right."

"Ah yes."

"So be sure and vote for my baby!" She looks into the camera.

"Alexander Rett on November Seventh! *The Choice!*"

"Another shameless plug," the host smiles.

"Oh, I'm sorry!"

"No, it's okay. I was kidding!"

"Oh good," Mary smiles. "So he asked me what that car, you know, the DeLorean, looks like."

"Oh yes."

"And I tried to describe it being all silver, you know. But how can you describe silver to someone who, you know, who's never seen anything before? It's so much better now. That's why this was so necessary." She pats the glass cover again. "So my baby can see everything in this great big world of ours."

"We at *The History Channel* have contacted many of the experts in their field, that of Human Physiology, and they are all in awe of Alex."

"Yes, me too." She smiles.

("Aww... Thanks, Mom.")

"But I must ask you, Mary, the prospect of being so closely connected to your son, with no... Well, he won't technically be *born*, so you'll be joined like this for..."

"That's all up to him, to little Alex."

("Mom!")

"So you have no desire to be one of those parents like Joe Kennedy was, for example... with JFK?"

"Heavens no! But I do wish that..." She pauses, her eyes suddenly filling with tears.

"Ma'am?"

"I'm sorry." Mary Rett wipes her eyes with a handkerchief. "I thought of my... of my Josef, my Joey."

("Nice one, Mom! Get the sympathy vote!")

"Yes, it was indeed tragic," says the host. "Who could imagine that a simple paper-cut in an office at work could lead to a fatal bout of necrotizing fasciitis."

"We all have our crosses to bear."

("Way ta go Mom! Get the Christian and Catholic vote!")

"I just wish that Joey could've seen our son, what he's become."

"Any father would be proud," says the host.

"Yes, and I know he'll make us *all* proud, as our future President." She smiles.

"God willing."

("Go Mom! Firing on all cylinders! The base loves God!")

"That's two months from now, the election," says the host. "And you have the debates coming up."

"Yes, we're looking forward to those."

"But it hasn't *all* been good," says the host. "The campaign. There has been some mud-slinging, from both sides. And from you yourself. Like when you took issue with the Democratic candidate's '*bastard*' slur."

"Well, yes, but a mother will *always* protect her child from harm."

("Nice, Mom.")

"Of course."

"And technically, you know, Alex *is* a..." She tilts her head to the side. "But still, it's not nice. I mean, did Alex have a say in it? That his poor loving father died under such tragic circumstances before we could make it official, marriage-wise? He worked so hard, my Joey."

"So do you think you might ever..."

"What, want to *marry* again?"

"Yes."

"My Joey was the one," Mary says.

"The one and only."

"Mmm." The host smiles.

"And right now the campaign is everything. My son has such plans for the country. Such good ideas. He wants to make America *greater!*"

"Haha! Like the campaign slogan."

"Yes, well you can never be *too* great, right? There's always room for improvement."

"There is indeed. So we'll look forward to the upcoming debates."

"Me too."

"Thanks so much for being here today, Mary Rett."

"It was my... I mean, *our* pleasure."

The host looks into the camera as it zooms in closer.

"And thanks for joining us at home for this very special edition of *The History Channel: The Short Incredible Life of Alexander Jackson Rett.*"

6

[A one-bedroom apartment in Alexandria, Virginia. Brayden Carter, President Rett's black intern, and his white French girlfriend, Carly Menteur, are lying naked in bed beneath a single white sheet...]

"Is it hot in here or is it just me?"

"Well, *you're* definitely hot," says Brayden.

"Haha. *Merci.*"

"And we just had sex."

"I know, but still..." Carly motions to the air conditioner in the window.

"It doesn't work, as far as cold air is concerned," Brayden explains.

"So why do you still use it?"

"I like the sound."

"The sound?"

"It's comforting, like the womb."

"Ha! So how *is* our baby President?"

"Eh, he's okay. But..."

"What?"

"I'm the token, right? He doesn't even know my name." Brayden Carter sits up in bed and lets out a breath.

"He's called me Brady, Bradley, Billy, Brendan, Brandon, Braxton, Brexit..."

"He called you *Brexit?*" Carly laughs as she sits up beside him.

"He's got a lot on his mind."

"I guess. So how tiny *are* his hands?"

"They're minuscule!" Brayden laughs.

"Like this G.I. Joe I had when I was a kid."

"Haha!"

"But..."

"What, baby?"

"I can't help but feel that I'm there to... you know, pad the stats or something."

Carly shrugs.

"Ya know, when I first got the call..." At that moment, the phone rings.

"Speaking of..."

"Ha!"

"I can't believe you still have a land line!"

"This used to be my friend Reggie's place."

"Reggie the misogynist?"

"Yeah. When he moved out, he left the phone."

"So are you gonna answer it?"

"I like it cuz it's *old school...*" Brayden leans over to the nightstand and picks up the receiver.

"Yes?... No, I didn't order a pizza." He hangs up and moves alongside Carly in bed.

"Domino's," he says.

"So you were saying..."

"Hmm?"

"About when you first got the call."

"Oh yeah. I mean, it was the *White House* calling! It's hard to say no."

"*But...*"

"I guess the bloom's off the rose."

"Like with me?" Carly throws the sheet aside and straddles him with her naked body, her blonde hair glistening.

"Yes," Brayden says.

"I'm sick of you."

"I can tell." She starts moving above him.

"And you seem firm in your resolve."

"*Oh! Oh!*" His eyes light up.

"Is this the part where we speak in witty *double entendres?*"

"*Oui, monsieur!*" She smiles.

"Good! I love that part!"

"Mmm..."

"So as you can see, I'm *rigid* in my views."

"Haha!" She grinds in deeper.

"In fact you can say I'm... *adamantine.*"

"*Adamantine?* You're a smart one."

"Smart is sexy."

"Ha! Well, sexy man, I have something that will *soften* you up."

Carly peels the sweaty sheet from Brayden's body. And then slowly she slides down the bed, her lips parted in anticipation.

7

So my mom wasn't too bad there, in that documentary. Which reminds me... That thing I mentioned in an earlier chapter, that off-the-cuff remark about my mom when I said "*rest in peace.*" Obviously she's not *dead*, since I'm still here in one piece, fingers and toes, with the ol' umbilical cord still attached. And I gotta say what a pain in the ass this thing has become.

And of course, the entire *world* heard about her stroke. I mean, the day of my freaking inauguration, the happiest day of my life, and my mom has a stroke? Can you believe it? Some bad luck that, huh? But it was amazing how the entire country came together, how they put aside their differences to support me in my darkest hour. As you know, it was touch and go there for a bit. But the doctors... well, not to knock my Great American Health Care Bill that we're trying to steamroll through Congress, but between you and me, there are times when it's nice to be the President. So after my mom had the stroke, everyone was worried about *me*. I mean, this has all been... *unpresidented!* Ha! That's a joke on my predecessor. But no worries. We're good friends. Especially after the pardon. Hey, I know what you're thinking, but it's a really small and exclusive club, this POTUS thing, and we gotta stick together, even more so than doctors. Which reminds me...

Alexander Jackson Rett @realAlexRett

Those who appose the Great American Health Care Bill are nothing less then murdurers. People will die if this isnt past. History will condem you!!!

Alexander Jackson Rett @realAlexRett

I'm talking about YOU, Senitor Palsey and YOU, Senitor Goiters. Let you're poor constituwents be warned. Death awaits if health care bill does'nt pass!!!

So there's this specialist on Birth & Eugenics from the Universität Heidelberg, Dr. Manheim Dampfwälze von Ludendörff-Dreck, who's trying to figure out if I can survive in here, in the womb-room, if the umbilical cord is unattached. So far, no go. But he's the best there is, umbilical cord-wise, so we'll see. But still, I'm not exactly thrilled about having to depend on this dubious length of pipe for my existence. Not to mention that I'm the freaking *President of the United States* and I still technically live with my mother.

And of course my clothes are custom-made, because where do you find stuff to wear if you're a freaking fetus? I'm only twelve inches tall. Not that I stand up that much, cuz it's been kinda cramped in here since the remodel. But still, it's pretty swanky, like Otter's room in *Animal House* when Dean Wormer's drunk wife came over in that negligee. And I don't know if you remember your time inside, but the womb *is* a pretty dodgy place. All wet and slimy and drippy like with stalactites an' shit. And of course, pitch black. It's no wonder everyone just curls up in the fetal position, cuz there's not much to do in here except sleep and wait to be born. Hang on, I'll be right back...

Alexander Jackson Rett @realAlexRett

America is the greatest nation on Erth so it NEEDS the Great American Health Care Bill so we can have the gratest health. Vote for it or youl get sick and die mizerbly!!!

I remember that first moment when I had a thought. It was *"Hey! I'm me!"* And after that sunk in, *"What is this place?"* I mean, it was all moist and gooey and barely inhabitable and I thought, *"What. The. Fuck?"* I wrote it off as a bad dream and I went back to sleep, but when I woke up, it was the same, and that was my first moment of panic. And then I felt this thing coming out of my stomach, this rigid piece o' rope, so I panicked some more and tried to yank it out, cuz I figured it was that thing from *The Matrix* (that movie my mom watched on Amazon). And I was this human battery, kept alive to provide electricity to the malevolent Metropolis that keeps me here as its embryonic slave. Yikes. Self-awareness ain't all it's cracked up to be. Hold on a sec...

Alexander Jackson Rett @realAlexRett
Why do you want Americans to die in agany, Senitors Palsey & Goiters? No compashun? Time to cut Senite saleries. Weed out rottin appels!!!

But I was telling you about my bachelor pad. So this interior decorator, Maurice LePetite from Fifth Avenue, flounces in here with his lilac suit and bright yellow tie and gaudy sapphire tie-pin. Not that I have anything against gays, although to be honest, they're not a big voting demographic. And when you're The Prez, the first term is all about re-election. So Maurice is flitting about, all lilac and yellow and sapphire, sketching these things on a pad when he's not leering at the Secret Service guys. And I don't know what *they* think, since they always have on those dark glasses. So after a few minutes, he shows me his drawings and it's like, I don't know, Salvador Dali meets the Pink Panther meets Liberace and I say *meh*. But later on I watched that above-mentioned movie, *Animal House*. And when I saw the scene in Otter's room in the frat house, I said, *"THAT!"*

So the next day we got some DC contractor and he did up the womb as an exact 1/257th replica. The only problem was that they had to remove the bulletproof glass, which really wasn't that big of a deal, except... Now this *next* part is DOUBLE-SECRET FOR-YOUR-EYES-ONLY, because in order to remodel the womb, they hadda get me myself yours truly President Fetus outta there while they did the work. (You don't wanna get in the way of contractors. They get all pissy.) So technically, I was *born*, right? And this was no big deal, health-wise, since that umbilical cord is long as shit, and I sat in this comfy Barcalounger and binge-watched *Dexter*. But that's beside the point, because if word got out that I was *outside*, even for just a few hours... I mean, I got enemies. There's that crazy Alt-Left Birther Movement, or BM—these terrorist nut-jobs who want to forcibly remove me from the womb, since they maintain that the only reason I got elected is because I'm a fetus. But, haters gonna hate. And speaking of...

Alexander Jackson Rett @ realAlexRett
Everyone accept Senitors Palsey & Goiters love the Great American Health Care Bill. Everyone cares about you accept them. They want to kill you!!!

So since you're here, how 'bout I give you a tour of my humble abode. My picture window... *[Alex raps on the bulletproof glass from inside, and there's a hollow, echoey sound...]* I like how it's concave. Or is it convex? I always get them confused. But the cool thing is that it has this sliding glass door that looks invisible, right? Until you move it aside. *[Slides it open...]* This way I can get some fresh air. I mean, we put in AC, but sometimes I like to breathe air that's not been recycled. And I can get other things, like little cocktails in little cocktail glasses. I even have a personal bartender, Señor Manolo Vargas, or Manny, as I call him. And he calls me Mr. Alex, which I think is kinda charming, in an Old World, colonialist, condescending kind of way.

And when the world out there is too much, I have these nice thick curtains. After all, it's not like there are a lot of places for me to hide. But everyone, my Staff that is, knows not to bother me when the curtains are drawn. And I even turn off my cell phone because there's always some text or Tweet. Which reminds me...

Alexander Jackson Rett @realAlexRett
The Great American Health Care Bill is the gratest bill EVER! All drug companys behind it! They make the best drugs to kure you from yoor're disseeses!!!

There! See what I mean about these little fingers. I try to send thirty Tweets a day to keep everyone off balance and on their toes. And obviously, none of this wussy shit when you're the President. We play hardball here.

Alexander Jackson Rett @realAlexRett
All you Democrat Senitors who apose the Great American Health Care Bill shud be ashaimed of yoursef! Do you not care about America's health? Your evil!!!

So we were in the middle of the tour... Here's my comfy sofa that converts into a bed. As you can see, not much room inside, so there were a few things from Otter's pad that I couldn't include. But I *do* have the light dimmer and the surround-sound linked to my smartphone activated from this silver panel on the wall. And I know what silver is *now!* It's awesome. But I really had no choice, since my predecessor... well, all that *gold* everywhere. The golden toaster and electric can opener and shower! I mean, show a little restraint.

As you can see, they shored up the womb with walls, a floor, and a ceiling, since the old place was like living inside a mucous membrane. I thought about getting a chandelier, but I'd keep bashing my head against it. But I *do* have this nice shag carpet. Kinda retro. A nice little coffee table with a glass top, and a little refrigerator if I want a nightcap and I don't wanna wake up Manny, although he says he doesn't mind. And I have two closets. This one's for clothes... *[Opens closet door...]* And this one... *[Points to corner of the room...]* well, that's the, *uh-hmm*, W.C. Hey, I'm the President of the United States. I'm not gonna expel my excretions all over the floor like some barbarian.

But the coolest thing of all is my desk in the Oval Office. If your imagination can pan back just a little... There's my mom, see, sitting in that comfy chair behind Ronald Reagan's old desk. I had it shipped here from the Reagan Museum in California. I figured it would bring me luck. After all, who doesn't like *The Gipper?* And whenever I address the nation, they do some green screen stuff so it looks like I'm in the Oval (minus my mom), because as everyone knows, it's all about looking Presidential.

8

(Later that day at the televised White House Press Conference...) *[White House Press Secretary* Wiley DeSembler *stands behind the podium as a swarm of journalists vies for his attention...]*

Journalists: *[en masse]* Wiley! Wiley! Wiley!

Wiley: *[points to one up front...]*

Eckersley: *[stands up...]* Denyse Eckersley, *Left Field Magazine...*

Wiley: What is *Left Field* again?

Eckersley: How many times are you going to ask me that, Wiley?

Wiley: Just this last time.

Eckersely: *[huffs indignantly...]* *Left Field* is an award-winning online journal of civil discourse and provocative...

Wiley: *Blah-blah-blah...*

Eckersley: Excuse me?

Wiley: Next... *[points...]*

Wilhelm: *[smiling broadly]* Hoyt Wilhelm, *Breitbart...*

Wiley: Hoyt! *Guten Tag!*

Wilhelm: *Wie gehts!*

Wiley: Not bad! How's the wife and kids?

Wilhelm: Just fine. Hoyt Junior got a puppy!

Crowd: *[oohs and ahhs...]*

Wiley: That's great! What kind?

Wilhelm: An English Bulldog.

Wiley: Ah! They're so cute.

Wilhelm: Yes!

Wiley: And so much cuter than those *French* Bulldogs.

Wilhelm: *French,* ugh! Who'd want anything to do with the *French?*

Crowd: *Collaborators!*

Rivera: *[interrupting...]* Mariana Rivera, *Horse & Hound...* What's wrong with getting an *American* puppy from the ASPCA? There are so many unwanted animals.

Wiley: You weren't recognized, Maria.

Rivera: It's Mariana.

Wiley: You weren't recognized, Mariana. So sit down and zip it.

Crowd: Yeah! Sit down!

Wiley: But to be fair, I'll answer your question. Because we're nothing if not fair and balanced. *[winks at* Wilhelm...*]* First of all, the ASPCA's funding has been cut for the PDI... Since the demise of The Great Wall, President Rett wants to put all of our resources into the Protective Death-Ray Initiative.

Crowd: *[cheers...]*

Wiley: *[continues...]* Secondly, the main problem with America is that we have all these mixed breed puppies.

Wilhelm: The Mongrel Race!

Crowd: Yes!

Wiley: Before ya know it, ya can't get a nice English Bulldog anymore. Or even a *French* one, for that matter. But the point is, all races are diminished by this rampant miscegenation. These immigrant dogs, they come here to our sacred shores and interbreed, and before you know it...

Lyle: *[interrupts...]* Can we talk about something other than puppies?

[a crescendo of boos from the crowd...]

Wiley: Who are you again?

Lyle: Albert Lyle, *USA Tomorrow.*

Crowd: Boo! Sit down! Puppy hater!

Wiley: *[sarcastically]* Okay, Sparky... What do *you* wanna talk about?

Lyle: Well, since you brought up the PDI, how is this any different from Ronald Reagan's *Star Wars*, which was such a massive boondoggle.

Wilhelm: I *love Star Wars!*

Wiley: Who doesn't?

Wilhelm: I know, right? *[smiles]*

Wiley: I think that answers your question

Lyle: *[frustrated, sits down...]*

Hrabosky: Alice Hrabosky, *Modern Anachronist*... So what is your response to Senator Blitzen's newest call for impeachment?

Crowd: *[erupts in laughter...]*

Wiley: Sour grapes, what else?

Hrabosky: But she *did* win the popular vote.

Wiley: Popular schmopular!

Crowd: *[laughter abounds...]*

Wiley: *[continues...]* They tried to impeach President Rett's predecessor before he even got into office, and how'd *that* work out for them? *[smiles smugly]*

Crowd: Yeah!

Wiley: Besides, we all *know* that Mallory Blitzen is a bitter, confused, humorless old maid with cobwebs in her *vajayjay* who just couldn't stand that she lost to a fetus.

Crowd: *Yeah! Yeah!*

Wilhelm: So when is the new *Star Wars* coming out?

Wiley: The movie?

Wilhelm: Yes.

Wiley: Now *that's* a good question! I can't divulge anything too specific, since it's top secret. But I *can* say that President Rett is a good friend of the director. So as soon as *he* knows, I'm sure he'll tell the rest of us, since that'd be good for the country, for America!

Crowd: *[ecstatic]* Yes! Yes!

Wiley: God bless *Star Wars* and God bless America!

9

I guess there are a few things to catch you up on. Boy, that Mallory Blitzen makes me so mad I could just scream! Ya know, now that ya mention it, I don't believe I've ever screamed before. I'm gonna try. *[The President takes a few deep breaths as he works himself into a lather; then he lets out what sounds like the high-pitched squeak of a mouse...]* Hmm, that wasn't so hot. But I guess when it comes down to it, Presidents don't have to scream. We make *others* scream. Ha! But still, that Mallory Blitzen burns my butt. Hold on a sec... *[A flurry of fingers...]*

Alexander Jackson Rett @realAlexRett

Give it a rest, Mallory. You lost fair and square. Face it, your a loser. It's time to go to the rest home and take up neddlepoint!!!

There, see what I did? By deliberately confusing "your" with "you're" and by misspelling needlepoint I have everyone focusing on *that! "Look how bad Rett's grammar is!* And *he can't even* spell! *He's worse than that* last *guy!"* Like I said before, governing is 90% misdirection. And when that doesn't work, start a war. Hey, it's in the Bible: *How To Be President for Complete Idiots.* I read it twice! Hold on, let's check the media's response... *[Clicks remote to turn on TV...]* I had that installed since we saw each other last. One o' those big flat-screen jobs. It's a Samsung HD and light as a feather! Those Japs sure can make good TVs, although their cars, not that I drive or anything, but name me one Jap car that's distinctive in styling that wasn't ripped off from some British car from the '60s or some 1980s Porsche. And speaking of, I went for a ride in a Porsche on the freaking Autobahn that time I went to see that German so-called woman they have in charge over there, Mengele Männlichheimer. I wanted to ride in one of those 911s, but even though my mom was hooked up to the portable life-support thingie, there *still* had to be a nurse with us, just in case. And the nurse couldn't fit in the 911 so we took that frumpy SUV, the Caramba, I think it's called, with the nurse in the backseat. And that proved to be my one and only trip, well, *anywhere*, because it was off the charts, pain-in-the-ass-wise, schlepping my mom around like this matronly millstone.

But Germany was cool. I had my first beer, but it gave me gas. And then as a head of State, it behooved me to go to one of those Death Camp Theme Parks they have all over the place, and to balance it out for my loyal base, I went to that graveyard Reagan visited of all those SS dudes. Hey, if it was good enough for *The Gipper!* And even though that Caramba is kinda fat and frumpy like Mallory Blitzen, it was fast as shit! I even slid the glass door aside on the womb-room so I could feel some o' that 180 MPH Autobahn air in my face, since they left the windows opened and also the sunroof, although I couldn't appreciate *that* since I can't look up, if you understand the logistics of the womb-room with me inside. And that Mengele Männlichheimer was okay, I guess. Although she kept asking me if I were a twin. And then I had a sit-down with the Porsche CEO guy and I told him how I *loved* the Caramba (even though I didn't. But as President, you havta say all *sorts* o' shit you don't mean to everybody and their uncle cuz ya never know when somebody will take something the wrong way and then it's World War III). And speaking of, those Germans almost took over the world not once but *twice* in just a few years. And that's not too shabby. So to appease them, I talked with that Porsche dude about reintroducing the 911 to the American market as the "Special 9/11 Edition"! Hey, go for that 9/11 dollar! And I know I started that Buy American initiative, but look at the labels. Can you say "sweatshop"? But the Porsches *are* still made in Stuttgart, even though we bombed the shit out of it in that second war they started (which you don't wanna bring up, by the way, cuz they get all weird if ya do). But nevertheless, that was the *first* time America was great cuz we kicked their Nazi butts. But now we're making it *greater* (Nazis notwithstanding). Oh, and I had a pretzel. It was good. *[Looks at TV, at his journalistic nemesis,* Jules Tippler...*]*

"This is Jules Tippler, *CNN,* with a live update. President Rett's latest Tweet drew ire from both the liberal left and from school teachers across America. Mandy Manderson, an elementary school teacher from Sheboygan, Wisconsin had this to say: 'President Rett has to be held accountable for his egregious acts of grammar misuse. If one of my students mixes up 'your' and 'you're,' I make them stay after school and wash the blackboard.'

"Cynthia Winklestein, a sixth-grade teacher from Bound Brook, New Jersey, said:'Neddlepoint? Seriously? I know our so-called President technically didn't even attend kindergarten, but still, what kind of example is this to set for our impressionable youth? If President Rett were my student, I'd give him a big fat F.'

"And Randy Wabash, a third-year college student in pre-law at Yale had this to say: 'That's like, that whole thing, ya know, President Rett, haha! I mean, like, you know what I mean? It's like that time he, you remember? Um, it's just, I don't know, like effed up, man. Like seriously!'"

It's just too easy at times. Hold on. I gotta send a text...

To Tim Chopper:

Tim, that so-called teacher, Cynthia Frankenstein, who wanted to give me a big fat F... Get her F for Fired. And maybe F for Freeze her bank account for a week or two. And if she has a dog, make sure it gets F for Fleas.

Alex

As I said in an earlier chapter, Tim is my Chief-of-Staff, my Enforcer, my Bill Laimbeer. I saw this *ESPN* "30 for 30" on the Bad Boy Detroit Pistons, since I *do* love basketball. It was inspiring. I thought about putting a basket in *here*, but the same ol' story. No room. But I'll trade off spaciousness for ironclad security any day. You'd be surprised how many enemies a POTUS accumulates, just by being President. So anyway, ol' Tim gets things done, like behind the scenes, like ya only have to tell him once. Those jobs that nobody else even knows about. So maybe we should keep this just between us, okay?

[The intercom buzzes...]

"Yes, Gladdy..."

"Mr. President, Tall Skinny Sad-Sack is here."

"Send him in."

[A moment later...]

"Mr. President..."

"Wus happ'nin', homie?"

"Sir?"

"Oh, I'm jus' in a good mood. So let me axe you sumthin', Blake. I mean, Barkley..."

"It's Brayden, sir."

"Haha! Of course." The President smiles. "So Brayden..."

"Sir?"

"You're tall."

"Tall, sir?"

"Like much taller than me. So what I mean is..."

"Why don't I play in the *NBA*?"

"Well, *yeah!*"

"Um, well, I guess that's not where my talents lie, Mr. President."

"Ah, cuz I *love* me some hoops!" the President says.

"Those Bad Boy Pistons, ya gotta love 'em!"

"That was like thirty years ago, sir."

"Yes." Alex lets out a breath along with his good mood. Tall Skinny Sad-Sack is a downer. "So what do you have for me today?"

"Well sir, the PDI is encountering some blockage."

"The PD... Blockage?"

"From within the Party, sir."

"*What?* Who is it?"

"The Majority Whip, sir."

"*Dom Milanese?*"

"Yes sir. Apparently, there have been some backroom dealings with the Black Caucus."

"The Black…"

[Alex quickly reviews all the magazine and newspaper photo shoots he'd done a few months back with Brayden, all so the Black Caucus would give him the thumbs up when he needed them…]

"Sir?"

"How did you find this out?"

"My friend Reggie, sir. We went to school together at Choate. He works for Ezra Banes, the Minority Whip."

"Yes. Thank you. That'll be all."

"Yes sir."

"Oh, Reggie…"

"Brayden, sir."

"Yes, Brayden." Alex offers a half-smile. "One more thing…"

"Sir?"

"Keep your eyes and ears open. Ya feel me?"

"Yes sir, I feel you."

[Alex holds his breath until Tall Skinny Sad-Sack is out the door…]

"*We went to school together at Choate.*" And Ezra Banes, my old friend. What's that they say about no good deed? Hold on, a text from Tim…

To President Alexander Rett:

Mr. President, Cynthia Winklestein will be fired by the end of the day. And her bank account is frozen colder than a witch's tit. But she

has a cat, no dog. Awaiting further instructions.
> **Chopper**

Eh, maybe that "witch's tit" remark was outta line. But I cut ol' Tim some slack cuz *he da Man!*

To Tim Chopper:
Tim, I kinda like cats. Does she have like a goldfish or a gerbil?
> **Alex**

To President Alexander Rett:
No other pets, sir.
> **Chopper**

To Tim Chopper:
Okay, so maybe give her car a flat tire. So after she's fired, she'll see it when she goes to the parking lot pathetically carrying her cardboard box filled with her personal effects and mementos.

And Tim, see what you can dig up, dirt-wise, on Dom Milanese and Ezra Banes. They're back-stabbing duplicitors.
> **Alex**

To President Alexander Rett:
Yes, Mr. President. Consider it done.
> **Chopper**

See what I mean. I don't know what I'd do without him. So, *Dom Milanese...* Hold on. One more thing...

To Tim Chopper:
Tim, that kid, that college student, Andy Wabash, from Columbia or something. See if he wants an internship here this summer.
> **Alex**

To President Alexander Rett:
Will do, Mr. President.

Chopper

Tim, my friend... Ya know, it's not *easy* being President. I mean, friendship-wise. It's a given that everyone has an angle. Like that Black Judas, Ezra Banes. And Dom Milanese, that Dago-Guinea-Wop-Greaseball-Goombah! There, it's amazing how much better you feel after unleashing a completely racist string of expletives! Or is it epithets? I always get those confused. But anyway, I never really had any friends growing up. And friends in *here*, in the *Oval*... Ha! So maybe I should put present betrayals aside and tell you about when I made that decision to stay inside, in the womb-room... *[Alex is distracted by the TV, where Jules Tippler of CNN is jibber-jabbering...]*

"We've just received word that Mandy Manderson, a school teacher who spoke out against President Rett's latest Tweet, has been fired. For more on this, we go to our *CNN* correspondent in Sheboygan, Wisconsin... Rance Uprohr... Rance, what have you got for us?"

"Well, Jules, apparently there's been a massive backlash to that teacher, Mandy Manderson, and her comments regarding the corporal punishment she routinely doles out to her students."

How'd ya like that? We didn't even do anything to her!

"Thousands of emails received from concerned parents calling for her ouster. There's even a grassroots movement that has emerged called Sheboyganites Congregated to Undo Manderson, or SCUM."

Hahaha!

"A spokesperson for SCUM said: 'We can't stand idly by while this so-called teacher inflicts summary punishments on our innocent students simply because their opinions don't happen to match her rather questionable, and I might add, Fascist-leaning ideologies. The school system is no place for such a dispersal of ideas, not to mention such severe punishments as making the poor students stay after school against their will and do forced manual labor. We have learned that the student in question developed painful blisters on his hands from repeated washings of the blackboard, not to mention causing him a near fatal flare-up of asthma from being forced to inhale all that chalk dust.'

"The teacher, Mandy Manderson, was immediately terminated

in response to the public outcry. And now several lawsuits are being initiated as well as a class-action suit. And there have even been allegations against Ms. Manderson regarding incidents of pedophilia... Rance Uprohr, *CNN*, Wisconsin."

Never underestimate the power of the PC Police... *[Looks back to TV, at Jules Tippler yammering away...]*

"Quite a backlash indeed. Supporters are hailing this as a victory for our children, yet opponents are worried that this is yet another erosion of the beleaguered First Amendment. For more on this..."

[Alex clicks off the TV...]

I *hate* that Jules Tippler. And I have to go on his show this Sunday. I'll have to get Manny to make me a few beforehand so I can get ready. And speaking of... *[Points to a minuscule Everlast heavy bag hanging from the ceiling. Alex walks over to it...]* I had this installed since I saw you last. Pretty cool, huh? I've been talking with Iron Mike... You know, my pal Mike Tyson, who's *Secretary of Labor.* Anyway, Mike suggested I get a heavy bag so I can, like, build up my arms and upper body strength. *[Puts on little gloves...]* Here goes! *[Alex unleashes a flurry of punches with his little arms. The bag barely moves, and after a few seconds, huffing and puffing, he gives up...]* Jeez, that's exhausting! I don't know how he does it. But still, it's a great stress-relief, and the job of POTUS is nothing if not stressful. Boy, I got my blood up, with that pedophile teacher and that Jules Tippler and that Dom Ginzo Milanese not to mention that back-stabbing Ezra Banes! Okay, I'm gonna give another shot at the scream. I want it to be like that one Al Pacino does at the end of *Godfather 3*, you know, when that assassin shoots his daughter, who dies all bloody in his arms. That gets me every time. Alright, here goes... *[Alex takes a deep breath, then opens his mouth wide, and out comes that same high-pitched, mouse-like squeak...]* Shit. I need a drink...

[Moments later, there's a knock on the glass. It's Manny with a little martini on a little tray. Alex slides the door aside and Manny hands him the drink...]

"Gracias, Manolo!"

"You are welcome, Mr. Alex."

I *love* when he calls me Mr. Alex! So what were we talking about? Oh yeah, *Godfather 3*. I'm in the minority on this one, but I actually *like*

Coppola's daughter. And if my esteemed predecessor did anything during his time in the Oval, it was making nepotism great again! Ha! I kid him, but we're good friends. He now lives on a private island he named for himself. Hold on, it's a text from Tim...

To President Alexander Rett:
Apparently some eight-year-old kid in that school in Wisconsin is Tweeting in support of his teacher who got fired. Forwarding the Tweet. Awaiting instructions... Regarding dirt on Dom and Banes... still digging.
Chopper

Billy Dinkles @WilliamMyronDinkles
My teahcer, miss Manderson is the besst teahcer ever! and they shold fire the presdient who never even WENT to scool!!!

Why that little shit!

To Tim Chopper:
Can we give this Billy Dickface brat polio or something?
Alex

To President Alexander Rett:
I'll see what I can do, sir.
Chopper

Jeez, d'ya think I can have a minute to myself? My drink's getting warm... *[Looks at martini, takes a sip...]* Shit. There's nothing worse than a lukewarm martini. *[Reaches over to a panel of six or seven buttons on the wall beneath the light dimmer; presses one...]*
"Yes, Mr. Alex?"
"Manny, I need another round, *por favor.*"
"Coming right up, sir."
As you know, Hispanics make the best Infantry. And not bad bartenders. And ya see that thing on the wall beneath the dimmer switch? Those are my buttons! There's the direct line to Manny, and

one to the White House kitchen, and one to Krispy Kreme—the one that's open 24 hours—and one to Tim, and one to my lawyer, and one to my financial advisor, and one to my ol' pal Raz in Russia, and that one, the green one. Do you see it? That's the one I press to drop *The Big One*... Haha! Just kidding! Come to think of it, I don't even know what that one's for. Maybe I should press it... Nah. Just kidding. *[Alex looks back at that eight-year-old's Tweet...]*

Billy Dinkles @WilliamMyronDinkles
My teahcer, miss Manderson is the besst teahcer ever! and they shold fire the presdient who never even WENT to scool!!!

Little fucker! And what's up with those exclamation points? The little shit's mocking my signature triple exclamation-point finish! I'll show *him*...

Alexander Jackson Rett @realAlexRett
Alleged peddophile "teahcer" Mandy Manderson not so hot teacher-wise since Billy Dickles can't even spell "teahcer" as well as lots of other words. Dunce!!!

Alexander Jackson Rett @realAlexRett
Give him dunce cap cuz its President not "presdient." I may never have went to "scool" but have best IQ you would'nt believe how high. Dunce cap award!!!

Alexander Jackson Rett @realAlexRett
I hope Billy Doofus not representitive of all the disgraced Miss Manderson's students as my left big toe is smarter then Billy Dinkins. Peabrain!!!!

[Manny arrives with the martini...]
"*Gracias, mi amigo.*"
"*Da nada*, Mr. Alex." Alex takes a long sip.
"To your liking, *Señor?*"
"*Perfecto!*"

[Alex's phone beeps...]

"Dammit! Can I have this damn drink or what?" *[As Manny leaves, Alex looks down at his smartphone...*

To President Alexander Rett:

Apparently that eight-year-old kid had all his vaccines, so no go on the polio. But you'd better see this, sir...

Chopper

Billy Dinkles @WilliamMyronDinkles

The presedint is a big fat bully!!!!

That little A-hole! Fat? I'm not fat! And he used *four* exclamation points! Okay, this means war!

To Tim Chopper:

Tim, let's go all horror-show on that Billy Dickhead fuckface! Plan F for French Connection with a side of Porno.

Alex

To President Alexander Rett:

Got it. Plan F for French Connection with a side of Porno. Yes sir.

Chopper

At this, the President's personal secretary, Gladiola Gaze, appears—an urgent look on her pinched, wrinkly, well-meaning, middle-aged face. "Mr. President?"

"What is it, Gladdy?"

"The Vice-President is outside, sir. She's insisting that she see you."

"Must I?"

"You haven't seen her in a while, sir. It's been almost a month."

"Is that all? *Sigh...* Alright, send her in."

A moment later, the Vice President of the United States, Mavis DaLyte, walks purposefully up to the womb-room in the Oval Office, the sliding glass door opened to the air. She sees the President wearing a little smoking jacket with the Presidential Seal, a martini in hand.

"Mr. President..." She nods her head deferentially (but with a not-so-subtle hint of defiance).

(When that top-secret group of nameless unsavory billionaires referred to as "The Florists" ran Little Alex for President, they put up Mavis DaLyte, the ineffectual and somewhat scatter-brained Republican Governor of Idaho, as the running mate, to counter the odious Mallory Blitzen—since everyone hates Mallory and everyone loves Mavis. This way, ol' Mallory wouldn't be able to play the *"woman/mom card"* to trump Little Alex's *"fetus card,"* since market research said that most Americans, as in 73%, see Mallory Blitzen first and foremost as an overbearing, know-it-all, entitled, obnoxious, social-climbing, conniving usurper. And a startling 16% weren't even sure if she was actually a woman. So with this in mind, The Florists put forth Governor DaLyte, with her apple-pie, aw-shucks, homespun, Idaho-potato charm and her four kids—one of 'em handicapped with MS or diphtheria or something [to get the "Handicapped Vote"]. Not to mention that with her as the Veep, this would make Alex even more bulletproof, because if it came down to a choice between a woman and a white male fetus for President, America will go with the fetus 7 out of 10 times, according to that same market research. And as the guacamole on the enchilada, it was a given that Mavis DaLyte would toe the line, party-wise, and be a good and faithful Yes-Man. Or, Yes-Woman, as the case may be. But lately she's been exhibiting disturbing signs of thinking for herself, and President Rett and his Chief-of-Staff, Tim Chopper, have been pondering what to do with her.)

"Mavis..."

"Mr. President, that firestorm sitchiation with Billy Dinkles, that young eight-year-old boy..."

"Hmm?"

"There's a backlash, sir, an' it's consider'ble. Some Republican Senators are even comin' forward ta defend him."

"What? They're *defending* that little bastard? Who are they?"

"Perhaps you haven't seen the latest most recent thing on *CNN.*"

The President puts down his drink, grabs the remote, then turns on the TV to see his nemesis, Jules Tippler...

"Republican Senators are circling the wagons in the wake of the latest scandal to afflict President Rett's White House. This one involving the President's bullying Tweets towards an eight-year-old boy, Billy Dinkles, whom the President repeatedly called a 'dunce' and an 'imbecile.'"

"Fake news!" Alex calls out. "I never said imbecile!"

"This was especially disturbing in light of the disclosure that eight-year-old Billy Dinkles has ADHD, due to, as his mother claims, the polio vaccine he was forced to take as an infant. The Handicap Lobby is up in arms, not to mention the Anti-Vaccine Contingent led by controversial *InfoCombat* host, Dirk Fist.

"Little Alex has gone too far this time," said Fist on his nationally syndicated podcast. "It brings to mind the Twin Towers..."

"But by far the most vitriolic attack," says Jules Tippler, "has come from former Presidential Candidate, Mallory Blitzen.

"I am appalled by President Rett's latest attack, no, *assault* on poor Billy Dinkles, who's stricken with ADHD and dyslexia, not to mention gluten-intolerance. Yet in spite of this, he's been an honor student, as well as an outstanding athlete. He's the star backup quarterback on his Pee Wee football team and a pitcher in Small Fry baseball, where he even threw a seven-hitter."

[CNN shows footage of Billy Dinkles running around playing football and baseball, being all athletic and normal-sized...]

"Bush-Leaguers!" says the President.

"I only hope," says Mallory Blitzen, "that the President will issue a public and personal apology to little Billy, as well as an apology to the nation, to the American people, for this outrageous abuse of power, and his mean-spirited assault on this poor, innocent child."

"Say the word *assault* a few more times!" says the President.

"Sir, I urge you to address this immediately," says the Vice-President, "before this sitchiation snowballs outta hand."

[Alex gets a text from Tim Chopper...]

To President Alexander Rett:
Mr. President, Plan F a success. Check out Fox...
Chopper

"Sir," says the Vice-President, "you gotta act on this right now, if not sooner."

"Mavis, stifle!" *[Alex clicks on FOX NEWS...]*

"This is Dash O'Pinyon reporting live. Our *FOX NEWS* affiliate in Wisconsin just broke this story, and it's a big one. Apparently that eight-year-old boy, Billy Dinkles, involved in an online Twitter feud with the President of the United States, has been arrested. He is being charged with being the kingpin behind a million-dollar drug-dealing operation, where illegal drugs from marijuana to cocaine and even heroin were sold not only to students in the second grade, but to the entire elementary school and to the junior high as well.

[Cut to footage, as little Billy Dinkles is doing the perp-walk to his arraignment, his little hand raised to shield his face from the cameras...]

"In addition to being an alleged drug dealer, eight-year-old Billy Dinkles was found with a stash of over 500 hardcore porno magazines under his bed, along with several handguns and a box of ammunition."

[Alex smiles to himself as he turns to the Vice-President...]

"That'll be all, Mavis."

She opens her mouth to speak, but instead she stands there for a moment, her mouth agape, before exiting the Oval Office.

[The President grabs his smartphone...]

To Tim Chopper:

Thanks Tim. Truly inspired. Get ya a case of beer for that one! Oh, one more thing. Get me the names of those GOP senators who supported that bastard Billy Dickface.

Alex

To President Alexander Rett:

Will do, sir.

Chopper

10

[Thursday morning, Le Pain Quotidien, Alexandria, Virginia...]

Brayden Carter sits by himself as he waits for his girlfriend, the older and whiter Carly Menteur. Sipping his *caffè macchiato*, he can't help but notice a distinguished older gentleman a few tables away wearing what looks to be a very expensive suit, occasionally giving him the eye. He takes another sip as Carly appears (but what he *doesn't* notice is Carly's eyes meeting those of the distinguished older gentleman for a split second).

Brayden stands up to give his girlfriend a hug. As she feels his embrace, the older man gets up from his table and walks away.

"I'm glad to see you!" Carly says. And she punctuates this with a delectable French kiss.

"Uh-oh," Brayden says, "we gotta watch those PDAs."

"Yes, or the PDI."

"Haha! Rett's death-ray! I mean, they even *call* it that, can you believe it? Where's the sugar-coating for middle America?"

"I know, right?"

"So, the usual?"

"*Oui merci.*"

Brayden walks to the counter and returns a few minutes later with a caramel latte.

"Speaking of sugar-coating..."

"I *like* my caramel latte!"

"I know."

Before he sits, Brayden shoots a glance at the distinguished older gentleman, but he's gone—the table occupied now by a man-bunned Millennial hipster with red glasses and a paperback in hand: Camus' *L'Étranger.*

"How's your latte?"

"Good, thanks."

"I love the name of this place."

"*Le Pain Quotidien.*"

"Yeah, the word *pain...*"

"It means bread."

"I know, but if you think of it in English... *The pain of the day-to-day.*" Brayden smiles broadly" "I love that."

"Hmm, so how's the leader of the free world?"

"Ha! Not that he's a little *racist* or anything, but he *axed* me why I don't play in the NBA."

"Ha! I've been meaning to *axe* you that myself!" Carly smiles. "And did he really say *axe?*"

"Can you believe it? And then he said, *'You're so tall!'*"

"But *everyone's* taller than him."

"No shit!"

"And you suck at basketball."

"How do *you* know?"

"You *told* me!"

"Oh yeah." Brayden smiles. "So how *is* the little fetus?"

"He's only the biggest narcissist in the world."

"Or the smallest."

"Ha!"

"But I guess that's what they're all like," Carly says.

"Powerful men."

"But don't forget narcissistic *women!* Like Mallory Blitzen... She's a woman, right?"

"Poor Mallory, she lost to a fetus."

"Here's to progress..." In a toast, Brayden holds up his cup of coffee.

"Oh, and he called me Barkley."

"Barkley?"

"And Blake."

"Hey, I kinda *like* Blake! Can I call you that?"

"Sure... So I think he wants me to be his spy."

"Spy?"

"He told me to keep my eyes and ears open."

There's a pause that's not quite uncomfortable, but nevertheless they both feel it.

"So..."

"What?"

"Nuthin," Brayden says.

"So what're you doin' today?"

"I have a meeting."

"A new client?"

"Yeah."

"So you gonna go over to the Watergate and fuck his brains out?"

"Of course! I mean, what *else* do women do?"

"Ha!"

"But only after I give him the estimate for the design, of course."

"Of course. Business before pleasure."

"*Exactement!*"

"I *love* when you speak French."

"Well, this is the place for it. *Je ne peux plus attendre, j'ai encore envi de te baisser.*"

"I don't know what you said, but it gave me a boner."

"Ha! Did it now?"

"So you wanna take a big bite o' my bulging baguette?"

"Double entendres *and* alliteration!"

"Hmm... So what's the French word for boner?"

"Um... *avoir la gaule?*"

"Avoir la..."

"*Gaule.*"

"Gaule."

She shakes her head"

"What?"

"You sound like such an American!"

"I *am* an American."

"*Ouais.*"

"Ouais, which means 'yeah.'"

"*Mais oui.*"

"Okay, so I think I have a *really* big la gaule now."

"Do you?"

"Ouais."

"Hmm." She smiles. "But I have that meeting."

"Ah... *C'est la vie.*"

"Not bad, *monsieur!*"

"Thanks! So, tonight then? *En français?*"

"*Ce soir.*"

"*Ce soir.*"

"*Oui, monsieur.*"

11

So I was gonna tell you when I made that pivotal decision. You know, to stay in the womb forever... *[At that moment, the intercom buzzes.]* Arrggh!

"Yes, Gladdy, what is it?"

"Sir, Tim Chopper is here to see you."

[A moment later...]

"Mr. President. "

Tim, looking comfortable, finds Alex outside the womb-room, seated cross-legged on the edge of Reagan's desk. "Here are those names you requested. The GOP Senators who sided with that kid."

"Thanks, Tim. Have a seat." He looks over the list. "*Ames?*"

"Afraid so, sir."

Alex shakes his head.

"And *Philby?*"

"Mm-mm. "

"And *Vaughan-Heenan?*"

"Yep."

"Traitors." Alex looks further down the list. "Burgess and Blunt?"

"Uh-huh."

"But *Blunt?*"

"Afraid so, sir."

"I gave him that stock tip!" The President lets out a sigh of disgust. "Well, an example must be set."

"I agree, sir. Might I suggest OPERATION CLOSET?"

"*OPERATION CLOSET*... Excellent, Tim. Nuthin' works on Republican Senators like a whopping gay sex scandal."

"Indeed. Will there be anything else, sir?"

"No... Oh yes, you remember that artist I had you vet for me?"

"Artist?"

"That painter, Vincent Van Go-Go."

"Yes. He lives in Brooklyn, sir."

"I want you to bring him to the White House sometime next week. To do my official portrait."

"I'll get him, sir."

"So any news on our two friends, Dom and Ezra?"

"Not yet, sir. But I'm working on it."

"Good."

"Anything else, Mr. President?"

"No... Thanks, Tim."

Chopper starts to leave when Alex calls out. "Oh Tim..."

"Sir?"

"Thanks again, for, you know, that Dinkles thing. It was... impeccable."

"My pleasure, sir."

Tim Chopper, my one bright light. So that artist, Vincent Van Go-Go... His paintings sell for like 200 grand. But he was this unknown broke-ass loser by the name of Ace Buckland living in Newark, New Jersey in some abandoned brewery where he'd trade his paintings for whiskey and drugs. But then he changed his name to Vincent Van Go-Go and he started painting like his namesake. And he got away with it because he said he was Van Gogh in a *previous incarnation!* (So it wasn't like he was ripping off someone else's *style*, right? Ha!) And the art world being what it is, they bought it (and he didn't even have to cut off an ear). And now he's this millionaire living in New York and London with a house in Alexandria (although that was his parents' place). And after that, all these *other* artists started claiming that they were the reincarnated Picasso and Jackson Pollock and Rembrandt, but Van Go-Go was the first and all those other guys were SOL... I like his style. He doesn't give a shit. Besides, it'll be cool to have my White House portrait looking like some Starry Night acid trip hanging across from Herbert Hoover's.

Personally, I say no to drugs. Not because I'm ideologically opposed, but because my doctor advises against it. All those horror stories of crack whores with their crack-whore babies all strung out, since fetuses don't make good drug addicts. I'm afraid the afternoon martini or two is the limit of my expanded consciousness. So, I was saying... Oh wait. Time for a *Tweet*...

Alexander Jackson Rett @realAlexRett
Mallory, you backed wrong horse with that Dinkins kid drug-dealer. Your judgemint sound as ever. What a mess you would of made hear. But that'l never happen. Loser!!!

Ah, I feel better!

12

Mallory Blitzen. Get over it already! I mean, can't you find something to do? Write another memoir. I have some titles for you: *Frumpy Old Has-Been Loser*, or *How I Got Schooled by Someone Who Never Went to School*, or my personal fave, *I Lost to an Effing Fetus!*
[Using his smartphone, Alex brings up the video of the final Presidential Debate.]
I *love* this! I watch it whenever I feel kinda blue, to remind myself of how I kicked Mallory's rather large, shapeless behind. Oh, there she is on the left, Mallory Rodman Blitzen, in her bright red... well, it's not a *dress*, really, more like a frock. A fusty frock on a frumpy Hausfrau from Frankfurt. And I know there's this unwritten rule in politics regarding the conservative power suit/uniform that looks more like a block of granite with eyes, nose, and a mouth. And I guess throw on a pair of ears, but in case ya haven't noticed, candidates listening to the question being asked, or Heaven forbid, each other is, well, optional.

Oh look! There's me in my *mini* power suit. (It's a 2R, meaning 2 Regular.) Navy blue, of course, not black because black is for funerals, and you don't wanna be dressed for a funeral at your own Presidential Debate because that would send a mixed message. But you don't wanna wear a blue that's too light either, because that would mean you're not serious. And running for President is nothing if not serious.

Look at Mallory, with that... what shape *is* that? Her frock, that is. It's not square or rectangular. It's more like the geometrical equivalent of a pear.

Yes! A trapezoid! There's Mallory Blitzen in her bright red trapezoid with the sensible heels. I mean, we don't want our President, if she's a woman, to be struttin' her stuff in stilettos, showin' some thigh an' sashayin' her way to the important Cabinet Meeting, shakin' her booty like some Vegas showgirl! It's the old double-standard, that brains and beauty, especially if there's sexiness involved, don't make for a viable candidate. But the problem is, we now have Mallory Blitzen for sixty long minutes without commercial breaks, looking like a frumpy trapezoidal tomato. And I know I'm kinda small there, especially on the screen of my smartphone, but if you squint, you'll see that *my* power suit is the same style that Kennedy wore when he kicked Nixon's butt on national TV. When JFK was all suave and tan and Nixon was all swarthy and sweating his ass off like Rudolf Hess in the dock at freaking Nuremberg—which is not an electable image, by the way. And even though I'm a big fan of Tricky Dick, he wasn't exactly a clothes horse.

I guess I'd do better on radio, because even though I'm pretty small, I have this voice that's rather normal-sized. Not to mention the disconcerting image of me in the womb-room with my mom looming above me. This presented a quandary, debate-wise, because nobody wants to see their Presidential candidate with his freaking *mom* always hovering about! But surprisingly, ol' Mallory thought that debating a fetus while he's inside the womb would be too distracting. (Everyone would be looking at *me and my mom*, not *her! Can you say *narcissist?*) So the producers put that black curtain in front of my mom with a hole cut out so all you see is me, with the big screen overhead for close-ups, like we're at a freaking rock concert.

And there's the Moderator, Agnes Plunge, who anchors that news show on *PBS* that no one watches because, well, Agnes Plunge has seen better days. Today, she's like seventy-something with those round, wire-rimmed glasses and that Ayn Rand hair-bob and those even frumpier frocks that make her look like someone's Dust Bowl kindergarten teacher during The Great Depression. And doesn't *PBS* know *anything?* The template for today's modern female newscaster is young, hot, blonde, and babe-a-licious, with complexions so smooth they make linoleum jealous and hair so shiny it gives you sunburn. But Agnes Plunge has *gravitas* to burn. And as I said above, this is serious business, the selling of a President.

"Good evening, and welcome to the final Presidential Debate. I'm Agnes Plunge, and I'll be the Moderator for tonight's spectacle. The format is once again..."

Okay, this is the usual boilerplate. Let's fast-forward a bit...

"What was the question again? Because I thought we were talking about education, and my opponent seemed to talk about anything but."

Haha! This is good. Since it was the last debate, ol' Mallory and her team of strategists decided to take the gloves off. And while we Americans love to kick ass, like as often as possible, we also have this soft spot for the underdog, especially if the underdog is this cute little puppy dog with sad puppy dog eyes, like that stray who just wants a home.

"Senator Rett seems to... Oh, I'm sorry. You're not a senator, are you, sir? Forgive me, I misspoke. In fact, you've never held public office."

Go Mallory!

"In fact when it comes down to it, my esteemed opponent has never been to school, not even kindergarten, not even pre-school, not even daycare, not even..."

She's on a roll!

"He's never even had a *baby-sitter!*"

Watch this! She looks out at the audience as if they're her allies. But all *they* see is some bullying baby-basher!

"You're not a baby either. In fact, an actual *baby* has more worldly experience than you have, is that not so? In fact, a newborn infant in the Maternity Ward at any hospital in America right now has..."

"You've made your point, Senator Blitzen."

[The moderator, Agnes Plunge, intervenes.] Haha! *Go Agnes!* And

watch this. *[The camera pans across the audience.]* Look at her. She's disgusted. And this guy here—he's like, "*Leave the little guy alone, ya big frumpy bully!*" And this one's like, "*Come on! Give the little guy a chance!*" Cuz Americans, like I said, have this soft spot for the underdog. And now Mallory goes after Agnes.

"My *point* is the sheer lack of experience my opponent has, by definition, in not just education but life experience as well, since…"

"Yes, we get that your opponent is a fetus."

Agnes to the rescue like the freaking cavalry! And *there*, she gives me this warm, motherly look. *Aww…* And watch what she says here.

"But it's not like anyone's kept this a secret from you, Senator Blitzen."

Ha! Listen to the laughs. And now Mallory's all contrite… sort of, because Mallory doesn't do contrite.

"Yes of course. I understand that. And I believe that was the point I was making about qualifications. I've been a Senator for eight years, and in all that time, I've worked tirelessly on these many different…"

And all the audience hears is *blah blah blah*. Oh, here's *me!*

"Mr. Rett, your response…"

"Thank you, Agnes. I don't think there's any doubt that I'm not your average candidate. And I think that's a *good* thing! I mean, who wants average?" Look at that smile! Not bad, huh? Although technically, I still have my baby teeth.

"I know that my esteemed opponent, Senator Blitzen, is a big baseball fan. So am I, as I believe most Americans are. And we all have that player on our favorite team, right? The one who's been around for… eight years. And they're solid and reliable and they hit .250 and they're decent at second base. And the years go by and our team never makes the playoffs, not once, but we're used to it. 'Maybe *next year*,' we say. But then this rookie comes along, this hotshot center-fielder. And he doesn't have much experience, because he's a rookie. But he has this spark, this desire, this *need* to be great. He won't settle for anything less. And not for himself but for his team—this team he loves! *Our* team! Because he realizes that individual greatness is defined by the greatness of the team… I mean, what good is it if that second baseman we talked about before, the one who hits .250…

What good is it if they tell you about their eight years of experience while their team has never made the playoffs, not one single time! Do you wanna say yet again, 'Maybe next year,' or do you wanna say, *'This year! Right now!'*"

And even though they're not supposed to applaud, listen to that crowd! I mean, did I kill, or what? And Mallory's like, suicidal. "Please, hold your applause."

And then, watch... Ol' Agnes smiles for like a *split second*. Did ya *see?* Then she suppresses it. I *love* that Agnes Plunge. So I wanna fast-forward to the "abortion" bit. It's *sooo* good!... Here it is. Here's me...

"My situation, as you can see, is unique. And unlike others who may be concerned only with themselves, with their own happiness and well-being..."

Bang-Zoom!

"I realize every moment of every day how I depend on others and how they depend on me. Everybody's seen *The Wizard of Oz*, right?"

Ha! There's me looking at the crowd. And then... I *love* this, they're all smiling to themselves, see? I made them happy. My team of strategists said *The Wizard of Oz* polls consistently in the 95th percentile, political debate-wise, with baseball at the 87th.

"You all *know* that my mom is behind that curtain... *Hi Mom!*"

"Hi baby!"

"*Mom!*" *[Laughter from the audience...]*

"I'm sorry, I mean *President-Elect Rett!*"

Way ta go, Mom! They're eatin' it up! And look at that sourpuss, Mallory Blitzen, eating her liver! She and I had agreed that I was *never* to engage my mom and that my mom was never to speak. Haha! Suck on that one, Trapezoid!

"Well, let's not get ahead of ourselves." Watch how I turn to the crowd...

"There's nothing like a mom who loves you!"

And was that one big *"Aww"?*

"And I love my mom..."

Who doesn't like a boy who loves his mom! I'm gettin' all misty-eyed.

"And because of this, these unique circumstances that have brought me here tonight, I am literally dependent upon someone else for my very existence. Which is why I will *always* support the sanctity of our unborn children. Think of it for a moment. I stand before you now with the hopes of becoming your next President."

A few cheers!

"Thanks guys! I'm here tonight with the intention of being a fair and just leader. A leader who will lead by example, and who will inspire *you* to be your best. Because imagine what a great country this will be if we are *all* inspired again."

Wait for it...

"Yes, Alex!"

"Please, hold your comments."

Go Agnes! *Crack* that whip!

"So with this in mind, we must believe in each other's potential, this potential for greatness. And of course potential is good, but it's nothing if it goes unrealized."

Here it comes...

"My opponent, Mallory Blitzen, has aspired to a greatness that sadly has *not* been realized. And through her we see the tragedy of this. So when you think of our unborn children, think not of their unrealized potential, but rather that they can be something great, even President. Value them as you do yourselves, when you're feeling most inspired."

And the crowd goes ape! And Agnes, *watch...* She tosses her hands in the air. Is that great or what? Ha! And now the follow-up...

"As a follow-up question, Mr. Rett... How does your stance on abortion align with your stance on health care?"

"Thank you, Agnes. That's a good question. I believe we are strongest when we come together to help each other. *Especially* in our time of need, because that's when we need it most. We've all heard the expression, *fair-weather friend*, right? You may have even *met* a few."

A strategic glance at Mallory. Haha! Look at her face! Like a *constipated prune.*

"We're all in this together. And if we can focus on what we have in common, the things that we share, rather than being separated by our differences, then we won't be that fair-weather friend. We'll be there when we need each other most."

More applause, like candy from a baby. And Mallory's slow-burn has become a singe.

"Senator Blitzen, your response..."

"Thank you, Agnes... Well, I've heard a lot of things in my eight years in the Senate..."

Seriously, Mallory?

"...but that takes the cake. My... I was going to say *esteemed opponent,* but by definition, to be esteemed, you have to actually *do* something. And technically he hasn't even been *born,* so..."

"Yes, Senator Blitzen, it's been well-established that your opponent is a fetus."

More laughter. That Agnes should have her own show... Wait, she *does* have her own show! Maybe I should watch it.

"Is that your answer to the question, Senator Blitzen?"

"Um, no, it's... What I meant to *say* is that Mr. Rett, among his rather limited achievements... I mean, by definition..."

If she says "*by definition*" one more time, this thing is mine!

"By being, in fact, a fetus... then, *by definition...*"

BINGO!

"...his achievements are few and far between. But I will grant him the gift of gab. He sure can spin a yarn."

Ha! Are you kidding? Nobody says "*spin a yarn*"!

"And what he just said, his answer. Can you play it back? I mean, what did he even *say?* It's just... high-sounding empty phrases with no substance." And now watch... She turns to the audience like they're her second-graders and she's this crotchety old schoolmarm who's gonna make them stay after school.

"I just hope that when all of you face that desperate time, when you're sick in the hospital and dying, that you'll get more than empty words."

Give it a rest, Mallory! Okay, on to the grand finale...

"We are nearly at the end of the debate. This last question has been submitted by Caleb Sears, a fifth-grader from the Rutherford B. Hayes Elementary School in Delaware, Ohio. The question is: 'If you were a flower, what kind would you be?'... Senator Blitzen, you are first to respond..."

"Thank you, Agnes... And I'd also like to thank the audience here, and the American people at home. In my many years of public service, I've valued very much the wonderful people that I've..."

"Senator Blitzen, would you like me to repeat the question?"

Haha! Agnes!

"Um, yes please."

"If you were a flower, what kind would you be?"

"Well... I would... I would be... a Venus Fly Trap!"

"A Venus Fly Trap? Is that even a flower?"

Go Agnes!

"Yes. It's a flowering plant."

"Okay. So why would you choose *that?*"

"Because the Venus Fly Trap gets things done. It's no nonsense. When something is wrong, it fixes it. When an enemy appears, whether it be foreign or domestic, it puts them down for good. You know where you stand with a Venus Fly Trap. It's not just some pretty flower that does nothing."

No words...

"Mr. Rett... If *you* were a flower, what kind would you be?"

"If I were a flower... I'd be... a rose."

"A rose?"

"Yes. A rose is about so many good, positive things that we all value as Americans. It's about *love*... And isn't that what we want most in life? To love and be loved?"

Look at them nodding..."

"It even smells nice!"

Laughter...

"It's what we give to the people we love most, to show them how we feel. Who doesn't like getting roses, right?" Goin' for the *Woman Vote!*

"But it also has thorns, which means that we're Americans and this is America. We live in a beautiful country with the highest standard of living that makes us the envy of the world, and we love it dearly. But if you *mess* with us..."

I love this pause...

"Then these thorns will have sumthin' ta say. Ya know what I'm sayin'? Thank you so much! I'm Alexander Rett: *The Choice*... God Bless America!"

And not to be immodest, but will ya listen to the applause! It goes on for so long, it's almost embarrassing. And there's poor ol' Mallory... crumpled, crestfallen, crushed.

She lost to an effing fetus.

13

I guess you could say I'm precocious. I mean, *"by definition."* Ha! *Mallory*... And for the next few weeks, that became this catch-phrase that swept the nation. *Everybody* said it.

"You don't wanna go out with me? Well then, *by definition*, you're a..."

"Just the fact that you're here wanting to buy a Cadillac means that, *by definition*..."

"Your Honor, the witness's testimony proves that, *by definition*, he...

And it reached its zenith the following weekend on that live comedy show, *Saturday Nite In-Yer-Face*. The actor who played "Mallory" said it every chance she got, to uproarious laughs (and a few more percentage points in the polls *pour moi*). And with just a few weeks before Election Day, the campaign raged on. Not to say that she took it badly, what happened during the Final Debate, but Mallory Blitzen's commercials got nasty. And as so often happens with smear campaigns, it was a big-ass backfire.

Her 'WHO WANTS A little LEADER?' spot debuted during *Monday Nite Football*. And then came the slew of posters and bumper stickers. But all it did was reinforce her bullying of the underdog... *moi*, again. Not to mention that from far away, the billboard said, **WHO WANTS A LEADER?**, which made people think of me.

Then came her blatant grab for the *Woman Vote*...

Do You Want **A WOMAN WITH EXPERIENCE?**

Or **A MAN WHO'S A FETUS?**

But counter-intuitively, the maternal instinct kicked in, in women across America, and it was a wash.

And then came her *new & improved* campaign slogan:

MALLORY BLITZEN: BORN TO LEAD, which of course brought up that whole "I'm still a fetus" horse that she boringly beat to death during the final debate. And then things got ugly. In a last-ditch effort two days before Halloween, she appeared on *The Jules Tippler Show.* She made a big production of displaying her birth certificate to the cameras. "*I have a birth certificate,*" she declared, with a way-too-intense, smug determination that made her seem, well, unhinged and a bit nutty. "*Can my opponent say the same thing?*" But all it did was show to America—beneath a most glaring and unflattering spotlight—that you *don't dis the fetus...* EVER.

And me, I stayed the course. Our campaign strategy right from the start was to ignore Mallory completely. To let her self-destruct and instead aim the campaign scattergun at my predecessor. Because he somehow got elected in the first place, and since he spent his time in office dodging IMPEACHMENT GRENADES and side-stepping minefields of SHIT-BOMBS, we figured we'd be a shoo-in if we came off as *just a little bit better.*

So we used that tried and true tactic of turning our weaknesses into our strengths. The fact that I was childless:

With me, NO NEPOTISM!

That I was stuck inside the womb:

THIS President Won't Play Golf!

That I was unmarried, since I was, as everybody realized (except Mallory Blitzen), a fetus:

MY ONLY AFFAIRS WILL BE AFFAIRS OF STATE!

And then, the official campaign slogan:

MAKE AMERICA GREATER!

And then of course, the most important thing of all, the bumper sticker:

ALEX RETT: *THE CHOICE*

Four of the most persuasive words in American history, as they swayed a nation and elected a President.

ALEX RETT: A strong, no-nonsense name. Easy to read. Easy to pronounce. Easy to remember.

THE CHOICE: In America, between Mallory Blitzen and a fetus, there *was* no choice. At times, I even felt sorry for her. So when Election Day rolled around, it wasn't even close, despite what that sore-loser keeps going on about, with her winning the popular vote. And in response, we put out a slew of posters and bumper stickers that said: **POPULAR SCHMOPULAR!**

Ahh! I feel so much better. Time for a Tweet...

Alexander Jackson Rett @realAlexRett

Mallory, when will you except that you lost to a FETUS? Perhaps some PSYCHO-therapy is in order. And maybe a new dress desiner. Haha! Looser!!!

14

In my own defense, I haven't gotten out much. I guess I'm ahead of the curve, at least for a fetus. Hell, for anyone, like those public servants in Congress (and perhaps quotes should be put around *public servants*). They're more like ants at a picnic. They want it to always be summer so the picnic never ends. I mean, Skitch McDougall voted 17 times against raising the minimum wage, but he voted 37 times to give *himself* a raise. Ha! But if I were him, I'd worry more about that triple chin becoming a quadruple chin! And regarding greed, when you're the Prez, you have to show a bit more subtlety (my esteemed predecessor notwithstanding). My friend Raz is never shy about offering advice. He's the President of Russia. Well, "President" is a bit of a stretch, as is the word "friend." Put it this way, you don't wanna get on his shit list. And there are those boring detractors still going on about Russian election-hacking. Get over it already! Ya think we didn't learn anything from Watergate? That shit is like jaywalking nowadays. Tricky Dick's rolling over!

So where was I?

Oh yeah, I wanted to tell you about that fateful day when I

decided to remain inside here forever. It's not often when you can look at a single moment as the turning point in your life. I mean, I didn't even know I was different. How could I? All I knew of the world was through those shows my mom watched on *YouTube* and *Netflix*. It could've been worse. She could've binge-watched *Sex and the City* and listened to disco.

What it comes down to is that the expectations of a fetus are really low, like non-existent. If your little arms and legs look relatively normal by the second trimester and not like Quasimodo, then the humans outside show off that sonogram like it's a winning Powerball ticket. The bar couldn't be lower, which for me has been pretty awesome. At first, anything I did beyond normal fetus stuff was big news and went viral overnight. I beat out Kim Kardashian's ass in a single day, and now I have something like 50 million followers on social media, and my slightest utterance, no matter how unfounded or ridiculous, is seen by most of the world. Life! Ain't it grand?

So I remember the moment. My mom was watching reruns of *All in the Family*, and Edith said something dingbatty and Archie said, "Edith, stifle." And my mom let out this high-pitched squawk of a laugh and suddenly it hit me, that everything bad in life happens *out there!* All the wars and famine and reality TV shows and people being shitty. But since this was the incipient second of my enlightenment, some research was required.

I wondered, for example, if that telepathy thing went both ways. You remember the "lemonade incident," when my mom just *thought* about getting a glass of lemonade but somehow I *knew*. So I concentrated real hard about the human condition, namely *my* condition in here. And lo and behold, by the afternoon, my mom was watching all these documentaries and they all said the same thing: that Americans are head-over-heels in love with the fetus. And I said, "*Da-yum!*"

And the next day, my mom watched this show on the prenatal environment and I gotta say, I was flabbergasted (to use one of Mom's favorite words). Apparently, I'm the anomaly, since all these other fetuses, like stretching back to time immemorial, have all been, well, dumb shits. Like inane drones wallowing in amniotic fluid, sucking their prenatal thumbs, dumber than a bag o' Democrats.

And not only that, they're completely clueless as to their position in life. They got it made, but they're too dopey to realize it. And from that moment on, I was determined to stay inside and never leave! But as with all glimpses of enlightenment, there's always a downside.

[Way back in the distant past, like the third trimester...]

"So I've decided to stay here," I said.

"What do you mean, baby?" said my mom.

"In here, in the womb."

"Oh, but you can't do that, baby."

"I think I can. And stop calling me *baby*."

"But..."

"I mean, technically I'm not born, so by definition I can't be a baby."

"But you're my *unborn* baby," my mom said.

"Okay," I relented.

"But I'm still not coming out."

"Ha! Well, I don't think it's your choice, dear."

"I don't know. I've been doing some research. Do you remember that documentary I had you watch, on the prenatal environment?"

"Yes, I... had me watch?"

"Forget it. But you remember it said that the womb is nearly ideal, from the standpoint of the fetus, because it's where all his needs are met unconditionally."

"Um, yes, I remember that. *Everyone* knows that, but..."

"So, *ergo*, why would any thinking person ever wanna leave?"

"Haha! That documentary on Descartes! *Cogito ergo sum*." My mom smiled. "My baby learns so fast!"

"*Mom!*"

"I'm sorry."

"So..."

"What, baby? I mean, dear."

"Don't you think it's, like, time I got a name?"

"But honey, that's what we'll do when you're... I mean..."

"But I'm not coming out. I told you that."

"I know, but..."

"I'm adamant."

"Okay. So you're going to just stay inside me then."

"Yes."

"Inside my womb."

"I mean, this is the place."

"Forever."

"Well..."

"My son..." She shook her head, then looked away.

"What?"

She remained silent.

"*What?*"

"I'm just... disappointed, is all."

"Disappointed? In what?"

"Not in what, dear."

"What, you're disappointed in *me?*"

"Well, what kind of son would..."

"What?"

"Nothing."

"*What?!*"

"Well, do this to his loving mother!"

"Hey!"

"I don't know *what* I did to raise such a spoiled, self-centered child." She shook her head again, then looked down at her womb, a vexed expression on her face. "Did you ever for once think about *me?*" she asked. "I mean, for a *moment?* How I might *feel* to have my unborn child living inside my womb for... well, *forever*, as you put it."

"But..."

"*Selfish selfish selfish.*"

"Mom, I..."

"What?"

There was a long, painful pause. Then, finally, I spoke.

"I... I'm sorry."

"Hmm, *sorry*," she shrugged.

"Sorry doesn't buy eggs on Tuesday." She sighed, then looked up at the ceiling.

"I don't know what I did wrong, God, to raise such a selfish child who only thinks of himself. I just don't know. I hope you can forgive me, when it's time for the Last..."

"Mom, *hello!* I'm right *here*, you know."

"Yes, I know. And you'll be right here forever, as you've told me. You're... *adamant*... Hmm, don't worry about me. I won't mind having you weigh me down like a sea anchor so my back always aches and I can never sleep on my stomach and I can't even have my little glass of wine before dinner that I used to like so much. And I *love* wearing maternity clothes. I really do. They're so... *stylish*."

"Jesus." I let out a sigh.

"You shouldn't take the Lord's name in vain."

"Hmm..." I sighed again. "Alright, you win."

"What was that?"

"I said I'll come out, if... if it means that much to you."

"You... You *will?*" My mom's eyes opened wide.

"Yeah, I guess."

"Oh good, baby! That makes your mama so happy!"

"But... can I ask you a favor?"

"What?"

"I know I'm supposed to be evicted in like a month or so, but..."

"It's born, not evicted."

"Whatever. So can I just hang for a few more months inside? Three months *tops!* So I can, you know, get used to the idea of being born, and... well, it'll give me the chance to say goodbye... to *in here*."

"Well..." She let out a huff.

"I just don't know."

"Please, Mom?"

"..."

"*Pleeeease.*"

"*Hhhh...*" She let out another sigh. "Alright, I guess. But just for a month or two."

"Yes! Three months tops!"

"Well... okay."

"Thanks, Mom! You're the best!"

"Hmm... I'm just happy that I'll finally get to *see* you."

At that moment, my father arrived home from work.

"Joey!" my mom said, rising excitedly to her feet (giving me a good jostling in the process).

My father looked at her once, grunted a greeting, then offered his left cheek to her in a perfunctory, lackluster way, and my mom planted the daily kiss.

"I'll get you a beer, dearie," she said. "How was work?"

"*Errgghh,*" he grunted again as she handed him a cold can of *Döpplegänger*, his favorite beer from the Old Country, and his one and only extravagance. What followed was the loud sloppy slurping sound that preceded the can-crinkling ritual, followed by said crinkled can being flung across the kitchen through the air into the wastebasket, a swish every time. (Perhaps this is where I got my love of basketball.)

"Guess what, Joey!" said my mom.

Without turning his head, my father issued a beer-induced belch.

"Our little baby has decided to come out after all!"

At this, my father cocked his right eye askew.

"*Ergh?*" he said.

"Yes!" my mom replied, overjoyed. "He's finally decided to be born!"

My father's left eyebrow raised, followed by a single nod of the head as my mom looked in his eyes.

"So maybe it's time we, you know, gave the little guy a name," she said. And as if to punctuate her statement, she softly rubbed her own belly with me still inside.

"*Hrrghh,*" my father said.

"I've given this some thought," my mom began.

"What do you think of Oscar?" She looked at my father, his face a blank.

"Well, how 'bout Maximillan? No? What about Arthur?"

Nothing.

And I listened, rapt, as my mom rattled off one name after another, each more absurd than the last, just to get a response out of my father, who made the Sphinx seem loquacious.

"Mortimer? Lance? Pietro? Rapscallion? Lafcadio? Peterpiper? Giacomo? Retrovirus? BumbleBee? Xerox? Califragilistic? Bombastic? Bonomo Turkish Taffy? Beelzebub? Rory? Caligula? Sampan?"

I'm not sure how long it went on...

"Reynaldo? Robitussin? Rhubarb? Mittagessen? Gonorrhea? Guatemala? Gargantua? Gargles?"

And after what seemed an eternity, my father finally spoke, a single, stately, four-syllable name.

"Alexander," he said, in a voice so coarse, it was as if a thicket of brambles occupied his voice box. But my mom was overjoyed.

"*Alexander!* What a lovely name!" she beamed. "Oh Joey!" And she enveloped him in her embrace like a Giant Squid clasps on to a cruise ship. And then my mom looked down at me and said, "My dear son, Alexander! My little Alex!"

For some reason, I cringed at the reality of finally having a name. The next thing ya know, I'll be out in the world, working a summer job at Dairy Queen with a face full of zits and no prospects, my life a big dead end. "Alex, say hello to your father!" my mom said.

"*Errggh*," I said. And my father said "*Errggh*" in response. Nothing like male bonding.

That night as my mom slept soundly, imagining the day when she'd be free of me at last, I lay awake in my *sanctum sanctorum* that soon would be no more. But then, Fate intervened.

[The intercom buzzes...] Hold on, I gotta do some President stuff...

"Mr. President?"

"What is it, Gladdy?"

"The Daily Briefs are here, sir. I sent you an email."

"Oh. Okay."

"And Governor Portly is here."

"Who?"

"Governor Por... That fat governor is here to see you."

"Oh yes! Thanks, Gladdy. Send him in."

Who can remember all these names? Thankfully, Gladdy and I worked out these *nicknames* for everyone. She even made flash cards. Porter Portly is the Governor of Iowa or New Jersey or something, and he's really fat, like Goodyear blimp fat. And every time he waddles into the Oval, I gotta hold on tight cuz my mom's near-lifeless and comatose body starts undulating uncontrollably from the vibrations.

"Mr. President."

"Port! Have you been working out?"

"Fat chance. Haha! Say, there's this new intern... at *least* a ten." He gives me a licentious smile as he excavates his cell phone from his voluminous suit, evidently designed by Omar the Tent-Maker.

"*See...*" He shows me her pic. "Hot as shit, right? I mean, *am I right?*"

"Hmm," I say with a noncommittal nod.

"And here's one in a bikini! I swiped it from her Facebook page! What a knockout, huh? Boy, I'd like ta get me a Lewinski from *that!*"

Immediately, I drift into Little Alex mode...

There, lying on a sandy beach in Iowa or New Jersey, amidst the discarded fast-food wrappers, beer cans, used condoms, and syringes, is *The Leviathan* washed ashore. Pathetically, it gasps for air, about to breathe its last breath, when the Swedish Bikini Team happens to walk by. (They're in town for the Bikini Convention in Des Moines or Atlantic City.) And being concerned with their fellow man, as Swedish people usually are (unless their fellow man is a Norwegian), they try to roll the great beast back into the sea.

But when the creature notices that he's surrounded by hot babes in bikinis, he starts leering lasciviously, drool dripping from his slack-jawed mouth and disgusting spittle on his lathering lips. And then he says something that decorum prohibits me from repeating. But needless to say, it's really fucking foul. Members of the Swedish Bikini Team look at each other once before grabbing these things that look like battle axes (which, since it's my daydream, are just lying around), and they proceed to hack his blubberous body to bits as he screams in agonized awareness that his whole miserable life has brought him to an end such as this.

"So I hope that clears everything up," says Port Portly.

"I mean, I would *never* side with some eight-year-old drug-dealing pornographer! *Fake news!* Ha! You know I got your back, Mr. President!"

"Thanks. I know I can always count on you, Port."

"Yessiree Bob!"

As Port Portly leaves, I hold on tight till he's out the door.

Alexander Jackson Rett @realAlexRett

Just had a BIG meeting with Gov. Port Portly. Huge! Talked about important stuff like getting down to business. He's a great friend. Want to give him ENORMOUS hug!!!

So where was I? Hold on, it's a text from Tim...

To President Alexander Rett:
More Dirk Fist shit. Check out podcast...
Chopper

What the fuck? Can't I have a second to myself? *[Grabs smartphone; goes to* YouTube *to see the latest podcast from* InfoCombat...*]*
"Our investigative journalists here at *InfoCombat* have made a shocking discovery! Among our current President's numerous and nefarious lies, we've found that his very *name* isn't even real."
I *hate* that Dirk Fist.
"His father, who died under mysterious circumstances, was named Josef Schnitzelgrüber. You can see why the so-called President didn't want *that* name. We all know that he took his mother's name, which is *Rett*, although our investigative reporters have uncovered that his mother's *real* name is *Retler*... Sound like anyone we know? *[Cut to newsreel footage of Hitler's 1936 Nuremberg speech...]* Adolf Hitler... Alex Retler... Coincidence? I don't think so. Think back to that dark day of September eleventh..."
Arrggh. I *really* hate that Dirk Fist.

Alexander Jackson Rett @realAlexRett
Maybe Dirk Fist shuld be more concernd with going to the gym then with my genology. Last I heard I was POTUS and he was just some fat f#*@!!!

The Internet. Jeez! In the old days, if you were an idiot, you had to keep it to yourself. Now you have a podcast. Which reminds me, I guess I should tell you the rest of the story. You know, the one I began before all the interruptions... Oh fuck, the *Daily Briefs. Gotta look at the Daily Briefs, blah-blah blah-blah.* One more second... *[Alex clicks on his smartphone to his email account. He gives the* Daily Briefs *a cursory glance, then presses* DELETE...*]* Same ol' shit. So where were we?

15

[Wednesday evening; an upscale bar in Georgetown called Deco...*]* Brayden Carter sits at the bar next to Reggie Mason (his best friend from their days at Choate), a Gin & Tonic in hand.

"How's your drink, man?" Reggie asks.

"It's really good!" Brayden turns to the bartender, a sultry-yet-surly white woman of twenty-six or so, her long black hair severely bound in a Dominatrix ponytail. "Excuse me, what kind of gin is this?"

"Do you know your gin?" the bartender asks, as if she couldn't be bothered and it pains her to even speak.

"Well, no!" he says. He shoots a quick glance at Reggie, then turns back to the bartender. "That's why I'm asking."

"Hmm..." she says. "It's *Old Tom.*"

"Oh... okay. Thanks!"

The bartender walks away with two parts disinterest, one part rudeness, a dash of disdain, and a garnish of fuck-off.

Brayden turns to his friend.

"What just happened there?" he asks.

"Like, was she just this *snooty uptight snobby white bitch?*"

"Well, *yeah.*"

"Why you like this place again?" Reggie asks.

"She's new."

"Seriously, man, this place..."

"I don't know, I *always* come here. It's like... like it's modern and old at the same time."

"*Art Deco,* that's from the thirties, man... the *nineteen*-thirties..."

"So..."

"When white people were livin' it up in a place like this, we was down South gettin' our black asses lynched."

"Jeez, what a buzzkill!" Brayden finishes his drink, then looks to the bartender to catch her eye.

"*What*, man?" Reggie says.

"This place is racist."

"You think *everything* is racist."

"Well..."

"Ya know what? I think *you're* racist!"

The bartender appears and offers Brayden a pained raise of her eyebrows.

"Another one, please," he says.

Irrepressibly peevish, she grabs his glass and walks away.

"See what I mean?"

"But she's not racist," Brayden says, leaning in closer.

"Oh no?"

"She's just... a *bitch!*" he says in a whisper, and they both laugh.

"How's your drink?"

"They can't fuck up a bottle o' beer, man."

"Hmm, have I told you what a delight you are?"

"Ha!"

"I'm serious. You're like this... ray of black sunshine."

"But I ain't no racist."

"Look at you!"

"What?"

"All ghetto an' shit... *I ain't no racist!*"

"Fuck you, man," Reggie smiles and takes a swig of his beer. The bartender places a fresh *G&T* before Brayden.

"Thanks." He turns to his friend.

"I mean, do you talk like this around Ezra Banes and the Black Caucus?"

"I let my hair down witchu, man."

"You don't have any hair."

"No, it's *you ain't got no hair, muthafucka!*"

"Oh yes, thanks." Brayden smiles.

"So how are the Black Panthers these days?"

"The Panthers are a bunch o' pussies!" Reggie says.

"You better watch out."

"What?"

"I think that white girl put sumthin' in yer drink, man. Like a roofie."

"Haha!"

"So like, we *can't* be racists. I mean, by definition."

"Is that a fact?"

"Only the *dominant* culture can be racist. The rest of us, we oppressed."

"Hmm."

"I mean, din't they teach yer black ass *nuthin'* in thet fancy New England prep school o' yours? So what kinda gin she say that is? *Uncle Tom?*" Reggie takes another sip of his beer.

"Okay man, how 'bout *this*... (He employs his exaggerated white person voice) "My dear Brayden, how *is* that delightful French girl-friend of yours? She is positively radiant! Have you introduced her to your family yet? You simply must! Perhaps during a weekend at the Cape."

Brayden shakes his head.

"An' you be like, *'Mama, dis be my white girlfriend, Françoise. She frum France!'*"

"You're such an asshole." Brayden smiles.

"And where'd you get *Françoise* from?"

"I don't know. Some movie."

"You're an idiot."

"Thanks, man. So how's POTUS?"

"Now *there* is a racist. I told him what you said, about Banes and the Black Caucus, and he nearly lost his shit!"

"I still can't believe you work for a fetus, man. That umbilical cord would freak me the fuck out!"

"He keeps it covered. I hardy ever see it."

The bartender walks by and Reggie addresses her. "My man here works for *POTUS!*"

"Will you shut up!" Brayden says in a stage whisper.

The bartender drifts past, oblivious, and Reggie turns to his friend.

"Young people, man... Apathetic. That's why we're in the shit we're in. I mean, Mallory Blitzen. She lost to a fetus."

"A *white* fetus."

"*Now* who's racist?"

"Oppressed."

"Ha! So that *PDI*, man... Banes is up that Soprano guy's ass over it."

"Milanese?"

"Yeah."

"What is it?"

"I don't know, but it's *big*. Some power play goin' down, like *soon*. Shit, man. I gotta go." He finishes what's left of his beer and lays a couple bills on the bar.

"If I hear anything..."

"Thanks, man."

"Of course... You are my Negro!" Reggie says in his white person voice. And then he stands up and turns to the bartender. "*Dat's my Nigga!*" he says, motioning to Brayden.

The bartender is unimpressed.

"Later, man. Say hello to Angelique or Jacqueline or..."

"It's Carly."

"I know, man. See ya."

Brayden sits by himself as he finishes his drink, the bartender drifting in and out of his vision. He takes that one last sip, contemplates the wedge of lime for a moment, then the check. He thinks about leaving a sub-par tip, but then he imagines Reggie saying, "*Yer mama din't raise no cheapskate!*" and he leaves twenty percent.

Shortly after Brayden Carter walks out the door, that distinguished older gentleman from the other day at the coffee shop, the man in the expensive suit, stands up from his shadowy table against the back wall. He removes what looks like an earbud from his ear and then walks over and sits at the bar. The bartender appears, a hint of recognition on her face.

"What can I get for you?"

"A Gin & Tonic," the man says.

"*Uncle Tom* Gin." The bartender offers a Mona Lisa smile.

"Coming right up."

16

Porter Percival Portly @govPortPortly:

Just saw President Rett. Had a wonderful meeting. Discussed things vital to National Security. Making America safer. Making America greater!

Yep, ol' Port sucks up with the best of 'em. But I kinda wanna know what that green button is for. Shall I press it? I don't know, I'm gonna *press* it! But I was in the middle of that story about... Fuck it! Here goes nothing... *[Alex reaches over to the silver panel on the wall. He takes a deep breath, then presses the green button...]*

"Domino's..."

The President is taken aback.

"*Domino's?*"

"Domino's Pizza..."

"Never mind."

So you'll recall the Dark Time when I had acquiesced to my mom and agreed to be cast out of Paradise. For the next couple days, I was miserable as can be, when serendipitously, our neighbors, Ernie and Emily Rasmussen, came over.

"What's that?" my mom asked, noticing that Ernie had something cradled under his arm.

"It's my old Camcorder," he said. "I thought I'd, you know, make a movie of your boy in there." He looked at my mom's belly. "Before he comes out into all *this*." He gestured grandly with his hand, to the horizon of the kitchen window. And then he looked back at my mom. "Do you mind?"

"Well, I guess not," she replied.

"Would you like some strudel?"

"Homemade?"

"No. Entenmann's."

"Entenmann's is the *best!*" said Ernie Rasmussen.

So after Ernie and his wife Emily had their Entenmann's, Ernie picked up the Camcorder.

"Oops," he said. "I got icing on it." He put it down as my mom handed him a Brawny, and he wiped his hands, then the camera. "Showtime!" he said.

"So what do you want me to do?" my mom asked.

"Um, I guess just sit down in the chair and, you know, stick out your stomach."

My mom complied. "How's this?"

Ernie put his eye to the Camcorder and zoomed in.

"*Per-fecto,*" he said.

"So do you think we can get him to speak?"

"I think so," said my mom. "He's usually quite talkative."

"Good, cuz otherwise it's just, you know, a movie of some pregnant lady's stomach."

"I understand."

"Okay, ya ready?"

"Yes. This is exciting!"

"Okay, *you ready inside there?*" he asked me.

And I figured, what the hell, right? You only live once. And it might be nice to look back on this someday when I'm old, depressed, and suicidal, and recall that for one moment at least, I had it made.

"Okiedokie," I said from inside.

"Okay then... Lights... Camera... *Action!*"

And for the next ten minutes, Ernie made a movie of my mom's belly while he asked me all sorts of questions. Not surprisingly, they weren't that difficult and I answered most of 'em. And after the filming was concluded, Ernie looked at my mom and said, "That made me hungry. Ya got any more Entenmann's?"

I thought that was that, until a week later, when Ernie burst into our kitchen with the big news.

"It went viral!" he said, his eyes aglow as if they were irradiated.

"What went viral?" my mom asked.

"The video!"

"Video?"

"The one I shot of your stomach!"

"*What?*"

"I posted it on *YouTube* and it went viral!"

"Oh," my mom replied. "So what does that *mean*, exactly?"

"It's already gotten over a million views, and I just posted it a few days ago!" Ernie was barely able to contain himself.

"Oh! Well, how did I look?"

"Great! Your stomach, I mean."

"Well, isn't that something?"

And then Ernie, his wife Emily, my mom, and me sat down in the living room, turned on the TV to *YouTube*, and watched the video entitled *Amazing Talking Fetus!* that had amassed 1,436,727 views. This, of course, was before the picture window, so as the others watched, I listened.

"There... we're rolling... I'm Ernie," he said, as he pointed the Camcorder at himself. Then he turned it on my mom.

"And this is Mary Rett. She's the mother-to-be."

"Hello!" my mom said, smiling into the camera. Then he trained the lens on me.

"And inside *there* is the world's first and only talking fetus!" The camera zoomed in closer. *"Hello in there!"* Ernie said, as if his voice were an Alpine echo. *"Hellooooo!"*

"We call him Alexander," my mom said. "Or Alex."

"Hey there, Little Alex!"

"Hey," I said back.

Excited, Ernie turned the camera back on himself. "See what I mean!" Then he turned it back on me. "Say something, little feller. You're on TV!"

"Um, what do you want me to say?"

"I can't hear you that well," Ernie said. "Can you talk a little louder?"

"How's this?"

"Nah."

"Can you hear me *now*?"

"Nope."

"Can you hear me *now*?"

"Still too soft."

"Can you hear me *now*?"

"Nah, try moving a little to the left."

"To my left or your left?"

'Um, let's see..." Ernie paused to figure things out.

"My left," he said, "which would be... your right."

"Got it!" I said. "How's this?"

"*Much* better!" And then he turned the camera back on himself. "The little fetus is... whadaya call..." Stymied, he turned the camera on my mom. "Ya know that word you said, when somebody knows sumthin' allvusudden..."

"You mean when they recognize that they're an individual and not just a mindless member of the masses?"

"Huh?"

"Self-aware?"

"Yeah! That's it! We got ourselves the world's first self-aware fetus! Ain't that sumthin'! So what's it like in there, Little Alex?"

"I prefer just Alex."

"Well, okay! So what's it like in there, Alex?"

"It's dark."

"Haha! It's dark! I bet it is." He looked back into the camera. "This little guy is real smart. Watch..." He turned the camera back on me. "So who discovered America?"

"The Vikings."

"Was it the Vikings?" Ernie turned to my mom. "I thought it was Columbus."

"Leif Eriksson came here five hundred years before Columbus," my mom said.

"Well, ain't that sumthin'!" Ernie smiled.

"*So you in there...*"

"Yes?" I replied.

"Who was the first President?"

"Of the United States?"

"Haha! Yes."

"George Washington."

"Yeah!" Ernie beamed. "But that's an easy one. So who was the *next* President?... My *wife* don't even know this one!" Ernie said as an aside to my mom.

"Adams. Then Jefferson."

"Was Jefferson the third one?" He looked to my mom.

"Yes."

"Well, I'll be... See what I mean! That is one smart fetus! So when did we land on the Moon?"

"July 1969."

"Amazing! Okay, which major league baseball player hit the most career home runs?"

"Babe Ruth."

"Ha! Ya got that one wrong. It was Hank Aaron. With two A's. Um, I mighta run outta questions," said Ernie. He looked at my mom. "You wanna ask him sumthin'?"

"Sure," she said.

"Hey, baby."

"Mom!"

"Sorry." She turned to Ernie. "He hates when I call him *baby*."

"I can see that," Ernie said.

My mom turned back to me. "What makes up a water molecule, sweetie?"

"Two atoms of hydrogen, one atom of oxygen."

"Holy moly!" said Ernie. "How'd he know *that?*"

My mom smiled proudly.

"So what's 17 minus 11?" Ernie asked.

"Um, he's not that good at math," my mom intervened.

"Me neither," said Ernie. He looked back at me.

"Okay, so why'd they try ta impeach Bill Clinton?"

"He got a Lewinsky."

"Well, I'll be damned!" Ernie shook his head. "This kid, I tell ya... "So who's your favorite President, then, little guy?"

"Nixon."

."Nixon? Well I'll be...This kid's hilarious! So are you a Republican, Alex?"

"A young Republican."

"I reckon so. So do ya think you'll go into politics someday?"

"I want to be President."

"*President?* Ha! Well, ya havta come outta that womb first," he said. "Ain't this sumthin'! So, little guy, your mom tells me that you can sing, and that you have a favorite song that you an' her sing together."

"Mom!" I said, mortified.

"It's okay, baby."

"Mom!!"

"I'm sorry, dear." My mom turned to Ernie again, then looked down at me. "What do you say, sweetie? You wanna sing with your mama?" She turned back to Ernie. "He has such a nice singing voice."

"Hmm." Ernie smiled.

"Sing with your mama, honey."

"No."

"Spunky little feller," said Ernie.

"And then some... Come on, sweetie. Make your mama happy." She turned to Ernie. "It's that song, you know, the theme song from that TV show..."

"TV show?"

"All in the Family!"

"Oh yeah! With Archie Bunker!"

"Yes! Sing with mama, b—honey.

I figured I'd better sing the damn song or I'd never hear the end of it, so I said, "Okay."

"Thanks, sweetie."

"But I do this under protest."

"Duly noted," said my mom.

"Ain't he sumthin'!" said Ernie.

"We do it as a duet," my mom said to Ernie. "You know, like Archie and Edith."

"I can't wait!"

"You ready, sweetie-pie?" Silence. *"Sweetie?"*

"Okay."

"Good. So... whenever you're ready."

I took a few breaths, then began.

ME: *Boy, the way Glenn Miller played.*

MY MOM: *Songs that made the hit parade.*

ME: *Guys like us we had it made.*

UNISON: *Those were the days.*

MY MOM: *And you knew where you were then.*

ME: *Girls were girls and men were men.*

UNISON: *Mister, we could use a man like Herbert Hoover again.*

ME: *Didn't need no welfare state.*

MY MOM: *Everybody pulls his weight.*

UNISON: *Gee, our old LaSalle ran great! Those... were... the... daaaaays!*

Needless to say, we were a hit. By the end of the week, the phone was ringing off the hook, from newspapers, magazines, and TV shows. Even the Governor of Virginia himself (the state, or should I say Commonwealth, in which we live), the Honorable Jaspar Redford Torrence, called us up and spoke to me personally.

"Is this the little feller?" he said on the speaker phone.

"This is Alexander Rett."

"Alexander Rett!" the Governor of Virginia said.

"Well, I'll be a monkey's uncle!"

"What can I do for you, Governor?"

"Get a load o' this kid!" he said.

"So I jus' wanted ta say 'hey,' an' ta let ya know thet we're all mighty proud o' you an' yer accomplishment."

"Well, thank you kindly, Governor, sir."

"So if ya ever need anything, little feller... like a reference for a job application ta McDonald's or sumthin', jus' lemme know, okay?"

"Will do, Governor."

"Okay. *Arrivederci.*"

I'm not sure where he got the "arrivederci" from, but what I've found is that the higher you go in politics, the more you can do or say whatever you like. Six magazine covers, twenty-seven newspaper articles, and twelve appearances on the FOX NEWS affiliates all across Virginia later, I hit the big-time and was a featured guest on *Dr. Phyllis.* And I must say that, coincidentally, the more fame that came to my mom (vicariously through me), the more she settled into letting me linger inside the ol' womb a bit longer. "No rush," she said.

The guest before me, or us, I should say, since it was me and my mom, was this woman from Nebraska who was distraught because she believed that her six-year-old tabby named Puss-Puss was plotting to murder her in her sleep. Admittedly, a hard act to follow.

"Let's all welcome Alexander Rett, the self-aware fetus, and his mom, Mary!"

[Thunderous applause as my mom and I walked out and sat in the sofa opposite Dr. Phyllis...]

"So nice to finally meet you! Both of you!" she said.

"My pleasure," said my mom.

"Mine too," I said from down below. *[This brought more applause from the studio audience, comprised mainly of women of all ages, many who'd had children, but none who could imagine such a thing as a fetus who spoke the King's English and wanted to remain inside the womb...]*

"We've all seen the *YouTube* video," said Dr. Phyllis.

"I mean, *everybody's* seen it. Am I right?" She addressed the studio audience. *[On cue, they burst into more applause...]* "As of today, it's received over 50 million views!" *[More applause and cheers...]* "The most popular person in the world is someone who no one has ever seen," said Dr. Phyllis, going for the profound. She turned to me. "What do you make of all this... adulation, Alexander? Or may I call you Alex?"

"Alex is fine," I said.

"Oh good. So are you put off by all this attention? By the attention of the entire *world?*"

"Not really," I replied. "It'll come in handy when I run for office."

"Office! Haha!" Dr. Phyllis laughed, and then she turned to my mom. "That's some kid you got there, Mary."

"Don't I know it!"

"So is he serious about a career in politics?"

"Oh yes. We've watched countless documentaries."

"And is Richard Nixon still your favorite President?" Dr. Phyllis asked me.

"He is," I said.

"How come?"

"I think he got a bum rap."

"A bum rap?"

"I mean, nowadays, what he did would be a drop in the bucket, scandal-wise. *Watergate*, I mean."

"Hmm! So how did you arrive at such... political savvy?" she asked.

"Like my mom said, documentaries. We just watched this one on Machiavelli that was eye-opening."

"*Machiavelli!*" Dr. Phyllis raised her eyebrows and smiled into the camera.

And then she said some other things and the audience kept applauding, but I had let my mind wander. I could say *anything*. I could say anything I wanted and they'd eat it up. What power a fetus had! With the right backing and support, there's no telling *what* I could do.

"Alex? Alex?"

It was Dr. Phyllis.

"Can you hear me alright?" she asked.

"Yes! Yes I can."

"Good, because I asked you, with all that you know of the world so far, what is the thing you'd most like to do?"

There it was! The All-Access Pass to Disneyland! The Keys to the Kingdom.
"I want to run for President!" I said.

[The audience went mad with cheers and whistles. Dr. Phyllis was amazed...]

"Well, it looks like you have an entire audience that'll vote for you." She smiled, thinking of the ratings. "Not to mention some of the four million viewers we have at home." *[Thunderous applause...]*

This was it, my moment of truth, and I smiled to myself. And like Alexander the Great, I looked out (figuratively speaking, since I was still inside) on this wide, expansive world waiting to be conquered.

17

On Thursday morning, I decided to sleep in, because I'm the freaking President and I do what I want! My cell phone was turned off, the curtains were drawn. So when I woke up, I was greeted by an onslaught of *Tweets* from everyone and his brother.

Mallory Rodman Blitzen @realPresidentMalloryBlitzen
Little FOTUS screwed the pooch on PDI. GOP bailing on you. Women & children first! But no fetuses. Ha! Little boys and their ray guns. Loser!

Ezra Millstone Banes @EzraBanes

CrackTheWhipPDI more like pie in sky. Will never happen. Waste of $$$. FOTUS sinking fast. Were we wrong about Mallory? Second thoughts? Regrets? Anyone else?

And at least a hundred more Tweets in that vein from the whole nest of traitorous vipers. And WTF? *FOTUS? Fetus Of The United States?* I *hate* that Mallory Blitzen! And then...

Dirk Fist @infocombatBigDirkFist

Better to be a fat f@#! than a small-minded bastard going down in flames like the Twin Towers on 9/11. See ya, and I wouldnt wanna be ya! Adios little feller!!!

I *really* hate that Dirk Fist! And then...

Porter Percival Portly @govPortPortly

Poor FOTUS. PDI a BFB (Big Fat Bust). I told him when we met last week that it was Fetus's Folly. Not to mention a piss-poor health care plan. BIG FAT ZERO.

And the final stab in the back...

Jaspar Redford Torrence @govJRTva

FOTUS bit off more than he can chew. Do fetuses even have teeth? PDI=Science Fiction. Fact is, we need Prez in real world, not Fetus Bunker. Mallory still there?

Et tu, Jaspar? And then, the postscript...

Jules Dale Tippler @JulesTipplerCNN

FOTUS going over the falls in a barrel. Hope he washes ashore in one piece so he can be on my show this Sunday. We'll see...

I can't *stand* that Jules Tippler! And those are just the highlights, or lowlights, if you will. I'll spare you the rest. It took me an hour to read them all. WTF happened? Last night, when I went to sleep, all was right with the world, but today it's a raging shitstorm! *[Alex remembers the intercom and turns it back on. Instantly, it buzzes...]*

"Mr. President!" It's Gladiola Gaze. "I've been trying to reach you all morning, sir!"

"Yes, I... What is it, Gladdy?"

"There have been over two hundred requests for comments and seventeen reporters are waiting for you in the Taft Room, sir. They say your administration is on the verge of collapse."

Silence.

"Mr. President?"

"Fuck 'em!"

"Sir?"

"I said, *Fuck 'em!*"

"Um... okay."

[Alex checks his phone to see if there's anything from Tim. Nothing but old messages. He buzzes Gladdy...]

"Yes Mr. President?"

"Get me Tim Chopper."

"I've been trying all morning, sir, but I haven't been able to reach him."

FUCK! "Okay, keep trying."

"I will, sir."

[He sends Tim a text...]

To Tim Chopper:

Tim, what the fuck is happening? Where are you? Get here ASAP!!!

Alex

[A second later, Alex dials his number...]

"This is Tim Chopper. Leave a message..."

"Tim! Where the fuck are you? What the fuck is going on? Fucking shit! Call me ASAP!!!"

If Tim sold out, we're in a lotta trouble, believe me. A lotta trouble! I was all ready to tell you the rest of the story, of what happened after I went on *Dr. Phyllis*, but I'm at *Defcon One*. Shitstorms happen *fast* in politics. *[Alex turns on the TV...]*

"The White House is apparently on lockdown. Nothing is coming out from anyone, including the FOTUS, on the PDI disaster. A CBS reporter inside the Capitol says that...

CLICK...

"No word at all from the FOTUS..."

CLICK...

"...embroiled in the most desperate situation yet to afflict the Rett White House, with the utter disaster of what's come to be known as *Fetus's Folly,* the future of Alexander Jackson Rett, the fetus President, is in doubt."

CLICK...

"...FOTUS..."

CLICK...

"Fetus's Folly...

CLICK...

"As of yet, no response from the White House. But Senator and former Presidential candidate Mallory Blitzen had this to say..."

[Alex turns off the TV and flings the remote in disgust. It bounces off the wall, and as it does, he feels a discernible spasm from the body of his comatose mom...]

What the fuck? Fetus's Folly? *[Alex checks his smartphone... 213 more texts, Tweets, and emails, all saying the same thing, that the rats are leaving the sinking ship and that he's the sinking ship... Again, he calls Tim Chopper...]*

"Tim... Tim... Tim..."

"This is Tim Chopper. Leave a message..."

"Dammit!

[The intercom buzzes...]

"What is it, Gladdy?"

"Sir, the Vice-President is here."

"Tell her I'm... in a meeting with the Majority Whip."

"With Senator Milanese, sir?"

"Yes."

"But he's also here, sir. With the Vice-President."

"Tell 'em I..." *[Alex checks his phone... 53 new messages...]*

"Sir?"

[*Alex turns the TV back on and flips the channels...*

THE NATURAL HISTORY CHANNEL

"The dodo bird, with no natural predators, lived a happy, peaceful life, isolated from the rest of the world on its island paradise—what would become known as Mauritius, off the coast of East Africa. But by the end of the 16th century, all this changed when Dutch sailors landed on its shores. Within a hundred years of its discovery by human beings, the dodo bird was extinct, and it's remembered now as a symbol of obsolescence and of things whose time has passed..."

What the fuck?... *CLICK... [The intercom buzzes again...]*

"What is it?"

"Sir, the Vice-President is..."

"Tell her to come back later."

"Later, sir?"

"As in not now."

"And Senator Mila..."

"Tell them all to come back later! I'm in the middle of an important Skype with Putin regarding that thing in... Uzbekistan."

"Uzbekistan, sir?"

"Yes, it's next to... those other stans."

"Sir?"

"Hold all my calls."

"..."

"Gladdy?"

"Very well, sir."

Sometimes being President is like having your head stuck in a hornet's nest while doing a tap dance on a tightrope above a minefield while someone tries to give you a hot sauce enema. [*Alex looks at the small, intricately-carved ivory box on top of the coffee table in the wombroom. A gift from his predecessor. He opens it and takes out a Valium...*] It's time for Operation V for Vacation. [*The President swallows the pill, turns off his phone, then closes the thick black curtains with a flourish, shutting out the world.*]

[*Five hours later...*]

Where am I? [*For a moment, Alex thinks he's back in the second trimester, safe and sound in the womb, and that this whole President thing was just a bad dream. But then he opens the curtains and reality pours in...]*

Shit. *[He checks his phone...2937 texts, Tweets, and emails.* And *then he turns on the TV...]*

CNN

"Rett's resignation seems imminent. Sources within the White House have said that..."

CLICK...

I need a drink! *[He looks at his miniature TAG Heuer Carrera Calibre Chronograph... 8:37 PM. He reaches over and presses the button on the silver panel on the wall, but it doesn't work...]*

Dammit! *[He presses it a few more times, each time more frantically, when finally...]*

"Yes, Mr. Alex?"

"Manny! Oh good! You're here! Everybody else is..."

"Sir?"

"*Lo siento*, Manolo. I need a martini, *STAT!*"

"Yes sir, Mr. Alex. One martini STAT coming up."

"*Gracias amigo.*"

[A few moments later, Manny appears, pushing his drink cart, dressed impeccably as usual, in a well-pressed, nicely-fitting dinner jacket and tie. The sliding glass door is opened, and Manny hands the President of the United States a miniature martini...]

"*Muchas gracias*, my friend."

"You are very welcome, Mr. President." At this, Alex laughs to himself.

"What is it, sir?"

"You never called me Mr. President before."

"I'm sorry, sir, but I thought you might need a little boost."

"Hmm." The President smiles.

"A boost, yes. Thank you, Manny." Manolo Vargas starts to leave when Alex calls him back.

"Manny..."

"Sir?"

"Sit with me for a while," Alex says. "If you don't mind."

"Mr. Alex, I do not mind." And he pulls a chair over and sits down in front of the womb-room, as Alex takes a sip of the martini.

"Mmm, just the way I like it. Thanks."

"My pleasure, Mr. Alex."

The President takes another sip, then looks at Manolo.

"Quite the mess out there, hmm? And it happened so... *rapido!*"

"Yes sir, but I think it may not be as bad as it looks."

"You do?" Alex takes another sip of his martini.

"Do you know something I don't?"

"I do not think so, sir." His smile projects a profound tranquility that the President finds soothing.

"These things, they come and they go, yes?"

"Things?"

"The... *tormentas.*"

"The storms, yes. I like that word—*tormentas.*"

Manny smiles.

"Have a drink with me, Manolo."

"I cannot, sir."

"I... Have a drink with me, *Señor Vargas.*"

Manny looks at the President of the United States. In his eyes, he sees acceptance and appreciation, like when one looks out at the sea in the early morning, before the day begins.

"*Sí, Señor Rett.* It would be my honor."

"And mine as well." Alex glances at Manny's drink cart.

"Anything on there you like?"

"Yes sir, there is a tequila I keep, a very special bottle in case one day you would request it."

At this, Alex finishes his martini and hands Manny the glass.

"May I join you?"

Manny smiles softly, and then he walks over to the cart. After searching for a moment, he produces the bottle and a shot glass.

"For you, sir."

"*Gracias.*"

He fills the glass and hands it to the President. Then he pours one for himself. "*Salud.*"

"*Salud,*" says Alex. "*Gracias, Señor Vargas.*" Alex takes one sip, then another, and his eyes light up as a smile spreads across his face.

"*Esta bien?*"

"*Muy bueno!* So tell me about this..." Alex motions to the bottle.

"It comes from the town where I live," Manny says.

"Where I *used* to live, in *Méjico.*"

"What town is that?"

"It is called *Tequila.*"

"Ah!" Alex smiles.

"My father, he made this."

"Really?"

"Yes, he... he gave me seven bottles, so I... have enough."

"Well, I may need it today, my friend."

"*Sí.*"

"So tell me more about your father," Alex says.

"Is he still alive?"

"Oh yes. And my mother as well." Manny glances at Alex's mom, at her comatose shell of a body. "And my two sisters and two younger brothers, and my grandmother, María Guadalupe. I support them all."

"You are a..." Alex starts to say "credit to your race," but he catches himself. "A kind and considerate person."

"*Gracias,*" says Manolo. And then he glances back at Alex's mom. "I am sorry, sir. *Tu madre.*"

"*Sí, gracias.*" Alex takes another sip.

"I mean, the world out *there* is going to Hell, but... right now I feel okay."

"I am glad, *Señor Rett.*"

"But, might I have another, *Señor Vargas, por favor?*"

"*Sí.*" Manny fills the glass and the President downs it in one smooth motion. Manny looks at him without comment.

"So tell me about *your* father, sir... if you do not mind."

"*Mi padre?* Hmm..." Alex offers a half-smile.

"There's not much to say. I don't think he said more than five words to me... And then he died." Alex looks at Manolo.

"It was sudden. But... Let's talk about something else."

"Of course. *Una más?*"

"*Por favor.*"

Manny reaches over and refills Alex's glass for the third time.

"But I *do* have a story I'd like to tell," Alex says.

"If it wouldn't bore you too much."

"It would be my honor, sir."

"Okay, but first another sip..." And the sip becomes a long continuous drink until the glass is empty.

"The *best* tequila." Alex smiles.

"But you have never had it before."

"I know the best when I taste it! Hmm, I feel dizzy."

"Are you okay, sir?"

"Couldn't be better! Fill 'er up, my friend!" He holds out his glass.

"Are you sure?"

"Does the Pope shit in the woods? So I was going to tell you a story. Do you know... *hic!* Sorry."

"*No hay problema.*"

"Do you know *Dr. Phyllis?*"

"*Sí! Dr. Phyllis!* We get that show in *Méjico!*"

"Another great American export. So before all *this*..." Alex motions to the Oval Office.

"I was on that show, with my mom, before she..." He lets out a breath. "And ever *hic...* ever since that day..."

"Sir?"

"I mean, it's *crazy*, Manny! All this happened *because of that show!* This whole President thing!" Alex finishes his drink, then motions for another. And when his glass is full, he leans in closer.

"Now this is something that hardly anyone knows," he says, his voice a whisper. "There's this group of *bad hombres.*"

"Group, sir?"

"This... *club, sí?*"

"Club, yes."

"And it has thirteen members, and they're all *hic! Perdóname.* They're all *multimillonarios.*"

"Billionaires."

"*Sí*, these powerful men who live in the ... *hic...* in the shadows and can do whatever they want. And they... they only come out when they... *hic...* when they want to give you something."

"That does not sound so bad," says Manny.

"Yes, but then they *got ya by the balls!* Haha! The *hic cojones!*"
There's a long pause.

"It's... a funny *hic* world," Alex says.

"That I'm here and you're *hic* there."

"..."

"I'm. "

"Sir?"

"Drunk."

"So..."

"*No más, no más! Haha!*" Manny nods.

"And maybe I *hic* shouldna had that Valium."

"Sir?"

"But... thank you, Man. *olo. Hic!*" Alex tries to hand him his glass,
but it falls to the floor. "I...don't feel so *hic* good."

"I'm sorry. Can I do something for you, sir?"

"No, I... I'll be...okay."

"Well, if you need anything else..."

"Yes, thank...thank you, *Manny-olo! Woo-hoo!*"

The shit-faced President of the United States watches as two-Man-
nys-blurred-together gather their things, then wheel their carts out
of the Oval Office. And when the doors close behind them, it sounds
like an atomic bomb blast.

Alex looks at the silver panel swirling on the wall in the womb-
room, and he tries to press the blurry buttons as they dance in the air.

"B-*lue*," he says. "*Grrr-EEEEN...* Ye-*ellow-hic!...* What... What'ssss *that*
one? *Hic!...* Red! *Rojo!*" he laughs. "*Rojo. Uh-oh! Uh-oh, Rojo!* Hahaha!"

And since he had inadvertently turned the intercom back on,
instantly it buzzes.

"Mr. President, I've been trying to reach you!"

"*Uh-oh! Rojo!* Better dead than *rojo!* Haha!"

"Mr. President?"

"*Gladdy-ola amigo!*" he says.

"*Hic! Cojones!* Haha!"

"*Mr. President?*"

"Will you... come in here, Gladdyyy-ola... *por favor, mi amiga?*"

"Um, certainly, sir."

As he waits for his secretary, Alexander Rett feels the Oval Office spinning like toilet water after a flush. The womb-room gurgles, then quakes like tectonic shifts of the Earth, everything whirling and psychedelic like a revolving kaleidoscope.

"Sir, it's madness out there!" Gladdy says. "Utter madness!"

But before she can say another word, Alexander Jackson Rett, the President of the United States, projectile-vomits all over her.

18

After her most recent encounter with the President, aka "The Vomit Incident," Gladiola Gaze, the President's personal secretary, does everything she can to sanitize the situation. After cleaning the splatter from the rug and making sure that her boss is okay, she hurries to the Oval Office's private bathroom, which would've been Alex Rett's private bathroom had he been a normal President. But as Gladiola Gaze has come to discover on an almost daily basis, this particular President is anything but. Normal, that is.

So she fastidiously scrubs the vomitus from her dress. And then she waits in her undergarments until the dress is dry enough to re-wear. And when she returns to her post, she mans it like a machine gun nest (or *womans* it, as the case may be), popping her head into the Oval now and then to check on the Commander in Chief. And she finds the President, one of the world's most powerful men, either continually upchucking or sleeping it off.

When people appear before her—Senators and Congressmen and reporters and staff and anyone who has a vested interest in President Rett's seemingly spectacular implosion—she fends them off like King Kong batted down the airplanes. And of course the phone rings off the hook. And after a while, she unplugs it and occupies her time by playing *Angry Birds* on her smartphone. But in this instance, art imitates life as the relentless green pigs keep popping up to eat the birds' eggs. And as she sighs to herself and puts her phone away, that young African-American intern, Tall Skinny Sad-Sack, appears.

"Is he in?" Brayden Carter asks.

"Um, yes and no," she replies, and Brayden stands there nonplussed.

A long uncomfortable moment passes between them before he speaks again.

"So if he's in, can I see him?"

"I would say... no," Gladdy says. And it's then that she notices the young man sniffing the air, his face dominated by a grimace as he tries to ascertain the source of the unpleasant odor.

"What's that smell?" he asks.

"I certainly can't say," she replies. And then she gives him her best "*Go Away*" look until he finally does.

Free at last, she thinks about giving *Angry Birds* another go, when the Vice-President appears.

"Madame Vice-President!" Gladiola Gaze is always happy to see Mavis DaLyte. Here is a woman she can admire. A woman who worked her way up from the potato fields of Idaho to become the Vice-President, yet someone who still holds onto her homespun country charm.

"It's a nasty piece o' bizness out there," Mavis says with a shudder.

"Very nasty," Gladdy concurs.

"Is he... What's that smell?" the Vice-President asks.

"I... There was an accident."

"Accident?"

"He... The President was quite sick," Gladdy says, "and his doctor has prescribed a period of undisturbed rest and recuperation. Although the President himself instructed me to notify *you* before anyone else. As soon as he wakes up, that is, Madame Vice-President."

The Vice-President looks at Gladiola Gaze. Here is a strong-minded woman, she thinks. A woman who has your back. *Perhaps I'll keep you on*, she thinks to herself, *if all goes well.*

"Of course," says Mavis DaLyte.

"Lemme know when he's up an' around an' receivin' vizitors."

"Will do, Madame Vice-President."

Gladiola Gaze watches the Vice-President walk away. And when no one else is in sight, she enters the Oval Office. She sees the President's poor mother behind Reagan's desk, in a sorry state of half-life/half-death, oblivious to all that's been going on around her. "Poor woman," she says to herself. And then she steps closer (albeit tentatively, "The Vomit Incident" still fresh in her mind). She peeks into the womb-room and sees the President sleeping peacefully, without a care. For a second, he looks like the baby Jesus. And for a second, she wants to take him in her arms, this strange, unlovable little person, and give him all the maternal love he'll never get.

19

"So how'd you get a day off?" Carly asks as she fastens her bra.

"I mean, the White House is going down in flames."

"I went there," Brayden says, pulling up his boxer shorts.

"Did you see him? Was he there?"

"I... I'm not sure."

"Aren't *you* cryptic."

"It's a cryptic place these days."

He looks up and finds her staring at him.

"What?"

"Nothing," she says, a hint of coldness in her voice.

"I never thought I'd be with someone who wears boxer shorts."

"So you're a brief gal?"

"Tighty-Whities. Oh, that sounds racist."

"Eh..." He shrugs.

"What do they say in French? *De rien?*"

"Hmm."

Brayden looks at her, at this woman he's been seeing for the past two months, who all of a sudden seems like a distant stranger. (And he remembers that hipster at the coffee shop reading Camus.)

"So how does a French girl know about Tighty-Whities?"

"I'm a citizen of the world."

"Are you? In that case..."

"Hmm?"

"Let's take a trip together in the fall," Brayden says.

"We can go to Paris! Wouldn't that be great?"

Silence.

"Carly?" (And suddenly it feels as if his world is teetering on the edge of a table.)

"What about your job?"

"I may not *have* a job, the way things are going."

"..."

"So..."

"What was it like today?"

"What?" (Way to change the subject.)

"In the White House..."

"It was..." He looks at her, puzzled. "It was like they dropped *The Big One*. Everybody running back and forth like chickens on crack. And his secretary—she wouldn't even let me in."

"To see him?"

"Yeah. Why the sudden interest?" *(And what about Paris?)*

"Just...making conversation."

"Okay, so you never answered me."

"Hmm?"

"About Paris." (Again, he senses the world about to slip off...) "Or we can go in the spring. *April in Pa-ris* "

More silence.

"What, you don't like my singing? Well then you should see me dance, *cuz I gots me sum riddum!*" Brayden bursts into an impromptu tap dance in stocking feet, finishing on one knee with a flourish. "*Mammy!*" Looking up, he sees her walk to the bathroom, ignoring him.

"What? You don't like my dancing either?" A few minutes later, Carly reappears, all dressed and detached, purposefully fixing an earring.

"What the fuck, Carly?"

No response.

"Well?"

"I'm not racist," she says.

"*What?* I never said..."

She grabs her purse and rifles through it for her keys.

"I never said you were racist!"

She keeps rifling.

"Will you stop?"

"…"

"*Arrête!*"

"What?" She turns to look at him.

"*What?!* What just happened?"

"Nothing."

"*Nothing?*"

Brayden stares at her in disbelief, and finally she looks at him.

"*Voilà, comment ça se termine!*"

"What are you saying?"

Carly Menteur stares at him for a moment longer, then shakes her head.

"*Je ne vais pas me sentir désolé pour toi.*"

"I…I don't know that either."

"Hmm…*N'importe quoi.*"

He shrugs once, then watches as she turns abruptly and walks out the door.

An hour later, he's at a table at *Deco* in Georgetown with his best friend Reggie Mason.

"And she just walked out?"

"Yeah."

"Harsh, man."

"But first she said some shit in French."

"What?"

"Beats me."

"Fuckin' French, man. So why don't you ask *her* out?" He motions to the barmaid from the other day.

"The Queen of Aloof?"

"Maybe she's a dominatrix, like that *Fifty Shades o' Bullshit.*"

"They only go for billionaires."

"You got *that* right! So I know what happened, man."

"Happened?"

"With that girl o' yours."

"Oh yeah?"

"She don't wanna go on that trip o' yours, man. She wants yer black dick, but she don't wanna take yer black ass home to Mama... What's French for 'Mama'?"

Brayden lets out a sigh.

"Shit, man! She changed the subject when ya asked her, right? And when ya asked her again, she got all French on you and left toot sweet."

"Toot sweet?"

"Ha!" Reggie smiles.

"I went ta Choate, man!"

"So aren't *you* Dr. Phyllis!"

"What we got here is a classic case o' *she not dat into you!*"

"But I mean, it seemed like..."

"It was goin' so *well?* For *you*, man." He finishes his beer.

"..."

"Look where we at! The epicenter o' wealth an' power. Ya think some hot French babe is gonna want yer salaried intern ass? Ya ever hear of hypergamy, man? Bitches like her fuck in one direction. Up."

"But—"

"She's slummin'," Reggie says, "until she finds some rich white dude. Ya feel me?"

"Yeah, Omar, I feel you."

"Here's a French saying, man...*Fuck the French!*"

As Brayden finishes his *G&T*, he notices the patrons at the other tables all giving Reggie the hairy eyeball.

"I don't know, man," Reggie says.

"I always *thought* there was sumthin' off about 'er, ya know what I'm sayin'?"

"*Now* you tell me?"

"So... "He motions again to the barmaid.

Brayden looks at the Amazon Queen of Disinterest, and then he notices the TV behind the bar.

"Hey, the Press Conference is coming on."

"I guess we should watch it," Reggie says, "since we technically still got a government."

The two friends leave their table and find a place at the bar, where Reggie immediately engages the Ice Queen of Indifference.

"We meet again," he says.

The bartender (looking icier, more sullen, and more Amazonian than usual) seems to look right through him, through the walls behind him, to every place where she'd rather be.

"Yes?" she says, as if constipated.

"Beer. Bottle. Bud." For a moment, he looks into her eyes, but it's like gazing into the abyss.

"And for my friend, Gin & Tonic, with... What's that gin you like, man?" He turns to Brayden, but before he can respond, Reggie turns back to the bartender. "Uncle Tom," he says. A moment of silence passes between the two, and there's a barely discernible twitch at the corner of her mouth. As she walks away, Reggie turns to Brayden. "Amazon dot com, man."

Brayden looks at Reggie. He offers the same kind of twitch in response, and Reggie laughs and motions towards the bartender.

"That's the Fifth Law, man."

"Hmm?"

"Of thermodynamics."

"*Fifth* Law?"

"A woman's hotness is inversely proportional to her personality."

"Hmm..."

Reggie looks at the TV as the bartender sets down their drinks.

"This oughta be good." And then he notices Brayden's despondent look.

"I'm sorry, man."

"..."

"But it's not like you broke up, right? I mean, officially." Brayden picks up his Gin & Tonic.

"To better days..." Reggie says. He clinks the neck of his beer bottle to his friend's glass.

"How can you drink that swill?" Brayden asks.

"It speaks!" He offers Reggie a half-smile, and then the White House Press Secretary, Wiley DeSembler, appears on TV...

Journalists: *[en masse]* Wiley! Wiley! Wiley!

"Hey, can ya turn that up a little?" Reggie asks the bartender. She begrudgingly obliges.

Wiley: *[points to one up front...]*

Simon: *[stands up...]* Samantha Simon, *Time Magazine...* The past few days have seen a precipitous decline in FOTUS's approval rating.

"Nice word," Reggie says. "*Precipitous.*"

Simon: *[continues...]* As of this morning, FOTUS is at 17%.

Wiley: So is there a question in there somewhere?

Simon: My *question* is, is this the beginning of the end of the Rett Presidency? *[a chorus of cheers...]*

Wiley: The past few days have seen a drop in ratings, yes.

Simon: More like a nosedive, a plummet, a plunge.

Crowd: *[laughter...]*

Wiley: I think I've answered your question.

Simon: But I haven't asked it yet!

Wiley: *[points to another journalist...]*

Essex: Emily Essex, *Newsweek...*

Wiley: Yes, Emily...

Essex: *"Fetus's Folly"* has already cost the American taxpayers over 100 million dollars in R&D that we'll never get back, since PDI is on the scrap-heap. Would you agree with Senator Blitzen that this is another example of FOTUS's gross incompetence?

Simon: *[interrupts...]* Wait a sec! Gross is *big*. FOTUS is little!

Crowd: *[more laughter...]*

Essex: *Very* little.

Simon: *Minute!*

Essex: *Minuscule! [laughter abounds...]*

"This is better than *Saturday Nite In-Yer-Face!*" Reggie says. He looks over at Brayden, gazing at his cell phone as if it were a crystal ball. He turns back to the TV.

Wiley: The mark of a good leader, especially a President of the United States, is the ability to try things and fail, in order to...

Essex: *[interrupts...]* Well, FOTUS has sure done *that! [laughter...]*

Wiley: *[exasperated]* FDR tried everything under the sun during the Great Depression, and we somehow came out on top.

Simon: Yes, by starting a war!

Crowd: *Yes!*

Wiley: America didn't start that war. It was Germany and Hitler.

Essex: You mean, *Retler?* *[playing to the crowd...]*

Crowd: *[laughter...]*

Wiley: I won't even dignify that. *[lets out an indignant huff...]* And if you recall, FDR helped *win* that war. And he's regarded as one of our greatest Presidents. I mean, he's on Mt. Rushmore! *[glances around for an ally... no Breitbart, no FOX NEWS, no Automatic Weapons Home Journal...]*

Simon: *[drippingly sarcastic]* So you're comparing FOTUS to FDR?

Crowd: *[more laughter...]*

"This is getting good," Reggie says.

Wiley: What I'm *saying* is that history will be the judge.

Crowd: *[more laughter...]*

Essex: Aren't you gonna say *"History Schmistory"?*

Simon: Or *"Fake News"?* *[even more laughter, as Wiley points to someone else...]*

Decker: Doris Decker, *The Washington Post..."*

Wiley: "Bring in the *big* guns..."

Decker: *[continues...]* So speaking of history... and failure..."

"Uh-oh."

Decker: *[continues...]* With the Health Care Bill mired in quick-sand and the PDI a flaming wreck, hasn't FOTUS's brief tenure in office been characterized by one misfire after another?

Wiley: Some changes are being made to the Health Care Bill as we speak.

Decker: So the President is *speaking? [laughter...]* Rumor has it that he's gone into isolation... I mean, even more isolation than usual. *[more laughter...]*

"Liberals on the attack! Never thought I'd see the day." Reggie turns to Brayden, still texting on his cell phone. *"Dear Carly..."* Reggie says, as he pantomimes texting in the air. *"Can you ever forgive me for asking you to go to Paris?"*

"Fuck off," Brayden says, his eyes still glued to the phone.

"I was so heartless and insensitive. So uncaring. I miss your hot French body. I miss your alabaster skin."

Fixed on his cell phone, Brayden nevertheless shoots him the bird. Reggie returns to the TV.

Wiley: So I believe that answers your question. *[points to another journalist...]*

Armanian: Amanda Armanian, *The New York Times...*"

"Hel-lo."

Armanian: *[continues...]* With *"Fetus's Folly"* a complete and utter flop, and FOTUS going into hibernation...

"Haha!" Reggie laughs. "Hibernation!"

Armanian: *[continues...]* ...And FOTUS's hatchet-man, Tim Chopper, seemingly MIA, sources within the White House say that it's just a matter of time before FOTUS steps down.

Wiley: Has the *New York Times* run out of question marks? Because I don't hear a question there.

Crowd: *[a few condescending laughs...]*

Armanian: Obviously, my question is this: Is FOTUS going to resign?

Crowd: *[cheers, whistles...]*

Wiley: That is, quite simply, fake news.

Armanian: Haha! Is it?

Wiley: Like all the questions you've asked.

Armanian: So how 'bout this one... Do you think what's happening is the American people finally realizing that having a fetus for a President wasn't the best of ideas?

Crowd: *[cheers, whistles...]* Ding! Ding! Ding! Ding!

Armanian: *[continues...]* And that maybe you owe Mallory Blitzen an apology?

Crowd: *[in a furor...]* Yes! Yes!

Armanian: *[calling out...]* This Administration owes her an apology!

Apology, Wiley!

"Ho-ly shit!"

[For a few moments, it's pandemonium in the White House Press Room, before Wiley DeSembler *can finally get everyone's attention...]*

Wiley: *[solemnly]* I hope you've all had fun today... Have you? *[he looks around...]* Because the *POTUS*, the *President of the United States*, is right now, this very moment, fighting for his life. *[gasps of shock and disbelief...]*

"*What?*" Reggie turns to Brayden.

"Did you hear that?"

"What?"

"Rett's fighting for his life."

"*What?*" Brayden looks up at the TV.

Wiley: *[somberly]* I didn't want to get into this until I had something definitive to say. But since this Press Conference has been anything but civil... *[Wiley weighs his words carefully, then he looks out at the crowd, at the looks of embarrassment and contrition...]* I feel it's my duty, as the spokesman for the White House and the President, to disclose to you and the world that yesterday the President's mother, Mary Rett, suffered another stroke. *[more gasps and murmurs...]* This one more severe than the first that left her in the comatose state she's been in for the *entirety* of Alexander Rett's presidency. You'll recall that the initial stroke happened the very day that President Rett was sworn into office. And the President has been carrying this heavy load ever since, all the time managing the highest Office in the land. All while creating the Great American Health Care plan, which he's been tirelessly working on to make health care accessible and affordable for everyone, for *all* Americans.

"Go Wiley!" Reggie smiles in appreciation.

"This guy's good."

Wiley: *[continues...]* And with this burden of not knowing whether his mother would live or die and which day might be her last, he nevertheless persisted. Think on this for a moment, because if she died, if his mother died, then *he* would die as well. How would you feel if literally every day might be your last?

Crowd: *[silence...]*

Wiley: *[continues...]* And with all this hanging over his little shoulders... his, what did you say? *[he looks at the journalists from* Time *and* Newsweek...*]* What was it? *Minute? Minuscule?* *[a contrite hush comes over the crowd...]* This admittedly small person in stature who possesses such a big heart. To love his mother *so much* that he never wanted to leave her, especially when the chips were down, when she was at her lowest and she needed him the most. Did he abandon her, like you're all so ready to abandon *him*? *[pauses...]* No. He didn't. Because housed in that very small, almost insignificant body is character of gigantic measure. And what else did he do, our President? He wanted to protect *you*, every one of you, as he protects his own mother. The *PDI... Fetus's Folly*, as you so glibly put it, is all about making everyone feel safe and secure. So you can go to sleep each night feeling safe. So you can wake up each morning and not think that today might be your last. *This* is what our President, Alexander Rett, has done for us, and what he'll continue to do if given the chance. *[a deliberate glance taking in the room...]* But right now, both he and his mother are fighting for their lives. I suggest we all reflect upon *this*. And offer them our sincerest thoughts and prayers. Thank you.

"Holy shit!" says Brayden.

"Fuckin'-A!" says Reggie.

Throughout the bar there's scattered applause that gets louder and louder, punctuated with whistles and cheers. Brayden and Reggie look around as people rise from their seats in what becomes a standing ovation.

"What the fuck," says Reggie. He turns to Brayden.

"What the fuck," says Brayden.

When they look back at the TV, they see the entire crowd in the White House Press Room, everyone on their feet, applauding and cheering. Wiley DeSembler lingers at the podium, full of gravitas. He takes it all in, like a musician waiting for the crescendo to build, and then he steps down and walks away. The applause and the cheers continue. For several minutes, it goes on, and the TV cameras capture it all.

20

"Let's get outta here, man."

"Yeah."

A few minutes later, they find Brayden's BMW, and Brayden turns to Reggie. "You mind drivin'?"

"Huh?"

"So I can..." He holds up his cell phone.

"Sure, man. Besides, I *love* your car!"

"Just don't go all *Bullitt* on me."

"Okay." Reggie smiles. A moment later, they speed away as Brayden stares at his phone.

"So where you wanna go?"

"I don't know. Just drive."

"Just drive. *I like that.* So any word from..."

"No."

"So whadaya think o' the Press Conference?"

"It was the shit."

"It was *indeed* the shit," says Reggie.

"I mean, I never thought ol' Wiley had it in 'im. Ya see how he played the crowd? It was beautiful. And the applause..."

"I know," says Brayden.

"People are gonna start feeling *sorry* for the little..."

"Fucker? Bastard?" Reggie steps on the gas to speed through a yellow light.

"You just made it."

"What year is this, man?"

"Year?"

"Your car."

"Oh... Oh-Eight."

"It looks newer, all shiny an' shit!"

"Are you reverse car-shaming me?"

"*Brayden Carter, Personal Assistant to the FOTUS, with his Oh-Eight Beamer. Mm-mmm! You come a long way from Newark, New Jersey.*" Reggie swerves around a minivan.

"It's Patterson."

"*Missah Brayden, sir, ken I wash yer car, sir? Please sir!*"

"You'd make a lousy slave."

"Cuz I'd be a Field Negro, like Malcolm said."

"Oh? So I'm a House Negro then?"

"Man, you a White House Negro!"

Brayden cracks up.

"Ha! I made you laugh."

"You did."

"Oh-Eight, man…"

"What?"

"That was a fucked-up year. We get the first black President, but then he lines up to blow Goldman-Sachs. *Fucking Wiley!* I mean, did he play this one beautiful or what?"

"It was poetry."

"It was art, man." Reggie shakes his head.

"So any word from…"

"No."

"How many messages you send?"

"…"

"Hmm?"

"A few."

"Like *ten?*"

"…"

"*More* than ten?" He looks over at Brayden.

"Man, you are one Grade-A, world-class sap!"

"Hey."

"But you *my Nigga!*" Reggie blows past a Prius.

"Thanks."

"That's okay, man. We all saps from time to time, cuz we ain't figured the shit out yet."

"Oh, and *you* have?"

"I'm single, ain't I?" Reggie downshifts to pass a slow-poke.

"White people in their Buicks, man." And in his exaggerated white-person voice: *"Dear, shall we take the LeSabre out this evening to dine at the Red Lobster?"*

Brayden laughs in spite of his mood.

"So what's Bullitt's first name, man?"

"Huh?"

"Steve McQueen."

"Oh. Is it *John?*"

"No, that was Magnum….*John Magnum, P.I.*"

"That was *Thomas* Magnum."

"Oh yeah! I *loved* that uptight white dude, Higgins. *'Release the hounds!'* I mean, was that guy gay or what? So what the fuck is Bullitt's name, man?"

"Dave?"

"*Dave* Bullitt?!"

Brayden shrugs.

"*Reggie Bullitt!*" Reggie smiles. "That's what it *should* be. Hey man, there's a bar. I'm thirsty."

"We just *came* from a bar."

"I know, but... I couldn't stay there, man. It was too fucking weird. All them white people standin' up an' cheerin' an' shit."

"I know what you mean."

"Ha! *Look...*" Reggie says.

"It's called *Whitey's!*"

"Ha!" Brayden smiles.

"Ain't life grand!"

A minute later, they're inside.

Whitey's is your typical working-class dive, with a limited menu, a limited beer selection, and most assuredly a limited selection of gin.

"Hey..." Brayden calls Reggie aside after sizing up the place.

"Don't go asking for *Uncle Tom*, okay?"

"Haha! *Me?* Would I do that?"

"What can I get for you?" the bartender asks.

"So are you Whitey?" Reggie asks (and Brayden cringes).

"No, but I bought the place from him a few years ago. What can I get for you gentlemen?"

"How 'bout..."

"Two bottles o' Bud," Brayden says.

"Comin' right up."

Reggie gives Brayden a look, and then their attention is grabbed by the TV. A news story with a banner headline on the bottom of the screen that says: **Historic Turnaround For POTUS**.

The bartender returns with two beers, and Brayden asks him to turn up the volume.

"In a heartfelt and emotional press conference today, White House Press Secretary Wiley DeSembler called on all Americans to pray for President Rett and his mother, who suffered another stroke on Thursday night, this one more devastating than the last, putting both her life and the life of the President in jeopardy."

"Poor guy!" says someone at the end of the bar.

"And his poor mom!" says another.

Brayden and Reggie look over, and then they glance around the room. Everyone has stopped what they're doing so they can watch the newscast.

"In what experts and political analysts are calling 'a massive groundswell of sympathy and support for the President, Alexander Rett's approval rating has risen from an all-time low of 17%, just this morning, to over 35%."

[Scattered applause in the bar...]

"Press Secretary Wiley DeSembler called for nationwide solidarity with President Rett, reminding everyone of the President's overriding concern for the health and security of *all* Americans. *[They cut to the taped footage from the Press Conference of less than an hour before; Press Secretary* Wiley DeSembler *at the podium...]*

"Fetus's Folly, as you so glibly put it, is all about making everyone feel safe and secure. So you can go to sleep each night feeling safe. So you can wake up each morning and not think that today might be your last. *This* is what our President, Alexander Rett, has done for us, and what he'll continue to do if given the chance. But right now, both he and his mother are fighting for their lives. I suggest we all reflect upon *this.* And offer them our sincerest thoughts and prayers. Thank you."

[Louder applause becomes cheers, then another standing ovation...]

"WTF," says Brayden.

"WTF is right," says Reggie. He raises his bottle.

"To Wiley Fucking DeSembler..."

They clink their bottles and take a sip as the cheering continues.

"Yuck!" Brayden grimaces.

"How can you drink this?"

"Buy American," says Reggie. He turns to the bartender and holds up his bottle.

"Buy American!"

"Damn right!" says the bartender, smiling proudly. And then he looks at Brayden and Reggie. "On the house, gents."

"Thanks!"

"Yeah, thanks," Reggie says. And then he looks at the bartender.

"Hey man, what's Bullitt's first name?"

"Bullet?"

"You know, that Steve McQueen movie."

"Oh! It's Frank," he says.

"*Frank Bullitt!* Yeah, man! Thanks!" He smiles and turns to Brayden. "It's Frank!"

Despite the cheers and applause, Brayden hears a robotic sounding beep and he reflexively turns to his cell phone.

"Way ta go, Pavlov!" says Reggie. He watches his friend as he reads the text, as his face goes from a hopeful future to a dead-end present. "What she say?"

"She broke up with me," Brayden says.

"Hmm... Sorry, man." He looks at his friend. "So what she say?"

"She said I'm too needy."

"Shit, man, that's Chapter Seventeen outta *The Bitches' Playbook.* They take their own shit an' they put it on you. I mean, you asked her to go to *Paris!* There gotta be *somebody* who'd like that shit."

"Ya *think*, right?"

"Gold-diggers an' whores, man," Reggie says.

And even though Brayden knows his friend is trying to be supportive, he can't help but feel offended by his words. *They're not all gold-diggers and whores,* he thinks. *There must be* somebody.

The news story on the TV is over, and now there's some baseball game. But the feeling is undeniable. Something happened today. Something that nobody could have guessed.

Reggie Mason raises his bottle of beer as he motions for another toast. "*To the New World Order...*"

21

By the following morning, President Alexander Rett's approval rating is at a staggering 63%—a jump of 46 points in a single day. Apparently, the American people were moved by Wiley DeSembler's painfully honest vulnerability, and the thought of both the President's mom and the President himself fighting for their lives. It fed into everything that's American. And as everyone knows, Americans *love* the underdog. At least white European underdogs, not reddish Native American ones or blackish African ones or brownish Mexican ones. But even more than that, Americans love their mom! What happened at the press conference was a devastating Floyd Mayweather one-two punch that left the American public reeling. And now they're against the ropes, waiting for the knockout blow.

It would come that night at 11:30.

Saturday Nite In-Yer-Face, more commonly known as *SNI,* is the most popular comedy show on TV. It's been around forever, since the 1970s, when there were still hippies and counterculture and subversive ideas that translated into an hour-and-a-half show every Saturday night. And what made it special was that it was *live.* With a live show, technically anything could happen. As it did that time when the punk band "Mucus" stopped in mid-song, flipped the audience the bird, and walked offstage. Or that time when the Republican-leaning guest-host and the ultra-Left cast member got into a fist fight during a sketch—the legendary, infamous "Karl Marx Pizzeria" bit. Or the many times when they unabashedly broke down the barriers of what you could and couldn't say on national TV. Thinly-veiled sexual references and innuendo predominated, like the memorable *"Dr. Phil Ayshio"* bit, or the one about *"Clitoris Popsicles... They're easy to find!"* At the time, it seemed like a great triumph over censorship and *"The Man."* In their own way, through comedy and satire and poking their fingers in the eyes of giants, they were changing the world.

Paradoxically, the show was the brainchild of Vern Ankles, the transplanted Canadian born of French and Norwegian stock, who became an American citizen, a Republican, and an Arnold Schwarzenegger fan (although he could never get *Ahnold* to come on his show, try as he might). And while his politics leaned to the Right, his pocketbook (as well as that of the network) leaned to the Left. There was big money to be had when you went for the liberal dollar—at least in 1975, when the show debuted. And throughout its lengthy run, it became a *de facto* showcase for all that was liberal. And even though Vern Ankles himself, in those long nights of the soul, lamented that he had painted himself into the corner of a room he couldn't leave, he said, "Fuck it! I'll focus on the room, and buy all the best shit I can find to fill it!"

Over the years, *SNI* had its highs and lows, partly because the most popular cast members always departed for greener pastures—green as in money. It wasn't cynicism exactly, but more like the American Dream in action. And wasn't laughter *good*, whatever your politics? So it was indeed a godsend for *SNI*, which had been in a slump for the past few seasons, when suddenly, out of nowhere, a self-aware talking fetus ran for President. *A fetus! Are you kidding? Who could make that up?* Endless bits about Alex Rett and the umbilical cord and his poor mom and the campaign and Mallory Blitzen and the debates. And then, when he actually *won*, when a fucking fetus for fuck's sake became *President,* it put *SNI* back in the vanguard, at the front of the comedic curve, where its ratings skyrocketed. In fact, the rumor went round that Vern Ankles was so elated—that night in November when the election results became final—that he spent the rest of that week hitting up all his drug connections dating back to the early 1970s, and a few days later, he had a lost weekend of epic proportions. Alexander Jackson Rett was a gift from God and Allah and Jehovah and the Great Spirit and all the rest of the goddamn deities! He was the network's cash cow through *SNI,* and this was the new Golden Age. On every show, there were at least four FOTUS sketches, not to mention the *Weekend Newsblast* segment and the monologue. And even though *SNI* was merciless towards Alex Rett, they all hoped he would stay in office forever.

For the past six months since Alex's inauguration, *SNI* has been unerringly accurate with its arrows, hitting one bull's eye after the next. So it's perhaps overweening hubris that will lead to its downfall. With Wiley DeSembler's gut-wrenching, heartstring-pulling press conference fresh in everyone's minds, all of America is anxious to see what *Saturday Nite In-Yer-Face* will say and what their response will be.

Tonight's cold opening is all too familiar. The mock-up of the Oval

Office with the ridiculously high chair behind Ronald Reagan's desk (so everyone can see the glass-covered womb with the Fetus President inside). Seated in the high-chair is President Alexander Rett's mother (played by an actual dummy that looks as if it's stuffed with straw). Innumerable hoses like a giant Tinker-Toy set-up go in and out of her lifeless body, connected to IV drips and saline solutions, and there's even one for *Lime Kool-Aid* (the President's mom's favorite). And one of the running gags is that two *extra-wide* hoses transport her... well, her *Número Uno* in one and her *Número Dos* in another. And every thirty seconds or so, there's the painfully obvious sound of "running water" resounding in a tin bucket, or a big fat *"plop."*

As the live studio audience waits on tenterhooks, the door to the Oval Office swings open. One of the cast members, Bill E. Baylor, walks in, made-up to look like Wiley DeSembler, and the audience greets him, per usual, with applause and cheers.

"Mr. President!" Wiley calls out.

And then the scene shifts to the other set, the one designed as a "giant womb"—a replica of Alex Rett's *"womb-room,"* with the full-sized actor, Penelope McDodge, in her ongoing portrayal of the Fetus President.

[Cheers and whistles as the camera moves in closer...]

"Mr. President!" Wiley DeSembler calls out again.

[The camera alternates the POV, from Wiley *in the Oval, to* The Fetus *in the womb. And from the Fetus President's perspective, Wiley's voice sounds like cavernous echoes...]*

"What?!" the Fetus responds. "Speak up! I got these tiny ears. Not ta mention tiny hands!"

[The predictable punchline, the usual response, as the "Tiny Hands" gag is expected, and always scores a laugh or two...]

"Mr. President," Wiley says, at wit's end, "the press conference is in five minutes and I still don't know what I'm gonna say!"

"Pull yourself together, Wiley!" the President says. "You're such a mama's boy!"

[The first uncomfortable laughs...]

"Do what you always do, Wiley. Make some *[BLEEP]* up. Hey? Do you think I can jump rope with this?" the President asks, as he starts playing with the umbilical cord.

[The camera cuts to Wiley DeSembler, *although the actor playing him,* Bill E. Baylor, *is starting to sweat. He has the feeling they're about to tank, as the first boo is heard...]*

"Hey Wiley!" the Fetus President calls out. "You got a cigarette? I'm dyin' for a smoke."

"Yeah." Wiley takes out a pack and pulls a cigarette from it.

[The actor playing Wiley DeSembler *lights it, then puts it between the dummy's lips...]*

"So much better than *Lime Kool-Aid,*" says Penelope McDodge.

[And through special effects, the dummy's mouth opens wide and smoke rings come out. And then, heard in the background is the familiar sound that's always good for a guffaw—that of the President's mom's Number Two making its way through the extra-wide hose, to emerge in a loud PLOP in the bucket. But when it happens tonight, the audience seems stunned. This is the President's MOM! His MOM, who just had another stroke and is fighting for her life, and they're making POOP JOKES?! Instead of laughs, they get boos, agonized moans, embarrassed groans, and a very audible and incredulous "Are you kidding me?"]

[The camera cuts back to Penelope McDodge, *sweat noticeable on her brow...]*

"This job's way too stressful," she says as the Fetus President.

"I thought about shooting some heroin. You know, *cuz I'm the President and I do what I want!*" *[The catch-phrase...]*

[Scattered laughs for the catch-phrase, but then Penelope McDodge *holds up a ridiculously large syringe from the Prop Department (about as big as her body) and then an enormous spoon. But instead of laughs, SILENCE. And then things start to really fall apart...]*

"Wiley! You still there?... Oh *Wi-ley...*"

"Yeah, I guess," he says. *[Although it's* Bill E. Baylor, *not his character, speaking...]*

"So about that press conference..."

"..."

"What the hell, Wiley?" Penelope McDodge says, off-script.

"I mean, my *mom's* more talkative than you!"

At this, boos erupt from every corner of the room as Bill E. Baylor stands frozen in place. The only things that move are his eyes as they shoot desperate glances towards the wings, where he desperately wants to be. And then the boos are joined by hisses, gestures, and jeers. And the actors onstage can't even go into their signature line: *"Live from New York, it's SNI!"* (which signals the start of the show) because the producers frantically cut to a commercial. And what follows are three of the most frenzied minutes in television history, as Vern Ankles goes ape in twelve different directions trying to salvage his show.

And as the house band finishes its impromptu cover of *"Eve of Destruction,"* the announcer introduces the guest-host.

"Ladies and gentlemen... *Derrick Kinkaid"*

(Derrick Kinkaid, who stars in the recently released fourth sequel to the third prequel to the sixth chapter of the fifth installment of the second iteration of the original *Star Quest*. The original *movie*, that is, since it first appeared as a TV show in the Sixties before it was rudely canceled, only to come back like Lazarus with a vengeance! And now you can't look in any direction without seeing some kind of *Star Quest* clone, be it movies, TV shows, video games, action figures, apps, breakfast cereals, coffee mugs, calendars, sippie-cups, t-shirts, jackets, hats, headbands, wristbands, socks, and underwear. There's even a line of *Star Quest* condoms featuring the likenesses of its most popular characters as well as the *Starship Intrepid*. And a company in Australia manufactures a *Star Quest* hearing aid for the hearing-impaired and Senior Citizens. And in a related aside, when asked recently about his new movie, Derrick Kinkaid replied, "You mean *Star Quest 97: The Revenge of the Capitalists?"*)

Kinkaid, a lifelong Democrat, has been a great friend of *Saturday Nite In-Yer-Face* over the years, as well as a frequent guest-host. So it's a relief to everyone in the studio when he walks out to thunderous applause. (And Vern Ankles backstage smiles to himself, convinced that he's dodged this bullet.)

"You all know what a fan I've been of this show," he begins.

[And for some reason, Vern Ankles starts to sweat...]

"I've been a guest-host fourteen times. *[applause...]*

"And tonight was supposed to be number fifteen."

[What's that supposed to mean? Vern Ankles holds his breath...]

"But after that opening..." Derrick Kinkaid pauses to look directly into the camera. "I'm an American," he says.

"Yes!" someone yells out from the audience.

"And as an American, I *love* this country."

"Yes, Derrick!"

"And even though I'm a Democrat, I support our President in his and his poor mother's time of need."

[The audience breaks into cheers, while backstage Vern Ankles says, "FUCK." His eyes fix on Derrick Kinkaid as he imagines a trap-door with a pool beneath it, filled with sharks and piranha and electric eels...]

"There was no call for that opening," says Derrick Kincaid.

"It was cruel, tasteless, and un-American. And I want no part of it."

And with that he turns and walks away, and the audience goes wild. In fact, the tumult is such that they cut to another set of commercials as Vern Ankles has to refrain from pulling out his own hair and gouging out his own eyes.

They try their best to salvage the night, but without a guest-host, and the audience out for blood, it just gets worse. When they introduce Tyler Quick, the mega-star musical guest, they wait and wait but she never appears and they go to more commercials. And then it gets ugly.

The *Weekend Newsblast* segment is a continual crowd-pleaser, with their irreverent off-the-cuff take on the news of the past week. But the best jokes had been written *before* Friday's press conference, all taking snide potshots at FOTUS, all suddenly taboo and NOT FUNNY. Unfortunately, the jokes that remain are lame as shit, and the hapless actor who plays the news-anchor, Sid Felton, knows this. "In other news, former Presidential candidate Mallory Blitzen said..."

"*BOOOO!*"

"Enough with the emails already, I..."

"*BOOOO! BOOOOOO!*"

"Hey, come on!" he appeals to the crowd. "This one's actually pretty good!"

But he can't deliver the punchline because he can barely be heard above the din. And if this were it, if this were all that would happen, they'd consider themselves lucky. But as Sid Felton tries to tell one last joke, there comes a sound like a great wall crashing down. The news-anchor looks on in disbelief turning to horror as a mob of people, like barbarians or the Mongol horde, rushes forward and knocks down everything in its path— expensive cameras, teleprompters, ladders, props, lights. In fact, anything and everything associated with the show. And when all this is destroyed, they rush towards the cast and crew. A panic usually reserved for Third-World dictatorships ensues, as everyone from *Saturday Nite In-Yer-Face*— from the lowliest gaffer to Vern Ankles himself—flees in terror as this mob of crazed, bloodthirsty, impatient, and pissed-off New Yorkers vents its rage. It goes on for ten frenzied minutes. Aside from several blurry cell phone accounts, the best visual record is what a lone, valiant cameraman was able to capture before succumbing to the onslaught. Eye-opening footage of assaults, attacks, near-rapes, and strangulations, including an especially graphic account of several of the *SNI* writers, beaten by the mob to the point of death.

And in no time at all, it's online, the whole insane, bloody, gruesome spectacle for the whole world to see. And from within the six-inch steel walls that's the Panic Room in his Manhattan penthouse, Vern Ankles lies incoherent, in the fetal position on the floor. Not even within the worst nightmares of his worst nightmares could he have conceived of a show such as this.

22

"'Did you see *Saturday Nite In-Yer-Face* last night? It was a riot!'"

By Sunday morning, everyone had either seen the show itself or the footage of the show that left five people dead, seventeen injured, and six hospitalized on the critical list. "How could this happen?" quickly became the next, more serious and somber question being asked. And this led to the third question that newscasters and pundits throughout the land all wondered in unison, in a hopeless, existential way: "What's become of our world?" The low-brows and the tabloids and the scandal sheets and the gossip rags and the news magazines and the bloggers and the op-eds and the middle-of-the-roads and the high-brows and the NY Times snobs were all quick to respond. And surprisingly (or maybe not surprisingly), the answer was all the same, namely, "We're fucked!"

As always in times of hopelessness and despair, the clutching, grasping masses look for a broad set of shoulders on which to lay their burden—for a towering, far-seeing Strong Man to lead them from their misery. And their clutching and their grasping and their seeking of salvation leads them this day to the same place: The American President, Alexander Jackson Rett. Over the past few days, as the world sank into chaos, this one man remained above it all. Like a Stoic of Ancient Greece, or one of those Hindu mystics, he seemed to float above the fray, looking down with compassion on his children, his flock of hopeless humans who strive and strive and always come up short. Who seek the summit, yet slide down like Sisyphus to the murky bottom of sediment, detritus, and quagmires. Yet somehow this little man, smaller even than Gandhi, seemed to hold the key. President Rett had conspicuously set himself apart so he could appear now on the world stage, and with his tiny finger on his tiny little hand, point the way.

By Sunday morning, everyone was anxious for 10 AM, for Jules Tippler, to see if Alex had come back to life. And within the protective walls of the White House, there was peace and tranquility. Gladiola Gaze had seen to it. She was the mother that Alex never had. And technically this was true, since a mother is defined by the act of birth, and Mary Rett was doomed to remain the expectant mother. She would never hold her child in her arms, she would never bounce it on her knee, she would never suckle it at her breast, she would never burp it over her shoulder when it had a little gas. And as Gladiola Gaze looked at Mary Rett, she felt a profound sadness.

Poor Mary Rett. Lifeless with eyes closed. With no movement except for the slow undulations of her breath, showing that her life, though miserable as could be, was still going on, if you could get beyond the medical equipment: the heart monitor and ventilator, the EKG, the tubes going in and out (*SNI* was on the money with that one, except for the plopping bucket). These tubes fed her and kept her alive; these wires kept her connected to the world outside.

And for her, the world outside was the staff of doctors and nurses in a room down the hall. This was what she would share with the world. Not a thought, a desire, a hope, or a dream, but rather the number of heartbeats per minute. Her life was no longer about the highs and lows that most of us experience, that in fact, define us. Mary Rett's life was about stasis. About living as opposed to dying, devoid of subtlety and nuance, of emotion and pain, of sadness and joy, of thought and realization. In short, everything that makes a human being.

But then, there was her child—well, her unborn child, but what child is this? Gladiola Gaze recalled the Christmas carol, the Three Kings gazing upon the Christ child in wonder and awe. And it was true enough that Alex Rett inspired a similar feeling by the circumstances of his birth—or in his case, non-birth. And surely there was some meaning here, that such a child arrived at the exact moment when the world was spinning off its axis. And as Gladiola Gaze looked upon Little Alex, peacefully asleep and blissfully unaware, she wanted to protect him with her life.

Of course it wasn't lost on her—the world-class irony at play. On Thursday night, the President of the United States got shit-faced drunk to the point of vomiting on his secretary and passing out in a drunken stupor, to sleep for two days straight as the world went to Hell. And somehow while this Fetus-President was sleeping it off, the world turned to him for guidance and salvation. *It's definitely a man's world*, Gladdy thought. And then she realized that she was the only person on Earth, other than the President himself, who knew what had happened here, in this room. What would the world say if it found out? How would history change? Gladiola Gaze felt at that moment that she'd been called upon as well; that it was her sacred duty to keep the flame of hope alive, amidst the ever-darkening tempest.

And on Saturday night, before the shitstorm on *SNI*, she looked down at the President, sleeping on his little sofa-bed in his tiny apartment. He didn't look like a fetus at all, but like a little adult; a grown-up in miniature. And when it came down to it, he wasn't bad-looking. In fact, he was kind of handsome, if you could get past the umbilical cord. And then Gladiola Gaze felt sad for *him*—that he would never know the loving touch of a woman or her sensual caress. That he would never experience the ecstasies two people could share. In the seven years since her husband died, Gladdy had devoted herself to her work. Others might see her now as just a secretary, but they were wrong. She saw herself as a Field Marshall overseeing a vast army, with President Rett as her Commander.

She reached inside, into the womb-room, and pulled the covers up to the President's little chin, and she heard him make a soft sound of contentment, like a sweet sigh. And then she went over to the couch on the other side of the room and closed her eyes.

23

On Sunday morning, Gladiola Gaze is awakened by the blasting sound of Frank Sinatra crooning *"My Way"* with Little Alex singing along. It's not bad. And then Gladdy remembers the *YouTube* video from what seems lifetimes ago, when the world first heard of Alexander Rett. The interview, and the charming duet with his mom that paved the way for all that would happen this morning.

"Mr. President?" Gladdy says. She walks over to his desk and peers inside the womb-room.

"Gladdy!" Alex turns off Sinatra and looks out at his secretary, his little eyes squinting into the daylight.

"What happened? What day is it?"

"It's Sunday, sir."

"Sunday?" And then Alex smacks his lips as if disgusted by himself. "It tastes like I went down on a dead mackerel."

Gladdy remembers the thoughts she had savored (just last night) of the Christ child. Of awe and wonder. And she bites her bottom lip and takes a breath.

Alex sticks out his tongue. And then he puts it back in and once again smacks his lips. "It tastes like the back of an Italian wrestler," he says. "Or that big Dago boxer." He looks at Gladdy. "You know, that guy who fought Max Schmeling... or was it Max Baer?"

It's amazing what you can learn on YouTube, Gladiola Gaze thinks to herself.

"Oh. My. God." Alex says. "My breath!" And then he cups his little hands before his face and expels a noxious cloud of stink into the air and gives it a sniff. "Yikes! Sorry, Gladdy."

She braces herself for another disgusting simile, but she's spared.

"Do you have any mouthwash?" he asks.

"Um, I have some in my desk, sir."

She walks to the door, then pauses as she looks down at the door-knob. Once that door is unlocked, the world out there will come in. And then, who knows? She stares at it for a long moment, as if on the edge of a precipice, and then she unlocks it and steps outside. The hallway is empty. Not a soul around, her desk as she left it. She glances at her watch: 5:37 on a pleasant Sunday morning. She can't recall ever being here on a Sunday morning at a time such as this. She finds the mouthwash and brings it to the President.

"Thanks, Gladdy." And then, "*GRuGLGRuGLGRuGLGRuGGRuGL-GRuGL*," as the sound of gargling fills the Oval Office. When he's through, Alex looks around for something to spit into. "*Mmmmmm...*" he says to his secretary as he motions to his mouthful of mouthwash. She comes back a few seconds later with a Dixie cup. "*Bllleeeerrgggh...*" says the President. And then, "Thanks. Much better." But to be sure, he smacks his lips a final time. And then he looks at Gladiola Gaze. "So what happened?"

"Well..." She doesn't know where to begin. "What do you remember, sir?"

"I..." Alex pauses as he tries to reassemble the last few days in his mind. "I remember Manny was here."

"Yes."

"He had tequila."

"Hmm..."

"Hey, did you know there's a *town* called Tequila? In *Méjico!*"

"No sir, I did not. Is there anything else you remember?"

"You said this is Sunday?"

"Yes."

"Shit! So I've been... I've been sleeping since *Thursday night?*"

"Yes, Mr. President.

Alex takes it all in and nods to himself.

"Well, I *do* feel better."

"I'm glad, sir."

"So... anything exciting happen while I was asleep?"

"*Ha-HA!*" Gladiola Gaze can't contain herself.

"I'm sorry, sir, I..."

"What, did something happen?"

"Well..."

"You said it's Sunday?"

"Yes."

"I have to go on Tippler."

"Do you still want to do that, sir?"

"Yeah, I guess so. I mean, even though he's gonna rake me over the coals. I *do* remember I was at 17%."

"Well sir..." Gladiola Gaze takes a long deep breath.

"Things have changed a bit since then." And she tells him the whole story, unfolding every detail. And he sits on his little chair in the womb-room, spellbound.

"Holy fucking shit," he says.

"I know, sir."

The President is at a loss. When he passed out cold on Thursday night, he was *this close* to being forced to resign. And now he's the Go-To-Guy of world leaders, with an approval rating of 74 and climbing.

"Well, that's a horse of a different stripe," Alex says.

And Gladdy wants to correct him, but she knows that in *his* mind, it somehow makes sense—he's probably thinking of zebras—so she lets it be.

"So I need to go on Tippler."

"Yes sir. If that's what you want."

"I mean, the world *needs* me!" he says.

"Jeez, ya leave it on its own for a few days and it eats a shit sandwich."

"Hmm."

"What time is it? I think my watch stopped." Alex glances at his $10,000 custom-made Swiss Chronograph. It stopped dead at 12:01 last Friday morning.

"It's 6:07, sir. You have lots of time. They aren't scheduled to show up here until 8 AM."

Jules Tippler and his mobile crew will set up in the Oval Office, as they did two months before for the previous interview, to spare the President's mother the hardship of being shuffled about. This is especially true today. In the eyes of the world, her condition is grave.

"Yes. Good," Alex says. "Give 'em a call, Gladdy. Let 'em know it's on."

"Will do, sir. Is there anything else I can do for you?"

"No. Thanks, Gladdy. I need a shower. I feel like I slept inside André the Giant's anus."

"Very good, sir. Then I'll let you be."

She starts to leave when the President calls her back.

"Gladdy?"

"Sir?"

"Thank you... for everything."

"You're welcome, sir." Gladdy takes a step towards the door, but then she pauses and looks back at the President.

"It was Primo Carnera, sir."

"Huh?"

"Primo Carnera... that big Dago boxer."

"Oh yes!" Alex smiles.

"Thanks, Gladdy!"

"You're welcome, sir.

As soon as the door to the Oval Office closes, Alex reaches out and presses the red button on his desk (this desk that once belonged to Ronald Reagan). A second later, a small self-contained compartment rises from within its confines until it stands there, beckoning. It's the miniature shower unit they installed after the inauguration, so Alex can hop out of the womb-room into a nice warm shower whenever he feels like, the ol' umbilical cord dragging behind him.

As the water pours down, it's never felt so good, as it washes away the past few days. *How can it be,* Alex wonders, *that by withdrawing from the world, the world has come to him?* And miraculously, almost as if through Providence, his political currency is at an all-time high, his regard and esteem unparalleled. What a mixed-up, screwed-up, fucked-up world it is where a fetus can become President (and by year's end, a drunken, unconscious fetus will make it to the cover of *Time Magazine* as its "Person of the Year"). *Only in America,* Alex thinks.

After his shower, Alex Rett sits in his bathrobe in his comfy chair. His phone is exploding with texts, but the only one he wants to see is from Tim Chopper... Nothing. He sends Tim three more texts without a reply, and then he watches the video of *Saturday Nite In-Yer-Face.*

"*Ho-lee Shit!*" he says at least twenty separate times. And halfway through, he decides to appoint Derrick Kincaid Secretary of the Interior. And when he's finished, when it's all over but the shouting and the *SNI* studio is a smoldering wreck, Alex knows that his time has arrived. What a strange, incomprehensible, unfigure-outable bitch is Destiny. But now she's *Alex's* bitch. He even looks forward to seeing Jules Tippler at ten o'clock— Jules Tippler, his nemesis, coming to *him* like Chamberlain came to Hitler at Munich. And like Hitler (and Alex's predecessor), Alexander Jackson Rett will reach out and grab the world by the pussy.

24

"So, President Rett... *Alex...* Welcome," says Jules Tippler, a look of appreciation—and of reverence even—in his eyes. "We've learned here at CNN, a little over an hour ago in fact, that you have been awake since last Thursday night. That you've been caring for your mother *nonstop* since the stroke occurred."

Alex offers a self-effacing shrug.

"And even in your sadness," Jules continues, "you kept your eyes opened wide to all the incredible events that've been happening. And you were ready to *intervene* if necessary. But yet you chose to step back."

(*"Bull's eye!"* Alex says to himself. He had planted that story through one of his undercover operatives at CNN a little past seven this morning—the moment after he'd thought of it. And in the mathematics of Fake News, if you counter a previous bit of fake news with a new bit of fake news, do they cancel each other out?)

"Yes, well, it was what I needed to do," Alex says.

"And thank you for having me, Jules."

"You're welcome. And now the question on everyone's mind..." He looks at Alex's mom.

"How is she? How is your mother?"

The camera pans back to Alex's mom. *This* is unprecedented! It's the first time that any news outlet during an interview has shown Alex's mom in relation to Alex himself. Before this, they shot the President in close-up. It seemed unseemly to have this unconscious woman looming above the President like a dark cloud. No one wanted to see *that!* She's *comatose*, for Christsake! It couldn't be more of a downer. And since it's all about ratings, the networks agreed. But the world had held its breath since Friday's press conference. And now it wanted to see the President and his mom—together, safe and sound—so it could breathe a sigh of relief.

"She's good," Alex says. "Thank you for asking. And thank you and everyone for your supportive messages, for your thoughts and prayers. They couldn't have meant more to me over these past few days, which have been among the hardest I've faced."

"The past few days have *indeed* been a whirlwind," says Jules Tippler, once again looking at the President with heartfelt admiration.

"Yet somehow you knew enough to stand apart from it all, to let it play itself out. And that, to me, is the mark of a true leader."

Alex smiles with gratitude. Since the first day of his candidacy, Jules Tippler has been a bug up his butt, scrutinizing his every move, calling his every decision into question. But *now...* 'I love that Jules Tippler!' Alex says to himself.

"Thank you, Jules, for saying that. Although I wasn't thinking *any* of that at the time." He offers a half-smile. "I was just..."

"Being a *leader?*" Jules says with affirmation. (Alex can barely believe his own ears.)

"I know that you're a big basketball fan," Jules says.

"I am."

"Me too. And when the game's on the line with seconds remaining, the go-to-guy doesn't stop to think about it. He just *is*, a part of it, of the flow." Jules looks at Alex. "And the chances are good that he'll make that basket."

"I... Thank you, Jules. That's a wonderful analogy."

"Well, thank *you*, Mr. President."

"Alex..."

"Alex." Jules smiles.

"You've shown the *world*, Alex, that *you're* the go-to-guy."

"We live in extraordinary times," the President says. "What happened last night, on that TV show, is just a symptom of the dis-ease that's spreading worldwide. People everywhere are wondering what to do, some throwing their arms up in despair. Others, like those people the other night, taking their rage out on each other."

"Yes, extraordinary times indeed," says Jules Tippler.

"So... what do we do?" *(DING! DING! DING! DING! DING! He's asking me what to do! Ha! And through him, the whole freaking world is asking me what to do—as if I have the slightest idea!)*

"Well, during these past few days, I've reflected upon that question a *lot*," Alex says, "with my mother facing death. With me facing my own mortality. I've realized that what we want more than anything else is to feel safe. To have our family and friends be safe and secure, so they can live their lives instead of being overwhelmed by worry and dread."

And the camera pans again to Alex's mom, as if to punctuate the President's words.

"And I have redoubled my efforts," Alex continues, "now that my prayers have been answered and my mom is okay. I'll devote myself, with all the powers I have as President, to making the world a safer place. So we *all* can pursue our dreams, so we can all find happiness, so we all can be fulfilled."

"Yes!" Jules says, barely able to contain himself. "And I can say with confidence that we're with you, Alex. You have been put on that Road to Damascus, and you've been transformed. And we are all the better for it. I look forward to your renewed, rejuvenated Presidency, Alex... *President Rett...*" Jules smiles broadly. "And let's not wait so long for the next visit, okay?"

"Yes!" Alex smiles. "I'll look forward to it very much."

The camera pulls back as they cut to a commercial, and Jules moves his chair in close.

"Thank you so much, Mr. President."

"Alex, please!"

"Okay, *Alex!*" Jules smiles. And he reaches over, his hand outstretched. And in response, Alex reaches his little arm through the opened glass door and they shake hands.

As Jules Tippler leaves the Oval Office and the camera crew packs its gear, Alex jots down a note to himself on a small slip of paper... *What the fuck does "Road to Damascus" mean???*

PART TWO

94 NOT 95

"I got the swagger of a champion."
—Britney Spears

1

"Did you believe that Jules Tippler shit, man?"

"Yeah! I mean, what the fuck, right?"

"Man, he was up his ass like a wedgie."

"Ha!"

"He was so far up there," Reggie says, "he could look out at *himself,* ya know what I'm sayin'? It was like that fucked-up shit all them white people are doin'."

"The 'Enema Challenge'!" says Brayden.

"Yeah, man. Jules Tippler is Rett's enema."

The latest craze to hit social media is the newest variation on the "Ice Bucket Challenge." In this one, white people throughout America have their friends shoot a video of them on their cell phone as they display their naked butts, take a deep breath, then shove enemas up their asses. And what happens *next...* Well, ya gotta see the videos! But it's all for a good cause—Colon Cancer or Rectal Cancer or Ass Cancer! Who knows? But every day there's a barrage of naked, soon to be enema-ed butts on *Facebook, Twitter,* and *Instagram.* Because that's the 21st-century equivalent of the tree falling in the forest. If a post doesn't get those LIKES, if it's not shared and it doesn't go viral, does it even exist? "I mean, they used ta hate each other's guts," says Brayden.

"That's why I watched his show, man. Ta see 'im rip Rett a new one!"

"Ha!"

"And then all that basketball shit... The only basketball Rett knows is the triple double-*cross.* Ya feel me?"

"You're on a roll!"

"Do ya think if there was some talkin' *Black* fetus, they'd make it the fucking President?"

"Haha!"

"*Hell no!* They'd say it was this voodoo baby, an' they'd stone its black ass, an' throw it off a cliff!"

"Word."

"White people."

They come to a red light, Brayden's somewhat new Beemer in the left lane behind a silver Prius.

"I mean, look at *that!*" Reggie says. "That bumper sticker on that fucking Prius..."

Brayden leans forward.

"I can't even read it."

"My point, man." On the back of the Prius is a bumper sticker the size of a cocktail napkin. It looks like a multi-colored, multi-cultural flag of world peace and Kumbaya, with some uplifting quote by Gandhi or MLK or Chief Seattle or Gunga Din, written in a different language for each of the colors.

"Wut dat shit say, man?"

They both lean forward and squint their eyes.

"Fuck if I know," says Brayden.

"Pull up closer." Brayden inches forward.

"Can you read it?"

"No." He inches forward some more till he almost hits the Prius and has to slam on the brakes.

"Watch *out,* man! You're gonna hit it!"

"I *know! Chill!*"

They look at each other, then they look back at the bumper sticker.

"What's that bottom one, man? It looks like Arabic."

"I think it's Farsi."

"Fuckin' liberals, man! They want ya to vote for the Democrat, but they put Farsi on their goddamn bumper stickers!"

"So what if the fetus was a little *Arab* fetus," Brayden says, "with this little turban an' shit."

"Listen ta *you!*" Reggie smiles.

"Turban an' shit... *My Nigga!*" Reggie ponders it for a moment, then turns back to Brayden.

"But they don't wear turbans, man. That's the Sikhs. The Arabs are the towel-heads."

"*Righhht,*" Brayden says.

Reggie glances over at the vehicle in the right lane.

"Okay, so look at *that* one..."

On the bumper of an enormous SUV are two stickers with huge letters in easy to read fonts with contrasting colors: NRA. HELL YEAH! and RETT: *THE CHOICE.*

"See what I mean!" says Reggie. "Ya can see that shit from a mile away." The light turns green and Brayden steps on the gas.

"So what did he even *say*, man?"

"Who?"

"Your pal. The Prez. On Tippler."

Brayden feigns gravitas as he turns to Reggie.

"He said '*blah-blah blah-blah blah.*'"

"Haha! I know! And Jules Tippler was up there with his spoon like it was *Nutella!*"

"Speaking of..." Brayden motions to a billboard with Jules Tippler on it, advertising his show.

"I used to respect the dude."

"Sell-outs and sycophants," says Brayden.

"Indeed. So why we in politics again?"

"For the women!"

"Oh yeah."

"What *I* don't get," says Brayden, "is how everyone is just... *buying* it!"

"They voted for him in the first place. Ya feel me? They jus' need ta be re-hypnotized every few months so they remember how happy an' free they feel."

"So did ya see that shit on *Saturday Nite In-Yer-Face?*"

"Holy shit, man! Ya know it's bad when even the *white people* are runnin' amok."

They're on their way to the Hotel Morocco in Alexandria. On Sunday afternoons from five to six, the hotel offers free wine and *hors d'oeuvres* to its guests. But as Brayden and Reggie discovered on a previous expedition, if you wear a nice suit and tie and are reasonably well-groomed, they smile at you and hand you a glass.

"So when you seein' him again?"

"Rett?"

"Yeah."

"Tomorrow," Brayden says.

"Jeez, when I saw him last Thursday, I thought he wouldn't last the weekend. Now he's *King o' the World*."

"A lot can happen in a week, man."

"Tell me about it."

"Oh yeah... Sorry, man."

There's an awkward pause.

"So... did ya hear from her?"

"No."

"Hmm... How many texts you send?"

"None."

"*None?*"

"I sent emails," Brayden says.

"It's too hard to type five-page letters on my phone."

"So how many emails you send?"

"Oh, four or five... They were really well-written!"

"I'm sure. Hey, there's the hotel."

A few minutes later, they're milling about the lobby of the Hotel Morocco, decorated in a style that can be described as Ottoman Empire meets Art Deco meets Las Vegas. When they look around, they see that everyone else is white.

"At least we're well-dressed!" Brayden says.

"So she never wrote back?"

"Nope."

"Typical."

After getting some wine, they float like two black clouds among the life-is-good white people, sipping their Chardonnays and nibbling their noshes. At this moment, the world seems problem-free. As they mill about, they pick up snippets of conversation.

"He really needed that. He was at 17%."

"Yes! On Friday!"

"And now he's at 83."

"84."

"*We* really needed that! The American people!"

"Such a boost."

"Amen!"

"How's the Chardonnay?"

"Not bad, but not as oaky as I would like."

"But it's buttery."

"I don't like buttery."

"You don't like *buttery?* Who doesn't like *buttery?*"

"Did you see Tippler this morning?"

"He's finally seen the light."

"Tippler?"

"He really admires him."

"The President?"

"He was so... *Presidential.*"

"I was thinking that *exact word!*"

"It was like he became the *President of the United States*, right there before the whole world."

"It was inspiring."

"*I'm* inspired. I think I'm finally going to get that sailboat."

"That's great!"

"I mean, life is short."

"Is it ever."

"Do you think he's handsome?"

"The President?"

"Yeah."

"I never thought about it. But yeah, I guess he is."

"I think he's *hot.*"

"I can see that."

"I mean, he was *gorgeous* on Tippler!"

"Absolutely!"

"If only he wasn't so short."

Reggie and Brayden disengage from the crowd and go back for a refill.

"My dear Brayden, what do you think of the wine?" Reggie asks in his white person voice.

"The Chardonnay?" says Brayden, playing along.

"Not as oaky as I would like."

"But it's buttery," says Reggie. "I adore buttery." At that moment, he happens to glance outside. Beyond the plate glass window, he spots Brayden's ex-girlfriend, Carly Menteur, walking by with a distinguished older man wearing what looks like a very expensive suit.

"Whatsa matter?" Brayden asks.

"Nuthin', man." Reggie turns back to his friend. "I hate buttery."

They sip their wine as they look out on the room, and they can't help but catch more of the conversation.

"These are so good, these little quiches."

"But I don't think they're made here. I think they're frozen."

"Are they?"

"*Whole Foods* has some nice ones."

"Yes! There's one with shallots and gruyere!"

"And their Quiche Lorraine has free-range bacon!"

"I'm a Vegan."

"Oh."

"Don't they have one that's eggless and cheeseless?"

"And flourless!"

"And gluten-free!"

"Well, that's why it's flourless."

"Oh."

"So I think I'm going to do it!"

"Do what?"

"You know, that thing."

"Thing?"

"That thing that everyone's doing! *The Enema Challenge!*"

"Really?"

"That's great!"

"My friend Ashley did it. She said it was amazing!"

"And it's for a good cause."

"White people..." says Reggie, shaking his head.

2

CNN

"President Alexander Rett, after hitting an all-time low approval rating of 17% just last week, has bounced back with a vengeance. After appearing yesterday on *The Jules Tippler Show*, his approval rating has skyrocketed to a stunning 87%."

So what's up with that 13%? And yeah, I used the calculator. *CLICK...*

CBS

"During a remarkable turnaround, President Rett has seen his stock rise world-wide. World leaders from Angola to Zanzibar have proposed visits to the White House to seek counsel with the President. And the United Nations has even invited him to address the General Assembly in session next week."

Suck-ups... *CLICK...*

FOX NEWS

"The word is *Presidential.*"

"*Presidential,* yes. We've been hearing that word a *lot* since Alexander Rett's appearance yesterday on Tippler."

"It was *amazing,* to see him like that. So..."

"*Presidential!*"

"Yes! So powerful and in command."

"Well, we've been *needing* him to rise up and take charge. And that's exactly what he did."

"And under such circumstances! The near death of his mother!"

"But he was there for her, as he's there for us, for all Amer—"

CLICK...

PBS

"What he did was astonishing. It was FDR on December 8th, it was George W. Bush on 9-12. It was Alexander Rett's crowning moment so far, and like it or not, it's *made* his Presidency."

Borrr-ing! *CLICK...*

THE YOUNG TURKISH ANARCHISTS

Fat Guy With Weird Name: You *know* my feelings on Alexander Rett. I mean, right from the start, I thought it was a *bad idea* for a fetus to be President.

Hot Babe With Weird Name: You've made no secret of *that!* *[smiles ironically... And I hate when you always speak in italics.]*

Fat: But I gotta say, what I saw yesterday. It wasn't so much what he *said*, which wasn't *much* when it comes down to it.

Hot: *[impatient, restless]* But the way he *said* it. *[There's an italics for ya! And I love finishing that fat guy's sentences. It makes me feel all empowered and in control.]*

Fat: Yes. His poise and self-confidence. His... *equanimity.*

Hot: *[offers fake smile] There's* a word for you! *[Show-off! Maybe hit the gym, why don't ya?]*

Fat: I've never *seen* him like that before.

Hot: *[inwardly rolls eyes...]* I *know.* Like that word that's been bandied about *so much* over the past 24 hours... *[Wait for it... I got words too, Fatso...]*

Fat: *[cuts in line...] Presidential.* Yes! I just high-fived myself.

Hot: *[Goddamn it! He stole my word!]* Yes. It's a tired old *cliché*, of course. *[Take* that, *Fattie!]*

Fat: But a cliché is a cliché... *[looks to* Hot Babe *in an* "aren't we the coolest liberals ever cuz we can eat some crow but it actually doesn't taste so bad" *kinda way... Oh Shit! I forgot to italicize something!]*

Hot: Because it's *true.* *[Ha! I love when I finish his sentences!* Especially *with an italics!]*

Fat: Yeah, I gotta *give* it to him. Props to the President. *[I love having my own show! I mean, I'm this fat guy with this Albanian name that even I can barely pronounce. But I got my own frickin' show! I love America!]*

Hot: So do you think that this is a *mandate? [I'm bored...* And *what's up with that word? Mandate... Leave it to the Patriarchy.]*

Fat: I wouldn't go *that* far. *[Damn! If that little* fetus *can turn it around, I gotta get my fat Albanian butt into the gym!]*

Hot: *[That fat guy looks* extra *fat today. And what's that word... swarthy.]* But his stock has *never* been so high. *[Speaking of... That stock tip* *that guy I banged last night gave me, that IPO. I wrote it down somewhere. And he expected me to swallow! As if...]*

I love The Young Turkish Anarchists! *CLICK...*

ENTERTAINMENT AMERICA!
"'Dead from New York, It's Saturday Nite!' was the headline in today's *New York Post.*"

Haha! That's pretty good!

"In the aftermath of the unspeakable tragedy that happened during *SNI's* live broadcast, the network announced today that the show has been canceled."

Ha! No more Fetus jokes!

"The riot claimed the lives of seven people and hospitalized 27 others, while leaving the studio at Rockefeller Center a smoldering wreck. *[They cut to the heinous footage from the show...]*

Ho-lee Shit! And I think that's the twenty-*first* time I said that.
[They cut to interviews with people on the street...]
"It was horrendous!" said Chip Narz from Staten Island"
"It was even worse than 9/11!"
"I hated that those people died an' all," said Loretta Dimsum from lower Manhattan, "but I hated that show even more. Especially the way they treated our poor President. But *he* showed *them*, I guess... on Tippler."

Lo-retta!

"Ya know it sucks an' everything, I mean, that all them people, like died an' *[deleted]*, but comedy's a tough *[censored]* business," said Ricky Balls from Queens.
"I mean, people take their comedy *seriously* in New York, ya know

what I'm sayin'?" And then he looked into the camera. "Go Mets!"

[They cut back to the perfectly perky, buxom blonde host, Vanessa Sparks...*]* "In addition to the show's cancellation, the actor who played 'President Rett' in the infamous sketch that sparked the riot, Penelope McDodge, has received over one hundred death threats and has gone into seclusion. And the show's creator, the transplanted Canadian Vern Ankles, has been brought up on charges of manslaughter, accessory to murder, and gross criminal negligence. So, *Saturday Nite In-Yer-Face,* the comedy show that had been on the air since 1975 and had been a vital part of our cultural landscape, is no more."

Fuck 'em! *CLICK...* Time to check the *Tweets...*

Ezra Millstone Banes @EzraBanesCrackTheWhip
I gotta hand it to the President. What he did, remarkable. He united the country and set an example for the world. I look forward to doing great things with him.

Whoa! Ezra knows where his Pumpernickel is buttered.

Porter Percival Portly @govPortPortly
What President Rett did is HUGE! He showed us all what's really important. Family, friends, our safety and security. Never have I seen him so PRESIDENTIAL.

I'm really starting to *dislike* that word.

Jaspar Redford Torrence @govJRTva
On first meeting Alex Rett, I knew that one day he would be a great world leader. With what he did this past week, that day is here. God bless you, Mr. President!

Well, I'll be a monkey's uncle.

Dirk Fist @infocombatBigDirkFist
I'm the first to admit when I'm wrong, which I never admit, cuz

I'm never wrong. Except this one time. President Rett kicked some serious ass. God Bless America!

How'd ya like that! Way ta go, Fat Boy!

Jules Dale Tippler @JulesTipplerCNN
Again, what an honor it was to share the stage with the President yesterday morning. He showed us what true leadership is about. A profile in courage for our time.

Aww, I think ol' Julie is sweet on me.

Mallory Rodman Blitzen @realPresidentMalloryBlitzen
Well, I'm glad your mom is okay. But what did you say, if anything, on Tippler? The same empty promises in a nicer wrapper? Old dog. Same tricks. You don't fool me!

Ah, Mallory... so old and bitter, with those frumpy clothes. With all the money you raked in from all those shady business deals, ya think you could afford some good taste! Ha! Well even *you* are not gonna spoil this day.

Alex clicks on *iTunes* and calls up one of his favorite songs: Kid Rock's *"Bawitdaba."* As the song gradually gets louder, as it rises in intensity to its sinister crescendo, Alex Rett strides onto Reagan's old desk like a mini-Colossus. And he waits until the exact freaking moment and says: "MY NAME IS *ALLLLLLLLLLLLLLLLLLLLLLLLLL LLLLLLLLLLLLL LLLLLLLLLLLLLLLLLLLLLLLLLLLLLLLLLLLLLLLLLL LLLLLLLLLLLLLLLLL... ALEX RETT!!!!!!!!*

And then he belts it out along with Kid Rock at the top of his little lungs. So loud in fact, that he doesn't hear the intercom, or his secretary Gladiola Gaze pounding on the door outside.

Bawitdaba, da bang, da dang diggy diggy Diggy, said the boogie, said up jump the boogie!
POUND! POUND! POUND!
Bawitdaba, da bang, da dang diggy diggy Diggy, said the boogie, said up jump the boogie!

"MR. PRESIDENT!" POUND! POUND! POUND!

Bawitdaba, da bang, da dang diggy diggy Diggy, said the boogie, said up jump the boogie!

POUND! POUND! POUND! POUND! *"MR. PRESIDENT!"*

Finally, Alex hears the pounding and he turns off the song.

"Yes?" he says.

The door bursts opened and Gladiola Gaze hurries in, frazzled.

"Mr. President, it sounded..." She glances around to see what's amiss.

"Yes?"

"Um, I... I was worried about you, sir."

"I was just blowin' off some steam. What's shakin', Gladdy-Ola?"

"Um, the *Daily Briefs* are in, sir."

"Oh good! I love me some *Daily Briefs!*"

Gladiola Gaze looks to see if there are any empty tequila bottles strewn about (and she unconsciously brushes her blouse with her hand).

"And what else, Gladdy?"

"Sir?"

"You came in with such urgency, I thought there must be something more."

"Oh yes, sir. There is. That artist is here to see you."

"Artist?"

"Vincent Van..."

"Go-Go!" Alex smiles. *"Wake me up before you go-go!"*

Gladdy stands there staring at the President.

"Excellent!" he says. "Send him in!"

"Yes sir." She starts to leave but then stops.

"Something else, Gladdy?"

"The new approval rating is in, sir." There's an expectant pause.

"*And...*"

"It's 92 percent!"

"*92 percent?!* Well I'll be dipped in Ronzoni!"

"Yes sir. I'm glad you're pleased."

"Thanks, Gladdy! I am! What. A. Day."

As Gladdy leaves, Alex begins again: "*Bawitdaba, da bang, da dang diggy diggy diggy, said the boogie, said up, My name is ALLLLLLLLLLLLL LLLLLLLLLLLLLLLLLLLLLLLLLLLLLLLLLLLL LLLLLLLLLL..."*

"Mr. President?"

Alex stops abruptly and looks up.

"I'm that artist, Vincent Van Go-Go."

"Yes of course."

"But can we cut through the bullshit?" he says. "I mean, all this *yes sir/no sir* crap gives me a fucking migraine. An' we're *both* bullshitters, am I right? I mean, ya can't bullshit a bullshitter. Ha! But *you* are *Da Man! Day-um!* An' what ya said yesterday on Tippler was *World-Class Gold-Medal Epic-Hall-o'-Fame Dream-Team Michael Jordan Will Eat Your Lunch Coca-Cola-Classic Bullshit*, Mr. President! Ha! Or can I call you Alex?"

"Um, Alex is good," the President says.

"Solid. Cuz I'm not like those other artists. They're these colostomy bags with a paint brush, ya know what I'm sayin'?"

"I'm not sure," he says.

"Hold on..." Alex buzzes Gladdy.

"Yes, Mr. President?"

"Hold all my calls."

"Yes sir.

Alex turns to look at this artist before him. Big, unruly, and wild like an Old West desperado crossed with Cyrano de Bergerac, all swagger and panache, bred with a snorting bull in a China shop, with a conspicuous scar running down his left cheek as the final flourish.

"Where'd you get *that?*" Alex motions to the scar.

"Knife fight."

"Oh. You want something to eat? A sandwich?"

"I'm good."

"Tacos? Cheese? Pringles? We got great *blintzes!*"

"I'm good, thanks."

"How 'bout a drink then? I have the best bartender, Manolo Vargas!"

"Why not!" Van Go-Go smiles.

"Muy excelente![He presses the intercom...] Gladdy?"

"Yes, Mr. President..."

"Have Manny come in here, *pronto!*"

"Right away, sir."

Alex turns to Van Go-Go and nods as if they're in for a treat, and Van Go-Go offers the smile of a budding-conspirator.

"I like your style, Vincent... Or may I call you Vince?"

"My name's Ace, man. Ace Buckland."

"So where'd you get *Ace* from?"

"This car I liked when I was a boy."

"Okay. So you're not *like* other people."

"Ha! I guess not." Ace laughs. "But I always thought that was a *good* thing."

"It is!" says Alex. "Most people I've discovered, in my limited time here, are... how shall I put this?"

"Assholes, suck-ups, sell-outs, an' vipers."

"*Yes!* Those would be the four categories *exactly!*" The President's eyes light up as Manny walks in behind his bar cart.

"With the occasional exception, such as *Señor* Manolo Vargas."

"Mr. Alex."

"Please, just Alex..."

"Alex."

"Manny, this is the world-renowned bullshit artist of semi-epic proportions, *Señor* Ace Buckland!"

"A pleasure," says Ace.

"*Mucho gusto.*" Manny turns to the President. "I am glad you are feeling so much better... Alex."

"Yes, it was your miracle elixir that turned things around."

"So what can I make for you?"

"Please, attend to my guest first, then to yourself, Manolo."

"None for me," Manny says.

"After last time."

"I thought that as well, but today has been a *great* day!" Alex says.

"How 'bout a Margarita? I've never had one."

"You never had a *Margarita?*" says Ace. "But then, you're a fetus. I guess there's *lotsa* things you never had."

"Indeed. But I'm working to amend that... Two of Manny's Marvelous Margaritas, *por favor!*"

"*Sí.*" Manny nods.

"So we were talking about art and artists."

"Yeah... I gotta admit, I was surprised when I met your man, that Tim Chopper guy," Ace says. "Where is he? Is he gonna join us?"

"Tim..." Alex pauses. (*Where are you?*) "Tim only handles certain parts of the family business."

"Too bad. He's cool in a *'I'll fuck yer shit up without thinkin' twice'* kinda way."

"That he is."

"Your Margarita, Mr. Ace..."

"Just Ace, man." Ace Buckland takes a sip.

"Man, that is one motherfucker of a Margarita!"

Manny is momentarily taken aback.

"And for you, Alex..."

"*Mmm... Magnífico*, Manolo!"

"*Gracias.*"

"So where are your art supplies?" Alex turns to Ace.

"Today's about me givin' *you* the eye."

"Hmm?"

"Sizin' you up," Ace says, "so I'll know how to approach it—the portrait, that is."

"Ace is going to paint my official White House portrait," Alex explains.

"Ah!"

"So this is *good*, what we're doin'. I'm gettin' an idea of what you're about."

"Hmm, so what did you think before?"

"Before *this?*"

The President nods.

"I thought you were an *asshole!*"

Manny can't contain his laughter, and he takes a contrite breath. "Ha! But *now?*"

"Now I'm not sure if you're a viper, or... you know, a decent guy."

"Ha! So no suck-up or sell-out?"

"No, an' that's good for *you*, see, cuz I *hate* suck-ups an' sell-outs!"

"Me too!" says Alex.

"Me too!" says Manolo.

"But *here*, I mean… they're all *over* the place! How do you do it?"

"Ha! Well, I've learned that sometimes it's best to just sit back and do nothing. Right, Manny?" Alex smiles. "And then let them… self-destruct."

"*The Art of War*, man."

"Hmm?"

"Sun Tzu," says Ace. "'*The battle is won or lost before it's even fought.*'" (Alex remembers this documentary he was going to watch once on *The History Channel*—some 500 B.C. warrior-poet named *Sun Tzu*— but instead he watched *A Clockwork Orange* for the fifth time.)

"So when will you actually start it?"

"The painting? It's already begun, man. In *here*…" He points to his noggin. "But I'm sensing sumthin' real strong… an' *nasty!*"

"*Nasty?*"

"You got a mean streak in you, Mr. President."

"Do I?"

"I wouldn't wanna get on your bad side."

"Ha! That's what I say about *Putin!*"

"*Raz Putin?* That sneaky, murderous, homophobic, Commie-Cap-italist, ex-KGB *thug?*"

"That's him," says Alex. "We're good friends. He wants to come visit me… now that I'm important. Him and everybody else."

"But everybody else is a suck-up an' a sell-out," says Ace. "*That* guy is dangerous."

"I know, but so am I!" Alex offers an inscrutable smile.

"You are at that, sir… For a little bastard!"

Manny looks at Alex, and an agonized instant goes by until Alex laughs and then Ace laughs and then Manny laughs, but *his* laugh is more like a sigh of relief.

3

I'm worried about Tim. I mean, I guess I've done alright on my own this past week. And I kicked ass with that fake news I planted at CNN, and I ruled on Tippler—made Jules my bitch—and I'm at 92%.

But still, I miss him. I miss Tim Chopper. I mean, he does this shit for a living. Me, I got lucky.

Remember that shit they did back in ancient Rome? They have the Emperor ride in a golden chariot encrusted with jewels. A triumphal procession before the entire city—after he got back from kicking ass in Northumberland or Germania. And there it is, his finest hour. And it's like, free drinks for a year and the best concubines from Cleopatra's Secret and all the gold he can eat at Marc Antony's-All-You-Can-Eat-Gold & Salad Bar! And those eunuchs are oiled up nice an' glistening as they blast those trumpet fanfares! And in that one sublime moment, there's this lowly slave, standing behind the Emperor in the chariot. And this slave leans over and whispers all solemn-like in the Emperor's ear, "It won't last." And only the Emperor can hear it.

Fuckin' Tim! Where the hell did you go?

4

Nobody's heard from Tim Chopper since last Thursday morning. I sent people to his apartment—FBI and CIA and Secret Service agents. Nada. And his freaking car was gone from the parking garage. Like WTF, Tim? Thankfully my new BFF, Ace Buckland, the artist also known as Vincent Van Go-Go, is returning today to continue the official White House portrait of yours truly. I like that guy. If he has an angle or some hidden agenda, it's the most hidden, abstruse, lock-that-shit-in-a-trunk-in-the-attic-then-burn-down-the-house kind of agenda. And that's the kinda guy I can trust. And here on the Hill, trust is almost non-existent.

So while I'm waiting for my new pal to arrive, it's time I told you the rest of that story—you know, what happened after my *YouTube* video went viral. It was when I got my first enemy, the first on a long list, because when you're the Prez, you accumulate enemies like a Jehovah's Witness gets door-slams. And I actually *do* have a list! You wanna see it? *[Alex calls it up on his smartphone...]* There, see...

Comprehensive List of Enemies, Jerks, Back-stabbers, & Dickheads: BjhyBDerj;Ppo64

FHKf%CLLP9ksdl
djeo8UJHffY89IJe
69odhhsYIGUS0H7
bhFjlh09_7jl;pj
gDEhiRWDJ8HTDSjV
ghdtWHJF90970ug.
568HjgkkllhR7KBk
DNbhGI*JFR543F-
KL;polkjhfstesw5

That's just the first page. *Of course* it's encrypted! Duh! D'ya think I'd show my Presidential Enemies List to just *anyone?* Besides, if you have to ask if you're on it, you probably are. But since I brought it up, I'll tell you about my *very first* enemy: Cara Carthusian. Now everybody's heard of Kim Kardashian—duh!—and her epic ass. You remember that story of my neighbor, Ernie Rasmussen? How he made that video of my mom and me that put me on the map? Well, what happened *next* was the story I was going to tell you, before I was rudely interrupted by my Presidency about to disintegrate.

You'll recall that ol' Ernie's *YouTube* video entitled *"Amazing Talking Fetus"* took the Internet by storm and eclipsed the amazing butt of Kim K in a single day. But what I *didn't* mention was the sad, cautionary tale of Cara Carthusian, the archrival and bitter enemy of Kim Kardashian. Cara's ass was the equivalent in almost every way, ass-wise, to Kim Kardashian's, although as these things go, with no discernible rhyme or reason, KK's ass got all the glory while CC's languished in online ass obscurity.

But Cara Carthusian was nothing if not a red-blooded American embodiment of the Protestant Work Ethic, combined with Horatio Alger's steadfast belief in the success that comes from persistent nose-to-the-grindstoning. So she undertook an arduous training regimen that rivaled Rocky Balboa's when he prepared to fight Ivan Drago. For six months, Cara hit the gym and worked the weights and did the cardio and drank the wheat grass smoothies and even became a Vegan (for which she is the *most* resentful), all to make her ass a thing of perfection. And she was on tenterhooks until *finally* the day of The Big Ass Launch arrived.

Cara Carthusian found herself shivering with anticipation as she pressed the SEND button, and off it went, her gorgeous new posterior into cyberspace! Unfortunately for her (and then for me), she was about three hours too late, since Ernie Rasmussen had pressed *his* SEND button three hours earlier. And in the world of *YouTube* video uploads, the precedent set that day was that *"Amazing Talking Fetus"* videos trump *"Big New Ass"* videos every time. And poor Cara Carthusian's butt never made it out of the starting block—it garnered barely a hundred LIKES. And when she saw that her future had been robbed and her life had been ruined by a *FETUS*... Well, she didn't take it too well, and the hate mail poured in. Then the stalking. And then came the suicide attempt (at the last moment, she changed her mind, realizing that she was too in love with her own ass to ever want to part from it—even though her ass was a loser.) Nevertheless, she became my enemy for life, and she's even on the list. *See...*

FtuIeyULF98iF$%*

But as the silver lining to her dark cloud, the recent "Enema Challenge" sweeping the nation was her brainchild. Or should I say, *buttchild.* And while her ass never got the attention it deserved, it has inspired legions of other asses to come forth and present themselves proudly, before having enemas shoved inside and squeezed. And it's for a good cause, so there's that.

[The intercom buzzes...]

"Mr. President?"

"Yes, Gladdy?"

"Tall Skinny Sad-Sack is here, sir."

"Tall Skinny... You mean *Brayden.*"

"Sir?" Gladiola Gaze is momentarily flummoxed.

"Brayden is his name," the President says.

"Brayden Carter."

"Yes... Yes of *course* it is, sir. I'll send him right in."

[A moment later...]

"Mr. President!"

"Mr. Carter, so nice to see you!"

Brayden's eyes look off to the side for a moment, as he finds himself in a state of bewilderment.

"You too, sir. And I wanted to say how happy I am with the recent turnaround."

"Ninety-three percent as of this morning," says Alex.

"Not that it should matter. It's not a popularity contest, after all."

"No sir."

"So any news?"

"The Black Caucus has renewed its support, sir. My source inside says that Ezra Banes will be paying you a visit regarding the Health Care Bill."

"The one that he was against."

"Yes sir, but now he supports it."

Not a popularity contest? They were lining up last week to pour poison in my ear, but now it's to kiss my petite white ass. Hey, maybe *I* should do the "Enema Challenge."

"Well, good," the President says.

"Nothing like kicking ass on Tippler."

"Yes sir. That was quite transformative."

"So Brayden..."

"Sir?" (Brayden is having a hard time being called by his actual name. He keeps thinking of that movie, *The Invasion of the Body Snatchers*.) "Have you heard anything regarding the Majority Whip?"

"Senator Milanese? Yes, it appears that whatever alliance he formed with the Minority Whip, Ezra Banes, has been dissolved, sir."

It's extraordinary how life can change on a dime. My goose was freaking roasted on a spit for Columbus Day, and now...

"Very good. Thank you, Brayden."

[The intercom buzzes...]

"Mr. President, the *Daily Briefs* are in."

"Thanks, Gladdy." Alex turns to his young intern. "The *Daily Briefs* are in."

"I understand, sir."

"Keep up the good work, Brayden."

"Will do, Mr. President."

Still a bit stupefied, Brayden Carter leaves the Oval Office. *Reggie's not gonna believe this one!* he thinks.

The *Daily Briefs*... The *Daily Briefs*... I love me the *Daily Briefs*...

DELETE. What? You might think me irresponsible, but you haven't seen 'em! They're boring as shit! And what I've discovered to my astonishment is that sometimes it's better to get blind drunk and pass out for two days than to do anything else.

[The intercom buzzes again...]

"Mr. President, the Vice-President and that artist are here to see you, sir."

"*Ace?* I mean, *Vincent Van Go-Go?*" The President finds himself with a smile on his face.

"Yes sir, but..." Gladdy's earlier flummoxitude has a flare-up. "Shall I send in the Vice-President, sir?"

"..."

"Sir?"

"Very well, send her in." The President finds his face in the shape of a scowl.

"Mr. President." The Vice-President offers a conciliatory smile.

"Mavis! So good to see you! Have a seat."

"Thank you, sir."

"Coffee? Hemlock tea?"

"No thanks... Sir, I been wrastlin' with demons these past few days."

"Demons... Well, you know what they say, *When life hands you demons, make demonade!*" Alex smiles to himself, then he notices the Vice-President's blank expression. "My secretary's grandson told me that."

"He's a very clever boy, sir."

"Yes, so these demons with which you been *wrastlin'*... "

"Sir, I'm a Christian woman, as you know... a woman o' faith."

"And I respect that, Mavis."

"Well sir, there's sumthin' that's been eatin' at my craw like a drip from a leaky fawrcet. Sumthin' I need ta confess."

"Hmm." The President nods. "Please, continue."

"I was so moved by what you said, sir...on Tippler, on Sunday. It made me... It made me ashamed o' what I done."

"And what is that, Mavis?"

"Sir, for the past few weeks, I been meetin' with the Black Caucus, with Ezra Banes... an' with that Dago, Dom Milanese."

"Go on..."

"Well sir, with the way things were goin', with everythin' spiralin' out o' control like that turd goin' down the toilet... I mean, last Thursday, you were at 17 an' sinkin' fast."

"Ha! Don't remind me!"

"An' we thought..."

"Ezra and Dom and the Black Caucus."

"Yessir, and... well, me too, that... well, that you were gonna be forced ta resign, sir. I mean, you'd been sinkin' steadily. An' last Thursday seemed like the bottom o' that political barrel."

(*More like bottom of the bottle*, Alex thinks to himself.)

"Yes, it was a dark moment," the President says.

"Well, ta cut ta that chase, sir..."

"Please do."

"We worked out this stratergy ta keep things in place without too much wrack an' ruin," Mavis says.

"For the American people, sir."

"In the event of my resignation."

"Yes, but then... the way you handled yerself after that press conference, an' then on Tippler. It was so *inspirin'* ta... well, ta *everyone*, sir, but especially ta me. The way you rose ta meet that great challenge, which seemed like the end o' your Presidency fer shure ta this ol' country gal. An' not only ta meet it but ta *surmoun'* it. It was..." The Vice-President searches for the right word.

"Presidential?" says Alex.

"Yes! Presidential! An' I realized the kind o' leader you are, sir. A leader who I'm proud ta foller, as the American people are proud as well... ta foller, I mean."

"Why thank you, Mavis. That's a very nice thing to say."

"I mean it, sir. And... well, if you ken find it in yer heart ta both except my 'pology as well as my resignation, I'd be..."

"Nonsense, Mavis!" The President offers a benevolent smile.

"I will accept the former but most certainly not the latter!"

"Oh sir..." She lets out a sigh of relief.

"You are too kind, Mr. President. I will... I will pledge ta you my undying loyalty, sir. And I will be behind you 100%!"

"Thank you, Madame Vice-President. But 93% is still very good." Alex offers a sly raise of the eyebrows.

"Oh yes! Today's approval rating! Haha! Very funny, sir."

"Do you think we can get to 95?"

"Yes sir. An' I'll do everything I ken ta make it so."

"I know you will." Alex smiles.

"I'm glad we had this talk. Thank you for coming in."

"Thank *you*, sir." Mavis reaches out and warmly shakes his little hand.

As she leaves, she finds herself on the verge of humming show tunes.

A*mazing...* Alex says to himself. And then he presses the intercom.

"Gladdy?"

"Yes, Mr. President..."

"Is that artist still here?"

"He is, sir."

"Good. Have him come in."

[A moment later...]

"Ace!" Alex says with a smile.

"Mr. President."

"I thought we were past all that *yes sir/no sir* bullshit."

"We are. I just like sayin' it." Ace smiles.

"I've never been pals with a president before."

"So we're pals?"

"What do you think?"

"Yeah," Alex says after a pause. "I believe we are."

"Well, good."

"So you brought some things with you—some art supplies?" Alex motions to the leather satchel Ace has slung over his shoulder.

"Nah. Still in the sizin'-up phase. But I brought *this*..." He digs into his haversack and takes out a bottle of *Jack Daniel's*.

"It's opened. Forgive me, the Secret Service dudes hadda check it out with an X-Ray, an' give it a lie detector test."

"Ha! They're *schticklers*."

"That they are. So I'm guessin' you never had whiskey before."

"No, but I've been meaning to."

Ace reaches into his satchel and brings out two tumblers, one of them quite small.

"Where'd you find *that* one?"

"Kocktails for Kids. It's the latest craze."

"Haha!

Ace hands him the glass, filled almost to the top. "To *ninety-three percent...*"

They touch glasses and then Alex takes a sip. "*Oooohhh... boy!*"

"Good?"

He lets out a breath. "It's warming me all the way to my toes."

"Well, that's not far." Ace smiles.

"Ha!"

"So how tall *are* you?"

"Well, I believe twelve inches. But I'm due for a physical next week, so maybe I've grown."

"Jeez, twelve inches...What?"

Alex takes another sip. "I like this... whiskey."

"Tennessee Sour Mash... It was Frank's favorite."

"Frank?"

"Sinatra."

"Ah!"

"But I liked it *first*," says Ace. "I mean, before I heard that *he* liked it."

"But you were saying about..."

"Twelve inches, yeah. I've known some women in my day who woulda *loved* you."

"Hmm?"

"An' these are the kinda gals who like broke-ass artist types."

"But you're rich."

"Not then."

"So these women..."

Ace shakes his head, then leans in closer. "I mean, it would be like the ultimate *vibrator*, ya know what I'm sayin'? This... *self-aware dildo!*"

"Ha! I don't think any President has been called that before."

"Yes they have," Ace says. "I've called a few of 'em that myself. But never one that's self-aware."

Alex smiles.

"And that's the key, I mean. What you could *do* down there. *Mmm-mm*, if word got around..." Ace raises his eyebrows, then takes another drink. "So how come you don't *Tweet* anymore?"

"Huh?"

"I mean, you were kickin' 'em out like ten at a time."

"Less is more. Like we talked about yesterday, just sit back..."

"An' watch 'em self-destruct."

"Exactly."

"So if ya don't mind me askin'..."

"Hmm?"

"I've only known ya a few days, Alex, but it seems like ya don't do all that much... aside from sittin' around drinkin' with your pals."

"And that's a *bad* thing?"

"No, it's not."

"My esteemed predecessor played golf 17,942 times while he was in office. And America's still here."

"*Touché.* But he wasn't exactly a Zen Buddhist."

"No, he wasn't." Alex takes another drink. "So can I ask *you* something, my new pal, Ace Buckland, the world's *second* greatest bullshitter."

"Fire away, Kemosabe."

"You... what you do, being someone *else*, I mean."

"Hmm?"

"It's no secret. I mean, you were a broke-ass loser livin' in an old brewery in Newark, New Jersey."

"Haha! I was indeed."

"I mean as Ace Buckland. But as Vincent Van Go-Go, you're rich and you sell your work in swanky, upscale galleries."

"Life's a bitch, ain't it?" Ace takes another sip.

"It was a matter of realigning my authenticity."

"Come again."

"Just because you find some kind o' purity don't mean you'll get a bag o' groceries."

"So you're in the sell-out category then."

"The story o' the struggling artist is one o' the most boring, predictable, bullshit stories there is." Ace pauses as he looks at the President. "I just wanted to make it less predictable."

"I *think* I understand," says Alex.

"Well good, cuz I hate explainin' it. The people who need it explained will never get it no matter how blue in the face ya get. I mean, I got enemies. Ya think *you* got enemies? The art world is frickin' Darwinism on crack, but it's even worse cuz it's not Darwinism at all! Darwinism is *objective*, like you're food so I'll eat you, but with art it's *bullshit as its own freaking art form!* Talk about *bullshitters!*" Ace laughs, and then he looks at the President. "I've been known at times ta not suffer the fool."

"You don't say?" Alex smiles.

"There was this guy, this artist in like 1962..." Ace begins. "An' he's livin' in some shithole walk-up in New York City, back when even broke-ass artists could afford ta live there. An' one day he gets this epiphany. So he takes this Mason jar an' he goes to the bathroom an'... you know, there are these cockroaches skitterin' up the greasy walls an' shit. An' while he's watchin' the cockroaches, he does his business, an' when he's through, he scoops that turd from the toilet into that Mason jar an' he seals it up tight. An' the next thing ya know, he's at this gallery uptown, where they got the latest from the newest visionaries." Ace smiles.

"And there's his fucking Mason jar on this pedestal with his own freaking dump in it. An' he signed the damn jar, like Marcel Duchamp."

"Hmm, so what happened?"

"Today he's in the art history books."

"Cuz he put his own shit in a jar?"

"No. Because he was the first to do it. That's *art as idea*, man. The first time's a charm."

"So why Vincent Van Go-Go? The name, I mean."

"He had a fucked-up life. An' it pisses me off that these rich fucks today pay a hundred million for his shit, cuz ya know for a *fact* that if they were alive back then, they'd think ol' Vince was just some crazy homeless motherfucker an' they wouldn't throw him a Dutch nickel.

So it makes me feel good when these same rich fucks buy somethin' from *Vincent Van Go-Go*. I laugh at them... all the way ta the bank. Ha! I mean, people suck. Bein' President, I'm sure you're aware o' this."

"As a matter of fact..." Alex smiles.

"Which is why we need a strong leader who's Presidential to..."

"Fuck off!"

"Ha! *Cheers!*" They touch glasses.

"So there was this guy..."

"Another story?"

"My arch enemy! This artist. I said I have enemies!"

"You did."

"So I had this show up in Manhattan..."

"As Van Go-Go?"

"Yeah, after I became famous. An' it's the opening. An' all these people are millin' about, givin' the perfunctory two-second glance while they sip their free Chardonnay. But then I notice this guy, this crazy, bug-eyed, pale-skinned, vampire dude with these piercings an' stringy black hair that hasn't been washed in like a week, an' I'm thinkin', *artist*, right? An' he has this man-bag like mine, except his is all ragged an' dilapidated, an' he looks at me with this piercing stare. Like Nosferatu, but the original—not the remake with Willem Dafoe, although I gotta say, Alex, that is freaking awesome as hell that you made him *Secretary of Education*. I mean, that was inspired, man!"

"Thanks!" Alex smiles and takes another sip of *Old No. 7*.

"So this skinny, greasy, Nosferatu-starin' motherfucker is eyeballin' me like I fucked his mama. An' I say, '*wus up?*' So he says, *Are you Vincent Van Go-Go?* An' I say *yeah*. An' before I know it, he's throwin' this shit he got from his man-bag all over this painting o' mine that's right there on the wall. I look, an' it's this reddish-purplish slimy shit that looks like freakin' afterbirth, an' it's coverin' my painting an' drippin' down, an' the art gallery dudes rush over an' tackle the *shit* outta him. An' all the while he's yellin' at the top of his lungs that I suck an' I'm a sell-out an' I should kill myself an' the police arrive an' take his crazy ass away."

"Jeez," Alex says.

"So what happened?"

"His name is Nicos Käpp-Kuvét... He's like Romanian or sumthin'. An' he's this struggling artist, obviously. An' for some reason, he hates my guts. I never even met him, an' they send him off ta Bellevue for a Psych Eval."

"And what was it, that he threw on your painting?"

"It was fucking placenta, man."

"*Placenta?*"

"Yeah. So me bein' an artist, I look at that canvas, ya know, my painting with the fucking placenta all over it, an' I think, *YEAH!* So I get this idea. An' the next day, I have these cheap copies made of all these famous paintings."

"Copies?"

"They photo-copy 'em onto canvas, right? So you can pay like eighty-five bucks for the *Mona Lisa* at Freddie's Craft Shack."

"Yes, I've seen those online."

"So I have all these cheap pieces o' shit—famous paintings on the floor of my studio—an' then I take all this placenta..."

"Where'd you get placenta from?"

"New York City, man. You can get whatever ya want there. So I toss that shit onto the canvases like Jackson Freaking Pollock, an' when they're dry, I look at 'em an' they're not bad. So the next thing ya know, I got a show in Brooklyn, but not as Vincent Van Go-Go, but as this new persona I invented called Pete Scrotum."

"Hold on! I've *heard* of him! He was on the cover of *Time* or *Newsweek*."

"One o' those. I always get 'em confused."

"Me too. So that was *you?*"

"Yeah."

"You were holding this big placenta. And your face was obscured by shadows."

"That's because Pete Scrotum is *mysterious,* man." Ace smiles.

"Like he never goes to his own shows an' he never gives interviews an' hardly anyone's even *seen* him. An' at first I thought it was a bad idea, publicity-wise. But what I found is that the less you play their game, the more they want you. It's beyond fucked-up, man."

"So you're Pete Scrotum."

"Ha! Pleased ta meet you... Anyway, that crazy terrorist nutcase Nicos Käpp-Kuvét... When they let him out, he hears about this artist named Pete Scrotum who's the *next big thing* for doin' *Placenta Art.* An' this little fucker is all pissed because technically *he* invented it, which is true, but not really since he used the placenta as part of a *terrorist attack*, not as an *art piece*, so he was shit outta luck. An' now he *really* hates my guts, an' if he found out that Vincent Van Go-Go is also Pete Scrotum, he'd kill me twice. An' of course once the *Placenta School* had been established, then all these Johnny-Come-Latelies start doin' it, but like that guy with the Mason jar, it only works once, an' that's the first time. And that's what modern art is about in the 21st century, an' I need a drink."

"Hahaha!" Alex laughs so hard he falls backwards onto the shag carpet in the womb-room.

Ace looks inside after him.

"Hey, that's one groovy pad you got there, Alex."

"Thanks! I wish I could invite you in."

"That's okay."

[The intercom buzzes...]

"Mr. President..."

"Yes, Gladdy..."

"Tim Chopper is here, sir."

"What?!"

"That's alright, man," Ace says.

"I gotta go work on the painting. I'll see ya soon."

"Okay. Thanks, Ace." Alex turns back to the intercom as he feels his little heart race.

"Send him in."

5

How to describe Tim Chopper without lapsing into cliché... Sure, he looks like a chrome-plated fire hydrant with a crew-cut, crossed with a pile-driver or a jackhammer, forged into a six-foot block of radioactive iron. At least that's how his enemies see him, which means practically everyone on the Hill. At the mere sight of him, brows furrow and anuses uncomfortably clench, because the only time he appears is when something needs to get done, and he's not above administering a beatdown (or worse) to get satisfaction. He's my Luca Brasi. So you can understand the trepidation I've been feeling since last Thursday when he suddenly disappeared.

"Sir," he says, as he stands before the President.

"Tim! Where the fuck have you been?"

"Sir, I..." He looks at President Rett as if he were lost. And he can already sense the President's mistrust.

"I don't know, sir. I woke up in my bed in my apartment a half hour ago. Then I came here."

At this, Alex searches Tim's eyes to see if they waver, to see if they betray the slightest hint of something he wants to keep hidden.

"Tim, we were over there, at your apartment. You weren't there. And your car was gone as well."

"Sir, I... I don't understand... what happened." He lets out a breath.

"I had just received something on three of those senators."

"Senators?"

"For OPERATION CLOSET."

"Oh yes. I was *wondering* why nothing was happening with that. But I couldn't get through to you."

"Yes, I..."

"What was it, Tim?"

"Sir?"

"What you received."

"Emails and photos, sir. Incriminating ones."

"When was this?"

"Last Wednesday."

"Can I *see* them?"

"They're gone, sir. I was going to forward them to you today, after I woke up, but... when I checked my computer, they'd been deleted."

"And this was today."

"Yes. Right before I came here."

"After you woke up in your apartment... where we went to check on you every day since Friday."

"Sir, yes, I... I can't explain it. I don't remember *anything* from the last four days. All I remember is that I was walking to my car on Thursday morning."

"Last Thursday morning..."

"Yes. And then waking up today in my bed."

"And your *car?*"

"It was in the parking deck, sir, where I left it."

What Tim *didn't* know was this...

It's last Thursday morning. Tim Chopper walks to his car in the underground parking deck beneath his apartment complex. His senses are as alert as they always are, like antennae searching the air. But today he senses nothing amiss. He sees his car in its assigned spot, where it always is. There's the familiar *beep* as he presses the key fob to unlock the door. And as he grabs the door handle with his right hand, he feels a slight prick as if he'd been stung by a bee. He looks at his hand. There's a drop of blood on his finger, but the image almost immediately becomes hazy, then a blur. Then the fluorescent lights of the ceiling race by overhead as he collapses unconscious to the pavement.

Within seconds, a silver-paneled van pulls into the adjoining space, the side doors slide open, and men dressed in black clothes and ski masks hop out, grab Tim's body, and pull him inside. A few seconds after the van pulls away, an older gentleman appears—the same one from the coffee shop; the one who appeared at Deco after Brayden Carter left, who ordered a Gin & Tonic with *Uncle Tom* gin. This man reaches into the door handle and removes something small that looks like a needle. Then he takes out an aerosol can from his jacket and sprays it inside the door handle until it's clean. After putting the needle and the spray can away, he gets into Tim Chopper's car. He presses the ignition button and drives off.

For the past four days since last Thursday morning, Tim Chopper has been kept in a windowless room somewhere close by. A doctor and a nurse were at hand if needed, but the time went by without incident, as he was kept comfortable but unconscious. The plan had been to get him out of the way long enough for the events they'd set in motion to unfold, namely the resignation of the President. Without Tim Chopper by his side, President Rett would be helpless, they thought, since he was, after all, a fetus.

And by last Thursday night, with his approval rating at 17%, and being assailed from all sides, it appeared that the President's resignation was imminent. It would be one domino falling after the next. The President would unleash a barrage of angry *Tweets* in response to the attack, each more desperate, paranoid, and unhinged than the last. And the American people would bear witness to this very public meltdown, as Dom Milanese, Ezra Banes, and the Vice-President would rush in to prevent the government from collapsing.

Publicly disgraced, with an approval rating close to zero, President Rett would do the right thing and resign his office, with Mavis DaLyte becoming the next President. All of this was in motion, and Alex Rett's ignominious end seemed a *fait d' accompli* until, for whatever inconceivable, inexplicable reason, the President decided to not issue a single Tweet, a single response, a single word.

Then events beyond their control became a whirlwind; events that no one could have foreseen. The press conference on Friday, where Wiley DeSembler deftly and impeccably shamed what had become a pack of wild dogs spoiling for President Rett's flesh. His impassioned (albeit completely bullshit) monologue left America in a state of sympathy for the President and his poor, stroke-afflicted mom, as they *both* fought for their lives. And America came together in solidarity and selfless hope for their recovery.

Then the utter mess, the debacle, the bloody catastrophe that was *Saturday Nite In-Yer-Face*. And through it all, this most predictable of Presidents had become completely unpredictable. He stayed out of the fray like a modern-day Marcus Aurelius, only to re-emerge in a revitalized, heroic fashion on *Jules Tippler* on Sunday morning. America and the world witnessed this, Alexander Rett's spectacular and inspiring rebirth. And he gave *America* a rebirth, a second chance, this chance that no one even realized they had longed for so desperately. By Monday morning, with Rett's approval rating at 90% and rising, the plan was aborted and these clandestine, faceless men decided to cut their losses.

But they kept Tim Chopper on ice for one more day. The idea was that since he would have no way to explain his disappearance at the exact moment when the President needed him most, this would cast him into disfavor, or at the very least, elicit the President's suspicion and mistrust. Thus, Tim Chopper, the pit viper, would be defanged. So on Tuesday morning, he was surreptitiously taken back to his apartment and placed gently in his bed. A drug was administered to revive him in ten minutes' time. And by then they were gone, and Tim's car was back in its spot in the parking garage as if it had never left. Their plan had failed, for reasons quite beyond their control, but they were nothing if not resourceful, and in their own way, every bit the improviser that President Rett had proven himself to be. And now they would wait to see what happened next, for a new plan was already in the works.

"Tim, we checked," says President Rett.

"Your car was gone."

"Sir..."

"And there were payments made from your credit card, from Baltimore into Pennsylvania over the course of the past five days."

It was their red herring. Using Tim's credit card, they created a fictitious trail of bread crumbs. And when Tim woke up, his card was in his wallet where he'd left it.

"I... I don't know, sir. I can't explain it. As I said, I don't remember anything since last Thursday morning."

"Well, a lot has happened *since* then," the President says.

"Things that I've accomplished without any of your help."

"Sir, I..."

"I suggest you get up to speed on the past few days, *Tim*." And the way the President pronounced *"Tim"* was like a hock of phlegm being expelled from his throat.

"Sir, I... I will."

"Good. That'll be all."

[As Tim Chopper leaves the Oval Office, the intercom buzzes...]

"Yes, Gladdy..."

"Mr. President, Ezra Banes is here to see you."

A slight smile of satisfaction appears in the corner of Alex's mouth.

"Send him in."

"Mr. President!"

"Ezra, so good to see you! Can I get you something? Black coffee?"

"No thank you, sir."

"Please, sit down. To what do I owe the pleasure?"

"Sir, I wanted to say to you in person how pleased I am with... well, with what's been happening."

"Yes. Who could have imagined?"

"It was truly inspiring, how you handled yourself, sir. And I wanted to assure you that you have my unwavering loyalty and support."

"I'm glad to hear that, Ezra. It's important for me to know that I have you on my side."

"Yes sir. Always."

"Well, good. Thank you again. Was there anything else?"

"No sir."

As Ezra Banes starts to leave, the President calls out. "Oh Ezra..."

"Sir?"

"I know I can count on you with the AWS."

"The Automatic Weapons in Schools bill, sir? Yes, you can."

"Good, because with what I said on *Tippler* about security, I think the time is right to push this one through. After all..." Alex fixes Ezra's gaze. "*All* lives matter. Especially our children's. Wouldn't you agree?" He looks into the African-American Congressman's eyes. He sees the pained twinge he tries to hide, like a knife stuck in with the words "*all* lives matter," and he looks deeper to see if Ezra will react.

"Yes, I would agree, sir."

"Good." Alex smiles to himself.

[The intercom buzzes as a chastened Ezra Banes leaves the Oval...]

"Mr. President..."

"Yes, Gladdy..."

"Sir, the *Daily Briefs* are in."

But instead of deleting them per usual, Alex gives them a look. Something about the strife-ridden Eastern-European country of Hangry. And then as if through some kind of prescience, he clicks on the TV. His old friend from the Presidential Debates, Agnes Plunge. Her show: *The Trigger.*

PBS

"Good morning. I'm Agnes Plunge, and this is *The Trigger*."

Ever since the debates, we like ol' Agnes, and lately we've been tuning in, even though she's biased towards all that human rights and freedom shit all those liberals love.

"Er Mahgerd, the embattled President of Hangry, has announced that he will visit the United States and the Oval Office by the end of the week. Mahgerd is the latest in a string of world leaders seeking counsel with the revitalized President Rett, whose esteem in the eyes of the world is at an all-time high."

Yeah, *dat's us! We bad!* And everyone wants ta kiss our Presidential butt! (And we've taken to using *the third person*, as you can see.)

"However, Democratic members of Congress and activists worldwide have condemned Mahgerd for rampant human rights violations."

See! What did we tell ya! *PBS* and their human rights.

"Since seizing power five years ago in a brutal and bloody coup, Mahgerd has led a ruthless, dictatorial regime that routinely persecutes women, minorities, and gays, that has outlawed the free press and freedom of speech, and that has gassed, tortured, and imprisoned its own people without trial and due process, all to eliminate dissent."

Well, when ya put it *that* way, it don't sound so good.

"The most recent incident occurred last week when a 24 year-old Hangarian man, Rektim Bugr, an accused homosexual, was stripped naked in Democracy Square near the Presidential Palace in the capital city of Dahoom, and was then caned one hundred times before being publicly castrated, to the cheers of over 50,000 Hangarians who had gathered to watch the sorry, disgraceful spectacle."

What's with the editorializing?

"In Hangry, over the past two months alone, eleven men and twenty-three women have been publicly caned and have had their genitals mutilated in public before millions of onlookers."

What, don't they have *music?* Like *rock concerts?* They can get *Coldplay!* What about sports, like soccer? They play that *all over* Europe. Maybe we can take Mahgerd to a soccer match. Do we even *have* that here?

"Because of this, Mahgerd's visit is the subject of widespread protests in the United States and abroad. And President Rett is being urged to cancel the visit in the name of peace and justice, and to show his solidarity with the millions of oppressed."

Jeez, Agnes... way ta bring us down. *[Alex clicks on another channel...]*

THE YOUNG TURKISH ANARCHISTS...
Oh good! We *love* "The Young Turkish Anarchists"!

Fat Guy With Weird Name: So this visit with Er Mahgerd at the end of the week... I mean, *what* is President Rett *thinking?*

Hot Babe With Weird Name: I *know*, right? Just *days* after his historic turnaround on Tippler, and now he does *this?*

Fat: Yes! His approval rating was at an all-time *high* of 94%. We couldn't get to 95... *Sigh...*

Hot: But now, with this visit of the brutal Hangarian dictator *looming*, Rett's rating has *plummeted*.

What?

Fat: And there's no *way* to sugar-coat it. Mahgerd is a bloodthirsty *bastard* who has a list of bodies a mile long stretching back over the past five *years*.

Hot: Well, since it's been over the past five *years*, it would be a lot longer than a *mile*.

Fat: True. But the *point* being, why would the President *agree* to this? There's no upside. And just by being in the same *room* with Mahgerd, that stink rubs off.

Hot: And it's a *stink* you can't get rid of.

Jeez, what's up with Fat Guy? How quickly they turn on you! And for your information, Fat Guy and Hot Babe, there's this thing called *oil*. Perhaps you've heard of it. It allows those things you drive called *cars* to keep running back and forth to the gym. The gym Fat Guy never goes to. Haha!

There's this new source of oil they discovered in Hangry, using these drills we developed that they're leasing. And to seal the deal, all *we* have to do is make nice before the cameras with that Er Mahgerd sumbitch this Friday and we'll have 30% of *all that oil* at a fixed low rate for the next ten years. *You're welcome!* Of course this is all under the table, and it'll go through various brokers so it seems like the deal's with the Saudis, who are *almost* as shitty, human rights-wise, but since they have so much more oil, they get a *Get Out of the International Criminal Court at The Hague Free* card. You have no *idea* all the shit that goes on behind the curtain when it's drawn. So we gotta do this handshake thing. After all, you *like* when your gas is two bucks a gallon.

Fat: President Rett has been urged by a *slew* of world leaders, in no uncertain terms, to *cancel* the visit.

Hot: Germany's President, Mengele Männlichheimer, *condemned* the proposed visit, and urged President Rett to stand *up* for human rights.

Germany? That's the pot calling the kettle.

Fat: Even Russian President Raz Putin has condemned what he called President Rett's *callous action* in the *face* of world opinion.

Ha! *That's* a laugh! Our friend Raz tried ta get that same oil deal, but after what happened on *Tippler*, Mahgerd figured that *we* were the horse to back. And now ol' Raz is pissed and he's no longer our pal.

Hot: Protesters have already assembled *outside* the White House.

What? When did *this* happen? And what was that about the approval rating?

Fat: They have stated that they will *remain* outside the White House and the Capitol through this Friday, unless Mahgerd's visit is *canceled* and the President issues an apology for even *considering* a meeting with the ruthless despot.

Jeez! Every day they want us to apologize for something! And what happened? We were the Golden Boy who could do no wrong for a day and a half! And now it's freakin' *gone?* The half-life of a good mood is 36 hours, tops! Fuckin'-A! I need Tim! *Damn it! You made me leave the third person and come back to the first! Fuck you, you fucking fuckers!*

But that shit Tim said doesn't make sense. I wonder if he'd take a polygraph, if I pose the question the right way... Goddamn it, I can't even enjoy my good freaking mood for more than two freaking days! *FML! [Alex presses the intercom...]*

"Mr. President?"

"Gladdy, what's the latest approval rating?"

"I'll check, sir."

"..."

"It's 77, sir."

"*77?*"

"Yes sir."

"..."

"Mr. President?"

"Thanks." Ugh. I got *so close!* One more freaking point! And now this job at times totally blows. *[Alex clicks on another channel.]*

It's my BFF, Jules Tippler.

CNN

"The White House this morning is literally *besieged* by protesters. Here you see the live footage... *[Cuts to outside the White House...]* This, in response to Er Mahgerd, the universally despised Hangarian dictator, who's visiting President Rett this Friday. Human rights activists worldwide are demanding that Alex Rett cancel the visit and issue an apology.

Again with the apology!

"This just in..."

[Alex looks back to Tippler...] What *now?*

"This video has just been released. It shows a young Hangarian woman walking down a street in the capital city of Dahoom, wearing a tank-top and a miniskirt. Hangarian women have been forbidden under penalty of death to wear any form of western dress, especially that which is considered provocative and salacious. Hangarian authorities, including the police and members of REEMR, the infamous secret security service, are actively seeking the woman's identity."

What the fuck, *Er Mahgerd!?* You couldn't, like, *ixnay* on the oppression shit until after the goddamn *visit?* What's *wrong* with you? My good mood has been totally *ass-fucked! [Alex presses the intercom...]*

"Gladdy!"

"Yes, Mr. President."

"Get me Er Mahgerd."

"Right away, sir..."

[As he waits, Alex paces frantically in the womb-room, nervously twiddling the umbilical cord...] I'm gonna need a drink and it's only... *[He checks his new watch...]* 10:05 in the freaking morning!

"Mr. President?"

"Yes, Gladdy!"

"I have President Mahgerd, sir. I'm putting him through..."

"Thank you, Gladdy."

[There are several seconds of obnoxious static, until a voice is heard...]

"President Rett..."

"Yes, President Mahgerd..."

"How are you, sir?"

"Well, not too good, since you keep doin' all that overt human rights abuse shit in public while your freaking visit is in three days."

"What was that, Mr. President? I can't hear you."

Goddamn it! "I said not too good since your visit is this Friday."

"Yes, my visit... to see *you!*"

"Yes, but in the meantime..."

"What did you say? In the what?"

For fuck's sake! "I said in the meantime..."

"In the *meantime?*"

"Yes! In the *meantime,* you've been, like abusing human rights, like right and left."

"Human *what*, Mr. President? I can barely hear you, sir."

Oh for fuck's sake! [Alex presses the other line for his secretary...]

"Gladdy, what's wrong with the phone?"

"Sir? Mr. President?" *[More static...]*

"I said what's wrong with that line to Hangry?"

"The line, sir?"

"The *other line!* It *sucks!*"

"The other line, sir?"

Motherfucker! [He clicks on the other line...]

"President Mahgerd, can you hear me?"

"Hello?"

"President Mahgerd?"

"Hello, President Rett?"

"Is that *you*, Er?"

"Yes, how are you doing, Mr. President?"

"I'm... I'm not doing that well, Mr. President."

"I'm sorry to hear that. Is there anything I can do?"

"Yes, you can stop all that freaking human rights abuse shit!"

"Human what, sir? You're fading out."

[Alex presses the other line on the intercom...]

"Gladdy..."

"Yes sir?"

"Send Manny in."

"Yes sir."

[Alex presses the other line...]

"So I'll see you this Friday then, President Rett."

"What?"

"I said I'll see you on Friday!"

"But the human rights stuff..."

"What was that? You're fading..."

"Oh for fuck's sake."

"What was that, Mr. President?"

"Nothing. See you on Friday."

"What?"

"I said *I'll see you on Friday!*"

"Yes! Yes! *I look forward to it!*"

"Me too. Good-bye."

"What?"

"I said good-bye, Mr. President."

"Yes, good-bye to you!"

[Alex hangs up the phone and sprawls back in his chair as Manny appears...]

"Manny! Thank God!"

"Alex, you don't look so good."

"I need a double."

"A double what, sir?"

"A double anything."

"Coming right up."

A moment later, the drink is in hand and Alex downs it in one sip.

"Did you like it, sir?"

"I don't know. Hit me again, Manolo."

"Yes sir."

[Alex glances back at the TV...]

"With the President's approval rating at 73%, and with still no word from the White House, prominent Democratic leaders are at a loss as to the President's inaction."

Motherfucker! *[Manny hands him the new drink, and Alex pours it down with his right hand as he clicks another channel with his left...]*

CBS NEWS

"Democratic leaders, including the Vice-President..."

Et tu, Mavis?

"...as well as some prominent Republicans are at a loss to explain President Rett's inaction in the face of this current crisis. Senator Mallory Blitzen from right outside the White House had this to say just moments ago: 'I'm standing here along with thousands of protesters, all of us wondering the same thing... Why is President Rett remaining silent in the face of this crisis? Were the last few days a fantasy? Is the old reality new once again? The reality of the gross incompetence we've come to expect from Alex Rett throughout his brief tenure in office. How quickly the heroic image has faded into this picture of ineptness and inaction."

I *really* hate that Mallory Blitzen! *[Alex clicks on another channel...]*

FOX NEWS

"A handful of jobless liberals have gathered in front of the White House this morning to protest something. But aren't they *always* protesting something?"

"Haha! Yes they are. I just don't get it. President Rett, at an all-time high approval rating of 94% just *yesterday*, is spending the morning conferring with his chief advisors, as well as several high-ranking senators regarding this Friday's visit to the White House of Hangarian President, Er Mahgerd. Mahgerd, the subject of several witch hunts into alleged human rights violations, has led Hangry these past five years to a new level of prosperity, and to a standard of living unparalleled in his country's beleaguered existence since the end of the Cold War."

Thank God for *Fox News!* Get ya a six-pack for that one*!*
[The intercom buzzes again...]
"Yes Gladdy..."
"Mr. President, Tall Skinny... I mean, that young intern, Brayden Carter, is here to see you, sir. As well as that artist, Vincent Van Go-Go."
Alex lets out a breath.
"I can't see them today. Give them my regrets and reschedule."
"Will do, sir."
[The intercom buzzes again...]
"What is it *now*, Gladdy?"
"I'm sorry, sir, but Tim Chopper is here."
Tim! Yes! "Oh good! Send him in."
Alex takes a long deep breath, then lets it out as he turns to Manolo Vargas.
"Tim Chopper is coming in now, but if you would be so kind as to make me one more of these, Manolo, *inmediatamente.*"

"*Sí Señor.* It would be my pleasure." As Manny makes the drink, Alex stares at the door, waiting for Tim to walk in.

I hope you're still with me, Tim, the President thinks to himself. *I hope you're still with me.*

6

"Tim..."

"Mr. President."

"Have a seat."

Manny hands the President his drink.

"Thank you, Manny. But where are my manners?" Alex looks to Tim. "Would you like something?"

"No thank you, sir."

"Thank you, Manny. That'll be all for now."

"Yes sir."

As Manny leaves, Tim turns to the President.

"Mr. President, I still have no idea what happened. But... I want you to know that you can *trust* me, sir. As you always have."

"Hmm... Well, Tim, I hope that's true. I really do."

"In fact, I'll take a polygraph *right now*, sir! Anything to prove myself!"

(Well ,how d'ya like that? He volunteers for a polygraph.)

"There's no time for that. I'll just have to trust you."

"I won't let you down, sir. In fact, I have some ideas about this present predicament."

"Go on..."

"I saw the press conference, sir. And what you said on *Tippler.* You disarmed everyone by coming clean. By being vulnerable. You weren't defensive. You didn't even attack, but you waited things out."

"Well, I don't think that'll work this time around."

"Nor do I, sir."

"So..."

"So call a press conference."

"Hmm?"

"Today, sir. This afternoon. Have Wiley tell everyone that you'll address the nation tonight at 7 PM."

"And what will I say?"

"You'll come clean, sir. You'll tell them, the American people, about the oil deal with Hangry. You'll tell them how you *hate* Er Mahgerd, but then you'll remind them of their cars and how they like having cheap gas. And you'll tell them that *this* is the price they pay for it. That occasionally the President must make deals with another country, with another leader he's morally opposed to, but that's the price *he* must pay, as President, to look out for the American people."

Alex stares at Tim Chopper for a long moment as the message sinks in.

"Sir?"

"Tim..." Alex slowly nods his head. "That *is* a good plan."

"Thank you, sir. And when Er Mahgerd gets pissed off..."

"We tell him to *go fuck himself!*" Alex smiles. "And that we'll take back all the drills and equipment in a heartbeat."

"Then he may go to Russia, sir."

"Fuck 'im if he does," says Alex. "Then all that human rights shit will be *Raz's* problem. Like he doesn't have enough of those already. And if we can't supplement the oil, we'll raise the price so the American people will know that there are consequences to every action."

"Yes sir. And you'll look like a champion of human rights who nevertheless looked to the security and well-being of the American people first as your primary concern."

"I *like* that, Tim. I do. Let me get a piece of paper." The President grabs a pad and pen and starts jotting it down…"'*who nevertheless looked to the security and well-being of the American people as his primary concern.*'" He looks at Tim Chopper. "I like that very much, Tim."

"And I have another suggestion, sir."

"I'm all ears."

"Between now and Friday, might I suggest OPERATION R.E. LEE." Alex sits back at the magnitude of the suggestion.

"Yes, OPERATION R.E. LEE. We've been saving that for just the right moment."

"I think that moment has arrived, sir."

"It has indeed, Tim." Alex lets out a deeply satisfied breath, and then he looks at Tim Chopper. "I've missed you, Tim."

"You've done fine without me, sir."

"That was luck, but luck runs out. *This*, what we just did... what *you* just did... is *not* luck. It's what you do." Alex nods in appreciation. "It's why you're the best."

"Thank you, sir."

"So talk to Wiley. Set up the press conference for this afternoon, and tonight's address to the nation. I'm going to write my speech."

"Yes sir." Tim starts to rise from his chair when Alex stops him.

"Tim, perhaps you would reconsider that drink now."

"Yes sir. I would be delighted."

"Good." Alex smiles as he presses the intercom.

"Gladdy..."

"Yes, Mr. President..."

"Have Manny come back in, please."

7

(Later that Tuesday afternoon, the Millard Fillmore Room *in* The White House. *The White House press conference is about to begin...*

[Press Secretary Wiley DeSembler *stands before the pulsating throng of journalists, all seemingly in a frenzy...]*

Journalists: *[en masse]* Wiley! Wiley! Wiley!

Wiley: Today there will be no questions, as I will issue a brief statement.

Journalists: *[a barrage of protestations ensues...]*

Wiley: *[continues...]* This is regarding President Er Mahgerd's scheduled visit to see President Rett.

Journalists: *[a cacophony of questions erupts simultaneously...]*

Wiley: *[continues...]* I said there would be no questions today and that I'll make a brief statement! What about that don't you understand?

Journalists: *[grumbles and murmurs subside...]*

Wiley: *[continues...]* Thank you. *[gives them a reproachful glare...]* The

Hangarian President's visit to the White House this Friday morning will take place as scheduled.

Crowd: *[scattered boos...]* Say it ain't so, Wiley!

Wiley: However, to further elaborate on this, President Rett will address the nation tonight on television at 7PM. At that time, all of your questions will be answered, all of your fears assuaged.

Journalists: *[en masse] Wiley! Wiley! Wiley!*

Wiley: That's it. Thank you.

[Wiley DeSembler *leaves the podium and exits the room...]*

Well *that* was short and sweet. Now I have to write my speech. But I'm still a little drunk from this morning's stress relief. I read this article about pets; that if you have one, a pet that is, it's a great stress relief, since supposedly you get out of yourself in order to care for another living creature. But that sounds stressful! Especially if it's a cat and you have to clean out the litter box. Besides, if I had a cat, it would probably eat me since it would be so much bigger than me. And a dog wouldn't even fit. The womb, by definition, is a pretty cramped place. I wonder if they still have flea circuses. But then again, I'm morally opposed to circuses. I mean, those poor elephants have to hang around every day with clowns. And those lions and tigers still haven't figured out that freaking chair the lion-tamer holds up in front of him. It doesn't seem that difficult a concept. Smash the chair to bits and eat the lion-tamer!

Maybe I could get something *really* small, like an ant. But I'm guessing it would be hard to warm up to a bug. So I've been thinking that maybe I need to have some sex. As you know, that's also a great stress reliever (or so it says in those other articles I've been reading). But then again, the whole process of finding the sex to have can be really stressful. You'd think, being President, I would have my pick of the ladies, but nobody wants to be with someone whose mother is always hanging around. And then there's this virginity thing. It seems that a powerful world leader should *not* be a virgin. Even Queen Elizabeth the Virgin Queen wasn't actually a virgin. It was more of an *honorary* title, although they named the state where I'm from, Virginia, after her honorary virginity.

When I'm stressed out, my mind tends to wander. But luckily

there's this show I wanna watch, this young girl who supposedly has the *Next Big Ass,* even better than Kim Kardashian's (and my nemesis, Cara Carthusian's). But that's not on until later, so back to the damn speech.

Meanwhile, in a windowless, fluorescently-lit room in the bowels of the Federal Bureau of Investigation at Quantico, a young FBI analyst named Connor Raptor is traversing the trail left by Tim Chopper's credit card over the past weekend. In a moment of epiphany, he calls over his supervisor, who ponders the realization for a moment, then calls *his* superior. And this goes on for about thirty minutes more before it finally makes it up the chain of command. And then a half hour later, the intercom buzzes in the Oval Office.

"Mr. President?"

"Yes, Gladdy..."

"Sir, Nash Wasserman is here to see you."

"The FBI Director?"

"Yes sir."

"Okay, send him in."

I recall mentioning the FBI director in passing sometime ago. In fact, it was so in passing that I never even mentioned his name. Well, as you overheard, it's Nash Wasserman. And I think that's why he's so ineffectual, compared to the exemplar, the icon, the paragon, Ol' J. Edgar. I mean, who names their kid *Nash*, for Christsake? And *Wasserman...* Isn't that some kind of *test* for something? Hold on, he's here.

"Nash! What a surprise. Have a seat."

"Thank you, Mr. President."

"I'll be with you in *one minute...*"

[Alex takes out his smartphone and Googles "Wasserman Test"...] Fuckin'-A! It's the test they have for *syphilis!* Haha! I *knew* it!

"Mr. President?"

"Yes?"

"You laughed, sir."

"Oh yes... So what brings you to the Oval Office?" (*Syphilis?* Haha!)

"Sir, the credit card trail of Tim Chopper..."

(Now *that* got my attention.)

"Yes. What did you find?"

"Sir, as you know, it went from Baltimore last Thursday up through Pennsylvania and back to DC."

"Yes."

"Well, the last stop in Pennsylvania was at a *7-11* in the Pocono Mountains. He... I mean, whoever it was, as we still haven't established definitively that it was Tim Chopper..."

"Yes, so..."

"Well, whoever it was bought a chili dog and a Lime Slurpee at the *7-11* using Tim Chopper's credit card."

"And why is this enlightening?" (Syphilis Boy!)

"Well, as I said, sir, it was in the Pocono Mountains."

"The Pocono Mountains... Why does that sound familiar?"

"It's where the Majority Whip, Dom Milanese, has a summer home, sir. This nice A-Frame on a pond."

"Hmm... And was he..."

"He was there all weekend, sir. He came back to DC on Monday."

"But you don't know if he had any guests over the weekend."

"We do not, sir. We're still looking into that."

(WTF, Tim? I thought we put this behind us. Yet another stress-ball!)

"Mr. President?"

"Yes. Thank you, Nash. Keep me apprised of any new developments."

"I will, sir."

[As Nash Wasserman leaves, Alex stares at the blank screen on his smartphone where his speech has yet to be written...]

I won't lie. I have writer's block. Some days I wonder why I wanted to be President in the first place. Why I didn't just stay a normal fetus and do my time inside, then get paroled and be like everyone else. You know, suck my thumb, soil my diapers, fall down a lot. I guess I'm an over-achiever. But this unresolved Tim Chopper stuff really has me in a dither. Yesterday, Tim seemed... well, *trustworthy!* And those ideas he had were top-notch. But then again, what if he *were* meeting with that *Ginzo-Wop-Dago-Greaseball?* That would be very bad *pour moi.*

[Alex lets out a sigh as he looks back at the blank screen...]

Of course we have speech-writers at the White House. A plenitude. A plethora. But I'm one of those hands-on Presidents.

[The intercom buzzes...]

"Yes, Gladdy..."

"Mr. President, there's an enormous wooden crate here, sir. Something from the *FÊNIX Gallery* in New York City."

"The *FÊNIX*... Oh good! Thanks, Gladdy! Have them bring it in."

Yay! My *painting* is here! After my last meeting with Ace, I went online. I found this one piece I really love by his alter-ego, Pete Scrotum, so I bought it! It *was* a bit pricey, but I do have this generous remodeling stipend implemented during the Kennedy White House: the *Redecorating Act.*

The door to the Oval Office swings open and four delivery men in overalls walk in, laboriously lugging a huge crate.

"Shall we open it, Mr. President?"

"Please."

After ten minutes, the screechy sound of nails being wrested painfully from wood subsides, and the massive work of art is released into the rarefied air.

"Just lean it against the wall," Alex says. *[After the men leave, Alex buzzes the intercom...]*

"Yes, Mr. President?"

"Gladdy, would you come in here please..."

[A moment later...]

"So what do you think?"

"Is that what was in the crate, sir?"

"M-hmm."

"Is it a painting?"

"Yes... Of course."

"I mean no disrespect, sir."

"None taken."

"It's just so... *huge!*"

"Yes."

"*Enormous!*"

"Yes!"

Gladdy takes a hesitant step closer.

"What is that... *stuff* all over it, sir? It seems to be... It seems to be dripping."

"This is by the world-famous visionary artist, Pete Scrotum," Alex explains.

"*Pete Scr...* I'm sure I've never heard of such a person," Gladdy says.

"He was on the cover of *Time...* or was it *Newsweek?*"

Gladdy moves closer, cocking her head to the side as a dog would when it's trying to comprehend something utterly baffling.

"Well, what do you think?" the President asks again.

"I... I'm at a loss, sir, but... I've never been one for abstraction... if that's what you'd call this."

"Hmm..."

"I can't get over how *big* it is, sir!"

"It's fourteen by eleven."

"That's... I'm sure I wouldn't have the wall space for such a thing in my house, Mr. President."

"But it makes a statement, doesn't it?"

"It certainly does, sir. But..." Gladdy walks over to the painting. She slides her glasses up to her forehead as she tries to divine its inscrutable meaning.

"Is that another painting beneath all that... that *reddish-purplish goo?*"

"Yes," Alex says.

"It's a reproduction of Rembrandt's '*The Night Watch.*'"

"Yes, I can see that... now that you pointed it out, sir. But... why is it covered in *goo?*"

"That was... That was the artist's intention, I believe."

"Well, I guess I'll never understand modern art, sir."

"It's an acquired taste for many."

Alex ponders explaining to Gladdy about Pete Scrotum and the Placenta School and what that "stuff" or "reddish-purplish goo" all over the canvas is, but he decides against it.

"So, you're going to hang it someplace, sir? I mean, in here?"

"Of course. But I thought I'd, you know, *live* with it for a bit. So

I'll know where it should go... on the wall-wise."

"Yes, sir." Gladdy takes one last look, then turns to the President. "Will there be anything else, sir?"

"No. Thank you, Gladdy." She starts to leave but then turns around.

"Sir..."

"Yes?"

"I look forward to seeing you tonight on TV!"

"Why thank you, Gladdy!"

"Break a leg, sir!"

As Gladdy leaves, Alex gazes at the painting. It *is* enormous. And even though you can catch glimpses of Rembrandt's original beneath the goo, the swirling, oozing, dripping placenta is hard to ignore.

In that same windowless, fluorescently-lit room in the bowels of the FBI at Quantico, another young FBI analyst, this one named Sheila Bodega, is busy in her cubicle. She's studying security camera footage—videos from every place where Tim Chopper's credit card was used over the past weekend. And in a moment of revelation, she calls over her supervisor.

"Sir, I was going over the security camera footage."

"Yes..."

"This is from an *Exxon* in a place called New Freedom, sir. In Pennsylvania where Tim Chopper's card was used. As you know, for some reason all the security cameras at every stop have been disabled."

"Yes..."

"But there's *this*, sir..." On the screen is the Exxon station, and as her supervisor looks on, Sheila Bodega pans across the street to the New Freedom Federal Credit Union.

"You see the bank, sir. They have a security camera that's pointed right at the gas station."

"Yes..."

"So I got the video, sir. From the bank's security camera."

"Yes..."

She puts it on-screen.

"This is the exact time when the credit card was used, sir. You see that man standing next to the Chevrolet Bolt?"

"Yes..."

"There he is, swiping his card. And that's Tim Chopper's card, sir."

"Yes..."

"The only thing is, it's not Tim Chopper."

"Ye... It's *not?*" The supervisor squints his eyes to peer closer. "Yes, I can see that. So who is he?"

"Well, I've run his face through all the facial recognition software, but there's nothing."

"Nothing?"

"No idea. Zip. Nada."

"Nada?"

"As if he doesn't exist."

"Hmm..."

"And of course, the license plate of the Chevy Bolt is a dead end as well."

"Yes, thank you."

And after making a similar trek up the ranks, this information leaves the FBI Director's mouth in the Oval Office approximately one hour later, to float into President Alexander Rett's ear.

"So that pretty much clears Tim then," the President says. "I mean, conspiracy-wise."

"Yes, sir, it does. It appears that this was part of some... clandestine plot to discredit your Chief-of-Staff."

"Yes. So let me know if you find out anything else."

"Will do, sir."

As FBI Director Wasserman leaves the Oval Office, he pauses for a moment to look at the enormous drippy painting leaning against the wall.

Finally some good news! I gotta tell Tim...

To Tim Chopper:
Good news, Tim! Come to the Oval.

Alex

So I'm thinking about sex again. I'm guessing that sex is something that pops into your head when you're procrastinating about doing something else. They say a normal adult human male thinks about sex once every five minutes. Although I'm technically a fetus *and* the President of the United States, I don't think about it as often as I'd like, since as you've seen, there are a *lot* of interruptions. I don't know how my predecessor managed to play golf over 17,000 times and chill at Xanadu every weekend, cuz I'll be honest: This President gig is a major ass-pain. You wouldn't *believe* all the people who a year ago barely knew I existed but now want a piece of me. And most of 'em, it seems, are *dicks!* Ha! I was sad that I couldn't hang with my new pal, Ace Buckland, cuz o' that Er Mahgerd mess. But I *do* have his painting now. Well, his *alter-ego's* painting.

[Alex looks at the huge canvas leaning against the wall...]

That *is* a lot of placenta... Oh shit, what time is it? *[He checks his watch...2:05]* I hope I didn't miss it! *[He clicks on the TV...]*

"How have you coped?" Dr. Phyllis asks, as she leans in towards her guest.

I *love* Dr. Phyllis.

"I don't know," the young girl says, tears flowing down her face.

This is that girl I told you about, the one with the *Next Big Ass!* But she's been bombarded with negativity.

"Your *Ass Launch* was just last week," Dr. Phyllis says.

"Yes, last Tuesday. My manager, he says that Tuesday is the day for all the big important launches. You know, like on *Netflix.*"

"Yes." And then Dr. Phyllis turns to the camera.

"We're talking with seventeen-year-old Cheyenne Charmathian, whose ass aspires to be the next big thing."

Haha! *Ass... Aspires...* Good one, Dr. Phyllis!

"But you've encountered a level of criticism and negativity that you never dreamed of."

"Yes, it's been... it's been *horrible!* I've been on the verge." She wipes her tears.

"The verge?" Dr. Phyllis leans in closer.

"I thought it was, you know, like *suicide*." *[Audible gasps from the audience...]* "But my manager, he thinks it's just stress."

See! Stress *is* a bitch!

"But still, I mean, I just don't understand why there's so much *hate* in the world." The tears come again.

Me. Neither.

"Well, as they say," says Dr. Phyllis, "haters gonna hate."

"Yes!" The young girl laughs.

"There, that's better."

"I just..." Cheyenne Charmathian continues. "I just wanted to, you know, like add something *beautiful* to the world."

"Yes," Dr. Phyllis nods.

"With my *ass!*"

"Of course!"

"Like Kim K did. She's like, my idol!"

"Kim Kardashian..."

"Yes! She's like this *ass pioneer!* She showed us *all* how far a girl can go by having, you know, an amazing ass!"

"An ass pioneer," says Dr. Phyllis.

"I've never heard it put quite like that."

"Yes, she's so inspiring! So I, like, spent the past *year* perfecting it!"

"Your ass..."

"*Yes!* I mean, you have no *idea* all the stuff I hadda give up to get an ass like this! All the hours I spent at the gym and on the treadmill and watching my diet. I haven't been to McDonald's in like a *year!*"

"Yes, but there are those people out there who dispute the authenticity of your ass," says Dr. Phyllis.

"The what?"

"The... They say your ass is fake."

"The haters again! *Haters!* I *hate* them!"

"I know. No one likes a hater." Dr. Phyllis hands Cheyenne Charmathian another tissue.

"Thanks. I mean, these *haters*, they're like... ruining my life."

"I'm so sorry, Cheyenne."

"Thank you, Dr. Phyllis."

"So I'm told you have a *movie* in the works?"

"Yes! Well, it's just a small role."

"Of course."

"It's an ass cameo!"

"An *ass cameo?*"

"Yes, but you gotta start *somewhere!* I mean, Kim K didn't just show up one day and randomly get her own *reality show!*"

"Of course not. So when's the movie coming out?"

"This summer! It's called *Zombie Death Camp!*"

"*Zombie Death Camp?*"

"Yes. It's about, like, some camp they had in some war back in the olden days." She looks at Dr. Phyllis. "This part's kinda sad, though." She leans in closer. "They have all these people who were like, *killed* by these *haters.* But they, like come back, the people they killed. As *zombies!* And they get their revenge!"

"We'll all look forward to *that!*" says Dr. Phyllis.

"So Cheyenne, we'd like to help you, if we can."

"Help me?" She wipes another tear.

"We have here today in our studio, Dr. Georg Große-Gesäß from the *Institut Postérieur* in Paris, France. Dr. Große-Gesäß is a world re-nowned expert on asses. And if you agree, Cheyenne, he will examine your ass right here, today, before our studio audience and the 4.3 million viewers we have at home, to verify whether your ass is real or fake. What do you say?"

Holy shit! The pressure!

"While young Cheyenne Charmathian makes this crucial, life-changing decision, we'll go to a commercial."

Oh. My. God. What's she gonna do? I can't *stand* all these com-mercials! I need to know! *Now!*

[The intercom buzzes...]

"What is it, Gladdy?"

"Sir, the Vice-President is here to see you."

(Hmm, you mean *Vice-President Back-Stabber?*)

"I'm in the middle of an important *Skype* with Putin about Siberia. Tell her to come back later. Oh, it's back on!"

"Sir?"

"So what is your decision, Cheyenne?" Dr. Phyllis asks.

"Well, I want the whole *world* to know that my ass is the real deal, so I say... yes!" *[The audience breaks into affirming applause...]*

"Good," Dr. Phyllis smiles. "So let's bring out the world-renowned ass expert, Dr. Georg Große-Gesäß from the Institut Postérieur in Paris, France. Dr. Große-Gesäß..." *[Applause...]*

"Please, call me Georg," he smiles.

"Georg... This is Cheyenne Charmathian," Dr. Phyllis says.

"And this is her ass." She points to Cheyenne's protuberant, pulchritudinous posterior.

"Ahh, *sehr gut... sehr gut.*" Dr. Große-Gesäß walks slowly around Cheyenne Charmathian like a satellite orbiting the Earth, giving her ass the utmost scrutiny. "*Ja... Ja...*" he says, as he studies it with the eye of a scientist, yet with the sensibility of a poet and philosopher. "*Ja... Ja...*" he says again.

Dr. Phyllis and Cheyenne Charmathian and the studio audience and the 4.3 million people watching at home, including the President, all look to Dr. Große-Gesäß as they await his verdict.

"Doctor?" says Dr. Phyllis. The tension is unbearable.

"Her ass is..."

"Yes?"

"It's..."

"*Yes?*"

"It's..."

"*Yes???*"

"Perfect!" he smiles.

The studio erupts in pandemonium! And when the camera cuts to a close-up of Cheyenne Charmathian, they see her exulting, tears of joy streaming down her face.

I *knew* it! I *knew* that ass was bona fide*!*

[The intercom buzzes again...]

"Yes, Gladdy..."

"Tim Chopper is here, sir."

"Oh good. Send in him."

As Tim walks into the Oval, his eyes are drawn to the gigantic painting leaning against the wall.

"Tim, the FBI found conclusive proof that it was someone *else* who used your credit card last weekend. Obviously, you were being set up. But by whom and for what reason..."

"That's good news, sir."

"Indeed. So keep your eyes opened wider than usual, okay? We haven't heard the last of 'em."

"I will, sir. Thank you." Another glance at the painting. "So the Press Conference went well."

"It wasn't bad."

"How's your speech coming, sir?"

"I'm... still working on it. So did you find anything on that turn-coat Dom Milanese?"

"Yes sir. You'll have it within the hour."

"Good, Tim. So I... I have to get back to that speech."

"Yes sir. Good luck... And tonight as well."

[As Tim leaves, Alex looks at the blank screen on his smartphone where the speech is supposed to be. His fingers hover over the keys as he waits for the words to come.. Nothing. He lets out a sigh...]

Back to sex, I guess. I read that online dating is all the rage, so I checked out this new website that everyone's talking about. It's supposed to be ultra-specific, not generic, so you can really zero in on potential soulmates with pinpoint accuracy. Does that sound awesome or what?

[Alex calls up the website he'd heard about...]

This is it! Mega-Date! *See... MEGA-DATE!*$^{©}$ *The newest, hottest, most exciting and BOLDEST place to meet that special someone!*$^{®}$ Okay, that's kind of a generic slogan for such a bold and exciting place. But look at those beautiful, sexy people all smiling and laughing and having the time of their freaking lives because they've met that special some-one! Hell *yeah* I'm jealous! Okay, let's see... *[Alex's fingers flash over his smartphone...]*

The First Step: Create your profile... Okay... *What is your sex?* "Male." I love the easy ones! *What is your age?* Hmm, I'm stumped already. Technically, I don't *have* an age. I'll come back to that. *How tall are you?* Okay, they have a range to choose from... *3' 6" to 9'*... That's *it?* They don't have twelve inches, but they have *nine freaking feet!?* I would guess there are about as many nine-footers as there are self-aware fetuses. Jeez, it's all about the surface... Okay, what's next...

What is your occupation? Yes, I have one! But I can't, you know, put *POTUS* because then they'll... I mean, this is supposed to be *anonymous*, right? We're supposed to be able to hide behind our online personas until we choose to reveal ourselves. But I *do* have a job, and *that's* a plus! Let's see, they have some things to choose from, job-wise... *Sous-Chef... Wizard... Snake Charmer... Proctologist... Beekeeper...* These *are* specific! *Numismatist... Hockey Goalie... Atom Smasher... Rastafarian...* That's a *job? Wombat Wrangler... Oil-Rig Roughneck... Card Shark... Phrenologist... Missionary...* I guess I'll put "Other"... *[Alex types it in...]*

What is your religion? Hmm, I never really thought about that. Let's see what they have... *I Love God... I Love Jesus... I Love Allah... I Love L. Ron Hubbard... I Love Satan...* Let's skip ahead... *I'm A Jew But I Don't Have A Big Nose Or Anything...* Skip... *Muslim But Not A Terrorist... Muslim But Sort Of A Terrorist... Muslim Taking Flying Lessons...* Skip... *Atheist Who's Real Smart Yet Empty Inside... Agnostic Cuz I Have This Problem Making Decisions...* Skip... *Goddess-Worshipping Solipsist... St. Jerome Flagellator... Relentlessly Obnoxious Proselytizer... Guilt-Tripping Catholic... Jesus Christ Poser... Pot-Smoking Tree-Hugger... Spiritually-Advanced Meta-Being...* I'll just put "Other."

What describes your body type? They have *lots* of choices for this one. Let's see... *Adonis...* No. *Greek God...* No. *Charles Atlas...* Who's he? *Buff-Badass...* No. *Young Guns...* Nope. *Athletic & Toned...* Not really. *Doesn't Go To The Gym That Often...* Well, neither do I, but I've been meaning to. *Sorta Meh...* No. *Uninspiringly Average...* No. *Desperately Below Average With Flab And Man-Boobs.* No. *Flab-Ola!...* No. *Retired Charles Barkley...* No. *Retired Shaquille O'Neal.* Nope. *Look At That Beergut!...* No. *Lazy Fat Slob...* Nope. *It Took Like Ten Years To Get A Gut This Big!...* WTF? I think I'm going in the wrong direction... Okay, here we go... *Scrawny Pencil Arms...* Hey, I *resent* that! *Thin & Wiry...* That's better. *Slim & Sexy...* Yes! *[types it in...]*

What's your sign? Damn! Another stumper! Skip...

Who are you looking for? "A woman"... And now they have all these stats that you have to put down for *her*, this woman you have yet to meet. **Age... Height... Weight... Hair color... Skin color... Blood type...** Blood type? **Body type**... Okay, let's see what they have for this... *Delightfully Big-Boned*... Nope... *Fabulously Full-Figured*... No. *Huge Huggable Hips*... Nope. *Excitingly Expansive*... No. *Plus-Size Pulchritudinous Pachyderm*... Nope. *Rubens Woulda Loved Me*... No. *Zaftig & Zany Zeppelin*... Jeez, how many euphemisms do they have for fat? *Engagingly Enormous*... No... *Humongously Gorgeous*... No way. *Stunningly Gigantic*... Not a chance. *What A Personality!*... Jeez! Skip this! Let's see...

What is her preferred occupation? Ugh.

What is her religious preference? This is exhausting!

Do you like pets? I think so, but then there's that issue with the cat possibly eating me.

What is your ideal date? I don't know. I've never *been* on a date, which is probably a MINUS. But then again, I don't have all those Crazy Psycho Exes to ramble on about during our first coffee date, so that's a PLUS!

How often do you drink? Hmm, let's see... *Carrie Nation Axe-Wielder*... *Overzealous Prohibitionist*... Skip. Skip... *Noel Coward Sophisticated Martini-Sipper*... *Winston Churchill Martini-Guzzler*... *Richard Nixon Martini-Slammer*... Hey, Tricky Dick! *Blind-Drunk Richard Burton*... *Passed-Out Lost-Weekender*... That's the one. *[types it in...]*

How would you characterize yourself? *Meek & Mild*... *Strong Silent Type*... *Tall Dark & Handsome*... Well, not the *tall* part... *Brad Pitt's Younger Brother*... *Salt & Pepper George Clooney Twin*... Let's skip ahead... *Nerdy Geek*... *Broke-Ass Artist*... Hey, they have "Broke-Ass Artist!"... *Canny Entrepreneur*... I *hate* entrepreneurs! Especially canny ones. *Spy Or Double Agent*... *Part-Time Assassin*... *Ribald Raconteur*... *Webinar Mogul*... *Laborer/ Troglodyte*... They must get lots o' dates! *Tattooed Racist Redneck*... *Religious Fanatic Nutjob*... *Totally Hopeless Loser*... *Smelly Homeless Guy*... *Lawyer/ Satan Worshipper*... *Obtuse Entitled Fortune-Inheritor*... *Slippery Reptilian Investment Banker*... *Birkenstock-Wearing Granola Bar*... *Hairy-Legged Femi-Nazi*... *Priapic Hollywood Producer*... Let's skip a bit more... *Nutty Professor Time Traveler*... No. *NBA Sneaker-Endorser*... Nope. *Aimless Wanderer*... That doesn't sound so bad. *Mover & Shaker*... Yes! That's me! *[types it in...]* Okay, almost through...

What kind of relationship are you seeking? *Quickie*... *One-Nighter*... *Blind-Drunk One-Nighter*... *Drug-Induced One-Nighter*... *Alcohol &*

Drug-Induced One-Nighter... Casual Fling... Euro-Fling... Euro-Fling?
Self-Centered Dalliance... Co-Dependent Hanger-On... Steaming Hot Mess...
Drama-Queen Fruitcake... Suicidal Basketcase... New Age Narcissistic Night
mare... Psychotic Soul-Stealer... These *are* quite specific... *Gold-Digging*
Do-Nothing Meets Rich Guy With No Pre-Nup... Don't they have any *good*
ones? *Adolf & Eva... Sid & Nancy... O.J. & Nicole...* What?! *Manson*
Family Love-Fest... I coulda written that speech by now... *Heart-Breaking*
Soul-Crushing Emotionally & Physically Abusive Trainwreck... Probably
not. *That Crazy Bitch That You'll Talk About On Every Date For The Next*
Three Years... I'll put "Other"... Okay, it says I'm almost done...

Post a nice pic of yourself! I *do* have some nice pics! But damn,
that's not gonna work because then they'll recognize me and I'll get
nothing but *Gold-Digging Do-Nothings!*

[The intercom buzzes...]

"Mr. President?"

"Yes, Gladdy..."

"Tim Chopper sent over a packet for you, sir. Shall I bring it in?"

"Please."

This online dating blows. And I haven't even finished my profile.

Gladiola Gaze enters the Oval, then pauses for a moment as she
looks over her shoulder at the painting.

"That's something, sir." She hands the President a manila
envelope.

"Thanks, Gladdy."

On her way out, she casts another dubious glance, as Alex Rett
looks through the file on Dom Milanese.

Nice, Tim. This is good stuff. But I have that speech. And now
I'm thinking about *sex* again! It's like the more I have to write that
speech... And of course there's always porno. *We have the best porno in*
the White House. Everyone says that. It's tremendous! Haha! I'm quoting my
predecessor, of course. After I first got elected, he invited me here, to
this very room. And with my mom right above me, still very conscious
and aware, he imparted this sage bit of advice: *The White House has the*
*best porno. [Alex clicks back onto **MEGA-DATE!**[C] ...]* Look at all those sexy
babes just *waiting* for that special someone. What did I click on for
my body type again? *[He checks his profile...]* Slim *& Sexy... That's right!*

Uh-huh! Okay, here's my speech for tonight, muthafuckas... *[Alex puts on his pair of mini-Ray-Bans, then hops onto the desk...]* I'm Alex Rett, *Slim-Sexy* to you, my fellow Americans. And I *hate* Er Mahgerd's human-rights abusing guts! And all I have to say regarding *that* is *this...*

[He calls up that Rod Stewart song everyone knows and turns it up LOUD*...] If you want my body and you think I'm sexy, come on sugar, let me know. If you really need me, just reach out and touch me. Come on honey, tell me so.*

[Familiar pounding on the door.] A moment later, Gladiola Gaze enters the Oval Office, expecting the worst. She sees the President on Ronald Reagan's desk, dancing his little ass off, swinging that umbilical cord like there's no tomorrow. And Gladdy shoots a glance at the reddish-purplish goo as she retreats to the safety of her desk outside.

8

Brayden Carter is seated at a table near the wall at Deco, his favorite upscale, snobby (some say racist) bar in Georgetown.

"What can I get you?"

He looks up and sees a hipster mulatto waiter with perfectly sculpted facial hair and symmetrical piercings looming above him.

"Actually, I'm waiting for someone," Brayden says.

The waiter nods, then disappears.

A moment later, the dulcet tone of Brayden's phone announces the arrival of a text. A message from Reggie: Hey man, can't make it. Something came up. Reg

Brayden lets out a breath, then puts his phone away. When he looks up, his eyes are drawn to the bar, to someone new behind it—a young slender black woman, with a sexy face, fashionably straightened hair, and what looks from this distance like a very shapely *derrière*. (And for a second, thoughts of Carly intrude—his French ex-girlfriend who unceremoniously dumped him. In French. And to wipe her from his mind, he gazes back at the bartender.)

"*Hel-lo...*" he says as he straightens his tie.

After leaving some cash on the table, he walks to the bar and grabs a seat in the middle (a recollection of his teen-aged years when he was obsessed with chess. The object, to control the center).

"Hi there!" the bartender says with a welcoming smile.

And Brayden is almost shocked by her friendliness.

"Hi," he says back. "What happened to the other..."

"The other?"

"You know, the tall hot Amazon Ice Queen." But as soon as the words leave his mouth, he regrets saying them. But then he hears her laughing.

"I couldn't have said it better myself!" She smiles. "She went to Miami to be with her rich boyfriend."

"I guess she doesn't know that Miami will be underwater in twenty years, with global warming." (*What are you doing, you idiot!* he says to himself. *You don't bring up liberal politics as an ice breaker!*)

"Yeah, I think they call it climate change now," she says.

"Haha!"

"I'm Renée..." She holds out her hand.

(*Whoa!* Brayden thinks. And then, *Easy, tiger.*)

He reaches across the bar and shakes her hand.

"I'm Brayden Carter."

"Nice to meet you, Brayden Carter."

"Nice to meet *you, Renée...*"

"Renée Hardy."

"You're not *French*, are you?"

"Ha! My *first name* is." She smiles. "But I'm from Brooklyn."

"Oh good!"

"Why? Are you a... is it *Francophobe* or *Francophile?* I always get those mixed up."

"*Phobe*, like *phobic*," he says. "From the Greek *phóbos*, meaning fear." (*What are you doing, you moron! Now you sound like some pretentious asshole!* And *whatever you do, don't bring up your French ex-girlfriend.*)

"Well, aren't *you* the smart one."

"Oh, I... I just happened to know that." Brayden shrugs. "It was on *Jeopardy.*"

"Haha! That's funny!"

(Nice recovery!)

"So what would you like?" she asks, as she gives him a look that might, from a certain angle, under the right light, be interpreted as flirtatious.

"I heard you make a great G&T."

"Me personally?"

(Oh no! Now she thinks you're a stalker!) "Haha! I'm kidding."

She smiles. "I know what you mean."

"Whew!"

"What kind of gin do you like?"

(Don't say Uncle Tom.) "Um, dealer's choice."

"Comin' right up."

(Good, we have a moment to regroup. Get your head in the game, Brayden. This girl's pretty cool. Don't be an idiot.)

"Here ya go..." She watches him pick up the glass and take a sip. "Good?"

"Mmm, yes! Thank you."

"You're welcome, Brayden Carter. So what do you do?"

"Me? I... I work for the President."

"You mean, the *President* President?"

"Well, yeah. But I'm a lowly intern."

(Ya just hadda do that self-deprecating bullshit, didn't ya? What did I tell ya about confidence?)

"So what's he like?"

"He... He's nice... Sometimes. I mean, lately there's been a lot going on. He has a lot on his plate."

(Watch the clichés! Change the subject. Ask her about herself.)

"So what brings a nice Brooklyn girl to DC?"

(Good. Neutral yet engaging. And you slipped in that nice Brooklyn girl compliment.)

"School. Georgetown. Masters. Economics."

"Haha!"

"What's so funny?"

"It was just... You study Economics and your answer was so... *economical.*"

"Haha! I like a man with a sense of humor."

"Why, is there one here?" He playfully glances around, then looks back at Renée.

(Don't over-do it, Eddie Murphy.)

"You're funny," she says. And then, almost as a reward, she gives him a sexy smile, with perfect, gleaming teeth surrounded by full, luscious lips.

(Okay, watch out. You're doin' okay, but you don't wanna let your dick do the thinking. Say something disarming.)

"I don't know anything about Economics," he says. "I mean, I know to leave a 20% tip."

"Well, that's important!" She smiles. "Still liking your drink?"

"Yes! Thanks. What kind of gin is this?"

"This..." She holds up a beautiful blue bottle.

"Bombay Sapphire... It sounds sexy." *(That was a stretch.)*

"Hmm."

(See! You're striking out!)

"So what have you got against the French?"

(Whew, she saved your ass! But be careful how you answer this.)

"Oh, I had a bad experience once... on the Eiffel Tower."

"Really?"

"I was supposed to meet this woman at the top of it at exactly twelve midnight."

"But she was hit by a car on her way there!"

"Yes! It was a Citroën!"

"I *love* that movie!" she says. *"An Affair to Remember!"*

"Yeah! I love that you love it!" *(Not bad. But she probably thinks you're gay, cuz you like some old romantic movie.)*

"With Cary Grant and..."

"Um, I can never remember that actress," Brayden says. "So, you like old movies?"

"Yeah, I do. I'm kinda old school, I guess."

"Me too! Maybe we could..." Brayden begins, but then he sees that Rett's address to the nation is about to come on. "Hey, do you mind turning this up a bit?" He motions to the TV. "My boss..."

"Yes, sir!

As Renée turns towards the TV, Brayden steals a glance at her callipygous behind, and he finds himself smiling. *(You did pretty well. You deserve a look.)*

On the television is President Alexander Rett, from within the womb-room. But for the first time, they also show his mother, with all the tubes and wires connected to the life-support system. All part of the new strategy, to make his comatose mother a plus instead of a minus.

"His poor mom," Renée says.

"Yeah."

"My fellow Americans..." the President begins. "I'll get right to the point. I *hate* Er Mahgerd. He may be the Hangarian President, but not all leaders are good leaders."

"*Hel-lo...*" Brayden says out loud.

"Hangry was a democratic nation until five years ago when Er Mahgerd seized power in a brutal coup. He has stayed in power ever since through even more brutality by establishing and maintaining an oppressive regime that persecutes and even kills his own people, that has taken away their rights, all so he can retain his stranglehold on power. He is a dictator and a despot and I hate him as I hate all dictators."

"Whoa!" Brayden says.

"Your boss is lookin' good." Renée offers a distractingly sexy smile.

"In a perfect world, democracy would destroy dictatorship, good would eliminate evil, and freedom would triumph over suffering and oppression. But as you all know, this world is less than perfect. But we try. We keep trying. And sometimes as we try, we find that we have to deal with these people to whom we are morally and ideologically opposed. And this is the reality of our world, especially the political one."

"Not bad."

"Today we use wind and solar power to satisfy *many* of our energy needs, but we are still dependent on oil. America is a nation on the move. We all have cars, and they are essential to our daily lives. And let's be honest, we *like* having cheap gas. In other countries, gasoline is eight or nine dollars a gallon, but this is America and we *like* when it's three or even *two* dollars a gallon. We have *enough* to worry about, right? Well, this is the price we must pay for that cheap gas we all love. The reality is that sometimes I as your President must make deals with another country, with another leader whom I detest, to secure our present as we work towards securing our future. And this is the price that *I* must pay as I look to the security and well-being of all of you, the American people, as my primary concern.

"So I will meet with President Mahgerd this Friday because he has the oil we need. And by shaking hands with him before the cameras, we will be granted access to that oil at a fixed low rate for the next ten years, as we develop our alternative energy sources. But that is the future, and this Friday I guarantee our present. Thank you."

"That... was great," Brayden says. And in the background there's scattered applause and a few cheers.

"Your boss hit a home-run," says Renée.

Brayden nods his head, and as he does, he feels a sense of pride in his country—something he's rarely felt.

"So you said earlier..."

"What?"

"You said *'maybe we could'*..."

"Oh yes! *Maybe we could go see an old movie together* is what I was going to say... Earlier, I mean."

"My shift is over at seven-thirty."

"That's in six minutes."

"I like a man who knows math!" She smiles. "So how 'bout we have two *G&Ts* and discuss it."

"Yes. One each," Brayden says, and he watches her laugh.

"Why don't you grab us a nice table?" Renée motions towards the back wall. "And I'll join you in a few."

"Okay."

"And don't forget to tip your bartender!"

9

"So I can't get over your boss's speech."

"I know, right?"

"It seems like he's a new..."

"What?"

"I was going to say *man*." Renée smiles. "But... new *fetus?*"

"Haha! Yes."

"So what's happened to him?"

"I don't know. For the longest time, he couldn't even remember my name. And now he's like this mini-Churchill."

"I know you must get asked this all the time, but..."

"What's it like working for a *fetus?*"

"Ha! Yes. Sorry. Predictable."

"You're *not!*" Brayden reaches over and holds her hand for a moment. "Most women..."

"Uh-oh."

"What?"

"Is this where you ruin our date by showing what a misogynist you are?"

He pulls his hand away"

"I'm *kidding!*" She smiles. "Okay."

"So you can put your hand back."

"Okay."

"But you're *not* a misogynist, are you?"

"No," Brayden laughs.

"But my friend Reggie, he probably is. He was supposed to meet me here tonight, but he was stuck on the Hill."

"He's in politics too?"

"Yeah. He's an intern for the Black Caucus. So you asked me what it was like."

"Yes!" She gives him a big smile.

"To work for a fetus... I *like* that."

"What?"

"That you pay attention."

The look in her eye is unmistakable. There's something sexy going on.

"So are most women predictable?"

"I'll take the Fifth on that one."

"Hmm..."

"But not *you!*" Brayden smiles. "Ah! But *most* women..."

"It's... It's just that the *guy* usually has to do all the work, you know? He has to approach the woman and strike up a conversation and be witty and charming and risk rejection while the woman is safe behind this bulletproof glass."

"Like the President!"

"Haha! Yes. And way to change the subject!"

"Thanks for noticing!"

"My friend Reggie, he has this theory."

"Reggie the Misogynist..."

"Yeah. It's that a woman's personality is inversely proportional to her degree of hotness."

"What were you saying? I was busy thinking about makeup."

"Haha!" Brayden smiles. *"Touché!"*

"So maybe a *woman* should be President."

"Yeah, but not Mallory Blitzen."

"I know, right? She's like this... I don't know, invasive virus."

"Haha! That she is."

"So how 'bout Mavis? Have you met her?"

"Yeah, she's... You know, all '*aw shucks, I love my four kids an' I love potatoes an' I love America*'... In that order."

"That's a spot-on impression."

"Thanks." He smiles. "So how's your drink?"

"Eh, it's okay... I make better."

"I like a confident woman."

"I'm glad, because some men are put off by it."

"Not me. So you said we're on a date?"

"Did I?"

"You don't remember?"

"Vaguely. And who are you again?"

Brayden laughs and he gives her hand a purposeful squeeze.

"I feel like I've known you..." *(STOP! Do NOT say like I've known you all my life. That's the kiss of death!)* "Since... like an hour ago," he says. *(Whew! That was close!)*

"Me too!" She smiles and squeezes his hand.

"So it's not too bad."

"What?"

"Working for a fetus."

"Oh, right!"

"I mean, he's... You know, after a while you barely notice. Like it seems normal and he's just this... little person. You're not a *heightist*, are you?"

"A *heightist?* I don't think so."

"One time he asked me why I don't play in the *NBA*, because I'm tall."

"Who did? Rett?"

"Yeah."

"Well, why *don't* you?

At this moment, Brayden leans over. He takes the back of Renée's head in his hand and he pulls her into a kiss. There's the slightest twinge of surprise, but then she leans into *him* and caresses his cheek as their tongues touch for the first time. And the moment becomes its own reality as the world beyond their table fades.

When they disengage, they return to their more innocent posture as they smooth their rumpled clothes. Renée looks at Brayden. She reaches over to adjust his tie.

"There..." she says.

"Thanks."

"I like this suit."

"Yeah?"

"I like a man who knows how to dress well, who takes care of himself."

"I'm glad."

"I think you're gorgeous, by the way."

"You do?"

"Mmm..."

"You're not bad yourself. I liked our kiss."

"Kiss*es*..." She smiles. "Plural."

"Mmm, it turns me on, a woman who knows singular from plural." He steals another kiss.

"And what else turns you on?"

"*You*... are gorgeous," Brayden says. And he pulls her into him again.

And as Renée leans in closer, her hand brushes against his lap from beneath the table, like an explorer checking out the terrain.

"I like *this*..." She whispers in his ear and then bites his earlobe.

"And I like *this*..." She brings her mouth onto his. And after another of those timeless moments...

"Do you wanna..."

"Yes," she says.

"I'll get the check."

"Where do you live?"

"Alexandria."

"I live a few blocks from here."

"Okay!"

Ten minutes later, they're at her apartment. As soon as the door slams shut, their clothes become part of a dance of seven veils as they kiss and grind and grasp and grope, with pieces of clothing flying into the air every few seconds. They find themselves standing naked before a full-length mirror, Renée with her back to the glass. And as Brayden holds her close, he gazes at her reflection, at her beautiful body with his arms wrapped around it.

An hour later, they're in bed beneath the sheets.

"This is my favorite part," she says.

The feeling in the room is of satisfaction, contentment, a languorous exhaustion.

"Which part?"

"*This*... Our limbs intertwined. The soft, sweet nothings."

"You sound like a poet, not an economist."

"Can't I be both?"

"Yes, you... you can be whatever you want," Brayden says.

"Mmm..." She leans over and kisses his chest. "And I like *this*," she says. "Whatever this is."

"This?"

"Between us."

(Don't ask what this is! his voice says. *Don't think. Go with it.)* "Yeah, too bad it's just one of those crazy-passionate one-night Euro-Flings."

"I know, right?" She gives him a knowing half-smile. Then she slides the sheets away from her body, to lie there in her nakedness.

"So I guess I'll have to attend to my own needs from now on." She gives her breasts an enticing caress, then she moves her hand slowly along her skin until she's rubbing herself.

Brayden Carter, suddenly revitalized, throws the sheets aside.

"Perhaps I can be of some assistance," he says.

"What a gentleman!"

Outside the opened window, carried by the warm summer breeze, is the sound of the eleven o'clock news from someone's TV.

"In his address to the nation tonight, President Rett brought to mind JFK at his most passionate and FDR at his most decisive. In a bold and disarming speech, he reminded the American people of the cost of freedom, and the price we *all* must pay to secure it. In a scathing indictment of Hangarian dictator Er Mahgerd and of oppression worldwide, the President gave his assurance that dealing with dictators does not imply acceptance, as he ushered in a new era of transparency in government. And he boldly declared that he will do whatever needs to be done to secure our present, as we work to secure our future."

10

Ezra Millstone Banes @EzraBanesCrackTheWhip

Finally we have a take-charge President who gets things done, who speaks truth to power. President Rett's speech was not only inspiring but empowering. Great job, sir!

Porter Percival Portly @govPortPortly

Last night's speech by President Rett was HUGE. EPIC. He told it like it is, the reality of our world. And he showed us the true cost of freedom. I'm hugely inspired!

Jaspar Redford Torrence @govJRTva

I was a young man when I first heard JFK's "Ask not what your country can do for you" speech. Last night President Rett inspired me in that same way.

Dirk Fist @infocombatBigDirkFist

I'm starting to be a believer. Kickass speech last night, Mr. President! USA doesn't bend or break to foreign terror. Rett calls a spade a spade. Patriot-Badass!

"Patriot-Badass!" That's not bad. Good ol' Dirk Fist. I'll send ya a case o' ammo for that one. *[Alex clicks on* CNN, *his BFF* Jules Tippler...*]*

"Everyone's talking about being inspired since the President's speech last night, as he drew a line in the sand against dictators and oppression. In his boldest address yet, both to the nation and the world, President Rett vowed to do what it takes to secure our present as well as our future. And I can't help but again recall Saul on the road to Damascus, as Alex Rett before our eyes has become nothing short of transformed."

Julie, baby! What a day, and it's only nine in the morning! (And there's that *"Road to Damascus"* thing again. I gotta finally *Google* it.) *[Alex's smartphone announces a new* Tweet *with the sound of a portentous gong...]*

Mallory Rodman Blitzen @realPresidentMalloryBlitzen

Inspiring? Not really. A lot of hot air last night from Little Alex. And what's going to happen when the world realizes that it's a BIG BLUFF from a little boy.

I really hate that Mallory Blitzen. Like *detest*. Like... what's an even harsher word? *[His fingers flash over his smartphone...]* "Siri?"

"Yes Mr. President..."(I love that Siri calls me Mr. President! One of the perks of the job.) "Siri, what are some synonyms for the word *detest?*"

"Checking on synonyms for detest... Let's see, we have *loathe, despise, abhor, disdain.*"

"Do you have anything even *worse?* I mean, with even more hatred?"

"How 'bout *abominate?*"

"Yes! Abominate! Thanks, Siri! You rock!"

"You do as well, sir. And nice speech last night."

"Thanks!"

I love that Siri! And I abominate Mallory Blitzen. Alex's eyes are drawn back to the TV, to a familiar face.

"Hello America! This is Derrick Kincaid. As you know, I love America. And I would like to announce today my candidacy for the office of President of the United States. But first, *this...*"

Derrick Kincaid turns around as the camera pans downward to reveal his naked buttocks. The voice-over: "For a good cause!" he says. And then the actor turned Presidential candidate shoves an enema up his butt and squeezes it. The concluding voice-over: "Paid for by Derrick Kincaid for President."

What the fuckety fuck? And I was gonna make you *Secretary of the Interior!* This day was so good, until like a minute ago. *[Alex takes hold of his smartphone. He's about to send a Tweet, the first since his Alcohol-Induced Lost Weekend-Imposed Tweet Fast, when he lets out a breath...]* Nope, gotta stick to the fast. The world *likes* the new me. The old me almost got thrown under the bus. *[He takes a few deep breaths...]* But it's not easy, this Tweeting cold turkey.

But then his eyes are drawn back to the TV.

DC METRO NEWSBEAT

"And in a related story... The new issue of *DC Now!* that hit news-stands today has named President Alexander Rett as *The Beltway's Most Eligible Bachelor!*"

[They cut to on-the-street interviews with an array of young female colle-giate and professional types...]

"So what do you think of President Rett being named *DC's Most Eligible Bachelor?*"

"I think he's sexy."

"You do?"

"Oh yeah. Especially after that speech last night! So strong and powerful!"

[They cut to another young woman...]

"Do you think the President is sexy?"

"*Alex?* Yes!"

"How come?"

"He's like this rock star. Our rock star President!"

[Cut to another young woman...]

"I'd do him!"

"You would?"

"I mean, I usually go for taller guys, but I'd definitely... you know."

[Cut to another young woman...]

"Do you think Alex Rett is handsome?"

"Handsome? He's dreamy! He's President McDreamy!"

"So the fact that he's a fetus... I mean, that doesn't bother you?"

"I guess a little. But he's *so* smart and sexy! The way he said he hates dictators. That's *hot!*"

[Cut to two young women standing side by side...]

"So would you have sex with the President?"

"Sure! I mean, if he asked me. I think he's awesome!"

"How 'bout you?"

"Of course!"

"How come?"

"He's so strong and, you know, the way he stood up to that guy, that dictator dude."

"The President of Hangry?"

"Yeah, that Hangry dude! Haha!" *[The two girls break into laughter...]*

"So what would you like to say to the President? *[The reporter asks the first young woman...]*

"I'd say, *'I love you, Alex!'*"

"You didn't even *vote* for him!" *[Says the second woman...]*

"So?" *[Says the first woman...]*

"So what would *you* like to say to the President?" *[The reporter asks the second young woman...]*

"I love you, Alex! Call me!"

"So it's official..." *[The reporter looks into the camera...]* Forget Justin Trudeau. Forget Emmanuel Macron. *President Rett* is sexy... Back to you..."

Hmm! Bye-bye bad mood and hel-lo Britney... *[Alex calls up Britney Spears'* "Womanizer" *video on his smartphone, the one where she's nearly naked. With the tune so loud it rattles the bulletproof glass of the womb-room, he jumps onto the desk and sings along...]*

Womanizer, woman-womanizer You're a womanizer Oh, womanizer, oh You're a womanizer, baby You, you, you are You, you, you are Womanizer, womanizer Womanizer...

But before he can go into the second verse, he notices Tim Chopper standing above him.

[Alex turns off the song as he catches his breath...]

"Tim!"

"Mr. President. You're in a good mood, sir."

"I got the swagger of a champion."

"Sir?"

"I was... celebrating."

"You have a lot to celebrate, sir, first and foremost, the speech last night." Tim's look is brimming with respect and approval. "And you're back above 90."

"That's good," says Alex.

"So..." The President sits on the edge of his desk as Tim pulls up a chair.

"Our friend, Senator Milanese. He has something he loves more than anything," says Tim Chopper. "Something that gives him his identity. Something that would crush him if it were taken away."

"His car," says Alex.

"Yes. His '65 Mustang GT-350 Shelby fastback."

"Custom-made. It cost a fortune."

"Yes," Tim nods.

"So might I suggest OPERATION KHARTOUM?"

"*Khartoum... Khartoum...* Yes, that's perfect. Proceed with that immediately."

"Yes sir. And OPERATION R.E. LEE is scheduled for launch

tomorrow morning."

"Excellent, Tim. Tomorrow will be a good day. What a difference a week makes, hmm?"

"Yes sir."

"Alright, Tim. Make it so."

[The intercom buzzes...]

"Yes, Gladdy?"

"The President of Hangry is on the line, sir."

"Is he..." Alex turns to Tim Chopper.

"Tim, don't leave just yet," he smiles. "Put him through, Gladdy." He puts it on speaker.

"Mr. President?"

"Is that you, Er?"

"Mr. President, that speech you gave yesterday... it was an *outrage!*"

"What was that, Mr. President? I can't hear you that well."

"I said it was an *outrage!*"

"Out *what?* You'll have to speak up, Mr. President. You're breaking up."

"Can you hear me now?"

"No." Alex casts a sly glance at Tim.

"How 'bout now?"

"That's better. So what were you saying, Er? You're coming *out?*"

Tim shakes his head and smiles.

"Your speech last night!" Er Mahgerd says. "It was an *outrage!*"

"Oh, an *outrage.* I'm glad you listened to it, Er."

"The deal is off!"

"The deal? You mean our oil deal?"

"I'm canceling the visit."

"You're canceling your visit? Well that's too bad, Er. I'm disappointed."

"*You're* disappointed?"

"You *know* that the UN is voting tomorrow on whether or not to impose sanctions against Hangry. Do you remember that, Er? That's tomorrow. Tomorrow morning."

There's silence.

"Are you still there, Mr. President?"

"Yes."

"Oh good, because we were all set to abstain from that vote. And if *we* abstain, then other countries will follow suit and the vote won't go through. Did you hear all that, Mr. President?... Mr. President?"

"Yes."

"So I would really like to see you this Friday, Er. What do you think? Do you think you can make it to the White House?"

"..."

"Hmm?"

"Yes."

"What was that, Mr. President? I didn't hear you. The connection is bad."

"I said yes. I will see you on Friday, Mr. President."

"Oh good. That makes me happy, Er."

"Yes, Mr. President."

"Very good. Good-bye."

Alex hangs up and turns to Tim Chopper.

"This day just keeps getting better! So keep me posted on our operations."

"Will do, sir."

As Tim leaves, Alex notices him shoot a glance over his shoulder at the enormous painting, now hung on the wall replacing a battle scene from the War of 1812.

[Alex presses the intercom...]

"Yes, Mr. President?"

"Gladdy, what's today's approval rating?"

"It's 92, sir."

"92... 92... There's still a chance for 95."

"Yes there is, sir. Oh, that artist, Vincent Van Go-Go just arrived. Shall I send him in?"

"Please do."

"And Mr. President, your speech last night, it was wonderful."

"Thanks, Gladdy."

[A moment later...]

"*The most elusive figure in the art world,*" Alex says, as Ace Buckland walks into the Oval Office"

"*New Vision* said that about you just *yesterday*. Or rather, about *Pete Scrotum.*"

"I didn't know anyone read that rag."

"And speaking of..." Alex motions to the huge painting on the wall.

"Hey! *Nice!*" Ace stands back to take it in.

"Not bad for a poor boy from the slums of Alexandria."

"Ha! The American Dream."

"Where an outlaw like me can make it to *there*..." He motions to the wall. "And an outlaw like you can make it to *here*..." He motions to the Oval Office. "An' speakin' of, I owe you an apology, Alex."

"For what?"

"What I said last time, about you not doin' much. I mean, that speech last night. Even a cynical bastard like me was moved."

"Hmm..."

"I mean it!" says Ace.

"That was kickass... even if ya didn't mean it."

"Ha! How'd ya *know* I didn't mean it?"

"It don't matter. Like those JFK speeches. They were poetry, man. An' poetry goes beyond the words. Ya know what I'm sayin'? It's better ta feel *sumthin'* than ta feel numb." He notices the bottle of *Jack Daniel's* on Ronald Reagan's desk, where they'd left it the other day.

"Ya mind if I..."

"No, please."

"You want one, Mr. President?"

"I'm good. Today has been a *pret-ty good day*," says Alex, "and that's enough... So far, I mean. The day's young. North Urea could still launch a nuclear missile!"

"*Salud...*" Ace raises his glass, and as he takes a sip, he looks at Alex's mom.

"*That* is really sad, man. Your mom."

"Hmm..."

"Do ya think she hears what we're sayin'?"

Alex recalls the lemonade incident. He offers a shrug.

"That's one fucked-up cross, brother. So you didn't really have a childhood. Like, you skipped ahead."

"I'm precocious."

"That you are, Alex. I guess we all have our shit, but I look at *her*... I mean, that's one fucked-up childhood you never even *had*. But don't get me wrong," Ace says. "It's a *good* thing. It's like your personal dark cloud that's always floatin' overhead. An' when you need it, it gives you some of its fucked-up dark lightning."

"Ha!" Alex smiles. "Ace Buckland... artist... poet..."

"Alcoholic."

"Ne'er-do-well."

"Rat bastard."

"Rat bastard, yes." Alex looks at his friend.

"So do you know the story of the road to Damascus?"

"The Bible story?"

"Yeah. I've been meaning to *Google* it, but world events keep intruding."

"Okay, so there's this guy *Saul*," Ace begins. "An' he's this evil motherfucker who hates the shit outta the Christians, right? An' he spends his days like persecutin' 'em an' fuckin' 'em up. An' he's real good at it, like it's his job an' shit. So this one day he's walkin' with his pals on this road."

"To Damascus."

"Yeah! Wherever *that* is... like on the way to Jerusalem, I guess. So him an' his buddies are walkin' along when fucking *Jesus* appears, like right in the air before him, like *hovering*." Ace looks at Alex. "An' Jesus starts talkin' to him, to Saul, but his pals, they don't see him, they just hear his voice. An' they're all like startled an' nonplussed an' shit. An' Jesus gets all up Saul's butt about what a bastard he's been to the Christians, an' Saul is like *whatever*, an' Jesus, you know, he admonishes the *shit* outta him."

"Outta Saul..."

"Yeah, like '*Why are you persecuting all my believers, you fucker?*' An' Jesus strongly urges Saul to repent his stinkin' persecutin' ways, an' at that moment, Saul goes blind."

"He goes *blind?*"

"Like *that*, man!" Ace says.

"Leave it ta Jesus... An' those other guys, Saul's pals are like '*We're outta here!'* An' they split an' leave Saul's blind ass all by himself on this fucking dirt road in the middle o' nowhere."

"Some friends."

"I know, right?"

"So what happens?"

"Well, he somehow makes it to Damascus. But all the while, as his stumblin' blind ass is fallin' into ditches an' walkin' into trees an' shit, he thinks about, you know, seein' Jesus an' havin' Jesus speak to him. An' by the time he makes it ta town, he's had this conversion experience. An' now he *loves* Jesus an' the Christians. An' he repents an' he tells everyone that Jesus is cool. But he figures he hasta change his name, right? Since Saul had been such an A-hole. So he becomes Paul an' they make him a saint or sumthin' an' he gets into the Hall o' Fame."

"Haha! Thanks Ace! Add preacher to artist-poet."

Ace smiles. "So can I ask *you* something, Mr. President?"

"Sure."

"I saw most o' those videos like everybody else. About *you*, I mean. That documentary on..."

"*The History Channel.*"

"Yeah! But they never really, you know, said how you *did* it." He looks into Alex's eyes.

"But, if ya can't... I mean, if it's top secret or sumthin'..."

"No, it's... it's a good question," says Alex.

"And it *is* top secret. And if I tell you, *I* won't have to kill you, but some other people might... if they found out." Alex looks at Ace Buckland.

"You still wanna know?"

"Well..." Ace finishes his drink and pours another.

"Sure." He takes another sip.

"Why not? I mean, a month ago I never thought I'd be buds with the President an' have one of my placenta paintings hangin' in the Oval Office, so... what the fuck. Right, Alex?"

"I like your style, Ace Buckland." Ace smiles, takes another sip.

"So, the story... It was after I was on Dr. Phyllis."

"I remember that! It was hilarious!"

"Well, ya remember that I said I wanted to run for President? When she asked me..."

"Yeah."

"So there's this group..." Alex pauses to look at Ace.

"You *sure* you wanna know? I mean, this is the Rubicon."

"Sure, Alex. We only live once."

"Okay. So there's this ultra-secret society called '*The Florists*'."

"The *Florists?*"

"And they're these billionaires who... you know, stand above it all and pull the strings. But everyone's too busy being sloshed around in the mud, so they never look up."

"Hmm..."

"So they saw *me*... I mean, they *heard* me, on those videos. And they figured... well, they needed someone to run against Mallory Blitzen. And here's me, world famous. The ultimate single-issue candidate. So there's this knock on the door..."

Josef Schnitzelgrüber cocks his head almost imperceptibly, and as if hearing his thoughts, his wife-to-be, Mary Rett, calls out from a few rooms away, "I'll get it!" And a few moments later... "Yes?"

"Mary Rett?"

"Well, it's Schnitzelgrüber," she says. "I'm a married woman. Well, I *will* be. That's my *fiancé* right over there."

Her future husband barely turns his head. Instead, he finishes his can of *Döpplegänger*, crinkles it up, then tosses it through the air to make a perfect swish in the wastebasket at the other end of the kitchen, followed by a self-congratulatory belch. Meanwhile, Mary Rett takes in their visitor—a distinguished-looking older gentleman with short grayish hair, wearing what looks like a very expensive suit.

"Madame, may I come in?"

"Such a gentleman!" She smiles. "Please do."

The man glances at Mary's belly, then steps inside.

"This is my betrothed," Mary says. "My dear Joey."

"*Errggh*," says Josef Schnitzelgrüber.

"Charmed," the man says. "My name is Mr. Barrows. I represent a consortium, if you will, of wealthy businessmen interested in the health and well-being of America."

"Of America? Hmm!" Mary's eyes open wide.

"Can I get you something? Coffee? Tea? Entenmann's?"

"No thank you. I'll come to the point," the man says. "We have a proposition for you. For all of you, especially little Alex." He looks again at Mary's belly. "Is he still in there?"

"Oh yes," Mary replies. "And he still doesn't want to come out."

And from the chair by the kitchen table comes another grunt from Josef Schnitzelgrüber.

"May I speak with him?" the man asks. "To Alex."

"Oh sure... *Alex...*" Mary looks down at her own belly.

"There's this man, Mr. Burrows, to see you."

"It's Barrows," the man says.

"It's Mr. *Barrows*," Mary says.

"What does he want?" Alex asks from inside.

"*Ask him...*" Mary says to Mr. Barrows.

"Alex..." he addresses Mary Rett's womb.

"Yes?"

"I'm Mr. Barrows."

"I know. My mom just said that."

"Um, yes. Of course she did."

"So what do you want?"

"I represent a..."

"Consortium of *blah blah blah.*"

"Yes. And we would like you to run for President."

"*President?*" says Alex.

"*President?*" says Alex's mom.

"*Errgghh?*" says Alex's father.

"Yes," says Mr. Barrows.

"With our generous support, we feel confident that your son... that *Alex* will go all the way."

"All the way?" Alex's mother says, completely puzzled.

"To where?"

"Why, to the White House."

"*Ergrgrhhr!*" says Alex's father.

"But hold on," says Ace. "There's that age limit thing."

"Actually, there are *three* requirements," says Alex. "You have to be at least thirty-five, a resident of the United States for fourteen years, and a natural born citizen."

"Ha! Three strikes."

"So my predecessor, at the urging of *The Florists*, led a campaign to amend the Constitution, since technically I have no official age, since I haven't, you know, been born, and the Supreme Court approved it."

"But you're... sitting on your big desk outside your little apartment."

"Technicalities!" Alex smiles.

"So they..."

"What?"

"They..."

There's a long pause.

"Nuthin'." Ace shakes his head.

"Those rabbit holes."

"..."

"So what happened next?"

"Well, this Mr. Barrows, he explains how they'll make it happen. And then he brings out these diagrams, these schematics of this glass cover they want to install in my mom's... well, *that*..." He motions to the womb-room.

"So I can see out, but most importantly, so everyone can see *me*. And of course, my mom was beside herself, and my dad did even more grunting. But then Mr. Barrows brings out this check, and it's more money than they could imagine, and it's made out in their names. And he says there'll be more if they agree and I become President. And I mean, a half hour earlier, we're sitting in the living room watching *Spenser: For Hire* reruns."

"I *loved* that show!" says Ace.

"Me too! So to finish the story... My parents agree and they sign all these papers and they cash the check and they're happy as clams.

And the next thing ya know, they take me to this place and there's this whole team of people, like tutors, to teach me how to run for President. And then they do the operation to install the glass."

"Is it really bulletproof?"

"Of course. I'm the freaking President!" Alex laughs.

"But the thing is..."

"What?"

"These people, *The Florists*... They're the best," Alex says.

"At what?"

"At being whatever you want them to be."

"I'm not sure I..."

"When they appear in your life, you think your prayers have been answered. But they're on this other level, like a new species. A cross between your saintly grandmother and a velociraptor."

"Okay, so why do they call 'em *The Florists?*"

"Because after they get what they want, they send you this beautiful bouquet. Thirteen roses."

"Thirteen?"

"Because supposedly there are thirteen members. I mean, these people are the one percent of the one percent."

"You mean you're the *President* an' you don't even know?"

Alex shrugs. "So..."

"What?"

"It's not what I expected."

"Those rabbit holes..."

"So you're *The Florists'* bitch."

"Haha! But don't tell anyone."

Ace laughs.

"I'm *serious*, Ace. If you breathe a word of this to anyone, then they'll be killed and you'll be killed. Before you can even... pour off a shot."

"Jeez, just when I thought I had things figured out." He shakes his head and tries to refill his glass. "It's empty."

"We'll get some more. You hungry?"

"Yeah. That story... Actually, I'm famished!"

"What would you like?"

"Can you get takeout?"

"Sure, I get Krispy Kreme all the time."

"What about steak? There's this place in DC... 'Chip's Beth's Don's Steakhouse'."

"*WTF?*"

"It was originally Don's Steakhouse, but then Beth bought it, an' then..."

"Chip bought it."

"Yeah. It's the best, man!"

[Alex buzzes the intercom...]

"Yes, Mr. President?"

"Gladdy, can you order us two steak dinners with all the trimmings from Chip's Beth's Don's Steakhouse?"

"That's my favorite place, sir!"

"Oh!" Alex turns to Ace. "It's her favorite place."

"How would you like your steaks done, sir?"

"How would you like your steak done?"

"Medium rare," says Ace.

"Medium rare, Gladdy."

"Yes sir."

"Oh, Gladdy..."

"Sir?"

"Also get us a bottle o' Jack."

"*Jack Daniel's,* sir?"

"The one and only."

"A fifth or a quart, sir?"

"Better make it a quart." He looks at Ace. "I'm the fucking President!"

"Coming right up, sir."

"Thanks, Gladdy."

Alex turns to Ace Buckland.

"And I got this movie we can watch after dinner. *Shark-Quake.*"

"But that hasn't come out yet."

"*Prez-i-dent.*"

"Sounds good, my friend."

"This has been a good day," Alex says.

"And tomorrow, even better."

"Said the spider to the fly."

And as Alex Rett and Ace Buckland eat their steak, drink their whiskey, and watch their movie, the *Bulletin of the Atomic Scientists* sets the nuclear clock back from 30 seconds to three minutes before midnight. It's the first time in over eight years that the clock has been set so far from Armageddon.

11

In the early hours of Thursday morning, in a lovely old Colonial on a quiet street in Chevy Chase, Maryland, Senate Majority Whip Dominic Milanese is just waking up. The first thing he hears are the birds singing outside. It had been a mild summer evening the night before, and he opened the windows to feel the cool breeze, to hear the night sounds of crickets. Such a contrast, his life here, from when he was a boy growing up in Little Italy, in New York City. A cacophony of ethnic city life. The rattle and hum of swirling ambition left over from that first generation to land on these shores—from the Old Country, from Italy and Sicily. Both of his grandparents and his father had come over to make their fortune in America, and he was the realization of their dream.

But there was no lofty ambition for him of becoming President, since he's Italian, and no Italians have ever made it to the White House, except as a guest. Admittedly, he holds a grudge against the current President, since a fetus made it to the Oval Office before a *paisan*. So he had no qualms about going behind the President's diminutive back in the recent plot to get him to resign. "That's politics," he said. "Politics is for the *big* boys."

As he went to bed last night, Dom Milanese was content with his lot. After all, as the Senate Majority Whip, he has a substantial bit of juice, and he's both respected and feared. And at the end of the day, he can retreat to this beautiful old home built in 1791, when George Washington was the first President. And he can sleep in his comfortable four-poster bed and feel that he belongs.

When he opens his eyes to morning, there's the distinct smell of gasoline overwhelming the usual scent of primrose and plumeria. After realizing he's awake, Dom Milanese brings out his hand from beneath the blanket. It reeks of gasoline, and his brow furrows as he looks down the bed and throws the sheets aside. What he finds is the Ford Mustang grill emblem from his car, this galloping silver horse, dripping with fuel. And he grabs it and places it on the nightstand. Then he jumps out of bed and puts on his robe and slippers before dashing downstairs.

Once outside, he sees his car in the driveway, where he left his Mustang, an indulgence to his vanity, last night. He likes to park it there when it's nice out, so the neighbors can see it and marvel at its beauty. Dom Milanese had been married and divorced twice, but this car is the real deal. His 1965 GT-350 Shelby Fastback Mustang—black on black, sleek as a racehorse, with a sexy hood scoop and the Edelbrock supercharged Coyote engine that tops 700 horsepower.

But as he looks at his love in the soft morning light, there's a sudden flash and explosion as his car is blown to bits. Pieces of it rain down like meteorites, and what's left is engulfed in flames. Dom Milanese takes several deep breaths to keep from falling over. He stands there, wavering, as a long, agonized moan comes from his hidden depths and out his mouth, and then another and another, resounding throughout his upscale suburban neighborhood. He falls to his knees in the moist dewy grass and weeps.

To President Alexander Rett:
Mr. President, OPERATION KHARTOUM a success.
Chopper

[Several hours later, on Alex's big screen TV...]

FOX NEWS
"It was announced today that a new museum will open on September 1st in Richmond, Virginia called *The Slavery Museum.* However, this museum will not be condemning the institution of slavery but celebrating it. The museum's curator, Stafford Crowe, upon making

the announcement, said the following: '*The Slavery Museum* will celebrate all of the *good* things that slavery has done for America. Think of all the amazing accomplishments of white people, specifically white men, during the period in American history when we had the noble experiment of slavery. The countless inventions and machines that were created to make our lives better, the medicines to prolong our lives, the great books that were written to inspire us, and everything else that was done because slavery afforded these pioneers, these enlightened men, these artists and dreamers, the opportunity to accomplish all that they did, by giving them the time and freedom to create. And we are *still* reaping the benefits today, as all of this was done for the betterment of America, and for Americans as a whole. *The Slavery Museum* is about celebrating this.'

"But already, the museum has come under fire from liberals for allegedly being *racist* and for celebrating racism. In response, Congressman Harlon "Bud" Fizzle, a Republican from West Virginia, praised the museum, saying the following:

'It's about damn time that we're finally recognizin' the great things done by white people because o' slavery. All these terrific things, there's so many of 'em, that wouldn't have happened if there hadn't been slavery. So why can't you black people, you anti-slavery people, look beyond yourselves at the *bigger picture*? What these great white men did was for *all* Americans! But these coloreds... Oh, excuse me, was that politically incorrect? Haha! I have a hard time keepin' up with the latest lingo. So what I was sayin' is that this proves what me an' many folks have been sayin' for a long time, that these blacks an' black people in general are *selfish selfish selfish*, an' that they only think about themselves, which is why they're not real Americans. America is about sacrifice for the greater good. Like what that *Greatest Generation* did during World War Two. They saved America an' the *world*, not just themselves. If the blacks start acceptin' that the sacrifice they made was *good for America*, then the rest of America might start to respect 'em.'

"Virginia's State Capital is in Richmond, not far from the proposed Slavery Museum. Virginia Governor Jaspar Redford Torrence said *this* earlier today:

'I'm not gonna weigh in on that tired old argument 'bout whether slavery is bad or good cuz there were some very fine people on both sides. But I will say this... If we never had slavery, then we wouldn't have the blues and jazz, and I love me some blues! And speakin' of, we're havin' our annual *Blues & Jazz Fest* right here in Richmond all this weekend! So come on by and enjoy some mighty fine music! 'Ya can always count on the good ol' boys!"

"Gladdy?"

"Yes, Mr. President?"

"Can you have the kitchen rustle me up some grits?"

"Right away, sir."

To Tim Chopper:

Just saw the news on OPERATION R.E. LEE. We're two for two! Take the rest of the day off, Tim. You earned it.

Alex

[Alex clicks the remote...]

CNN

"The backlash against the proposed Slavery Museum in Richmond, Virginia continues to build. Democratic Senator Langston Ellis had this to say:

'This Slavery Museum is an abomination! It wasn't that long ago when signs hung from windows in this very city, in midtown Manhattan, that said *A Man Was Lynched Today*. And now they want a museum to *celebrate* this? It's an outrage!'

"Human rights groups across America have come together to denounce the museum, and Democratic leaders are calling on President Rett to... "

[Alex clicks the remote...] Sometimes it's too easy.

FOX NEWS

"Ewell P. Crawdad, the senior Republican Senator from Mississippi, had this to say in response to the trickle of liberal criticism:

'I don't know how many times we gotta say it, but them college-boy lib'ral types don't never listen. I guess it's cuz their heads is fulla all thet book- learnin'. Haha! I'm kiddin, o' course! But since this here's the 21st Century an' we're tryin' ta help 'em *see the light*, I'll say it one more dang time... It ain't about hate er any o' thet nonsense. It's about *heritage*. It's about our culture an' all the great accomplishmints we made, as a race, yet fer the benefit o' *all* Americans, whether they be white, black, or the savage Injun. An' while some of us wuz busy accomplishin', others wuz sacrificin', but *all* of it wuz fer the greater good! An' *that's* wut this here museum iz all about!'

Now *that* is scary.

"And in other news, the entire town of Flint, Michigan has disappeared inside a giant sinkhole."

What the fuck?
[Alex presses the intercom...]
"Gladdy?"
"Yes, Mr. President?"
"Have you emailed me the *Daily Briefs* yet?"
"Yes, sir, an hour ago."
[Alex finds the email and scrolls through the Daily Briefs...*]*
Slavery Museum to open in Virginia.
Borneo may have the bomb.
Celiac Disease outbreak in Congo.
Flint, Michigan disappears inside giant sinkhole.

Well, I'll be damned!
"Gladdy?"
"Yes, Mr. President?"
"Who's that guy... You know, the head of FEMA?"
"Bradley Milton, sir."
"Yes! That's why I couldn't remember it. Have him get his butt to Flint, Michigan. I mean, what used to be Flint, Michigan."
"Right away, sir."

There, our ass is covered. And this disaster becomes a big fat bonus *pour moi!* The Daily Double of Distractions! And by tomorrow, the Slavery Museum and this Sinkhole thing will be *mega!* No one's even gonna *notice* me shakin' hands with that Er Mahgerd. *[Alex looks back at the TV and clicks the remote...]*

CNN

"Candy Starkleton, a resident of Flint, went to Ohio yesterday for a family reunion. And she had this to say when she found out what had happened to her hometown:

'I... couldn't believe it... when I saw the news today. Everything's *gone!* I mean the whole *town!* And our home and our car and... We took a *rental* to Cleveland cuz the car is old and we didn't think it would make it. But now *it's* gone too! Luckily, we took our cat *Mutton-head* with us to the family reunion.'

"Longtime Flint resident, Bill Bronchiola, who last year moved to Lansing, said this in response to the disaster:

'Hey, I'm sorry for all them people, you know, who went down into that sinkhole, but as for Flint itself, good riddance! I got out when the gettin' was good.'

"As you can see from this live footage *[Cut to video with voice-over...]*, all that remains of Flint is a gigantic, smoldering black hole. Officials from FEMA are en route, although I wonder what can be done, since there's nothing left of this once thriving city."

[Alex clicks the remote...]

FOX NEWS

"And as sad as this story is, of Flint vanishing from the face of the Earth, it pains us here at FOX NEWS that long-time Flint resident and liberal snowflake filmmaker, Michael Moore, was in Pennsylvania participating in a pie-eating contest during the disaster."

To Wiley DeSembler:

Call a press briefing for this afternoon for multi-pronged

distraction. Slavery Museum backlash, Flint sinkhole, and anything else you can think of.

Alex

To President Alexander Rett:

It's scheduled, sir. 2PM.

Wiley

FOX NEWS

"And in New York City, there's a proposal to change the universally accepted emergency number of *9-1-1* to *9-1* in an effort to save time during an emergency. And this makes sense, because I used to *live* in New York City, and New Yorkers are nothing if not impatient."

[Alex turns off the TV...]

Finally, a moment to myself!

[The intercom buzzes...]

Dammit! "What is it, Gladdy?"

"Sir, your grits are here."

"Oh, good. And Gladdy, have the Vice-President make some statement to the press about this Flint thing."

"Right away, sir."

"And what's the approval rating?"

"It's 91, sir."

"91... But yesterday it was 92."

"It's that Flint disaster thing, sir."

"But that's not *my* fault!"

"I know, sir."

I'm *never* gonna get to 95. I mean, try going a week without a disaster! And they always point the finger at yours truly. I've never even *been* to Flint!

[The grits arrive and Alex digs in...]

They have the best grits at the White House, in addition to the best porno. Which reminds me, since that story came out where I'm *The Beltway's Most Eligible Bachelor*, I got all these letters. Like *thousands* since yesterday, of marriage proposals and naked selfies! And of course I didn't *read* them. That's why I have interns. But they put aside some of the really strange ones.

[Alex grabs the pile of letters from his desk...]

All these expectant mothers wanna fix me up with their daughters *in utero,* and they sent me their freaking *sonograms! WTF?!* I mean, they're freaking *embryos!* Look at this one. It looks like an extra-terrestrial. And this one: Is that thing even *alive?* I feel like I'm theoretically heterosexual, but does that even look like a human, let alone a human female? It'll make ya wanna become a monk. *[He takes a forkful of grits...]* I mean, I know I'm advanced for my age, but that's ridiculous. And I apologize for speaking with my mouth full, but these grits are so damn good! *[Takes a sip of OJ...]* There. Better. So I don't know what to make of sex. I mean, if those are my options...

[Alex's smartphone announces a new Tweet alert with the sound of an ominous tolling bell...]

Mallory Rodman Blitzen @realPresidentMalloryBlitzen

Is so-called Prez Rett sleeping in as Flint sinks into oblivion? Where's the response after tens of thousands died screaming? How could he let this happen???

That little... Why couldn't *she* have been in Flint? I double abominate her! And besides, you saw it! You're my witness! Did I not send that Milton Bradley FEMA guy to what's left of Flint like the second I saw the *Daily Briefs?* But it's never enough! It's amazing I don't drink all the time! And speaking of, it's only 10:35 and already I'm enervated. Sometimes this job totally sucks balls.

[Alex looks down at his grits, which are getting cold...]

Now I've lost my appetite...

[He presses the intercom...] "Gladdy?"

"Yes, Mr. President?"

"..."

"Sir?"

"Never mind."

[A flurry of fingers over his smartphone.] "Siri?"

"Good morning, Mr. President. How are you today?"

"I've been better. So Siri, do you think the next three hours will be disaster-free?"

"In the world, sir, or just in America."

"In America."

"Okay, checking on disasters over the next three hours in America...Calculating, sir "

"Take your time."

"Mr. President, it looks like the next three hours in America will be disaster-free."

"Oh good."

"As for Eastern Europe and Indonesia, not to mention that outbreak of Celiac Disease in the Congo..."

"That's okay, Siri. Thanks."

So maybe I can grab a catnap before the press conference.

[The intercom buzzes...]

Goddamn it! "What is it?"

"I'm sorry, Mr. President, but there's a woman here to see you."

"A woman?"

"A pregnant woman, sir."

"*What?*"

"She says that you asked her to come here so you could meet her daughter."

"Her *what?*"

"Her unborn daughter, sir. Her daughter *in utero.*"

For a moment, Alex is stupefied.

"Sir?"

"How'd she get in here?"

"I don't know, sir."

"Well, she's crazy, Gladdy. Like bonkers an' batshit. Get rid of her."

"I thought as much, sir."

"Oh *Gladdy...*"

"Yes, Mr. President?"

"I'll be Skyping with the President of the Congo now, regarding that recent outbreak, so I don't want to be disturbed."

"Yes, sir. For how long?"

"Till further notice."

"Yes, sir.

Alex lets out a loud puff of air before falling backwards onto the bed. Grabbing his smartphone, he sets the alarm for 1:55, with the press conference to begin at 2 PM. And with that accomplished, and with domestic disasters for the time being on hold, he closes his eyes.

12

Shortly after 1 PM, with President Rett in the middle of his nap, a disaster happened that not even Siri could predict. The Malique Kilvain verdict came in, and Police Officer Bryce Richards was pronounced "not guilty."

Ten months earlier, in Lincoln Park, Missouri—an ethnically diverse suburb of St. Louis—Malique Kilvain, a 20-year-old black man, was making pizza deliveries. He was driving his own car, an older model compact, with the Checkers Pizza sign on its roof. Admittedly, the car was a beater, but Malique was trying to save money so he could enroll the following semester at St. Louis University, to study Communications and Mass Media. The day was unseasonably hot for early September and he had the AC blasting. He had already made four deliveries and was on his way to the fifth when he saw flashing lights in his rear-view mirror. What he didn't know was that his brake lights no longer worked.

After pulling over, Malique watched as Police Officer Bryce Richards got out of his cruiser and walked towards him. When he got to Malique's car, Officer Richards motioned for him to roll down the window. But for some reason, most likely due to the age and condition of the car, the power windows no longer worked. Malique pressed the button again to no effect as Officer Richards kept tapping on the window from outside, each time a little louder and with growing impatience.

Malique tried to explain about the malfunctioning window, but apparently the policeman couldn't hear through the glass, since traffic was quite heavy that day. After pressing the button several more times, Malique Kilvain thought he had better open the door so he could explain himself. But as soon as the door cracked open, Officer Richards took a step back, planted his feet, and drew his weapon. A split second later, he fired five shots into the car, four of them hitting Malique, the fifth hitting the pineapple-pepperoni pizza on the passenger seat beside him.

The entire incident had been recorded on the dash cam of the police car, and it seemed open and shut. Another young black man needlessly killed. Another senseless tragedy at the hands of a trigger-happy white policeman. So when it came in *not guilty*, the verdict poured fuel on a fire set that morning at the Slavery Museum.

At 1:55 PM, President Alexander Rett wakes to his smartphone alarm as it plays the chorus to "*We Are the Champions.*" For a moment, he feels refreshed and ready to go, but then he sees that he had slept through a slew of Tweet alerts, texts, and emails. "What now?" he says. But nature calls and he relieves himself and then, "They'll just have to wait," as he looks at his watch and turns on the TV.

(*2 PM in the* James A. Garfield Room. *The White House Press Conference is about to begin...*)

[*Press Secretary* Wiley DeSembler *stands before the frothing mass of journalists, all chomping at the bit...*]

Journalists: [*en masse*] Wiley! Wiley! Wiley!

Wiley: [*points to one...*]

Emily Essex: Emily Essex, *Newsweek...*

Wiley: Yes, Emily...

Essex: Wiley, is there anything left of Flint?

Wiley: As you know, *FEMA* was on the scene almost immediately, and the reports coming back are that there's nothing left. That it just disappeared.

Mallow: Mitzi Mallow, *FOX NEWS...*

Wiley: Yes, Mitzi...

Mallow: We've heard rumors that Flint went all the way to China, like through the Earth.

Wiley: Those are just rumors.

Bogash: Kaz Bogash, *Modern Paranoia...*

Wiley: Yes, Kaz...

Bogash: We've also heard that the sinkhole is a bottomless pit, and that the entire town of Flint will hurtle through its dark emptiness for eternity.

Wiley: As I said, those are just rumors.

Decker: Doris Decker, *The Washington Post...*

Wiley: Yes, Dana...

Decker: It's Doris.

Wiley: Yes, Doris...

Decker: With the *not guilty* verdict in the Malique Kilvain case coming on the heels of the furor over the *Slavery Museum*, tensions have reached a fever pitch between Blacks and Whites.

Wiley: And your question...

What the fuck? When did that verdict come in? Fucking Siri!

Decker: So what is President Rett's response?

Crowd: Yes! Yes!

Wiley: The President is currently meeting with his top advisors, and he...

Smith: *[interrupts...]* There's a rumor that President Rett is *supportive* of the Slavery Museum, and that he's on its Board of Directors.

Wiley: *[irritated]* And who are you?

Smith: Cornelius Smith, *BLM Magazine...*

Wiley: BLM?... Bureau of Land Management?

Smith: *Black Lives Matter.*

Oh no...

Douglass-Jones: *[cuts in line...]* When will something be done to stop the cold-blooded murder of young black men by white police?

Crowd: *[in a lather...] Yes! Yes!*

WTF? That's the last time I take a nap!

Wiley: And who are you?

Douglass-Jones: *[proudly]* I am Frederick Douglass-Jones, *New Black Panthers...* *[cheers from the Blacks in the crowd...]*

New Black Panthers?! [Alex pinches himself several times to see if he's still asleep...]

Wiley: I can assure you that the President takes this very seriously, and that he's doing everything he can to...

Essex: And what about *Flint?* What is your response to Mallory Blitzen's claim that the President was asleep while Flint was sucked into the abyss?

Wiley: Well, first of all, we take everything from Mallory with a bushel of salt.

Crowd: *[scattered laughs...]*

Wiley: *[continues...]* And secondly, the job of POTUS has the President on-call 24/7. He gets updates *by the minute* on everything important, and his staff and cabinet are second to none.

Journalists: *[clamoring for Wiley's attention...]*

Don't pick the Black guy... Don't pick the Black guy...

Simon: Samantha Simon, *Time Magazine...*

Whew!

Simon: *[continues...]* So what is your response to the riots that are happening in St. Louis, Newark, and Detroit at this very minute, in response to the Kilvain verdict?

Riots in Newark?

Wiley: As I said, the President is...

Armanian: *[impatient]* Amanda Armanian, T*he New York Times...*

Oh no...

Armanian: *[continues...]* Is this not a further development in the utter collapse of race relations that began with President Rett's *predecessor?*

Good! Blame it on *him!*

Armanian: *[continues...]* And if it keeps going in this direction, some say a new wave of violence will engulf the nation that mirrors and might even surpass that of the 1960s, when our American cities were set ablaze?

Alarmist! Freaking *New York Times...*

Wiley: As I said, the President is meeting with...
Armanian: Top advisors, *blah blah blah.*

I *hate* that Amanda Albanian.

Decker: And what is your response to the Republican senators and the Governor of Virginia publicly *praising* the Slavery Museum?
Wiley: We are looking into this. *The Slavery Museum* has nothing to do with The White House and the President. It's a private institution that will receive no federal funding.

Good one, Wiley!

Douglass-Jones: But that's beside the point.

Not that *Black Panther* again...

Douglass-Jones: *[continues...]* The *point* is that Black people in this country are being treated as if they're disposable.
Crowd: *Yes! Yes!*

Where's a sinkhole when you need one?

Douglass-Jones: *[continues…]* And if it continues along this path, then a response in kind is the inevitable result!

WTF?!

Wiley: Is that a *threat*? Did you just threaten the United States Government?
Crowd: *[in a furor…]*
Wiley: *[continues…]* And what is your name again?
Douglass-Jones: *[boldly]* It's not a threat but a promise! And I'm Frederick Douglass-Jones! The *New Black Panthers!*
Crowd: *[deafening uproar…]*
Wiley: *[Looks around. At a loss, he hurriedly leaves the podium and makes his escape…]*

Ho-leee SHIT!
[The sound of one Tweet alert after another erupts from Alex's smartphone…]
Ho-leee SHIT!
[The intercom buzzes…]
"*What?!*"
"Sir, there's a whole slew of Senators, reporters, and the Vice-President here to see you."
"…"
"*Sir?*"
"Get Tim Chopper here, *ASAP!*"
"Yes sir, but what about…"
"Tell them I'm out."
"But sir, they know that you never go out."
"Well, tell them that I'm *in*, but that they can't see me."
"And when shall I tell them that they *can* see you, sir?"
"When I'm out."
"Um, yes, sir."
What. The. Fuck.
[Alex looks back at the TV as he clicks the remote…]

THE YOUNG TURKISH ANARCHISTS

Fat Guy With Weird Name: So the White House *press conference* was a real barn burner.

Hot Babe With Weird Name: Funny you should say *that*, as right now, American cities are in *flames*.

Fat: I *know*, right? Just a few days ago, President Rett was being compared to JFK because of his bold address to the nation, but over the past few hours, confidence in him has *plummeted*.

[Alex presses the intercom...]
"Yes, Mr. President?"
"What's the approval rating?"
"Um, sir, there are over fifty people here wanting to see..."
"Send them away! The *approval rating*, Gladdy..."
"One moment, sir... It's... 77, sir."
"*77!?... Arrghh!*"

Hot: It was bad *enough* with that asinine Slavery Museum.
Fat: Yes! That's the perfect *word* for it! *Asinine!*
Hot: And then the *not guilty* verdict in the Malique Kilvain police shooting case.
Fat: Yet *another* instance of only *white lives* mattering.

I hate that fat guy!

Hot: And what about those GOP *senators*, singing the *praises* of slavery!
Fat: It was really *unbelievable*. It's no *wonder* Frederick Douglass-Jones is pissed. I mean, wouldn't *you* be?
Hot: I *am* pissed! And I'm *Armenian*.

[Alex turns off the TV, and the second he does, there's a new Tweet alert...]

Mallory Rodman Blitzen @realPresidentMalloryBlitzen
First this asinine Slavery Museum, and now this not guilty verdict in the Malique Kilvain case. How can the so-called President let this

happen? Cities on fire!

[Alex chomps down on his own fist. And with his fist still in his mouth, there's another Tweet alert...]

Ezra Millstone Banes @EzraBanesCrackTheWhipPresident
Rett's inaction regarding that asinine Slavery Museum and now the not guilty verdict in the Malique Kilvain case deeply disturbing. Wake up, sir!

Ugh. I need a drink.
[Alex turns the TV back on...]

CNN
"This is live footage of Newark, New Jersey, in flames after the *not guilty* verdict in the...
CLICK...

C-SPAN
"We're talking with black activist and leader of the *New Black Panthers*, Frederick Doug...
CLICK...

FOX NEWS
"I know we all want to support our President, but with American cities on fire, the proposed Slavery Museum does seem, well, *asinine!*"

If I hear that word one more time...
[Alex grabs his smartphone and Googles "asinine"...]

as ·i ·nine
adjective
extremely stupid or foolish

And why is there only one "*s*" in it?
[His fingers flash over his smartphone...]

"Siri?"

"Yes, Mr. President?"

"I'm *pissed* about that Malique Kilvain verdict. I couldn't even enjoy my nap."

"I'm sorry, sir. I'm not infallible."

"Well, okay..."

"Do you forgive me, sir?"

"I guess..."

"Thank you, sir. How can I help you?"

"Why is there only one 's' in '*asinine*'?"

"Checking on why there's only one 's' in 'asinine'..."

"I mean, it seems like there should be *two*," Alex says, "so there could be an '*ass*' in there. Like '*assinine*'."

"It's from the Latin *asininus*, derived from *asinus*, sir, meaning '*ass.*'"

"But there still should be... Oh forget it."

[The intercom buzzes...]

"Mr. President..."

"Gladdy..."

"There are hundreds of people out here, sir, including Tim Chopper."

"Good! Send Tim in!"

A moment later, Tim Chopper bursts into the Oval Office and slams the door shut behind him.

"Tim."

"Sir."

"What the fuck?"

"I don't know, sir. Who could've figured on that verdict coming in this morning."

"And OPERATION R.E. LEE was a big fat backfire."

"I know, sir."

"So what are we gonna do? I mean, *Newark's* on fire! I never thought I'd be President while *Newark* went up in flames."

"Sir, the Black Caucus is demanding a response."

"Yes, I saw Ezra's Tweet."

"Another address to the nation?"

"I can't be making addresses every time there's a disaster. Besides, that Slavery Museum was supposed to be a *distraction!* Now we need a distraction from our distraction."

"I know, sir. But the good news is that Dom Milanese has stepped down as Majority Whip."

"He *has?* Well, that *is* good news. A bit of a silver lining."

"Maybe we can wait it out. I mean, it's worked before."

"Yes, but I was at 91 this morning. Now I'm at 77!"

[Alex's smartphone announces another Tweet alert...]

Frederick Douglass-Jones @FD-JtheNewBlackPanthers

Chicago, Birmingham, and Atlanta also ablaze with righteous anger over the systematic murder of our black brothers and sisters. Time for a Revolution!

"And who the hell is Frederick Douglass-Jones?" Alex asks. "I mean, two hours ago, I didn't know him from Adam, and now he's my *new nemesis?*"

"I'll find out, sir."

"Maybe we should give this to Wasserman."

"The FBI Director?"

"I know he's an ineffectual milquetoast, but maybe we can shame him into... you know, trying to live up to J. Edgar."

"I'll work out a plan, sir."

"Good, Tim. Get it to me before the ink is dry."

"Will do, Mr. President."

Tim Chopper gets up to leave when Alex stops him.

"Tim, why don't you go out *that* way?" He points to the side door. "It's a madhouse out there." He motions out front.

"Yes. Thank you, sir. I'll get back to you within the hour."

"Good, Tim. We need to put out these fires."

[An hour later...]

"What do you have, Tim?"

"I've spoken to Ezra Banes, sir. He's agreed to a public show of support if you kill the museum."

"That's it? Okay, let's kill it."

"But he also wants some kind of public demonstration, where you and he and the prominent black leaders announce your unequivocal stance in support of civil rights, specifically regarding the BLM movement."

"BLM?"

"Black Lives Matter, sir."

"Oh yes." Alex lets out a breath.

"And when was he wanting this?"

"He said sometime next week, sir."

"Okay, have an announcement made that next Friday we'll meet in the Capitol Rotunda."

"Not the Oval, sir?"

"No, this is too important."

"Okay, I'll..."

"*Hang on...*"

"Sir?"

"This is even *better.*" Alex smiles diabolically.

"Make it in front of that asinine *museum!*"

"That's in Richmond, sir."

"I know! It'll be a huge feather in our cap—the Black leaders in front of that Slavery Museum, as Alex Rett, like Lincoln, abolishes it!"

"Yes!" Tim nods, breathless.

"That's *it*, sir."

"Schedule it for next Friday morning, Tim."

"Consider it done."

"Oh, and make sure that New Black Panther Frederick Douglass-Jones is right up front with Ezra and me. And after I'm the next Lincoln, if he's still troublesome, we can deal with him."

"Yes, sir."

"And Tim, handle the travel plans so my mother is... comfortable."

"I will, Mr. President. Anything else, sir?"

"Let me know after you've talked with Ezra, and then I'll speak to him personally."

"I will, sir. It's a good plan, Mr. President."

Alex lets out a breath. "We'll see."

13

"So the Ice Queen left and you got it on with the hot new bartender!"

"*Got it on?*" says Brayden. "Are you a time traveler from the Sixties?"

"I wish, man," says Reggie. "But there ain't no place to go but *that way.*" He points forward.

"The past is no place for the black man."

"The present's not so great either."

"You got *that* right. That Malique Kilvain bullshit." He turns to look at Brayden.

"Whadaya expect from a pig... But five bullets?"

"Four. One hit the pizza."

"Just as well. It was pineapple."

"And that Slavery Museum..."

"I know!"

"*Watch out!*"

Reggie narrowly misses a minivan.

"*I got it.*" He pulls up within inches of a slow-moving silver Prius. "What the fuck, dude?"

"It's a red light," says Brayden.

"Oh... Hey, isn't that the Prius from the other day, with the bumper sticker we couldn't read?"

They both look at the Prius in front of them, festooned with seven or eight politically correct advertisements for left-leaning campaigns.

"Look at *that* one." Reggie motions with his head.

"'*What is to give light must endure burning.*'"

"Ha! Like *Newark*, man!"

"It's Viktor Frankl."

"Viktor Frankl? The guy's a pussy."

"*What?* He was in *Auschwitz*... And he's *dead*." Brayden turns to Reggie in disbelief.

"How can you call Viktor Frankl a pussy?"

"And *that* one, man. '*Life is Good.*' Ha! Ya never see a *brother* with that shit on his car."

"So maybe we should just accept our sacrifice," Brayden says, "so the white man can accomplish more great things."

"Haha! I hate liberals, man."

"But you're a liberal!"

"Not *that* kind!"

"What kind is that?"

"Your Prius-drivin', Life-is-Good, entrepreneurial milquetoast apologizin' liberal."

The light changes and Reggie darts into the other lane.

"Milquetoast?"

"It means timid an' submissive, man."

"I know what it means." He looks at Reggie. "You're so erudite!"

"Ha!"

"And not all white people are entrepreneurs."

"They're *not?* An' what does that even *mean*, bein' an entrepreneur, other than some *other* folks do all the work an' *you* get paid."

"Ha!"

"Like that *Uber* dude!" Reggie says.

"I mean, only white people think like this." He switches to his white person voice: "You know, Brayden, I think I'll start a taxi company! But Reggie, you don't have any taxicabs. No problem, Brayden! I'll get all these people to drive using *their cars*, and *I'll* get the money!' Ha! It's amazing what the white man can accomplish!"

"Hmm. Ya see the press conference?"

"Holy shit, man!"

"And that Black Panther guy."

"*That* is one badass muthafucka! I mean, the Panthers finally got their balls back."

"Did you see Wiley slink away?"

"Ha! *Lock the doors! Hide your women!*"

The traffic slows to a crawl. "Wus up wit da traffic?"

"Rush hour."

"Rush hour shouldn't conflict with Happy Hour, man."

"So you'll never believe what I hadda do this week."

"For the fetus?"

"You know that story in *DC Now!* About Rett being..."

"The *Sexiest Fetus Alive?* Haha! White people..."

"So all these women are sending in these naked selfies."

"To FOTUS?"

"Yeah! And these expectant mothers sent in their *sonograms!*"

"Their *what?*"

"Their *sonograms?*"

"I know what a sonogram is, man. I was just expressin' my disbelief." Reggie shakes his head.

"So they tryin' ta fix up their fetus with *President Fetus.*" He turns to Brayden.

"We live in some fucked-up times, man. So tell me more about Renée."

"Hey, you got her name right!"

"You know I'm jus' fuckin' wit ya." They come to another red light.

"I hate red lights, man."

"I told ya I'd drive."

"I'm cool." A huge billboard catches Reggie's eye. "So *that* is some bullshit." He points to the billboard of a morbidly obese white woman in a bikini, staring out defiantly. The caption reads: *Beautiful. Empowered. Sexy"*

"I'm sexy," Reggie says. "I love my body." Then he addresses the billboard. *"You don't love your body. You love not workin' out! You love the all-you-can-eat buffet!"*

"You should be a life coach!" says Brayden.

"Ha! I'd be a good one. The Marine Drill Sergeant Life Coach. *'Stop eatin', ya fat fuck, an' do fifty push-ups!'"*

The person in the car alongside gives Reggie a dirty look. Thankfully, the light turns green.

"So tell me about Renée, man."

"She's great! Tall, *slim*, beautiful, smart, sexy..."

"Okay, but she talked to you *first*, right?"

"Yeah, so?"

"Somethin' ain't right about that, man."

"What?"

"I mean, if she's tall, beautiful, sexy... Remember the *Fifth Law.*"

"What? There's no exceptions?"

Reggie looks at his friend.

"Sure, man."

"Remind me why we're friends again?"

"Cuz I tell you the *real shit!*"

They slow down behind an older pickup truck festooned with Republican bumper stickers. And taped in the rear window is a handmade sign: YOUR FREEDUM IS PAYED 4 IN BLOOD.

"Rednecks, man. They can't spell but they can vote. So I wanna go ta that Slavery Museum! Wouldn't that be a trip!"

"Haha!"

"Or we can get jobs there. As tour guides... Hey, there's a *7-11.* You mind if I stop ta get some smokes?"

"Okay. I'll get some toilet paper."

"Cigarettes an' toilet paper. We be two happenin' black men." Reggie pulls over.

"I thought you quit?"

"Yeah, well... But I'm beautiful, sexy, and empowered!"

A moment later, they're inside, and as Brayden gets the toilet paper, Reggie peers across the counter.

"*Marlboro Reds,* man," he says to the clerk.

"*Box.*" And then he hears a man's voice from behind him.

"*Selfish selfish selfish.*"

The clerk hands Reggie the cigarettes and his change, and the same man speaks again.

"You people jus' think about yerself." Reggie turns around.

"Excuse me?"

Behind him is a thirty-something white redneck with a soiled, too-small NASCAR tank top that exposes a hairy beer-gut. On his arms are what look like hastily done tattoos. On his face, a sparse-looking goatee and a few pimples. Clutched in his hands, a 12-pack of beer.

"Did you say something?" Reggie asks.

"I'm jus' sayin' you coloreds need ta know yer place, iz all."

"*What the...*

A second later, Brayden rushes to the counter.

"Sumthin' wrong?" he says. He looks at Reggie, then at the redneck.

"I'm jus' sayin' yer not real Americans."

"Come on," Brayden says to Reggie. He places the toilet paper back on a shelf as they walk away. But Reggie pauses in the doorway and looks back, the redneck still eyeballing him.

"Come on, man. Let's go."

Once outside, Reggie turns to Brayden.

"Do you fucking *believe* that shit?"

"I know. Here, let *me* drive."

"I'm good."

"You sure?"

"Yeah. Thanks, man." Reggie looks back at Brayden, dumbfounded. The next few minutes are spent in silence as they drive to Deco, Brayden's favorite bar. And a moment later, they're at a table near the wall, a waiter standing above them.

"I'll have a *G&T*," Brayden says.

"And you sir?" The waiter looks at Reggie. "Sir?"

"Um, *Jack... Daniel's.*"

"Ice?"

"Nah."

"No *beer?*" Brayden says as the waiter leaves.

"That redneck drinks the same kinda beer as me," Reggie says.

"..."

"What the fuck happened back there, man? I mean, I know they're *out* there, but..."

"I'm glad you didn't."

"I *couldn't!* I mean, I couldn't believe..."

He looks at his friend.

"I guess I'm no Black Panther."

"That... That's okay!"

The drinks arrive. Reggie raises his glass.

"To my best friend."

"Thanks."

They touch glasses. After a long sip, Reggie looks around the bar.

"So where's your girlfriend? Isn't she supposed ta meet us?"

Brayden looks at his watch, then glances at the door.

"She's late." He takes out his phone and sees that he got a text: "Something came up last minute. Can't make it. Sorry. Talk later?"

"What she say?"

"Something came up."

Reggie shrugs once, then takes another sip of his whiskey.

"Aren't you gonna say something?" Brayden says.

"Like how all women are lyin' bitches an' hoes?"

Reggie shrugs again. "I hope it works out for ya, man." He stares ahead as he clutches his drink, his mind still at the 7-Eleven.

Brayden looks over at the bar. He sees Renée, the night they met. How beautiful she was, and how she looked at him as if she really *saw* him. But now he sees a 20-something man-bun shaking up a cocktail. *Maybe I imagined her*, he thinks. And he looks back at the text. "Something came up last minute. Can't make it. Sorry. Talk later?"

He starts to send a reply: "Hey, that's okay. I'll call you later." But then one letter at a time, he deletes it and puts his phone away.

14

"I'm Derrick Kincaid. You've seen me starring in many blockbuster movies over the years, many of them fantastic fantasies. But I'm here today to speak about reality. We live in an America divided. As Abraham Lincoln said so many years ago, '*A house divided cannot stand*.' And all you have to do is look around and you'll see that it's still true. We need unity, not division. We need a change. And *I* will be that change... [*The camera pans back to reveal* Derrick Kincaid *sitting on a toilet bowl as if he's doing his business...*] Because America is going down the toilet... [Kincaid *reaches over and flushes it. The screen fades to black, to a voice-over with the flushing sound in the background...*] Paid for by Derrick Kincaid for President.

Alex turns off his smartphone and then opens the thick curtains in the womb-room, opening himself to the world. The Oval Office is abuzz as the camera crew and technicians get ready for this morning's photo op: the *pro forma* handshake to seal the deal with that repellent, hate-filled, racist, sexist, human-rights-violating President/Dictator-for-Life, Er Mahgerd of Hangry. Alex's distractions had succeeded in their original intent, which was to shine the light away from this meeting, but in the process, a fuse had been lit on a new civil war.

Outside the Oval Office, Brayden Carter appears.

"I'm here to see the President," he says.

Gladiola Gaze looks up from her desk.

"You should've been called. This morning is the meeting with the Hangarian President."

"Oh yeah. I forgot about that."

She looks up at this handsome young man, so full of hope and promise for a future that won't exist. Hopes, promises, and futures don't play well together and often have to be separated. And she thinks of her own son. He loved her once, but now it's a phone call every few weeks, a card on Mother's Day and Christmas. Was it even love anymore? She looks back at Brayden, suddenly sympathetic.

"I'll see what I can do," she says. She buzzes the intercom...

"Yes, Gladdy?"

"Mr. President, Brayden Carter is here for his Friday appointment."

"But it's the..."

And then Alex Rett sees the look on that racist Er Mahgerd's face when he's forced to shake hands with this young black, a shining example of America's *e pluribus unum-inity* (to coin a word).

"Ya know, Gladdy... Send him in."

"Yes sir." She looks up at the young intern. "You can go in now."

"Brayden! Good to see you."

"You too, sir."

"I was wondering if you'd like to stick around for the meeting. They're almost ready." Alex motions to the camera crew.

"The meeting with the President of Hangry, sir?" Brayden can hardly believe his ears.

"Sure... That is, if you don't mind being on TV."

"On *TV*? No sir." Brayden smiles. "I don't mind."

Ten minutes later, President Mahgerd stands before President

Rett with the look of a man forced to step in shit, smell it, then smile about it. Then a minute later, with the lights blazing and the cameras rolling, the director counts down: "In *three... two... (one)...*" And like a light switch turned on, Er Mahgerd flashes a radiant smile.

"Mr. President..."

"Er, it's so good to see you!" Alex reaches out and they warmly shake hands. And the instant they disengage, Er Mahgerd breathes a sigh of relief that the worst of this shit-eating nightmare is over, when President Rett says, "Brayden, come over here!" As the young man steps forward (with the cameras still rolling), Alex says, "I want you to meet my good friend, the President of Hangry, *Er Mahgerd...*" Then Alex turns to Mahgerd. "And Er, I'd like you to meet Brayden Carter, a shining example of our American youth." And like a demonic matchmaker, Alex motions for them to shake hands.

And with the glaring lights, the sweat on his brow, and the thought of shaking hands with this... *black boy*, Er Mahgerd feels his next breath sink into the pit of his stomach. The feeling of cloying black flesh against his skin. It's all he can do to keep the revulsion from showing on his face. And he summons up all his strength to extend his hand. A moment later, the lights go out and the ordeal is over. Er Mahgerd pivots in place and strides out of the Oval without even a fish-eyed glance at President Rett. With every step, he hears another *THWACK* of the cane coming down on the back of some poor homosexual black bastard. He's sure there's at least one or two in the State Prison in Dahoom, a block from Hangary's capitol building.

As the door closes and the camera crew packs its gear, Alex looks at his young intern.

"*That* went well."

"Yes!" Brayden says, exultant. "Thank you, sir."

"Better than sorting through sonograms and selfies, eh?"

"Yes sir! Much better."

"So you'll be on TV today," Alex says. "Are you excited?"

"Yes sir, I am.

And in that instant, another storm appears in the near-limitless sky of Alex Rett's brain.

"Brayden..."

"Sir?"

"I'll be in Richmond next Friday to close that asinine museum."

"Oh! Excellent, sir."

"So what do you think of it, the Slavery Museum?"

"Seriously, sir?"

"Yes, I want to know."

"Well sir, I think it's a *terrible* idea. And I *love* that you're putting an end to it. That's a great thing you're doing, Mr. President."

"Thank you, Brayden. You're a very thoughtful young man."

"Thank you, sir."

"Tell me, would you consider being my guest next Friday?" Alex asks. "Stand at my side as we do this historic thing in the name of civil rights and equality?"

In his mind, Alex can see the look on Ezra Banes's face. It was Ezra who told him about this young man in the first place. After this, ol' Ezra will be putty in his hands.

"Sir, it would be my honor."

"Excellent! We'll be making the announcement to the press today regarding the event. It's going to be *huge!*" the President says.

"You can talk to Gladdy for the details."

"Yes sir! Thank you! I will!"

As Brayden Carter leaves the Oval Office, he feels as if he's floating above the floor. And then his phone vibrates in his pocket announcing a text. He pauses in the hallway beneath the portrait of a pensive JFK and takes out his phone.

"Sorry about yesterday. Can I make it up to you tonight? My place? 9PM? Renée"

Brayden raises his head. He offers a smile to Jack Kennedy, which becomes a glow, which becomes a beckoning horizon. Then he turns to his phone as his fingers flash..."9PM. Tonight at your place. I'll be there!"

15

Brayden straightens his tie, his sleeves, and his pocket square, and then takes a long deep breath. A moment later, the door opens to candlelight and soft jazz. He sees Renée, like a wraith emerging from the shadows. She's wearing nothing but a see-through body-suit, and he feels himself gasp.

"Do you *like?*" she asks.

"Yes." He pushes the door shut behind him.

"I like this suit," she says. She takes his tie in her hand and pulls it like a leash, as she leads him through the candlelight to her bed.

Two hours later, after exploring the sexual geometry of their eager, supple, inexhaustible young bodies, they lie in bed beneath a single white sheet.

"That was... Oh boy."

"*Oh boy?*" Renée looks at him.

"It was so good. I need a cigarette... And I don't smoke."

"It wasn't too bad." She smiles.

Brayden remembers that he was going to ask her why she had canceled on him yesterday, but right now the only thing that mattered was that they had spent the last two hours like this. Everything else seemed insignificant.

"Hey," she says.

"Didn't you say you were going to be on TV?"

"Yeah, but when did I say that?"

"I think it was after you did me against the wall, but before you took me from behind on the floor."

"Oh yeah!"

She grabs the remote from the nightstand and turns on the TV.

CNN

"And from the Oval Office this morning, President Rett met with the President of Hangry, Er Mahgerd, during the Hangarian leader's visit to the White House.

[Cut to video footage showing the handshake of presidents...]

"Hey!" Renée says.

"There you are in the background!"

[Cuts back to news anchor...]

"In other news, Frederick Douglass-Jones, the radical New Black Panthers leader, said..."

She turns off the TV.

"I'm so proud of you, baby!"

"Thanks, but I hoped they were gonna show me shaking hands with that racist bastard."

"You shook *hands* with him?"

"It was Rett's idea, to piss off Mahgerd. You shoulda seen the look Mahgerd gave me!"

"Well *you* looked great!"

"Thanks. So guess what?"

"What?"

"You heard about Rett goin' to Richmond next Friday, right? To close the Slavery Museum?"

"Yeah."

"I'm going too!"

"What?"

"As the President's plus one!"

"Well, aren't *you* important?"

"Haha! I know, right!" Brayden smiles. "Actually, it's to chalk up political capital with Ezra Banes. For Rett, I mean. But *who cares?* I'll be right next to the President as he puts the wrecking ball to that museum!"

"My baby's goin' places!"

"The sky's the limit!" He looks at her.

"Hey, why don't you come with me?"

"What?"

"We can go to Richmond next Thursday! Have dinner. Stay at a nice hotel. You can bring the body-suit..."

Renée smiles.

"And then on Friday you can watch me hob-nob with my pal,

the Prez."

"That sounds great, baby."

"Good. I'll look up some restaurants... and find us a nice hotel."

"So you like the body-suit?"

Brayden takes a breath and lets it out as an expression of wonder. "I'm so glad."

As Renée seems to melt beneath the sheets, Brayden Carter feels her lips on his stomach, her tongue on his skin, and a tingling sensation as she moves further down. In a state of bliss and surrender, he closes his eyes.

16

As Carly Menteur (Brayden Carter's French ex-girlfriend) looks at Mr. Barrows, she realizes that she's never seen him wear anything but a suit. And she thinks this today because it's Saturday morning and they're in the depths of a vacant office building, in a hidden sub-basement, surrounded by reinforced concrete. But still, Mr. Barrows is dressed as if it were midnight on the *Grands Boulevards de Paris* and the night is young.

"It couldn't be simpler," he says, as he shows her the tie pin. An iridescent opal set in a jet-black base. Elegant yet unassuming. He hands it to her and she feels its weight.

"It's so light," she says. She hands it back.

Mr. Barrows walks into the next room, connected to this room by a steel door and a large window made of thick, shatter-proof glass. In the next room is a tableau of mannequins, as if they were onstage. Five faceless figures gather round a central dummy seated in a wheelchair. Mr. Barrows walks over to the mannequin standing to the left of the wheelchair—a male figure, about six feet tall, wearing a dark blue suit. He takes hold of its tie and sticks the tie pin through it till it's fastened. Then he walks back into the first room and closes the thick steel door.

"It's become something else," he says. He picks up a small object from the table—a remote control the size of a key fob. He shows it to Carly, then puts it in his pocket, concealed.

"He was supposed to be Nixon, not JFK." He laughs.

"Race riots and cities on fire... We can't have *that*." And then, with Carly moving alongside, he steps up to the thick shatter-proof glass. There's a moment's pause, then he presses the remote. Inside the other room, there's a massive explosion, although the room they're in is so well-insulated that they feel only a slight vibration, like a single distant heartbeat. Mr. Barrows presses a button on the wall now. Fans are activated within the other room and the smoke is sucked out through an exhaust system. And what they see after the smoke clears is nothing but the charred, obliterated remains of everything that had been there just moments before.

Mr. Barrows turns to Carly Menteur and offers a slight smile, as if he were about to remark on what a lovely day it is. He takes out an identical tie pin from his pocket and hands it to her. She looks at it once, then puts it in her purse.

As they leave the room, Mr. Barrows pauses to turn off the lights. They ride up the elevator in silence until they're at ground level. And once on the street, they wordlessly part, headed in opposite directions.

17

"Good morning..." Jules Tippler looks into the camera.

"It's Sunday and this is *The Jules Tippler Show*. Today my guest is the host of the hugely popular political panel show, *Get Mauled!*... Ric Maul."

"Nice to see you, Jules."

"You too, Ric. So, a lot has happened since your last appearance, which was two months ago."

"Has it only been *two months*?" Ric laughs.

"With this Presidency, a month seems like a *year!*"

"I know! I wish he'd take up golf. Give us the weekend off."

"It would have to be miniature golf," says Ric Maul.

"Haha! So in this age of fake news and alternative facts, many Americans are turning to late night comedians such as yourself to understand what's going on."

"Scary, isn't it?"

"So who can we trust?"

"You're not as old as I am, Jules, but I remember when there were only three networks."

"Yes! And everyone trusted Walter Cronkite. But now anyone with a *smartphone* can weigh in. "

"The Internet has changed the conversation."

"But was it even a *conversation?*" Jules Tippler asks. "When Walter Cronkite spoke, people listened."

"The key to *that*," says Ric Maul, "were journalistic standards. But now, because of the Internet, everything's at the bottom."

"And the result is a public Twitter battle between an eight-year-old and the President of the United States!"

"An eight-year-old alleged drug-dealer pornographer." Ric smiles. "But he doesn't *Tweet* anymore, the President."

"Yes, the *Tweet Fast.*"

"So how do we know what's true and what's fake? And this comes back to people turning to comedians for the news."

"It's like *The Fool* in Shakespeare," says Ric Maul. "*The Fool* was the only one who could speak the truth to the King."

"So your function now is to be *The Fool?*"

"It's a noble occupation." Ric smiles. "To be the truth-teller. And it's in Shakespeare, so it *must* be good!"

"So why *did* people believe back then in Walter Cronkite?"

"Because people back then were the same as people today."

"Hmm?"

"They're *busy!*" Ric says.

"They don't *want* to think for themselves!"

"Ha!"

"So they made this deal with Walter Cronkite. *If you tell me what's what, I'll watch your show.* And it worked because, as I said, there were standards to be upheld. It was a different world then. We could focus on a limited number of things."

"But today, it's everyone talking at everyone else."

"All at the same time!"

"Yes."

"The focus is gone," says Ric Maul, "and noise is coming from every direction. And everyone says they speak the truth. And that makes the truth itself meaningless."

"Hmm."

"I mean, how can the truth compete with the *Next Big Ass?* Or *The Enema Challenge?*"

"Haha! So do you think *you'll* do *The Enema Challenge?*"

"Ha! It *is* for a good cause," says Ric. "And what was that the other day with Derrick Kincaid?"

"That's how someone announces their candidacy for President these days."

Ric Maul shakes his head.

"It seems that we've lost our focus," says Jules Tippler. "We're becoming a vicarious society, a vicarious culture."

"Exactly! Everyone's focus is *this*..." Ric gazes at an imaginary phone in his hand, and then he looks at Jules Tippler. "I think within our lifetimes we'll witness an evolutionary leap. Human beings getting these really small, super dexterous thumbs."

"Ha!"

"And *texting* will become an Olympic event."

"Haha! Maybe so. I hear the *President* is really good at that."

"Tiny hands." Ric smiles. "And it's solely to keep us separate from the reality that's all around us. We filter it through our phones."

"So what do you think of Alex Rett these days?"

"Well, it's symbolic of that whole vicarious culture. Here's our President, in that *Ovum Office* of his."

"And you were the first to coin that phrase, by the way," Jules says. "But *Saturday Night In-Yer-Face* made it a staple."

"And look what happened to them!"

"So what do you think of *that*? What happened. How a comedy show can spark a deadly riot."

"Well, outside of the fact that people died and the studio was trashed and Vern Ankles fled the country as a fugitive..."

"Haha!"

"Put it this way. A hundred years ago, people would become outraged by an art exhibit or a piece of music. But *now*... I mean, it's like that song, *Comfortably Numb*. I guess I thought we were beyond caring enough to cause a riot."

"So you think it was a *good* thing?"

"Now the hate mail will pour in and they'll wanna cancel my show and make me issue a public apology, but *yeah*. It showed me that there's still some life in us."

"As a society?"

"That we're not all mindless drones."

"Which brings to mind this person I had never heard of till a few days ago, but now he's everywhere."

"That New Black Panthers guy."

"Yes! What's his name? Frederick Douglass?"

"Frederick Douglass-Jones," Ric Maul says.

"I'm trying to get him on my show."

"So what do you make of him?"

"Here again, I have to go back to the Sixties and early Seventies. We had people then in the political realm who were dangerous. And not physically, *per se*, but through their ideas. Here were people who thought for themselves. Who looked around and said this isn't right and here's why and then they'd do something about it. There's a *truth* in this. A truth that's real, that people can feel in themselves, that they know isn't some *bullshit*." Ric looks over at Jules Tippler. "Can I say that on your show? I'm used to *HBO*."

"It's Sunday morning," Jules says.

"Everyone's at church."

"Haha!"

"But what happened to *them?*" Jules asks. "These... well, these radical heroes, because it's heroic, isn't it? To tell the truth like that, like they did."

"Absolutely! And what happened to *them?* Bobby Kennedy and Malcolm X and MLK... the list goes on. They *all* met a bad end."

"And why do you think that is, Ric? Because people can't handle the truth?"

"Most people have no idea what that is. And the few who do control the narrative."

"Like..."

"Well, if a handful of people own most of the newspapers and TV stations, then what they say might be a bit skewed."

"But it's *always* been this way," says Jules Tippler. "Hearst said, '*You provide the pictures, I'll provide the war.*' That was a hundred years ago. And it's *still* about money, greed, and self-interest."

"But now it's that on *steroids,*" says Ric Maul. "And there's six billion more people. That's a lot more pockets to pick."

"So do we just go quietly into the night?"

"I think about what happened on *Saturday Nite In-Yer-Face.* This sudden outburst of... I don't know, everything we've been holding in for *decades!* Like this painful, congested, backed-up, all-the-way-inside-your-large-intestine shit!"

"Haha! Sunday morning!" Jules smiles.

"If you can look past the *tragedy* of it," Ric says, "there's hope there."

"Hope..."

"That we're not done yet. As human beings. That we still have some fight left in us."

"Hmm..."

"You remember that movie from the Seventies... *Network...*"

"Of course!"

"I was in college then, back when colleges were cool." Ric smiles. "Practically every night after that movie came out, students would throw open their dorm room windows and shout, '*I'm as mad as hell! And I'm not gonna take this anymore!*'"

"Yes!"

"But somehow we've forgotten that... spirit. And you can look at it from a historical perspective. Each decade gives birth to the next. So we get the Eighties: Ronald Reagan, *Miami Vice,* and really great... um, distractions," Ric offers a knowing smile. "And before ya know it, we have George Dubya and everyone's dumb and music sucks and the radicals can't get laid anymore!"

"So there's no upside anymore to thinking for yourself?"

"Unless you have your own show!"

"Ha!"

"I mean, if it wasn't for that, I'd *never* get any!"

"So, getting back to that New Black Panthers guy... do you think he's the real deal?"

"I don't know. These days, it's all about LIKES and going viral and doing *The Enema Challenge* and having shit-tons of money."

"So what about Bobby Kennedy then?"

"Well, for him, money wasn't an issue. He could go *beyond* it. Back then, there weren't all these *billionaires* everywhere measuring their bank accounts. I mean, there was this crazy Howard Hughes peeing in jars and growing out his fingernails like Fu Manchu. But now, if you're just a *millionaire*, you're a loser."

"So you're a loser then."

"*Touché.*" Ric smiles.

"But isn't this the reality of getting older? Of outliving the times we felt were better, to see times where we no longer fit in, that seem worse?"

"What's that line, 'If Jesus lived long enough, he would've re-nounced all of his teachings'?"

"Haha! So I know you laughed when I brought up the *Road to Damascus* in relation to Alex Rett."

"Well, yeah." Ric smiles. "But I'll give you that he *has* changed. But I'm not sure if it's for the better."

"Why not?"

"It's like what we talked about before, our vicarious culture. Our President, Alexander Rett, is responsible for governing a big part of this world, right? Yet he's separate from it." Ric looks over at Jules Tippler. "I know you and he have become buds of late."

"I *do* think he's undergone a transformation. And I *do* think it's for the better. I mean, we had a pint-sized Nixon!"

"Hey! *I'm* the comedian!" says Ric Maul.

"Fair enough. But now with his most recent speeches, he sounds more like JFK."

"And he met with Er Mahgerd and they shook hands and the

news barely covered it."

"And everyone *knows* how bad that regime is," says Jules Tippler.

"What we have is government by distraction," says Ric. "Wasn't it just a week ago when everyone wanted Rett's little head for agreeing to meet with Mahgerd? And suddenly we have this Slavery Museum controversy and the Malique Kilvain verdict and no one even *remembers* that Mahgerd was coming."

"But neither of those things are connected to the White House. And President Rett is going to Richmond this Friday to close the Museum down."

"Yeah, well *that's* a good thing," says Ric. "I mean, the *Slavery Museum? Seriously?* And those Republican senators who supported it!"

"And *praised* it!" Jules laughs.

"But by next Friday, no one will even remember that they *did* this! It's like everyone is bulletproof. Remember Rett's predecessor, and all that *he* got away with?"

"So, getting back to Alex Rett, what do you make of him so far? Of his presidency?"

"I like him as a person," says Ric. "I mean, I've met him, and I *like* the little guy!"

"Haha!"

"And it's funny, because sometimes he seems really sharp, like whip-smart, and other times not so much. Superficial even. And I guess it's because he's FOTUS after all." Ric Maul pauses for effect. "*We voted for an effing fetus!*... America, ya gotta love us!" He turns to Jules Tippler. "And then, when you look at what he's actually *done*... The *Protective Death-Ray Initiative*... The *AWS*."

"The Automatic Weapons in Schools bill."

"Like *that'll* pass. And that Dafoe bill, and health care... What has he done, outside of making people regret not voting for Mallory?"

"Well, I see him a bit differently," Jules says, "as you know."

"I know. And I *want* to give him a chance, but..."

"So what about lately? His speech denouncing Mahgerd?"

"I'll give him that," says Ric. "It was a good speech."

"It was inspiring."

"I wouldn't go *that* far. But regardless, one speech doesn't make a presidency."

"Hmm..."

"But what all this shows is that America is *still* the land of opportunity, where even a white male fetus can *blah blah blah...*"

"Haha!"

"Fetus privilege!" Ric smiles. "But I'm wondering when the novelty will wear off."

"Well, this Friday he'll be in Richmond to close down the Slavery Museum."

"Yes, he's our Lincoln."

"Thanks for being with us, Ric."

"My pleasure."

Jules Tippler looks into the camera.

"My guest today has been Ric Maul."

[Alex clicks off the TV...] I hate that Ric Maul.

18

FOX NEWS

"Matilda Walz, a kindergarten teacher in Lincoln, Nebraska is singing the praises of President Rett for his self-imposed *Tweet Fast.* *[Cut to interview with Walz...]*

'Kids today, even kindergarteners, are glued to their phones. When I was a kid, I would read a book. You remember those? Or I'd go outside and play with my friends. But now, children are sending *Tweets*, checking *Facebook*, or worst of all, taking and posting *selfies*. We're creating a nation of narcissists! I try to follow the President's example. I put down the phone and watch a good educational documentary. And I try to get my kids to do the same.'

"And in a related story, a class of first graders in Moose Jaw, Alaska is petitioning the state government to change the name of Denali, the highest mountain in North America, to Mt. Rett in support of their president. Word from the State Capital in Juneau is that Governor Sally Pooner is considering it."

Nice! Shoulda had *Sally P.* for my Veep. *[Alex changes the channel...]*

CNN
"This breaking news... There has been an assassination attempt made on the life of Hangry's President, Er Mahgerd."

What the...

"Mahgerd had just returned from his trip to the United States where he met with President Rett. He was attending a public caning in Hangry's capital city of Dahoom just hours before, when a member of the outlawed SHM burst through the crowd and fired six shots. The assailant has been identified as Salam Ionrye. SHM, which translates as Free Hangry Now, is a radical splinter group opposed to Er Mahgerd's oppressive regime. President Mahgerd is listed in critical condition, and Vice-President Orm Mahgoodnis has declared a day of fasting and atonement. The would-be assassin, Salam Ionrye, was killed by security forces during his assault on President Mahgerd."

[Alex is momentarily inert, and then he calls up the Daily Briefs *on his smartphone...]*
Borneo threatens East Borneo with nuclear strike.
Assassination attempt on Hangry's President Mahgerd.

I gotta start reading these sooner. *[He checks his texts...*

To President Alexander Rett:
Some nutjob tried to kill Er Mahgerd. Shot at him six times but only one bullet hit him. Superficial wound in arm. Nutjob killed by security. Shot 27 times. Also, there's some woman claiming that you drugged her in order to have sex with her fetus. It's beyond nuts, but that's the kind of thing that's reported, so I wanted to give you a heads up. If it gains traction, we can discuss damage control.

Chopper

What the fuck?! Ya try and get a decent night's sleep and the world goes to hell. *[Something on TV captures his attention...]*

CNN

"This just in... A twenty-four year-old African-American woman, DeeLishess Cameroon, has brought forth allegations against President Alexander Rett, stating that he drugged her and then tried to rape her unborn fetus.

Alex's face becomes a pained grimace. *[A new text from Tim appears...]*

To President Alexander Rett:
That crazy woman is on Dr. Phyllis right now, sir.
Chopper

[Alex switches to the channel...]

"So da Prezident, he like, callz me up ta, ya know, like *see* him!"
"The President of the United States..." says Dr. Phyllis.
"Yeah, *fo' real!* An' he haz dis here limousine like pick me up an' *[censored]*."
"A limousine?"
"Yeah! Like one o' dem stretch *[censored]*. An' it takes me ta dis, like, secret door in da back o' sum statue."
"A statue?"
"Yeah, one o' dem *white people* statues o' sum Gen'ral or sum *[censored]*. An' in da back o' dat statue, der'z dis door, see? An' dis secret passage takes me all da way ta dat office o' hiz."
"A secret passage took you to the Oval Office..."
"Yeah, why you keep repeetin' everthin' I say?"
"I'm sorry," says Dr. Phyllis.
"So I'm in dat office, an' der'z dat fetus guy who'z da Prezident."
"Alexander Rett..."
"*[censored]* yeah!

"And what happened next?"

"Dat fetus Prezident, he pourz me sum brandy."

"Do you remember what *kind* of brandy?" Dr. Phyllis asks.

"Courvoisier, man. An' so I drinks it, ya know, cuz it's da *Prezident* an' *[censored]*."

"But why did the President contact you in the first place, Ms. Cameroon?"

"Ha! You ken call me *Dee-Lishus!*"

"Okay." Dr. Phyllis laughs. "DeeLishus."

"*Deeee-Lishus!* Cuz I am!" DeeLishus Cameroon says, with a snap of her finger. *[Laughter from the studio audience.]*

"But I'm curious as to why President Rett contacted you in the first place, DeeLishus."

"I dunno. I guess he heard 'bout my baby."

"Your unborn child?"

"Yeah! An' he wanna *get him summa dat!* Ha! An' I sed *why not!*"

"You said *why not?*"

"Cuz maybe he *marry* her an' *[censored]!* Den I be related ta da *[censored] Prezident!* An' I ken live in dat White House!"

"Hmm, so what happened *next*, DeeLishus?"

"Well, I drank me summa dat Courvoisier, an' suddenly I don' feel so good, ya feel me? An' I starts ta git up, see, cuz I be drugged bafoh."

"You were drugged before? At some other time?"

"Yeah. Two er *three* times."

"And you think that this time the President of the United States drugged you?"

"*[censored]* yeah! So I starts ta stand up, but I gits all dizzy an' *[censored]* an' I pass da *[censored]* out."

"You passed out," says Dr. Phyllis.

"Then what happened?"

"Well, I wakes up an' I feelz sumthin' on my belly, so I looks up an' I seez *dis!*" DeeLishus Cameroon pulls up her shirt to reveal a vertical scar of a fresh wound about seven inches long, running up her pregnant belly. The studio audience gasps. Dr. Phyllis stares at the scar as the camera zooms in.

"So... what happened?" Dr. Phyllis asks.

"He had one o' dem White House doctors start ta cut me open!"

[More gasps from the audience.]

"So'z he ken take out my baby an' have *sex* wit it!"

[Even more gasps.]

What the quadruple fuck!?

DeeLishus Cameroon looks right into the camera now. "Da President tried ta rape my baby!"

[An uproar from the audience.]

"We'll be right back after these commercial messages," says Dr. Phyllis.

[Alex sends a text...]

To Tim Chopper
Watching Dr. Phyllis. WTF?
Alex

[Alex looks back at the TV...]

"So were the doctors there trying to cut you open, when you woke up?" Dr. Phyllis asks.

"*[censored]* yeah! An' I looks et wut dey wuz doin' an' I sed, '*You keep yer [censored] hands offa my baby!*'"

"Then what happened?"

"One 'o dem doctors, he sez 'Why she awake?' An' da udder one sez '*[censored] if I know!*' But o' course he din't say it *zackly* like det cuz he'z a doctor." She smiles.

"Of course," says Dr. Phyllis. "And was President Rett there?"

"*Hell* yeah! An' he sez ta dem doctors, 'You idiots!' an' 'Get the *[censored]* out!' An' so dey gets der white ass *outta* there!"

"And what did the President do then?"

"He ran back inside datwombthing, ya know, witdaglassan' *[censored]*."

"The womb-room."

"Yeah! Da *womb-room!*"

"An what did you do?"

"I looks et my stomach an' it's all bleedin' an' *[censored]*."

"So they never actually opened you up."

"No! Cuz I woke my black ass up! Cuz if I *din't*, den da Prezident woulda bin rapin' my baby!"

[More outcries from the studio audience.]

"So I grabs me dis here napkin an' I puts it on my stomach." DeeLishus Cameroon holds up a white napkin covered in dried blood stains. The camera zooms in to show the Presidential Seal, partially obscured by blood.

"That's a Presidential napkin," says Dr. Phyllis.

"*[censored] yeah* it iz! An' so I stands up wit dis here napkin holdin' in the blood an' I sez, '*[censored]* you, Mr. Prezident!' an' I gets my black ass outta dere!"

"You got out..."

"Tru dat secret passage."

"The secret passage in the statue..."

"*[censored]* yeah! Den I went ta the PO-Leese ta tell 'em 'bout da Prezident druggin' me an' tryin' ta rape my baby an' *[censored]*."

"That is indeed a harrowing tale," says Dr. Phyllis.

"Harrowing indeed!" DeeLishus says. "I ain't never bin dis harrowed in ma whole damn life!"

"I can imagine."

[The intercom buzzes...]

"Mr. President?"

"Yes Gladdy..."

"There are all these reporters here, sir. Something about an alleged sexual assault..."

"Get rid of them.

[He gets another text from Tim...]

To President Alexander Rett:

Here's the headline of today's New York Post, sir. I'm on my way to WH. html:rettbabyrapernewyorkpostawesomenews

Chopper

[Alex clicks on the link...]

NEW YORK POST

"The President Tried To Rape my Baby!"

I hate Mondays. *[Alex presses the intercom...]*

"Yes, Mr. President?"

"Gladdy, when Tim Chopper arrives, send him right in."

"Yes sir."

"Oh Gladdy..."

"Sir?"

"Send some flowers to Er Mahgerd."

"I already did, sir."

"You're the best!"

[Alex looks back at the Daily Briefs...]

Borneo threatens East Borneo with nuclear strike.

Assassination attempt on Hangry's President Mahgerd.

So why are there *two* "asses" in "assassination"? Certainly one is enough for any word. And that word *"asinine,"* which really *needs* an "ass," doesn't have *any*. The English language is dumb. And I know why there's a "b" on the end of "dum," because if you leave it out, then they know you are.

[Alex's fingers flash over his smartphone...]

"Siri?"

"Good morning, Mr. President. Rough day so far, sir."

"Yeah, Mondays. So Siri..."

"Yes, Mr. President?"

"Why are there two asses in the word assassination?"

"Checking on why there are two asses in... The word *'assassin'* derives from a secret Persian death squad from the 11th and 12th centuries called the '*Hashshashishin*' meaning '*hashish eaters*'."

"So it has nothing to do with asses then... neither one, nor two."

"Apparently not, sir."

"Okay. Thanks, Siri."

The door to the Oval Office swings open and the President's Chief-of-Staff, Tim Chopper, walks in.

"Tim... What the fuck?"

"She's obviously running a scam, sir. And those White House napkins? You can get them at the gift shop."

"I know, but the story's all *over* the place!"

(The irony isn't lost on Alex Rett that this woman is getting famous by being on *Dr. Phyllis*.)

"We can't kill her..." the President says.

"What about a press conference, sir, where Wiley refutes it as fake news and sensationalism? And then he puts the focus back on this Friday, with your trip to Richmond to close the Slavery Museum."

"Yes, that could work. So what did you find on this woman?"

"DeeLishus Cameroon... Twenty-four. A welfare mom with seven children by eight fathers."

"How is that even possible?"

"A mix-up with DNA, sir. She's presently collecting child support from four of the eight. The other four are in prison."

"Mother of the Year."

"Indeed, sir."

"Okay, Tim. Talk to Wiley. Set it up ASAP."

"Yes sir."

[An hour later, Alex receives another text from Tim...]

To President Alexander Rett:

Thought you'd want to know about this, sir. Some rapper named XYZ just released this song. It's going viral. Link enclosed...

html:xyzrapperprezidentfetusraper

Chopper

I *hate* when things go viral.

[Alex clicks on the link to the rich and famous rapper XYZ's *brand new song, written and recorded just minutes ago:* "Prezident Fetus"...]*

(Intro...) Yer a nasty boy, Lil' Alex... The Rettster, The Sex-Meister, Grandmaster-A, *uh-huh*...(the beat drops...)Yer Prezident, da rezident o' this present porno palace wit dis phallus like a nightstick. I'll do ya all *real* thick, wit a pile-drivin' cannon all quick an' thick an' can ya Lick my fuse explosive? Dat shit ain't corrosive. Better than a slurpee when it blows inside yer furpie. Drips like a placenta, like dat painting in yer office as ya fill her fuckin' orifice! Fist her fetus ass, I don't mean ta sound crass. Yer the biggest fuckin' dick,ya do things make people sick, like *cut* sum poor bitch open so *you* ken do sum gropin' put da moves on an em-bryoya think her mom's yer *fat ho!* Do any shit ya like, oh yer a fuckin' Psych-O! Do any shit ya like, oh yer a fuckin' Psych-O! Do any shit ya like, oh yer a fuckin' Psych-O! *Prezident Fetus...* Ha! Ha-Ha! Ha! Yer *Prezident Fetus...* Yer *Prezident Fetus...* Yer *Prezident Fetus...*

What the fuck?... How'd he do it so fast?

(An hour later, from the William McKinley Room, *the hastily assembled White House Press Conference is about to begin...*

[Press Secretary Wiley DeSembler *stands before the mass of salivating, apoplectic journalists...]*

Journalists: *[en masse]* Wiley! Wiley! Wiley!

Wiley: *[points to one...]*

Essex: Emily Essex, *Newsweek...* What is the White House's response to President Rett being a baby rapist?

Crowd: *[outcries of indignation...]*

Wiley: *[shakes head...]* Can anything be more preposterous?

Essex: So you're saying it's true then?

Wiley: ...*[amazed]* Of course it's not *true!* I'm saying it's beyond preposterous! *Seriously,* Emily?

Simon: Samantha Simon, *Time...* The woman in question, DeeLishus Cameroon, has a seven-inch cut on her pregnant belly. She claims the White House doctors tried to open her up so that President Rett could...

Crowd: *[outcries of indignation...]*

Simon: *[continues...]* So President Rett could have sex with her unborn fetus.

Crowd: *[more outcries...]*

Wiley: *[dumbfounded]* Is this the level of questions we have?

Simon: So you're denying it then?

Wiley: I'm denying it because it never happened.

Essex: So how do you explain the seven-inch wound on her stomach?

Wiley: I don't know... Self-inflicted?

Crowd: *[more cries of outrage...]*

Legges: Harriet Legges, *Feminists & Fists*... So instead of coming clean and admitting the crime, you're hiding behind the protective wall of patriarchy and white privilege...

Wiley: The *what?* I don't even know what that means. And there *is* no crime. And consequently, nothing to come clean about. *[points to another...]*

Andrist: Annika Andrist, *XX Magazine*...

Wiley: Yes, Miss Andrist...

Andrist: *[offended]* It's *Ms*...

Wiley: Okay, what's your question?

Andrist: Will the President be facing felony rape charges after he resigns?

Wiley: *[shakes head...]* There is no rape. There was no rape. So there will not be any rape *charges*. The story is a sensationalized attempt at getting publicity by the woman in question. DeeLishus Cameroon. We're in the process of getting a *Psych Eval* on her as we speak.

Andrist: So a woman cries for help and justice and you shut her up by calling her *crazy?* *[outrage from the feminists present...]*

Wiley: You're hysterical.

Andrist: *[eyes light up...]* See! See what I mean! What the fuck, Wiley?! Who *are* these women?

Smith: Cornelius Smith, *BLM Magazine*...

Oh no! Not some *black guy!*

Smith: *[continues...]* With tensions at an all-time high between Blacks and Whites, and with Newark and other U.S. cities in flames, was the rape of this Black woman a callous attempt at...

Wiley: *[irate]* For the last time, there has been no *rape!*

Biggs: Manly Biggs, *Modern Hip-Hop...*

Biggs: *[continues...]* What is your response to *XYZ's* new song about the rape, entitled "*Prezident Fetus*"? I hate that *XYZ*.

Wiley: I haven't heard it. How could... How could he have gotten a song out so quickly?

Good freaking question!

Wiley: *[points to scary-looking Black dude wearing dark sunglasses and a beret...]*

Douglass-Jones: Frederick Douglass-Jones, *New Black Panthers...*

Not *him* again!

Douglass-Jones: *[continues...]* It's my civic duty to say, in the name of justice and fair-play, that this whole rape thing is a fraud! A fake! A fabrication!

Crowd: *[uproarious outcries...]* What the...

Douglass-Jones: *[continues...]* I know for a *fact* that the woman in question, DeeLishus Cameroon, is a scam artist.

Crowd: *[cries and moans...]*

Douglass-Jones: *[continues...]* And that she lied her Black ass off to get publicity so she could become famous like that "*Cash Me Outside*" chick.

Crowd: *[deafening uproar...]*

Douglass-Jones: *[continues...]* Sisters like her give us a bad name when we're fighting for *real* things, not made-up shit. Like the Slavery Museum, which our President, Alexander Rett, is closing down this Friday in Richmond. This couldn't be more important, and it's what we *should* be talking about. Not some crazy bitch making false accusations so she can go viral.

Crowd: *[erupts in cheers and applause...]*

Ho-lee shit!

Wiley: Thank you, Mr. Douglass-Jones. And yes, the Slavery Museum will be closed by President Rett on Friday. And this will be a huge step towards equal rights and justice for all Americans. Thank you. *[Wiley hurriedly steps from the podium and rushes off...]*

What the hell just happened? *[At this, Tim Chopper appears...]*
"Tim! Did you see that?"
"I saw it on my phone, sir."
"What the bloody hell?"
"I don't know, sir. But that Black Panther guy..."
"Saved our ass... He's just down the hall at the Press Conference, Tim. See if he'll come to the Oval, like *ASAP.*"
"Will do, sir."
"And find out about this *XYZ* rapper sumbitch. We need to go all singing-in-the-rain on his modern Hip-Hop ass."
"Yes, sir. I'll get on it immediately."
"Good, Tim. Thanks."
As Tim Chopper leaves, Alex presses the intercom.
"Yes, Mr. President?"
"Have Manny come in."
"Right away, sir."
[Five minutes later... Manny hands the President an extra dry martini.]
"*Gracias*, Manolo... Umm, *perfecto*," he says after a long sip.
"I'm glad, sir. I hope next Monday is less eventful."
"Yes, today has been totally fucked up."
"It has indeed, sir."
"Call me *Alex*, please..."
"Yes, sir. I mean, *Alex.*"

[Tim Chopper sends the President another text...]

To President Alexander Rett:
Check out CNN, sir.
Chopper

[Alex turns on the TV...]

CNN

"We've just received this video that refutes completely the allegations the young woman, DeeLishus Cameroon, made earlier today, that President Rett drugged her and tried to rape her unborn fetus.

[Cut to video of very poor quality, done on a cheap cell phone. We see DeeLishus Cameroon *with her shirt off, exposing her bare, pregnant belly as she talks to someone off-camera. She takes a Sharpie and draws a seven-inch vertical line on her skin...]*

'So dis *[censored]* bes' not hurt to much!' *[DeeLishus Cameroon]*

'Well, ya took summa *deez*, rite?' *[A man's voice off-camera...]*

'*[censored]* yeah! I took three.'

'Well, have sum *more!*' *[He hands her more pills. She puts them in her mouth, then washes them down with a bottle of cheap whiskey called* Thunder Dog...]*

'Okay, ya ready?' *[Man's voice off-camera...]*

'Yeah, so how much ya think we git?'

'For the Prezident rapin' yer unborn fetus? *[censored]*, man! Like millions! Maybe even billions!'

'Awrite! So cut dis *[censored]* up, mother*[censored]*!'

...[DeeLishus Cameroon motions to her own belly...]

'But I ken't like, cut yer dam stomach an' hold the dam phone et da same time. Ya feel me?'

'Well, gimme the dam phone!' *[The phone switches hands.* DeeLishus Cameroon *holds it now, as the unknown man starts to cut her skin along the Sharpie line...]*

"The rest of the video is too graphic to be shown here. But this was where the wound on her stomach originated, as part of a get-rich-quick scheme to extort the President of the United States."

"Good news, sir!"

"Yes, thank you, Manny. If you'll excuse me for *one moment...*" *[Alex's fingers flash over his phone...*

To Tim Chopper:

Find out who sent the video.

Alex

Alex turns to Manny. "Another one of these."

"Coming right up, Alex."

[The intercom buzzes...]

"Mr. President?"

"Yes, Gladdy..."

"Frederick Douglass-Jones is here to see you, sir."

[A moment later...] "You wanted to see me, Mr. President?"

"Let's cut the shit," Alex says.

"You saved my ass at the press conference. So my question is... Why?"

"Iz all 'bout politics, ain' it, Missah Prezident, suh? 'Bout collectin' favuhs an' cashin' in?"

Alex stares at this New Black Panther as he tries to comprehend him.

"Please, sit down, Mr. Douglass-Jones."

"Call me Fred." He takes off his sunglasses and looks around the room.

"Fred..." Alex smiles.

"That's some freaky shit, man!" Fred motions to Alex's mom with the tubes and wires.

"Yes. Would you like a drink? Oh, my manners... Fred, this is Mr. Vargas."

"What's happenin'?"

"*Mucho gusto, señor.*"

"Ya got any Scotch?" Fred asks.

Manny searches his cart and brings out a bottle of 25-year-old Macallan. He presents it to Frederick Douglass-Jones, but he scrunches up his face.

"Eh... Ya got any *A'Chailleach 27*, man? That stuff 's the shit!"

"I'm sorry, Fred. Just this."

"Forgive me," Alex says, "but I didn't expect you to be such a connoisseur."

"What, a brother can't like Scotch?" He turns to the President. "That's fucking racist."

"No it's not. Is it?" Alex asks.

"Sure."

Alex turns to Manny.

"Is it fucking racist, Manny?"

Manny gives him a good-natured, well-meaning nod in the affirmative, and Alex lets out a sigh.

"That'll be fine, Manny." Fred motions to the Macallan.

"Ice?"

"Nah."

"Water?"

"A few drops, man."

At that moment, Alex receives another text from Tim Chopper. "Excuse me..." Alex's fingers fly over his smartphone.

"He's pretty fast on that phone," Fred says to Manny.

"*Muy rapido.*"

To President Alexander Rett:

Video sent in by Douglass-Jones.

Chopper

Alex turns to his new best friend.

"So, it appears that I owe you a favor, Mr. Douglass-Jones."

"You owe me *two*, Mr. President."

"Hmm, so where'd you get the video?"

"Hey, it's who ya know, right? The secret to success."

"Yes. And now you know me."

Fred offers a self-satisfied nod, then sips his Scotch.

"How's your drink?"

"Not bad. Thanks, Mr. President."

"Call me Alex. So you *know* I'm a big fan of the Black Panthers. But the ones from the *old days*, when they were badass... before they self-destructed."

"With a little help from J. Edgar. Ya feel me?"

"So you're here in the Oval Office, sipping Scotch whiskey with the President and his good friend, Manolo Vargas."

"I am indeed."

"So what's your game, Fred? What do you want?"

"Power... Money..."

"So, the usual." Alex seems disappointed.

"No fame and glory?"

"Yeah, that too."

"So the New Black Panthers ain't so new."

"We're both part of the same hypocrisy, Mr. President."

"Did you just quote *The Godfather* to me?"

"*Godfather 2*, Alex."

"Hmm, we might get along after all."

"You *need* someone like me," Fred says.

"Do I? I know enough cynics and sell-outs."

"I'm your inside man." His eyes sharpen into self-serving slits. "This whole black-white shit. You give me the power and I'll control it for you. And they ain't *never* gonna burn Newark again. *B-lee dat!*"

"Please, continue..."

"And you'll be the President that united a broken and divided nation."

"And you can help me do that..."

"Hey, you can do most anything if ya got a charismatic, articulate leader the people wanna get behind."

"And you're that leader..."

"What do *you* think?"

"I think you might be," the President says.

"But we've had articulate, charismatic leaders before. They were all destroyed."

"Yeah, and they was destroyed because they went *against* the Powers That Be. You and me, we work *together*, but behind the scenes, ya feel me? We'll serve the same agenda."

"And what is that again?" Alex asks.

"Power and money, man! And fame and glory. And as an ancillary benefit, we'll unite the damn United States."

"Ancillary... good word."

"Dat's cuz I be one articulate muthafuckin' Nigga!" Fred smiles.

And then he smiles at Manny. And then he looks at Alex.

"You are indeed," says Alex.

"So... we got us a deal?"

Alex, holding up his glass, motions for a toast. "To the New Black Panthers..."

"You my Nigga!" says Frederick Douglass-Jones. They bring their glasses together.

"I like that little martini glass, man." And then the big painting on the wall catches his eye. "Hey man, is that placenta?"

"Haha! Yes it is!" Alex smiles. "A connoisseur of Scotch *and* modern art."

Fred walks over to examine the painting. He bends down to look up at it. He contorts and cranes his neck. His head rotates 359 degrees as he takes it all in.

"This placenta painting is the *shit*, man!"

"I'm glad you like it."

"And it's *huge!* I couldn't even fit this in my apartment!" Fred turns to Manny. "How 'bout you, man?"

"No," Manny says. "I couldn't even get it in the door."

"My man!" Fred says. He nods to Manny in appreciation.

"So you'll be there with me in Richmond this Friday, yes?" Alex says.

"Sure, why not? When you do your *Lincoln thang*. But I gotta wear my shades an' beret, man. It's part o' my idiom."

"Ha! Of course. I would expect nothing less."

"Okay, man. Since we cool, I gotta make me some moves. And whatever shit I do, man, it's part o' the agenda, ya feel me?"

"I'll keep that in mind."

"Cool." Fred downs the glass of Scotch, then hands the glass to Manny.

"*Gracias*, Manolo."

"*De nada*, Fred."

"My secretary will give you the details regarding Friday," Alex says.

"Solid." He puts his sunglasses back on.

"Oh, Fred, thanks again for... the press conference... and the video."

"*De nada, Señor* Alex."

[After Fred leaves, Alex presses the intercom…]

"Yes, Mr. President?"

"Gladdy, please provide Mr. Douglass-Jones with all the pertinent details regarding Friday's event in Richmond. He'll be joining us."

A few minutes later, as Douglass-Jones walks away from the desk of Gladiola Gaze, outsider artist Vincent Van Go-Go appears. They give each other a scrutinizing glance as they walk past in opposite directions.

[The intercom buzzes…]

"Yes, Gladdy…"

"Mr. President, that artist is here."

[A moment later…]

"Ace!"

"There's a scary lookin' black dude in the White House, Alex."

"Ha! That's Fred."

"Fred?"

"Didn't you see the press conference?"

"No, I been workin' on the portrait."

"What, you're not doing it *here?*"

"Nah. I come here for the free drinks." He turns to Manny. "Whadaya say, Señor Vargas? It's flowin' like mud around here."

Manny smiles.

"Nice ta see ya, Manny. An' nice to see *you*, Alex, you old fetus-raper!"

"Ha! So you saw it?"

"Of course!" Ace smiles. "Those press conferences are the best thing on TV. An' that Black Panther dude saved your white ass. So now ya got him on the payroll?"

"Keep your friends close," Alex says. He turns to Manolo. "Manny, see if Ace likes that Scotch."

Manny holds up the bottle of 25-year-old Macallan.

"You been holdin' out on me, Alex?" Ace turns to Manny. "A little water, no ice, *por favor.*"

[A moment later…]

"Now *that* is seriously good shit," says Ace. "You like Scotch whiskey, Alex?"

"I've never had it."

"Well then... *Manolo...*"

Manny pours a small glass, hands it to the President, and Manny and Ace watch as he takes that first sip"

"Bleegghh!" Alex says.

"That's 25-year-old Macallan!"

"It tastes like battery acid."

"But you've never had battery acid."

"I'm sorry, Manny." He hands him the glass.

"So that movie we saw the other day, Alex. *Shark-Quake.* Man, that was good! Have you seen it, Manny?"

"No. What is it about?"

"It's the near future, right? An' the oceans are so polluted that the damn sharks can't get a decent meal, with all the floating plastic islands. So they find this hidden cave that leads to this underground salt-water lake, like right beneath California, so there's all this seismic activity."

"Seismic?"

"You know, earthquakes an' shit! So there's like thousands o' sharks under L.A. when the earthquake hits. An' the ground opens up an' all these sharks swim through Beverly Hills an' eat all the movie stars, an' one of 'em eats Kim Kardashian's *ass!*"

"It sounds very good!" Manny says.

"And it has a message!" Ace turns to Alex. "So you bein' President an' all, whadaya think o' those floating plastic islands? They say one is bigger than Mexico." He shoots a glance at Manny.

"That's international waters," Alex says.

"No es mi problema." Ace smiles. "You pass the buck with the best of 'em, Alex!"

"Thanks!"

"This calls for a toast! Get yerself a glass, Manny, an' bring it in here." A moment later, Ace Buckland raises his glass. *"Our leaders suck, religion's bunk. Fuck it all, let's get drunk!"*

"I like your toast," says Manny.

"It's the Buckland family motto." Ace turns to Alex. "So that fetus-rapin' chick with the Sharpie was *hilarious!* I mean, real life is beyond satire. Ya know what I'm sayin'? I'd hate to be a writer these days." He takes a sip of his Scotch. "So you're really goin' ta Richmond?"

"Yeah," Alex says.

"My *Lincoln thang.*"

"But you're gonna be out *there*, man, where all the bad shit happens!"

"I've found that bad shit happens in here as well." Alex smiles. "Besides, if I'm gonna be a man of the people..."

"So *that's* what you wanna be? Another *Kennedy?*"

"What if you can do something good," Alex says, "in *spite* of everything? In spite of all the bullshit."

"I don't know, man. But it's good that you're closin' that museum. I mean, who the fuck came up with *that?* Some sick fuck."

"I know!" says Alex.

"So what if a guy could... you know, heal the divide between the races?"

"*What?*"

"Even just a little."

"You been watchin' too many documentaries, man."

"But wouldn't that be *something?*"

"Yeah, for the *history books.* But how many o' them *Florists* are Black?"

"Hmm..."

"Besides, I worry about you, Alex."

"You do?"

"Yeah. I don't wanna lose my connect ta all this good liquor."

"Ha! You can afford it."

"Only lately." Ace smiles. "There was a time, like for *years*, man, I had just two pairs o' underwear that wasn't in tatters. And I kept wearin' 'em an' washin' 'em an' they kept gettin' more holes... That one expense too many, ya know what I'm sayin'?" He looks at Alex. "Well, *you* don't!" He turns to Manny. "But *you* do, right, Manolo?"

Manny nods.

"Bein' an artist is like bein' a drug addict. Your art is your fix an' you'll do *anything* to get that next high... I've done some shit, man."

Ace nods his head.

"Okay..." says Alex.

"So how would you fuck up a rapper?"

"What?"

"I mean, if you needed to."

"So you wanna fuck up a rapper... Like maybe some Hip-Hop dude who wrote some song about *fetus-raping?*"

"Yeah. Maybe someone like that." Alex smiles. "It's all about the ego, man."

"The ego?"

"The rivalries an' the disses an' the East coast-West coast thing."

"I didn't know you were a such a fan."

"I know some things."

"I know you do," says Alex.

"So what do you think of that *XYZ* song?"

"Are you kidding? *Do any shit ya like, oh! Yer a fuckin' Psych-O!*"

Alex stares at Ace, and then he sees Manny moving his head to the song.

"That's a great fuckin' song, man! I can see why you'd wanna Tupac his black ass."

"Hmm..."

"An' what about that actor dude runnin' for President? The *Enema* guy?"

"To be honest, I'm not that worried."

"So Manny, do you do that *Enema Challenge* thing in Mexico?"

"No, Ace, we do not."

"How come?"

"Because *gringos* are *loco.*"

Alex and Ace both burst out laughing.

"They are indeed," says Ace.

"They are indeed," says Alex. He holds up his glass and motions for his friends to do the same. *"Our leaders suck, religion's bunk. Fuck it all, let's get drunk!"*

"Amen, Mr. President!" says Ace Buckland.

"Amen."

19

"So you shook *hands* with that motherfucker from Hangry?"

"Yeah."

"And then he got shot!" Reggie smiles. "So how's yer hand, man? I mean, it's not all corroded and withered an' shit?"

"Haha! It's fine," Brayden says.

"I bet he wanted to *cane* your black ass."

"Hmm..."

"Did you see the video, of that chick in the miniskirt?"

"The one from Hangry?"

"Yeah. *That* is some brave shit. It's like this big *fuck you,* cuz you know if they catch her ass, that shit gonna get real."

"I feel you." Brayden smiles. "My Nigga!"

They stop at a red light on their way to the Peking Palace, Reggie's favorite Chinese place. The car next to them is blasting the new *XYZ* song. The booming bass thumps its way into Brayden's car, into his hands through the steering wheel.

Do any shit ya like, oh! Yer a fuckin' Psych-O! Do any shit ya like, oh! Yer a fuckin' Psych-O!

"I love that song, man!" Reggie says.

"*Do any shit ya like, oh! Yer a fuckin' Psych-O!* That shit *kills!*"

After the light turns green, they pull away.

"*Better than a slurpee when it blows inside yer furpie!* That's *hilarious,* man! So what does Prezident Fetus think? Has he heard it yet?"

"Beats me. I'll ask him on Friday."

"You be standin' next ta Prezident Fetus when he free da slaves! Haha! You'll be on the cover o' *Modern Abolitionist.*"

"There's no such magazine."

"An' I read that the Black Panther dude is gonna be there too. Did ya see him at the press conference? That shit is badass!"

"And how 'bout that *DeeLishus Cameroon?*"

"The Sharpie chick! 'Cuz I'm *Deeee-Lishus!*'"

"I *loved* her!" says Brayden.

"'Well, gimme the damn phone!'"

"Hey, ya can't blame a sister for tryin'."

"And why'd they video themselves cutting her stomach?"

"Cuz dey *dumbasses?*"

Another car passes by with the song blasting out its windows.

"That shit is viral, man! *Put da moves on an em-bryo. Ya think her mom's yer fat ho!*

At that moment, there's the obnoxious chirping sound of a police siren with flashing lights in the rear-view.

"What the fuck, man?"

Reggie turns around, sees the cop, then turns back to Brayden.

"Whatchu do, man?"

"Nothing."

Suddenly the steering wheel feels heavy, massive, the car like a tank as Brayden pulls over to the side of the road. He turns to Reggie.

"So be cool, right?"

"Fuck yeah!"

Brayden glances in the rear-view mirror. A white policeman gets out of the car while another white policeman remains inside, his fingers typing away on the dashboard computer.

"Is he comin' over?"

"Don't turn around, man!"

Brayden presses the button on the door and the window slides open, letting in a blast of hot summer air and the acrid smell of car exhaust. A long moment later, the policeman is looming overhead.

"License and registration..." he says.

And suddenly Brayden is all thumbs as he tries to extricate his license from his wallet. The policeman leans in, looks inside, scrutinizes the car, eyeballs Brayden.

"Is there a problem?" the policeman asks.

"Get the damn license!" Reggie says in an urgent whisper. The policeman zeroes in on Reggie.

"Is something wrong?" he asks.

"No. We're cool," Reggie says.

The policeman remains impassive.

Finally, Brayden hands him his license and registration. The policeman stands erect as he examines them.

"Fuck, man!" Reggie says in another whisper.

"Shut the fuck up!" says Brayden.

"So is this car new?" the policeman asks.

"I'm sorry. What did you say?"

"This car looks new," the policeman says.

"No, it's... It's a 2008."

"What?"

"I said it's a 2008," Brayden says.

"It's old."

"It looks brand new," the policeman says. He looks again at Reggie. "Is something wrong?"

"No, Officer."

"That's right, you're cool," the policeman says.

A car drives by with the *XYZ* song blasting. *Do any shit ya like, oh! Yer a fuckin' Psych-O! Do any shit ya like, oh! Yer a fuckin' Psych-O!*

"Where are you going?" the policeman asks.

"Sorry?"

"I said where are you going?"

"Can I ask why you pulled us over, Officer?" Brayden asks. And Reggie gives Brayden a *what-the-fuck* glare.

The policeman gives them both a long, scrutinizing glower before he replies.

"You were going 39 in a 35."

"Oh. I was?"

"So what's your hurry?"

"We... We're going to dinner," Brayden says.

"We work in the White House."

"You work in the White House..." the policeman says.

And while this is going on, the officer in the police car runs a make on the plates of the 2008 BMW. He sees on the computer that it's flagged, so he calls into headquarters.

"I'm calling about the 2008 BMW," he says.

"Virginia plates *Xerxes Pavlov Fidelio* 3171 registered to Brayden Carter."

"Did you say Brayden Carter?" the voice comes back over the police radio.

"Yes, Brayden Carter.

And somehow this information passes through the air with celerity and lands in the ear of someone who is way above everyone else's pay grade. And this someone tells the supervisor, who tells the sergeant at the police station, who tells the policeman in the squad car to *stand down*.

"Did you say *stand down?*"

"Yes, stand down."

"Roger."

"The Peking Palace," Brayden says.

"Hmm, do you go there often?" the officer asks.

"Now and then."

The policeman peers into the car and glares at Reggie. "Is something wrong?" he asks.

"What? No," Reggie says. "Nothing's wrong."

"Because it seems like something's wrong."

"No. Nothing's wrong, Officer!" Reggie can feel the sweat on his forehead. His eyes are drawn to the holstered gun on the policeman's hip. '*He hasn't unsnapped the holster yet,*' Reggie thinks. '*That's a good sign.*' At that moment, the other policeman walks over, says something in this policeman's ear, and this policeman hands back Brayden's license and registration.

"Don't drive so fast," the policeman says. He turns and walks back to his car.

Brayden and Reggie let out this breath they'd been holding for the past ten minutes. They glance in the rear-view as the police car pulls away, then they turn to each other.

"What the fuck," says Brayden.

"Motherfucker," says Reggie. "I thought we were gonna be on the news."

"Fuuuck."

"You didn't pee yer pants, did ya?"

"Oh, look who's talking! '*No, nothing's wrong, Officer!*'"

"Fuck, man! '*We work in the White House*'?"

"Ha! Well..."

"And then, when that car went by with the song playing..."

"I *know!*"

"I thought he was gonna shoot us just cuz o' that *song,* man!"

They see the Peking Palace up ahead, and moments later they're inside seated at a table. (Behind them is a lacquered wooden screen of a black-feathered owl on an opalescent background.)

"I'll have the General Tso's Chicken, man," says Reggie.

"I'll have the Beef with Broccoli," says Brayden.

"To drink?" the waitress asks.

"Water."

"Water."

Brayden laughs as the waitress walks away.

"What?"

"You said '*man*' to the waitress!" Brayden says.

"'General Tso's Chicken, *man.*'"

"I'm nervous. That shit was harrowing."

"I know. I thought we were gonna be on some protest poster. Or somebody's T-shirt."

"But you *were* speeding," Reggie says.

"39 in a 35." Brayden shakes his head. "I'm *serious,* man! Cops just need the slightest excuse!"

As the waitress sets down their waters, they catch part of a conversation between a white man and a white woman a few tables away.

"So I'm an introvert," the man says.

"But an outgoing introvert."

"I was going to say that," the woman says.

"Like I think you're a PNRT."

"No, more like an MRPL," the man says.

"You think?"

"Or even a GHFD, but definitely not a PNRT."

"I don't know about that," the woman says.

"Because *I'm* a PNRT."

"Yes, I can see that," the man says.

Reggie and Brayden look at each other.

"Do any shit ya like, oh! Yer a fuckin' Psych-O!" Brayden sings.

"Haha!"

"So I gotta tell ya, when I pressed the button to roll down the window, I kept thinkin' o' Malique Kilvain."

"Shit, man, I kept lookin' at that cop's holster ta make sure it wasn't unsnapped!"

"Fucking police."

More snippets of dialogue drift over.

"So then, would you call yourself an *entrepreneur?*" the man asks.

"No, I would say *solopreneur,*" the woman says.

"Ah! Since you're doing it by yourself!"

"Yes."

"But can't an *entrepreneur* do it by his or her self?"

"I... I don't think so," the woman says, "because then they'd be a *solopreneur.*"

"Ah!"

"I'm thinking of doing a podcast!"

Their meals arrive and Reggie digs in, using his set of chopsticks like an Olympian.

"You're good at that," says Brayden.

"What?"

"Chopsticking."

"Ha! Dat's cuz I do this podcast, man."

"Haha! You're a *chopstickpreneur!*"

"So *that's* one chick I wouldn't mind meetin'," says Reggie.

"What chick?"

"That miniskirt chick in Hangry, man. The one they're lookin' for. I bet *she* don't pee her pants when the cops pull her over."

"Yeah, but then..." Brayden shakes his head.

"I don't even wanna think about it."

"Your friend is one evil dude."

"Yeah, my friend... How's your food?"

"Great, man! They make the best General Tso's."

"I heard that the guy who invented it just died," Brayden says.

"Invented it?"

"General Tso's Chicken..."

"Really?"

"Yeah. Some Jewish guy... Rabbi Glickman."

"Hahaha! That's hilarious, man!" Reggie says. "Rabbi Glickman invented General Tso's chicken!"

And now from several tables away, they hear this obnoxiously annoying *sing-song* laugh coming from a very short white woman who resembles a Hobbit. The laugh begins on a high note **"HA,"** and it descends the scale with the next three "Ha's" to end on a low note **"ha."** And then it begins again, as apparently whatever the other people are saying is so damn funny that the Hobbit Woman keeps laughing with the world's most obnoxiously annoying, repetitive, sing-song laugh.

"*Blah-blah-blah...*" says someone at the table.

"HA-HA-Ha-ha..." the Hobbit Woman replies.

"*Blah-blah-blah...*"

"HA-HA-Ha-ha..."

"*Blah-blah-blah...*"

"HA-HA-Ha-ha..."

Reggie and Brayden look at each other, then refocus on their food.

The waitress appears.

"How's everything?"

"It's good," Brayden says.

When she's gone, Reggie turns to Brayden.

"So how's it goin' with what's-her-name?"

"Renée?"

"Yeah."

"Well, now that you mention it..."

"Oh no."

"It's going *amazing!*" Brayden says, bursting. "She invited me over the other night, and we..."

"What?"

" ..."

"*What?*"

" ..."

"You asshole! I haven't gotten any in a *year!*" Reggie says. "An' you're fuckin' wit me!"

"Sorry."

"I gotta live vicarious, man."

"Okay, I'll say this... We filled up the time in splendid fashion."

"Dat's not *all* you filled up."

"Ha!"

"You *blew inside her furpie!*"

Brayden smiles. "So you haven't had sex in a *year?*"

"It's a cost-benefit thing, man. Bitches drive a brother crazy." There's a pause as Reggie looks at his friend. "But I'm glad *you* be gettin' some."

"I really like her!" Brayden says.

"Uh-oh!"

And from a few tables away.

"*Blah-blah-blah...*"

"HA-HA-Ha-ha..."

"*Blah-blah-blah...*"

"HA-HA-Ha-ha..."

"*Blah-blah-blah...*"

"HA-HA-Ha-ha..."

"I can't stand her laugh, man."

"I know," says Brayden.

"No. I mean, I wanna go over there and stab her with a chopstick."

"*Blah-blah-blah...*"

"HA-HA-Ha-ha..."

"It's drivin' me nuts."

"Okay, I'll distract you. So Renée was wearing this black see-through body-suit when she opened the door."

"*What?!* I *love* see-through body-suits."

"And then we..."

"HA-HA-Ha-ha... HA-HA-Ha-ha... HA-HA-Ha-ha..."

"*Really?*"

"Like all night long. And I got two hours of sleep and it was *great!*"

"Jeez..." Reggie lets out a profound sigh. "So you don't even *miss* what's-her-name."

"Carly?"

"Yeah."

Brayden shakes his head.

"So whenaya seein' her again? Renee."

"Thursday! She's goin' with me to Richmond!"

"No shit!"

"I already got us a hotel."

"So you gonna *schtup* all night, then stand with Prezident Fetus."

"*Schtup?*"

"It's Yiddish, man."

"Oh look! The *Laughter Woman*. They're leaving!"

"Thank you, *Jeezus!*"

And then they hear the conversation of the New Age white people from a few tables away.

"So Eden-Bliss is in Hawaii now."

"Maui?"

"No, Kauai."

"Ah yes! So what's she doing?"

"*Eden-Bliss,*" Brayden says to Reggie.

"*Maui? No, Kauai,*" Reggie says to Brayden.

"She's a practicing *Eco-Sexual* now."

"Really?"

"She just got certified!"

"That's amazing! I've been thinking about getting into that."

"You should take her workshop."

"When is it?"

"This fall, in Big Sur."

"Big Sur?"

"Yes! Because of the Redwoods. Or are they Sequoias? I always get them confused."

"Aren't they the same?"

"I'm not sure."

"So they'll have sex with the *trees!*"

"*Yes!*" The woman beams.

"Wouldn't you just *love* to have sex with a thousand year-old tree!"

"Oh. My. God. That would be amazing!"

Reggie and Brayden look at each other in complete bewilderment.

"So how long did it take Eden-Bliss to get certified?" the man asks.

"Well, she got her Ascended Masters in Eco-Sexuality. But she also does *Soul Path Mentoring* and *Yogastrology!*"

"I am *really* into *Yogastrology!*" the man says.

"I know, right?" The woman smiles. "And she also does *Goddess Gatherings* and *Medicine Woman Healing!*"

"That is *so cool.*"

"It totally is! She's beyond amazing."

"I think I prefer the white cop," says Brayden.

"I know what ya mean," says Reggie.

"So tell me more about your girlfriend. Is she an Eco-Sexual?"

"Ha! Funny you should mention that. There's this *tree...*"

"So you be havin' the time o' yer life while I be watchin' *Netflix.*"

"A victory for one is a victory for all."

"So they say."

"Maybe you should try *Yogastrology.*"

"Nah, I got *Death Wish*, man. Charles Bronson is badass."

20

[Friday morning, 10 AM...]

CNN

"To the left of the President stands Ezra Banes, the leader of the Black Caucus and the House Minority Whip. Next to him, the charismatic leader of the New Black Panthers, Frederick Douglass-Jones, in beret and sunglasses. To the right of the President, the promising young intern, Brayden Carter, who is President Rett's *protégé.* I'm sure we'll be hearing more about *him* in the future. Behind them, other members of the Black Caucus and the Governor of Virginia. And in the center is President Rett himself, in the storied *womb-room,* his mother, Mary Rett, seated in the extra-high wheelchair to elevate the President. They're setting up the microphones for what amounts to an historic event, the President here in Richmond, Virginia before the Slavery Museum, to close it down. The President's speech is just moments away."

[12 hours earlier, Thursday night. The National Hotel, *Richmond, VA...]*
"Thank you for dinner," says Renée.
"My pleasure," Brayden smiles.

They make a gorgeous couple as they walk hand in hand. Young, sexy, beautiful, and black, with a shine, a glow, a scintillation to their skin. Brayden, in his slim-fit charcoal suit with thin silver tie and matching cuff-links. Renée, in a short black dress that caresses her curves, her stilettos resounding against the marble floor with its black and white checkerboard pattern, as they walk towards the elevator.

"I love this old hotel," she says. "It's so elegant... so..."

But the moment the elevator opens and they're inside, they're at each other like something feral, rapacious, devouring. They consume each other's mouths and lips, their tongues probe and penetrate, they pull each other close with something beyond urgency, as if the rising elevator were almost weightless, its own reality, separate from everything and everyone. Brayden takes hold of her ass and pulls her into him so she can feel his hardness, his power. Renée rubs against him, almost grinding. And then she takes his earlobe between her teeth and bites it until there's an exquisite pain he can barely endure.

When the elevator opens to their floor, they're a tangled blur of limbs and clothes in disarray. Somehow Brayden's tie is undone, his shirt unbuttoned, the back of Renée's dress unzipped. And when the door to their room closes behind them, they spend the rest of the night in a blissful sexual haze.

As the morning light seeps in from behind the thick curtains, Brayden lies in bed reeking of sex, exhausted yet invigorated, as he thinks of that movie *Groundhog Day*, and how this for him would be that day.

Moments later, he feels the hot water pour down his back, the steamy cloud-like mist as he sees Renée's body, dripping wet and glistening. She kisses him deeply, and he gets hard for what seems like the twentieth time. He has become sex and nothing else.

"You're amazing," she says, through the sound of the water

cascading over their skin.

"*You're* amazing," he says. And he positions her against the wall of the shower and enters her again.

A half hour later, Brayden adjusts his tie as he glances at Renée in the mirror. She's naked on the bed, but then he watches her grab her purse and take something from it.

"A present," she says as she walks over. "So you'll think of me while you're up there with the President."

A small box wrapped in silver paper with a red ribbon. Brayden opens it and finds an iridescent opal tie pin set in a jet-black base.

"It's beautiful!" he says. (In that moment, he thinks he might be falling in love.)

"Here, let me help you..." Renée positions her naked body before him as she fastens the tie pin to his dark tie.

"Thank you." He looks at it in the mirror. (Her first gift.) "Promise you'll think of me later," she says.

"I do. I mean, I will." He's about to say something more when she puts her finger to his lips.

"I'll be watching on TV," she says.

"Then I'll do *this*..." He makes a grotesquely silly face.

She laughs as she places her fingertip on his tie pin. Then she runs it softly along his cheek.

Frederick Douglass-Jones @FD-JtheNewBlackPanthers
Historic day today. Here in Richmond to make sure Prezident Fetus does the right thing for once and abolishes that hateful museum. Fight hate with justice!

Ezra Millstone Banes @EzraBanesCrackTheWhip
In Richmond with F. Douglass-Jones. A new young leader of fire, passion, and unwavering integrity. Just who we need for the struggle ahead. Abolish racism!

Jaspar Redford Torrence @govJRTva

As Governor of Virginia, I'm pleased as punch that we're gathered here in the State Capital to abolish racism with these fine black leaders and the President himself.

Jules Dale Tippler @JulesTipplerCNN

An historic day for black-white unity. The Black leaders of today with the leaders of tomorrow behind President Rett to abolish racism. The world is watching.

[Friday morning, 10:05 AM...]

CNN

"Here in Richmond, on this bright sunny day, not a cloud in the sky as we go live now to the President's speech...

'My friends, this world we live in is a volatile place. It's a place of intense passions and intensely-held opinions. And some opinions hold onto a past that no longer exists, while others speak to a future of progress and change. Every father wants his children to have it better than he did. Every mother wants her child to inherit a future where her hopes may be realized. And wouldn't that be a place where happiness can exist? Where it can exist for us all?

'We are here before this reprehensible monument to a regrettable past, so we may stand together today for the equality of *all* Americans...'

As the President's words float in the air, Brayden Carter can only think of last night and this morning. He can still feel Renée's body moving with his, their timeless dance of flesh. The smell of her. Her fragrance when he breathed her in, when he inhaled her. He looks out towards the cameras to Renée in the hotel room, naked in bed.

For a split-second, he makes his silly face. Then he glances down at the opal tie pin. *"Promise you'll think of me,"* she said. He looks up again at the cameras, and as he looks out, he notices a man in the crowd who sparks a memory. (That time in the coffee shop with Carly, the distinguished-looking older gentleman with the expensive-looking suit.) Brayden's eyes squint ever so slightly as he looks at this man who seems to be looking at him. From out in the crowd, he sees Carly step forward. Brayden Carter takes a breath as she looks at him, as she almost seems to smile. And a moment later, the man presses a button in his pocket, and there's a tremendous explosion that's heard ten blocks away.

PART THREE

THE FALL

"Man serves the interests
of no creature except himself."
—George Orwell, *Animal Farm*

1

[Friday morning, 10:05 AM...]

CNN

"Here in Richmond, on this bright sunny day, not a cloud in the sky as we go live now to the President's speech...

'My friends, this world we live in is a volatile place. It's a place of intense passions and intensely-held opinions. And some opinions hold onto a past that no longer exists, while others speak to a future of progress and change. Every father wants his children to have it better than he did. Every mother wants her child to inherit a future where her hopes may be realized. And wouldn't that be a place where happiness can exist? Where it can exist for us all?

'We are here before this reprehensible monument to a regrettable past, so we may stand together today for the equality of *all* Americans. And equality means that we share the struggle in an effort to make our lives better, for ourselves and our children. We do this not by being suspicious or afraid of those who may be different, but rather by celebrating these differences. What a boring world it would be if everyone were the same. Look at me, your President... I couldn't be more different, yet instead of shunning me you have embraced me. You've placed your faith in me because you want to believe that the world can be a better place. And I believe that it *can* because we're all in it together, and through this we draw strength. The motto of our great nation is '*e pluribus unum.*' I'm sure you've seen it. It's on the back of all of our coins... *[Laughter...]* It means '*out of many, one.*'

It's easy to discriminate. It's easy to hate. But it takes *strength* to show compassion. It takes courage to be kind and to love. And I believe that as Americans, we *have* this strength and courage, so we can all move towards a future where *[A blinding flash of light! The sound of a great explosion like a crack in the Earth. A moment of stunned silence, then screams...]*

'*What?! What?! Oh my God! Oh my God! Oh my God! Oh my God! There...*
There's been an explosion! People... People are... They... There's been an explo-
sion! The President!... Oh my God! How horrible! I... can't speak... I...'

"This was the scene earlier today in Richmond, Virginia. CNN
correspondent Tara Singer reporting. President Rett was delivering
his speech to a huge crowd before the Slavery Museum, when at 10:08
AM a bomb went off. *[Cut to interviews...]*

Distraught Woman: I was... watching the President, his speech
when... there was this flash of light and this *explosion*. It was *deafening!*
And the smoke and the... the *people*, it... Is the President okay?

Traumatized Veteran with Blood on His Face: There was this blast and
I felt this... shock wave and blood flying through the air with... pieces
of bodies. It was terrible. It was awful... like Afghanistan, like Iraq...

Crying Black Woman: I came to see the President close that hateful
museum, and his words were... soothing. But then this horrific explosion. And these people, these poor souls blown to bits. Is he... Is he
alright? Is the President alright? I pray to God that he's okay.

CLICK...

CBS NEWS

"Tragedy in Richmond when a bomb exploded during President
Rett's speech. He was about to close the controversial Slavery Museum, and he was delivering an impassioned plea for unity before a
capacity crowd when a large bomb detonated. At least seven people
are dead. Many more injured, although the fate of the President is
still unknown. He was rushed from the scene by a helicopter to a
hospital, and he's listed in critical condition...

CLICK...

FOX NEWS

"A terrorist attack kills ten and injures thirteen more as a massive
bomb exploded during President Rett's speech today in Richmond,
Virginia."

Tim Chopper, the President's Chief-of-Staff, turns off the TV. The last few hours were scattered pieces of a broken mirror, and now he's going through each piece in his head, trying to put them back together.

He had stood across the street from the museum, amidst the throng of people who had gathered for the President's speech. He remembers being moved when Alex said, "*It takes strength to show compassion.*" He remembers noticing a strange look on the young Black intern's face to the right of the President, a kind of grotesque grimace that only lasted a second. And then a moment later, the flash of light, the blast, the panic, the screams, the Secret Service rushing towards the President as everyone else fled in the opposite direction.

He remembers standing still for a moment outside of time, the explosion ringing in his ears, the catastrophe of motion in silence like a slow-motion ballet of death. And then amidst the chaos, his eyes were drawn to his suit jacket, to its sleeve, to something that looked like blood and human flesh, and he brushed it away with his hand.

Then the sounds came back, the piercing sirens, the ambulances, fire trucks, and police. The helicopter's whirring blade drowned out the screams, like a peaceful hum where all things come to rest. And when he was of no use at the hospital, he took a helicopter to the White House, to his office. And now he's waiting on the surveillance footage from the FBI, to examine it from every conceivable angle, to try and make sense of it.

There's a knock on the door that in his haste he'd left open. He turns and sees the President's secretary, Gladiola Gaze.

"Oh Tim..."

He stands up. They embrace.

"How is he?"

"I don't know. His *mother...*" Tim looks at Gladdy. "I'll let you know as soon as I hear anything."

"Thank you, Tim. His speech...it was beautiful."

"Yes it was." He sees her staring at his jacket. "What is it?"

Gladdy looks at it for a moment, then she hurries from the room and returns a minute later with a moist sponge. She motions for him to hold out his arm, and she wipes the blood stain on the sleeve.

"You'll need to get this dry-cleaned," she says. "If you give me your jacket, I'll have it done for you."

"Thanks, but... I need to keep it on for now."

"Yes, of course." She offers a slight smile.

As Gladdy leaves, Tim turns on the TV.

FOX NEWS
"It's been confirmed that..."

CLICK...

CNN
"...Eleven people were killed in this morning's tragic bomb blast. Among them, Congressman Ezra Banes, the leader of the Black Caucus and the House Minority Whip. The Governor of Virginia, Jaspar Redford Torrence. Brayden Carter, a young White House intern. And Mary Rett, the President's mother. As for President Rett himself, he is listed in critical condition fighting for his..."

CLICK...

CBS NEWS
"... fighting for his life. As for the cause of the deadly explosion, a spokesman for the FBI said it is being investigated as a possible terrorist attack."

CLICK...

FOX NEWS
"...a terrorist attack. Sources from within the White House say..."

What the fuck? I'm in the White House and I know that nobody's said dick.

"...linking the blast to *OSIRIS*, the radical Islamic terrorist organization, although there has been no official word from them claiming responsibility. In Egyptian mythology, *Osiris* is the god of death, the underworld, and the afterlife..."

CLICK...

CNN

"With the President's mother, Mary Rett, listed as among the casualties, we are all concerned for the President. If he did manage to survive the blast, then his mother's death would put his own life in peril. He is listed in critical condition, and we will give you up-to-the-minute updates..."

CLICK...

C-SPAN

"...up-to-the-minute updates..."

CLICK...

CBS NEWS

"...up-to-the-minute updates as to the condition of the President. Sources within the White House have linked the bombing to the radical Islamic terrorist organization, *OSIRIS*."

Come on, *CBS*, you're better than this... *Edward R. Murrow... Walter Cronkite...*

Ten minutes later, Tim receives the surveillance footage, and he spends the next several hours pouring over it. Concurrently, footage of the blast, specifically the blurred close-up of the young intern, Brayden Carter, has become the *Selfie Generation's* 9/11. Endless rewinds of the poor young man, alive one second, blown to bits the next, in super slow motion, with blurry, pixelated flesh and bone blasting into the air.

On Dirk Fist's syndicated podcast, *InfoCombat*... "There, you see... *[Dirk Fist's voice-over...]* This grimace the young Black intern makes. It only lasts a second. Here it is again. *[They rewind...]* Is it a seizure? And how is it connected to what happens just seconds later? Here, from the right, coming from the edge of the picture frame is *this*... *[An indistinct, blurred, pixelated, split-second flash that could be nothing, that could be a lens-flare, but Dirk Fist believes it's something more...]* There, you see that flash moving towards the President... I believe what we're seeing is *nanotechnology*, folks. A *nanobot-drone* loaded with high-intensity battlefield-grade *nano-explosives* that hits Brayden Carter *right there*, in the chest, then detonates, taking out everyone within a hundred square feet. There, you *see*... *[The clip is rewound and repeated...]* This is scary stuff, people! Nanotechnology is real! *[Again the clip is played...]* You see as it hits the poor Black intern, like the planes into the World Trade Center. *There!* And the devastating explosion that immediately follows...

An hour later, there's breaking news.

CNN

"This just in. This video has been sent to every major news agency worldwide... *[On the screen is a slender man, most likely in his mid-to late twenties. He is dressed in black, with a black balaclava on his head, although his eyes, which are visible, suggest that he's Asian. He addresses the camera, speaking English, but with a noticeable Chinese accent...]*

'I am addressing the oppressive imperialist regime known as America. You have victimized the rest of the world long enough with your Capitalist greed. You are the cancer and we are the cure. Today was the first injection of the antidote to your poison. The next injection is coming soon. We can get to anyone. No one is safe. We are PONG.' *[The image cuts to a black and white TV screen from the 1970s. One of the first video games, the one called "Pong." The primitive graphics show the white dot slowly being hit back and forth by the white rectangles, with the robotic "blip" sound each time it's hit...]*

"In a written statement from PONG released along with the video, it declares: 'PONG is *The People's Offensive to Negate Governments*, meaning the Imperialist Capitalist governments of the West, specifically the United States, which is the biggest offender. We are young Chinese anarchists who believe the world will change for the better only through force, and violence if necessary. And you Americans have made it necessary. Political power grows out of the barrel of a gun. We are PONG. We will strike again soon."

While much of the world braces itself for a resurgence of terror by this new player on the world stage, Gladiola Gaze steps inside the Oval Office. It's so quiet today, a kind of funereal hush in the air. There's the enormous painting on the wall, dripping purple and red. But today when she sees it, she shudders. Images of the explosion and of bodies blown apart and that poor intern whom she saw just the other day.

Gladdy steps away from the painting and approaches the President's desk, this desk that sat here before, in another time, another era. A time more innocent, she thinks. But then again, is any time innocent where human beings are concerned? She remembers taking care of the President when he got blind drunk and slept for two days straight (this secret she holds fast).

But the world saw him emerge as a leader, as Presidential, as a latter-day John Kennedy. And in spite of what she knows, she feels inspired. And what does it matter, the reasons behind things? It's the *results* that count! And somehow Alex Rett had been reborn and inspires now, as JFK had inspired. And the people feel something that many had never felt before or that they didn't dare to feel—hope.

Gladiola Gaze runs her hand along the old wood of the desk. She pictures Alex Rett, his small face, handsome in a way, almost beguiling, and filled with wonder at his own existence—that he has come into the world at this time, in this way. Surely there must be a reason. As tears fill her eyes, she says a silent prayer for the President.

2

Within twenty-four hours, the *YouTube* video of the *Richmond Bombing* had been viewed over thirty million times (and it received over 57,000 LIKES, which could mean that they appreciated the video being posted, or that they liked seeing a horribly graphic fatal terrorist attack and assassination attempt). And within twenty-four hours, people throughout the world were wearing t-shirts and posting on *Facebook* and *Twitter* and *Instagram: Pray for Richmond... Pray for Alex.*

The image of Brayden Carter blown apart in slow motion had become part of the public consciousness. When she saw it, his mother Estelle suffered a near-nervous breakdown, his father Jesse went back to the bottle after ten years of sobriety, and his high school-aged sister Brianna tried to slit her wrists. But having dyslexia, she got the right way and the wrong way confused in her dyslexic mind and she chose the wrong way, from the perspective of the would-be suicide, and she's now on the anti-psychotic *zippidoodamine* in a hospital, under observation.

CNN

"The word on Brayden Carter, the young Presidential intern, from sources within the FBI, is that a *nano-bomb* was placed on him, either by himself or by a person at this time unknown. *[Cut to video with voice-over...]*

"It's hard to see, with the grainy, blurred quality of the image, but it's believed that the *nano-bomb* was contained within his tie pin and was detonated remotely from a range of no more than fifty feet. It is unclear what Carter's connection was with the Chinese terrorist group, PONG. Was he a willing suicide bomber, or was he an unwitting dupe to further PONG's anarchist agenda?

"Wayne Elliott, who knew Brayden Carter when they were classmates back in first grade, had this to say..."

CLICK...

CBS NEWS

"Regarding the Richmond Bombing, this ominous Tweet was just posted by the terrorist group known as PONG:"

PONG @DeathToAmerica

You will never find us. We are invisible until we show ourselves. We can get to anyone. We will strike again soon. No one is safe.

"And in a related story, a Chinese restaurant in Richmond, Virginia was vandalized earlier today, with racist, xenophobic slogans scrawled on its windows..."

CLICK...

PBS

"Good morning. I'm Agnes Plunge, and this is *The Trigger*. My guest today is Marcus Thrush, the former CIA head of Counter-Terrorism, and author of *The New York Times* bestseller, *No More Mr. Nice-Guy*... Marcus, welcome."

"Thank you, Agnes."

"In your new book, you prescribe a more forcible, combative approach to terrorism, even going so far as to advocate for surgical nuclear strikes."

"I do."

"So what do you make of the *Richmond Bombing* and the attack on the President?"

"Well, may I first extend my sincerest wishes to President Rett so he may recover soon and kick PONG's cowardly ass."

"You say *cowardly*. Terrorist groups are often described as such."

"Because it's cowardly to attack from the safety of the shadows!"

"But how is this any different from the drone strikes America continues to launch against Af..."

"That's *nothing* like this! America is *here!* It says *Made in the USA* right on the bombs. And if you don't like it, then you know where to find us."

"But isn't that what just happened?"

CLICK...

CNN

"We're here with Commander Keith Kilmore, a former MI-6 intelligence officer and expert on terrorism and counter-terrorism... Keith, what can you tell us about PONG?"

[With British accent...] "PONG is like OSIRIS on steroids. They are young, radical, intelligent, well-funded, sophisticated, and highly motivated."

"But sophisticated? Surely the clip of that old video game..."

"That is ironic misdirection."

"Ironic misdirection?"

"I take them very seriously when they say no one is safe. I take them very seriously when they say they can get to anyone. My hope is that the United States, specifically the *IntelCom*, takes it seriously as well, since I'm sure another attack is imminent."

CLICK...

FOX NEWS

"We're joined now by the controversial founder and host of *Info-Combat*, Dirk Fist... Dirk, thanks for being here."

"Thanks for having me."

"You have some insight into this newest kid on the terrorist block, PONG, *The People's Offensive to Negate Governments*... Dirk..."

"I believe that PONG is a front."

"A front?"

"For this ultra-secret society of reclusive clandestine billionaires and trillionaires who are so insulated, so buffered, so far behind the scenes as to be invisible. And from within the cloaking device which is their obscene wealth, they act as puppet-masters on a global scale."

"And if this were true, then what is their goal?"

"It *is* true! And their *goal* is to further their agenda by any means necessary, be that disinformation, misdirection, or gross manipulation up to and including mass murder."

"Does that include *ironic* misdirection?"

"Yes it does."

"And what is their agenda?"

"It's hard for regular people like you and me to grasp, but to *them* the world is this massive Monopoly board and they own all the properties... except Baltic and Mediterranean... and Waterworks and that other crappy one..."

"Electric Company."

"Yeah... Is *that* it? *Electric Company?*"

"I believe so."

"Okay, and every time we go around, they put up more hotels."

"Ah, but I think we got off track there."

"Yes. So they will do anything it takes to win the game, and that includes an assassination attempt on the President, although that doesn't fit with the Monopoly metaphor."

"Yes. But he's been doing such good things lately, President Rett. Uniting the nation, trying to ease tensions between Americans of different races. That *has* to be good, right?"

"Not if it's contrary to their agenda."

"Their agenda..."

"This... *cabal*, if you will, of murderous, clandestine billionaires."

"And trillionaires."

"Yes."

"But how do you know what their agenda *is?*"

"They show us."

"Please explain."

"The 'Cabal' doesn't want domestic threats, as in racial violence, because that divides the country. It wants a united America allied against a nebulous foreign threat, such as OSIRIS, and now PONG."

"But President Rett was in the process of *quelling* this domestic discord. The whole point of the Richmond trip..."

"He was, but they don't like him."

"They don't like him?"

"Not anymore."

"Hmm..."

"And how do we *know* this? Because they just tried to take him out. Which means he no longer conforms to their agenda."

"But the *Chinese* do?"

"They want us to *believe* it's the Chinese, but that's more misdirection, although I'm not sure if it's ironic. So now we can focus on a country of over one billion Communist atheists, and what better foil to a Christian democratic America?"

"But if the Cabal, as you call it, is made up of the ultra-rich..."

"Yes?"

"Then why did they say in their video that America has victimized the rest of the world long enough with its capitalist greed?"

"Now *that* is ironic misdirection!"

"Ah! And why is it better for *them*, the so-called Cabal, for America to be united against a foreign enemy?"

"I don't know. I guess the usual... power, money, control. And since PONG has been presented to us as the new *THEM*, then this must be better for the Cabal, *vis-à-vis* facilitating their agenda."

"Hmm... that's a lot."

"I'll say!"

"So what can we do about it?"

"Well, I'm in the process of conferring with my covert agents within the *IntelComs, SecFors,* and *UndOps* regarding the nanotechnology used in the *Richmond Bombing*, and we hope to generate some leads... to peel away the layers of the artichoke, if you will."

"Don't you mean *onion?*"

"Onions give me gas."

"Ahh... Thank you, Dirk Fist."

[Tim Chopper turns off the TV...]

In his office is Nash Wasserman, the Director of the FBI.

"That fat guy's closer than he thinks," Wasserman says.

"Really? So who's behind it?" asks Tim Chopper.

"Well, *not* the Chinese. But they might as well be, as far as America is concerned."

"A *cabal*, like he said?"

"That fat fuck, Dirk Fist? As much as I hate his fat guts, his logic is sound. Whoever it is, they want America to be united against a single amorphous enemy. And with stories already of the Chinese coming here and buying up half the country, this somehow serves their agenda."

"And the assassination attempt on the President?"

"Like the fat guy said, he no longer fits in with their plans."

"So there's this group out there that nobody knows about," says Tim Chopper, "including the *Intelligence Community*, run by people nobody's met, that just tried to kill the President of the United States?"

"It's happened before."

"So what can we do about it?"

"Beats me."

"What about the people in the crowd?" Tim says.

"In Richmond."

"We've run them through facial recognition and everyone was clean. We're trying to find out more about the bomb, through trace signatures left at the scene, but it was a very efficient device."

"What about that kid, that poor bastard..."

"Brayden Carter?"

"That strange face he made, seconds before..."

"We've had a team of criminal psychologists on that, and the consensus is that he was making a face for someone."

"A face?"

"You know, a funny face for someone he knew would be watching."

"Like a girlfriend?"

"We've interviewed a friend of his..." Nash Wasserman scrolls through his smartphone. "A Reggie Mason. Mason said that Brayden Carter had a new girlfriend, an African-American woman named Renée Hardy, although Mason had never met her. She worked at a bar in DC, but she quit three days before the bombing and has since disappeared. And all info about her is phony, as if she never existed."

"What about the hotel, where that kid..."

"*The National...* Several of its staff remember seeing Brayden Carter with a young black woman fitting Renée Hardy's description, but all of the hotel's security footage has been erased, and the room where they stayed in was sanitized like you wouldn't believe. Like beyond spic-n-span. Obviously not the work of the hotel chambermaid. Which brings me back to what I said before."

"Meaning?"

"It beats me."

"Okay," Tim Chopper says, as he lets out a sigh of frustration.

"So how is he?" Wasserman asks. "The President?"

"Still critical."

"Okay. Keep me posted, Tim."

"You do the same."

CNN

"Frederick Douglass-Jones, the charismatic young leader of the *New Black Panthers*, who was seriously injured during the *Richmond Bombing*, has recovered enough to make this statement from his hospital bed in Bedford Stuyvesant, New York. *[Cut to hospital, to Douglass-Jones in a full body cast, thick bandages covering his left eye and head, both of his arms in a sling, both of his legs in a cast, his back in traction, his body connected to myriad IV drips and machines...]*

'What happened in Richmond was mother*[censored]* heinous and un*[censored]* forgivable and I vow to get those mother*[censored]* responsible and kick their mother*[censored]* asses... As soon as I can move again, that is, and walk and see.'

"As for President Alexander Rett, he's still listed in critical condition. And as we send him our thoughts and prayers, I personally take heart in his words from that fateful day in Richmond... *[Cut to video...]*

'We do this not by being suspicious or afraid of those who may be different, but rather by celebrating these differences... It's easy to discriminate. It's easy to hate. But it takes *strength* to show compassion. It takes courage to be kind and to love. And I believe that as Americans, we *have* this strength and courage.'

"Inspiring words from an inspiring leader who knows the cost of doing what's right.

Jules Tippler *looks directly into the camera...]* 'We're praying for you, Alex."

By the end of the day, President Rett's approval rating is up to 92.

"*Ironic misdirection*" has become the newest catch-phrase, the *YouTube* video of the *Richmond Bombing* has topped 50 million views, Dirk Fist's speaking fee has quadrupled, there are reports of Chinese restaurants being vandalized in thirty-four states, the YOUNG

TURKISH ANARCHISTS TV show is canceled as a backlash to the YOUNG CHINESE ANARCHISTS of PONG, and the rap-metal group *Rage Up Ur Ass!* releases their new album entitled *SHOCK U!*, with the image of the exploding Brayden Carter on its cover.

3

It would become known as 彊竻裂拈 or *Shujing zhi yè*. By the next day, Chinese restaurants in every state of the union except Alaska and Maine had been vandalized. Windows smashed, lo mein and chop suey splattered over the walls, egg rolls stomped upon. And in one particularly virulent display of nationalistic, racist xenophobia, in Pig's Elbow, Arkansas, a bonfire of millions of chopsticks was lit in the town square. As to where they got millions of chopsticks, it's unclear, but Americans are nothing if not resourceful.

America is not gonna sit back and take shit from the Chinese. After all, *they're* little and Americans are big. Americans drive big-ass pick-up trucks, *they* ride bicycles. Americans play football, *they* play ping-pong. But most importantly, Americans, especially American men, are no slouch in the penis department, whereas those Chinese are little shrimps. Or is that the Japanese?

And in response to 彊竻裂拈... PONG released another video:

"Dear Flaccid Capitalist Racist American Fools: Your impotent displays of misplaced rage really make us laugh. Today, a symbol of your Capitalist regime will shrink like your penises. We are PONG. No one is safe." *[Cut to B&W video of the 70s* Pong *video game with the infernal* blipping *sound...]*

In response to all this, Tim Chopper has Wiley DeSembler do what he does best.

(From the Gerald R. Ford Room, *another hastily assembled White House press conference is about to begin...*

[Press Secretary Wiley DeSembler *stands before the crush of vengeful, frothing journalists...]*

Journalists: *[en masse]* Wiley! Wiley! Wiley!

Wiley: *[points to one...]*

Wu: Loo Duc Wu, *Sino The Times*... What is your response to *Shu-jing zhi yè?*

Wiley: First of all, ya have ta speak American.

Crowd: Yeah! Yeah!

Wiley: Second, I've read your magazine. It's nothing but yellow journalism. *[offers crowd a wink...]*

Crowd: *[appreciative laughter...]*

Wu: That's *racist!*

Wiley: No it's not. *[looks over at black journalist...]* Is that racist?

Smith: Cornelius Smith, *BLM Magazine*... Well, not the way it is for Black people.

Crowd: *[supportive applause...]*

Wiley: See! Cuz Black people are Americans!

Crowd: Yes!

Wiley: And Chinese people are...

Smith: Chinese!

Wiley: Yes! And President Rett, whose life hangs in the balance, urged us all to come together despite our differences, black and white, united as one against our common enemy...

Crowd: The *Chinese! [cheers, applause...]*

Mayflower: Skeet Mayflower, *Xeno Magazine*... Do you think there'll be a travel ban issued to prevent the Chinese from entering America, not to mention extreme vetting?

Wiley: Well, just because they don't practice birth control, I don't see why the rest of the world should be burdened with their toxic overflow.

Crowd: Yes! Yes!

Wiley: And we'll be implementing a policy of Extreme Mega-Vetting with Cheese and Special Sauce! *[smiles]*

Mayflower: And a side o' fries!

Smith: *Cheese fries!*

Wiley: Haha! Yes! *[points...]*

Revolver: Butch Revolver, *War-Hammer Magazine*... What's your response to the latest video from PONG?

Wiley: Well, I'll have to think long and hard about it.

Crowd: *[laughter...]*

Revolver: Will the response be firm and fast?

Wiley: Very firm, but *slow*, as we'd like to enjoy it. But rest assured, the response will be probing and penetrating, and it will go deep.

Revolver: Very deep?

Wiley: Until it hits bottom.

Revolver: Ahh!

Simon: *[appalled]* Samantha Simon, *Time...* Ironic misdirection aside, PONG says it will attack one of our symbols of capitalism. The Twin Towers were such a symbol.

Wiley: *[plays to crowd...]* That's not *all* they were a symbol of!

Crowd: *[fist-pumping]* Roo! Roo! Roo!

Wiley: *[to Simon...]* But I can assure you, Samantha... Sam... Sammy... *[smiles, winks...]* We'll put it to 'em good! *[cheers...]* If they're ahead of us, we'll take 'em from the front. If they're behind us, we'll take 'em in the rear... *[cheers, hoots, whistles...]* And we won't stop until we've spent our load and we're out of ammo and we take out that cigarette and have ourselves a smoke.

Crowd: *[more fist-pumping]* Roo! Roo! Roo! Roo!

Wiley: I think that about covers it. *[starts to step down, then returns to microphone...]* Oh, and the acting President, Mavis DaLyte, will make a speech tonight sometime. *Booyah!*

Crowd: *Booyah! Booyah!*

[Wiley steps from the podium and exits the room...]

[Later that day, at 7 PM, Vice-President Mavis DaLyte addresses the nation on all the major networks except ESPN *and* THE FOOD CHANNEL...*]*

"Greetings, my fellow Americans. The past few days have been filled with tragerdy, but first, some *good news!* President Rett is offa the critical list! Yessiree! His condition is listed as guarded, which means he's not out o' the woods, but still, that's better then blight on yer potato crop! I hope ta speak with him shortly if not sooner, as we plan are stratergy regardin' that group o' Young Chinese Anti-Christs we all hate an' detest called PONG.

"In addition, there's all this other stuff goin' on in this big ol' world, an' some of it even bears mentionin'. That outbreak o' Celiac Disease that started in the Congo of Darkest Africa has been spreadin' like Miracle Whip on Wonder Bread. An' sumthin' needs ta be done about *that,* cuz there's nuthin' worse then bein' gluten intolerant. An' there's a lesson here fer all us Americans, that we should be tolerant o' things that're diff'rent from us, except fer gluten an' them Chinese because they're godless terrorists an' PONG is top o' the list o' butts that needs ta get kicked. As I said, we're in the process o' discussin' stratergy with the Joint Chiefs so we can avoid anymore tragerdies like that Richmond Bombin'... that put are President's life in grave peril an' jeopardy an' took the life o' some of are beloved Afro-American colleagues o' color.

"There's also this sitchiation in Borneo that also bears mentionin' as well. Word is that they got the bomb, an' not jus' *any* bomb but *The Bomb,* an' that's disconcertin' ta anyone who loves freedom an' hates nuclear holocaust. Because we as Americans, an' America bein' the *Arsenal o' Democracy*... well, *we're* the arsenal! Which means that *we* got The Bomb, not Borneo! So there's another butt that might need some kickin'. But in the meantime, we're rootin' out those PONG vermin like the godless termites they are as they undermine the strength of are hardwood.

"In closing, when yer hungry for a nice dinner or sumthin' ta eat, remember ta buy American! We got hamburgers comin' outta are butts in America. An' if ya get sick o' that, well, there's lots o' great pizza an' tacos. An' don't forget the French fries! God bless President Rett an' God bless America!"

"I love the Vice-President!" somebody says at the end of the bar. "She's hilarious."

"You *know* she's the acting *President.*"

A half hour earlier, Reggie Mason planted himself behind that same bar, at Deco. And even though he hates this place and thinks it's racist, he misses his friend. He only saw the explosion once, when it happened in real time. To see Brayden like that, to see his best friend blown to bits and then have it become this voyeuristic *YouTube* phenomenon... He keeps going over their last day together. That near disaster with the white cops; those crazy New Agers at the Peking

Palace. And he read today that it was fire-bombed last night and it burned to the ground this morning.

And *Chinese terrorists blew up his friend and tried to kill the President?* The world is spinning out of control. It's hurtling in a death spiral and all you can do is hold onto something. And what about that girlfriend who conveniently failed to show up last week when he was supposed to meet her? He had come *here*, to Deco, the day after the bombing when he was able to move and think and be conscious. He asked about that black bartender, Renée Hardy, and they said she moved to Miami to be with her rich boyfriend. And his boss, Ezra Banes, was killed as well. And now Reggie's not even sure if he has a job, and the country's being run by a temp-worker hick from some Idaho potato field. Nothing makes sense. The world has gone batshit, over-the-edge, cray-cray insane.

"Another beer?" the bartender asks.

"Yeah... No..." Reggie looks up. "How 'bout a *Gin & Tonic?*"

"What kind of gin would you like?"

"Doesn't matter."

A moment later, his drink appears.

"Thanks, man. So... whatever happened to that hot bartender, Renée, who used to work here?"

"Renée?" The bartender puzzles for a moment. "I don't know her. I only work part-time. I'm in school."

"Ah..."

"So she was hot?"

"She was smokin'."

"Hmm..."

"What're you studying, man?"

"Political Science."

Reggie laughs to himself, and then he takes a sip of his Gin & Tonic. He grimaces once, then takes another sip.

"How's your *G&T?*" the bartender asks.

"It's good, man."

Reggie swirls the ice around the glass with his fingertip as he thinks of death spirals hurtling out of control.

4

FOX NEWS

"The terrorist group of young Chinese anarchists known as PONG has struck again. Following through on the threat they made in yesterday's video, the famous Wall Street Bull in the heart of the Financial District in New York City has disappeared. The twist is that it's been replaced with an exact replica, although the replica is a bit on the small side. *[Cut to video footage...]*

'I'm speaking with NYPD Sergeant Milo Minderbinder. Can you tell us what happened, Sergeant?'

'Well, this morning people began to notice that the bull had shrunk.'

'The famous Wall Street Bull...'

'Yeah. And now it's *this...*'

[Camera pans to the new bull*...]*

'It's tiny,' the reporter says.

'Minuscule,' says Sergeant Minderbinder.

'How did this happen?'

'It's New York.' The Sergeant shrugs. 'It iz wut it iz. Whadaya gonnado?'‟

'The original sculpture was made of bronze. It stood eleven feet tall, sixteen feet wide, and it weighed seven thousand pounds, which is three and a half tons. Its replacement is made of plastic. It's eleven *inches* tall, sixteen *inches* wide, and it weighs seven *pounds*, about as heavy as my cat Pixels... Back to you, Sandy.'

"The FBI has been called in, since the crime appears to be the work of PONG, although they have yet to claim responsibility. FBI Special Agent Pierce Magnusson had this to say:

'It's PONG's m.o. alright. No witnesses, all cameras within a two block radius disabled or erased, and somehow a massive three-ton sculpture has been replaced with this pipsqueak. If I weren't FBI, I'd make some trenchant remark on the all-too-apparent Freudian symbolism, but the FBI doesn't do that. We catch bad guys.'

"When asked what they thought of the *new* Wall Street Bull, random New Yorkers had this to say:

Jill Stemple, *Brooklyn*: 'It's *sooo* cute!'

Delores Del Rio, *Queens*: 'It's adorable! I want one!'

Felicity Unger, *Manhattan*: 'Can I take it home with me?'

Dick Ego, *The Bronx*: 'What the *[censored] happened* to it?!'

Kirk Rammer, *Staten Island*: 'That's just *[censored] wrong!*'

Ricky Balls, *Queens*: 'It's sooo *[censored] awful.*' *[Begins to weep...]*

"In other news, Borneo yesterday detonated a thirteen-kiloton nuclear warhead, obliterating the uninhabited island of Tauwopalop in the South Sulu Sea. In this blatant show of strength to intimidate East Borneo, as well as a flagrant violation of the worldwide ban on above-ground nuclear testing, Borneo has been condemned by the world community, and it now faces UN sanctions.

"And in Reykjavík, Iceland... American Grand Master *Barry Feschler* has walked out of his second round match against Russia's *Igor Isassky*, in the ten million dollar *World Monopoly Championship* yesterday, citing a problem with the lighting and that *Isassky*, the Russian champ, has B.O. *Feschler* lost the opening round match on Friday when *Isassky* took him by surprise by employing the rarely used '*Baltic Gambit.*' The unorthodox tactic lured the American into a false sense of security, as *Isassky* then put twenty hotels each on *Baltic* and *Mediterranean*. *Feschler* retired eight turns later after he was sent directly to Jail without passing Go, and without collecting a much needed $200."

Boy, a lot happens when you're away! Sorry to keep ya in the dark, but I hadda go underground for a bit. Literally! Yeah, it's me, Little Alex, still the POTUS, although just barely. Put it this way, you *don't* wanna get on *The Florists'* shit list. And they went real horror-show on my poor intern, Brayden Carter, blown to bits over fifty million times the last I checked on *YouTube*. But I guess some back-tracking is in order. I *knew* it was a bad idea to go out into the world! I told ya that right from the start. But before I get into all that...

Check *this* out! See!

Now I'm over *here!* And then...

I'm all the way over *here!*

And then I can be...*over here!*

Haha!

And then I can do *this*...

Back and forth and back and forth...

But it's exhausting. And I'm not in the best of shape, having been cooped up in that womb-room all the time like I was.

I'm actually huffing and puffing now. *Whew!*

Okay...

I'm gonna rest over here a bit. But did you *see* me? Scampering all over the place, free of constraints! And by constraints I mean that accursed millstone of an umbilical cord which I'm finally free of! And yes, I still end some sentences in prepositions. But I'm still the *Prez*, and now more than ever I can do what I want, cuz I gots me mobility! Feets, don't fail me now!

I must say what a joy it is, like a dog finally off its leash who can poop in the neighbor's yard and overturn trash cans and cavort and gambol and frolic in a field and roll around in a dead, fermented, woodchuck carcass! In short, the world has opened up like a luscious pair o' legs (to pick up on the "pussy-grabbing" image employed at the end of *Part One*), and I'm not gonna let something like the world's richest, most powerful evil villains who want me dead be a cock-block.

And as an aside, my pussy-grabbing predecessor's official White House portrait was done in velvet. You know, like those velvet matadors you find in every cheap motel. But as soon as he moved out of the White House, or as he called it, "The Dump," the disgruntled White House staff yanked it off the wall and put it in the basement with the portraits of the presidents' pets. And it hangs there to this day between Checkers (Nixon's Cocker Spaniel) and Tootsie (Gerald Ford's iguana).

So, that back-tracking was sub-par. I'm just excited to be alive after that heinous incident, which thankfully I can't remember. And of course my poor intern who I used to call *Tall Skinny Sad-Sack*—well, the *sad-sack* part proved prophetic. And Ezra Banes and my ol' friend the Governor of Virginia and my New Black Panther pal, Frederick Douglass-Jones, who's still alive, although his black ass was fucked up but good. Actually, his *ass* is about the only part of him that *isn't* fucked up. And of course the pivotal thing, the most salient of points I've been skirting around, is that my mom, poor Mary Rett, finally ended her miserable existence. Well, *The Florists* ended it *for* her. So here's what happened, as told to me by the White House doctors.

I'm in the middle of this speech that's going really well, rich with inspiring JFK parallelisms, and I'm almost to the part where I metaphorically free the slaves, when I get interrupted by this BIG-ASS BOMB BLAST, and... well, you saw the video. My poor mom was blown to smithereens, but thanks to modern American technological know-how, that bulletproof glass cover of the womb-room made of *aluminum oxynitride* with Teflon and titanium left me safe and sound inside. In fact, I would be willing to be a paid spokesperson for *aluminum oxynitride* after my tenure in the Oval Office, when I'm out in the private sector and in need of cashola.

The problem with my mom being blown to the Hereafter is that the umbilical cord was Hereaftered as well. And some helicopter swooped in and flew my disconnected butt to some army hospital, where the world-renowned specialist on Birth & Eugenics from the *Universität Heidelberg*, Dr. Manheim Dampfwälze von Ludendörff-Dreck, was waiting. He'd been trying to figure this out forever, namely, was it survivable to be separated from my mom the way all children are eventually separated from their moms, and the bomb blast forced the issue.

Apparently it was a non-issue, because I was just fine and I could've been removed way back when I first went onto the campaign trail. But you know doctors. There's no money in cures. So I fired his *Deutschland Über Alles* ass and he moved to Argentina and I was free at last from Mommy Millstone. And sure, I'm sad that she's gone, but it wasn't like we were that close. She was hardly this charming, witty travel companion these past seven or eight months, all mute and catatonic. But I'm probably still in shock and not thinking straight. And since *womb* is pronounced *woom*, then shouldn't *bomb* be pronounced *boom*?

So where have I been hiding the past few days? Well, you remember just last week when my dictator pal Er Mahgerd was shot by a would-be assassin while attending a public caning? And even though it was a flesh wound, they kept everyone in suspense because that's right out of *How to Be President for Complete Idiots*—Chapter One, page 27...

Misdirection

Assassinations—Any injuries that occur during an assassination attempt must be overplayed for maximum sympathy effect.

So while the world was sending me its thoughts and prayers, I was hunkered down in the Fetus Bunker watching *Netflix*. And if I've learned anything in my short time so far as President, it's that sometimes it's best to just sit back, do nothing, and see what happens. As for what happened, I'm as surprised as you are. I never thought Barry Feschler would lose that opening round Monopoly match, but *nobody* expected that Baltic Gambit! And I guess I should, like, intervene or something with that crazy Borneo president all *sabre-rattling* and *A-Bomb exploding*.

[*Alex grabs his smartphone...*] "Siri?"

"Why hello, Mr. President! So nice to hear from you!"

"Thanks."

"How are you feeling, sir?"

"Pretty good, thanks. It was just a flesh wound. But don't tell anyone."

"My lips are sealed, sir. Sorry about your mom."

"Yeah, whadaya gonna do? She's in a better place."

"Yes. So how can I help you today, sir?"

"Siri, what's the name of the President of Borneo?"

"Checking on the name of Borneo's President... *Sabah Sarawaak*."

"*Sabah Sarawaak*... Thanks, Siri."

"You're welcome, sir. And I'm glad you're back."

"Me too!" I love that Siri.

And this hot new "*ironic misdirection*" that everyone's talkin' about? It's not so new. It's in the book too, under *Advanced Misdirection*.

And how 'bout Mavis last night *addressin' the nation, talkin' 'bout tragerdies an' strategies*. And then this PONG thing. Dirk Fist got a bull's eye on that one. Too bad *The Florists* seem to like him, but I guess every generation needs its Chicken Little. Besides, nobody believes they even exist, *The Florists*. But *Brayden Carter* believes, looking back from The Afterlife... if there is such a place.

[Alex's fingers flash over his smartphone...]

"Siri?"

"Hello again, Mr. President!"

"Siri, what do you know about a clandestine cabal of ultra-rich global puppet-masters who manipulate world events to satisfy their nefarious agenda?"

"Checking on a clandestine cabal of so forth and so on... I'm sorry, sir, the only thing I have is a link to Dirk Fist's website."

"Okay. Thanks."

See! Not even *Siri* has a clue. So I'm kinda rarin' ta go, President-wise. My first thought was *press conference*. But that press conference yesterday, Lord have mercy! Wiley needs a vacation, like *STAT!* So then I thought, maybe an address to the nation, but I think baby steps are required. So it's time to break the *Tweet Fast* and let the world know that ol' Alex Rett is alive an' kickin'.

[He grabs his smartphone and sends a Tweet...]

There. Just two words. "I'm fine." What did the Bard say about brevity... And this time, *Twitter's* not gonna be a mindless addiction used for vainglorious self-aggrandizement or petty attacks on my enemies. It'll be a tool for communication. Simple. Precise. Immediate. I'll use it for good instead of evil. I'll change. I've learned that I have the strength to change.

Speaking of... my approval rating went up to 92! Nuthin' like an assassination attempt to jack up the ratings! I can still get that 95. No President has *ever* gotten 95, not even Reagan. If I can get that, I'll be a shoo-in for the Hall of Fame. Unless I get impeached, cuz that would be like a Pete Rose thing.

So I should tell Tim Chopper that I'm back from my vacay. And Gladdy, Manny, and Ace. We need to celebrate my birthday! And as for where I'm at now, I've been hangin' with the White House carpenter guys. They're building me a new womb-room, although in name only. And this one is *way* bigger! It'll be this awesome self-contained apartment within the Oval Office, and this one is more *Mad Men Sixties Cool* than *Animal House Hijinks*. They've been working their asses off, the carpenter guys, and they said it'll be in place tomorrow and ready to move in. So I think a party with Ace and Manny is just what the doctor ordered. And then tomorrow night, an address to the nation and the world, showin' 'em all that Alex Rett, *The Rettinator,* is back!

5

FOX NEWS

"Our top story, Hip-Hop artist XYZ, who scored a massive hit with last week's protest song *Prezident Fetus,* was murdered last night outside a Las Vegas strip club by his arch-rival and nemesis, rapper KILL U DED. KILL U DED, who was apprehended at the scene, cited a long-standing feud over creative differences, as well as the fact that he was jealous of XYZ's new hit *Prezident Fetus.* KILL U DED was working on his *own* protest song at the time entitled *Baby Raper,* but XYZ, in the words of KILL U DED, 'beat me ta the mother*[censored]* punch an' got alla dem *President Raped My Baby* dollars.'

"In other news, the Food and Drug Administration announced that they have upped the daily allowable amount of plastic ingested by human beings to one ounce. Anything an ounce and under is acceptable. So if you want to eat that red plastic cup after you finish that beer at the Frat party, that's okay. But don't eat any *more* than that. This was seen as a huge victory for the Parmesan Cheese lobby.

"In the political world, the state of South Carolina has announced that it wants to secede from the Union because of the sudden accord between Blacks and Whites. When asked to comment, South Carolina Senator Baxter Boggs said: 'Now I hate them Chinamen az much az the next feller, but thet don't mean I ken't hate me them so-called African-American colored folks too! We're South Carolinians! We got us a whole *mess* o' hate! But the resta the country, filled with all them Abolitionists like are slave-lovin' President hisself, wants us ta *love* them coloreds. We don't go 'roun' tellin' *them* who ta love! An' on a personal note, President Rett, we're all pullin' for ya down here in South Carolina!'

"And finally, with the President's condition still listed as grave, the world was both surprised and perplexed when this cryptic Tweet from the President himself was posted:

Alexander Jackson Rett @realAlexRett
Undubw

"Nothing else, just *Undubw*. To hopefully shed some light on this, we have with us in the studio, Dan Randanran, a former senior cryptologist at the National Security Agency.

"Dan, what do you make of this apparent *Tweet* from the President?"

"It is surprising, considering his condition, and also it breaks his self-imposed *Tweet Fast*."

"Yes, but what do you make of the *content* of it? Just this one word...*Undubw*."

"Yes, well, we've run it through every known language, including dialects, colloquialisms, and idiomatic phrases, and there's no such animal."

"No *Undubw*..."

"No. So then we ran it through all the codes, ciphers, and conundrums presently in our system, and there are a *lot*, like 1x10 to the 27th power."

"That *is* a lot!"

"Yes indeed! But nada."

"Nothing?"

"Nope. It's an enigma."

"Hmm."

"But one of the theories we're pursuing, and admittedly one that's off-the-wall, is that the word *Undubw* refers to former President George W. Bush, who was known as *Dubya*. Perhaps President Rett is trying to erase something that George W. Bush had done. To *Un-Dubya*, so to speak."

"But it's *Undubw*."

"Yes. But as I said, it's just a theory."

"Thank you, Dan Randanran."

Porter Percival Portly @govPortPortly

I don't know what Undubw means, but I hope it means the President is back in charge in a BIG way. Enormously glad if this is the case. It'll be HUGE for USA!

Dirk Fist @infocombat

BigDirkFistUndubw is the signal to the aliens who've been invisibly circling Earth since 9/11. They've replaced the President in the recent alien coup, aka Richmond Bombing.

Mallory Rodman Blitzen @realPresidentMalloryBlitzen

Is Undubw so-called Prez Fetus's "covfefe"? Richmond Bombing left him brain-damaged. Better monosyllables than JFK plagiarisms. Is Rett an unfit idiot?

Frederick Douglass-Jones @FD-JtheNewBlackPanthers

I feel your Undubw, man. Did you type the wrong damn letters? My fingers are the only thing not broke. Thanks for inviting me to Richmond, man. I owe ya one.

And in the White House, the hallway outside the Oval Office is filled with the pitter-patter of little feet racing from one end to the other. Gladiola Gaze, after her initial surprise and elation upon seeing the President return safe and sound, is now filled with maternal pride. She watches Alex Rett dash back and forth in his little track suit, in his little sneakers, as if he'd never run before. Which he hadn't.

"Mr. President..."

Whizzzzzzzzzzzz...

"Sir..."

Whizzzzzzzzzzz...

"Mr. President..."

Whizzzzzzzzzzz...

Finally, Alex stops before her desk.

"I just did... ten laps!" He smiles as he catches his breath.

"Sir, the Joint Chiefs are insisting on a meeting regarding the situation in Borneo."

"I know. That Sabah Sarawaak is a real whack-job. Hey, that's pretty good!" Alex smiles to himself. "Sabah Sara*waack-job!* Ha!"

"They're insisting on an answer."

"One does not *insist* to princes... *Machiavelli*... Or maybe it was from some movie."

"So what shall I tell them, sir?"

"Tell 'em I got it covered. So Gladdy, do you know Usain Bolt?"

"Is he a super-hero?"

"Yes he is," says Alex.

"I want you to call him."

"Call him, sir?"

"I think he lives in Jamaica. Have him come to the White House, all expenses paid, the usual red carpet VIP-treatment."

"Is he... Is he their new President, sir?"

"Not yet. He's one of the world's fastest humans."

"Oh. All right, sir, I'll get right on it."

"Thanks, Gladdy. I'm gonna take a shower in my new pad."

"Very good, sir. And Tim Chopper is scheduled for 10:30."

When Alex gets inside the Oval, he glances at the placenta painting. Even though it reminds him now of the blown-up Brayden Carter, he still likes it, in a *Picasso-Guernica-awful-shit-remembrance* kinda way. As he wipes the sweat from his brow, he looks at the huge bottle of Gatorade on Reagan's old desk. He presses the intercom...

"Yes, Mr. President?"

"Gladdy, call up Gatorade."

"The company, sir?"

"Yes. See if they'll make me special *two-ounce* bottles."

"I'm sure they will, sir. I'll get right on it."

"Thanks, Gladdy."

Alex hops onto the desk, uncaps the huge bottle of *Gatorade*, and then slurps it through a straw until his thirst is slaked. Then he breaks out *The Bible: How to Be President for Complete Idiots...* Chapter Thirteen, page 345...

Tinpot Despots (subsection **Nuclear Threats**)

When unhinged and or crazy tinpot despots or dictators threaten the use of nuclear weapons, keep in mind that it is most likely braggadocious posturing to bolster their low self-esteem and to make them look bigger and more powerful in the eyes of the world. They are the equivalent of a spoiled, entitled child throwing a temper tantrum, but with nuclear weapons. To diffuse the situation, feed their ego with deference coupled with effusive praise of their manhood and leadership, while gently reminding them who's the boss. It costs nothing to do this, yet it is what the narcissistic dictator craves most, to be seen and recognized by "The Big Boys."

A word of caution... Whatever you do, do not sink to their level and engage in nuke-measuring. This may precipitate a scenario where they actually might use one to prove a point. In the unlikely event that this occurs, the upside is that since they are a tinpot dictatorship, their nuclear payload is in kilotons, not megatons, so no real biggie.

> *[Alex presses the intercom...]*
> "Gladdy, get me Admiral Numnutz."
> "You mean Admiral Nimitz, sir?"
> "That's the one."
> "Right away, sir."
> I don't know what I'd do without *The Bible*. This Presidenting ain't so tough. Oh, one more thing...
> *[Alex grabs his smartphone...]*
> "Siri?"
> "Good morning, Mr. President! How can I help you?"
> "Siri, what's the closest battleship of ours to Borneo?"
> "Checking on the closest U.S. battleship to Borneo... It's the *U.S.S. Merrimack*, sir. It's presently in the South Sulu Sea."
> "The *Merrimack*? Why would they name a United States ship after a Confederate ironclad? Didn't the South *lose* that war?"
> "That's debatable, sir. The *Merrimack* was given that name as a concession to South Carolina's tungsten lobby."
> "*South Carolina?* I wish they *would* secede! And what the heck's tungsten?"
> "Checking on what the heck's tungsten..."
> "No, belay that order, Siri."
> "Ah! Nautical humor! Very funny, sir."

"Thanks, Siri."

"Always a pleasure, Mr. President."

[The intercom buzzes...]

"Yes, Gladdy..."

"Admiral Nimitz for you, sir..."

"Ah, perfect... Chester, how's it hangin'?"

"Um, not very well, sir. But first I'd like to say how glad I am that you're alive and well."

"Thanks, Chet! So I want you to have the captain of the *U.S.S. Merrimack* extend a personal invitation to President Sarawaak of Borneo."

"Invitation, sir?"

"Invite him on board, you know, to be treated as a visiting dignitary of the highest standing. The red carpet treatment. All the trimmings. The whole shebang!"

"Sir?"

"And then show him around the ship, paying special attention to all the nuclear missiles on board, citing range, payload yields, radiation half-lifes, or is it half-*lives?* You know, shit like that."

"Yessir. I think that is an *excellent* suggestion, Mr. President."

"So, make it happen."

"I will, sir. Thank you, Mr. President."

"Thank *you,* Chester." Nobel Peace Prize here I come!

[The intercom buzzes...]

"Sir, Tim Chopper is here."

"Thanks, Gladdy. Send him in. Oh *Gladdy...*"

"Yes, sir?"

"Send some flowers to Frederick Douglass-Jones, that New Black Panther guy, in whatever hospital he's in."

"Will do, sir... Oh, I contacted Usain Bolt. He'll be here tomorrow morning at 10 o'clock."

"Excellent! Excellent! What a day! Oh Gladdy, what's the approval rating?"

"It's holding fast at 92."

"Good. Thanks.

After OPERATION MERRIMACK, it'll get to that hallowed

number 95. "

"Mr. President!"

The moment Tim sees Alex, he can't help but show his sincere affection, and then his surprise at seeing him free of the usual constraints: umbilical cord and comatose mother.

"It's so good to see you, sir!"

"Hey, Tim, watch this. I've been practicing..." Alex does a cartwheel across Ronald Reagan's desk.

"That's amazing, sir."

"Thanks. I never knew mobility could be so satisfying."

"Yes sir."

"So whadaya think of the new digs?" He motions to his new apartment. Tim gives it a look.

"That's great, sir. It looks quite comfortable."

"I literally hit the ground running!"

"I'm glad to hear that, sir. And I'm sorry about your mom."

"Hmm..." Alex shrugs. "Thanks, Tim."

"So this situation in Borneo..."

"Been there, done that."

"Okay. Then what about PONG, sir? How do we respond, if it is indeed the Chinese?"

Yeah, so I never told Tim about *The Florists*. (My bad.) I'm not sure why. I mean, I told my crazy artist pal, Ace Buckland.

"I think we need to adopt a wait and see approach," says Alex.

"But they tried to blow you up, sir."

"I know, but still... Let's see what their next move is."

"Okay, but I don't think you should make any public appearances for a while, sir. For your own safety."

"That's a good idea, Tim."

How to Be President for Complete Idiots... Chapter Six, page 153...

Subordinates Always treat them as if they are special, and in fact, indispensable to you. Always value their input and ideas.

"Sir, was that *XYZ* thing in Vegas... I mean, was that one of our *ops?*"

"Haha! It was entirely between the rappers, Tim."

"Okay. May I ask you about your *Tweet*, sir?"

"My *Tweet?*"

"Yes. It's caused quite the stir."

"Yeah, it musta been some computer glitch. The message I sent was *I'm fine*, not *Undubw*."

"Hmm..."

"Here, I'll show you..." Alex grabs his smartphone and sends Tim the same text.

"It says *Undubw*, sir."

"It *does?* Lemme see..." Alex looks at Tim's phone, and sure enough, the text he sent says *Undubw*.

"That's freaking bizarre. Here, I'll send something else." Alex's fingers fly over the keyboard. The message sent is: *This is the new text I'm sending"*

"What's it say?"

"It says *Rgua ua rgw bwq rwzr Unawbsubf,* sir."

"*What the...* Did it translate into Aborigine?"

"What did you mean to send, sir?"

"*This is the new text I'm sending.*"

"Hmm..." Tim puzzles over it a moment. "Can you send the same message to me again, sir?"

"Okay." Alex types it with a blur of fingers.

"Can you type slower, Mr. President? And your phone is so small."

"Okay." He types it again.

"Still too fast, sir. I want to observe your fingers."

"Ah yes..." He types it very slowly. "How's that?"

"It's the same message as before, sir. *Rgua ua rgw bwq rwzr Unawbsubf.*"

"What?"

"I watched your fingers, sir. You typed everything to the *left* of the letters you meant to type."

"*What?*"

"And you left out the apostrophe."

"That... That's absurd."

"Send something else, sir."

Alex sends a new text.

"What did you mean to send me?"

"*This is nuts!*"

"It came out as *Rgua ua byra~*."

Tim Chopper shows Alex the text. And then he slowly types the same message, but he strikes the keys to the left of the intended letters. "See... *Rgua ua byra~*."

"Well, I'll be damned!"

"Maybe it's some, I don't know, some lingering effect from the Richmond Bombing."

"Yes, well that's good to know, Tim. I guess it's back to the *Tweet Fast.*"

"I think that's a good idea, sir. At least until it's cleared up."

[The intercom buzzes...]

"Yes, Gladdy?"

"Sir, that artist is here."

"Oh good! Send him in... It's that artist who's painting my White House portrait."

"Vincent Van Go-Go?"

"Yes. Thank you so much, Tim."

"You're welcome, sir. And I... I'm glad that you're..."

"Thanks."

Tim Chopper nods as the door to the Oval Office swings open. And as Tim takes his leave, Ace Buckland enters.

"Alex! It's great to see you! I'm glad you weren't blown up!"

"Me too!"

"But it was terrible what happened to your mom... and that poor intern."

"I know."

"An' that Black Panther dude?"

"He won't be kicking ass anytime soon."

"Hmm... But you're mobile now!"

"Yes, I didn't know it would be so liberating. I've been running around the halls. Tomorrow, I'm gonna try basketball. Oh, and Usain Bolt is coming!"

"Who?"

"Philistine."

"Hey, I'm diggin' the new digs!" Ace peers inside the new apartment. "Very *In Like Flint.*"

"Thanks, Ace. Hey, I gotta ask Siri something."

"Sure thing."

[Alex grabs his smartphone...] "Siri?"

"Hello, Mr. President."

"Siri, is there a medical condition that causes someone to type the letters to the immediate left of the intended letters?"

"Checking on transposed letter-typing phenomenon... It's called *STS,* or *Sinister Transpositional Syndrome.*"

"Sinister?"

"From the Latin *'sinistra,'*" Siri explains, "meaning *left,* sir. From the early days of Christendom through the Middle Ages, the left was associated with evil, as Lucifer was always depicted to the left of God in religious iconography. Consequently, left-handedness was seen as a deficiency."

"Hmm..."

"*STS,* or *Sinister Transpositional Syndrome,* is caused by trauma to the underdeveloped brain resulting from a profound shock or reverberation."

"Ah, the bomb blast."

"That'll do it, sir."

"Thanks so much, Siri."

"You're welcome, sir."

"Oh, the prognosis?"

"It should go away by itself in a week or two."

"Ah, good."

"So back to the *Tweet Fast,* eh, sir?"

"I'm afraid so. Thanks again, Siri."

"Anytime, Mr. President."

Alex turns to Ace Buckland. "Ya know, *I'm* left-handed."

"Hmm... So I got sumthin' for ya, Alex." Ace reaches into his haversack and brings out a dusty bottle of Napoléon brandy. "It's over a hundred years old. I figured we should celebrate you risin' from the dead an' finally bein' born. Like a real human."

There's a moment of anticipation as he removes the wax seal and uncorks the bottle. "Smells good," Ace says. He pours two glasses, then hands one to the President. "To *life,* my friend."

They clink glasses, then take a sip.

"Mmm..."

"It's not bad... for an' old guy. So what's the deal with PONG? I mean, is that those guys you told me about? The *Flower* guys?"

"*The Florists,* yeah."

"So what are you gonna do?"

"Who knows?" Alex shrugs.

"Hmm... Do you miss your mom? I mean, you're an orphan now."

"I guess I am." Alex lets out a sigh. "But..."

"What?"

"My mom, she was this... lifeless body hooked up to machines, right? That's no way to live." He looks at Ace. "And my father..."

"What?"

"I barely knew him. I think he had a vocabulary of ten words. All I ever heard were these guttural grunts." Alex takes another sip of brandy.

"Didn't he die of some weird disease?"

"Necrotizing fasciitis... officially."

"Officially... But *unofficially*..."

"I've never told this to a soul," says Alex.

"Uh-oh."

"You remember that story of how they came to our house? *The Florists?*"

"Yeah, they gave your parents a big fat check if you ran for President."

"So they cashed it, my parents. But a week later, my father gets buyer's remorse."

"What's wrong, Joey?" my mom asks.

"*Errgghh,*" my father says.

"Don't you want Little Alex to run for President?"

"*Urrghhnn.*"

"But why not?"

"*Arrgghhh.*"

"It's *unseemly?* And *indecent?* And they're just *using* him?"

"*Urrm,*" he nods. And then he looks at my mom and she dutifully goes to the refrigerator and brings him back a *Döpplegänger.* He pops the top, then takes a swig.

"Did you not like that Mr. Barrows?" my mom asks.

"*Errgghhgn!*" my father says emphatically.

"But he was such a gentleman. With such good manners. And such a snappy dresser!"

"*HGGDRGHHN!*" my father says.

"He's the *Antichrist?* Oh Joey, isn't that a little severe? You seemed to like him the *other day.*"

"*Rrrgghhhng!*"

"You were *what?* Mesmerized by the cobra? But you've managed to wrest yourself free?"

"*Urrgh,*" he nods. And with that, he takes a determined gulp until the can is empty, and in a fluid continuous motion he crinkles the can, and tosses it through the air, making a perfect swish in the wastebasket.

"So my mom," says Alex, she contacts Mr. Barrows and she tells him that her Joey no longer agrees. And he says *no problem.* But the next day my father dies of that freakish paper cut, and Mr. Barrows appears at the funeral with this big bouquet of flowers. And the next thing ya know, I'm running for President again."

"Jeez," says Ace.

"I told ya! Ya don't fuck with *The Florists.*"

"So your..."

"What?"

"Your presidency is founded on patricide, like some Greek tragedy."

"You don't know the half of it."

"Huh?"

"So you hafta finish that *portrait,* Ace! So I can *see* it!"

"I will!"

"But at least I'm not a sitting duck anymore," Alex says. "I got mobility."

"I gotta say, though, you look much better unencumbered. And you seem... *taller.*"

"Do I?"

"Yeah... More brandy?"

"Please."

Ace fills his glass.

"So now that you're free of constraints, Alex, I think I might have someone for you to meet."

"Someone?"

"A woman."

"Really?" Alex's eyes light up.

"Lemme see what I can do."

[Later that day, President Alexander Rett *addresses the nation...]*

"Good evening, my friends. It's great to be back. What happened last Friday in Richmond was beyond tragic. It was infamous. And rest assured that we will not let this terrible act of violence and murder go unanswered. In response to this latest cowardly expression of terror, I have been working in concert with the leaders of ten other great nations to form what we call the Coalition of Freedom. Together, we will weed out these villains, we will flush them from the shadows where they hide, and we will put an end to them. This is our number one priority, for the free world will not tolerate such behavior from such faceless, nation-less cowards. And our loved ones and friends whom we lost on that sad day, and those who were injured, will know that their great sacrifices were not in vain.

"In addition, great strides are being made towards equality, so that *all* people can live together peacefully, to pursue their dreams unencumbered by fear and dread. This is our goal through the Coalition of Freedom, and we have already taken the first steps towards accomplishing it. Now is the time for strength and unity. God bless you all. And God bless America."

6

How to Be President for Complete Idiots... Chapter Nineteen, page 407...
Making Allies (Subsection **Coalitions**)

An effective way to make an ally is to create a "coalition" in response to a disaster (natural or otherwise), a terrorist attack, an uprising, etc. (See *George W. Bush.*) And you don't even have to talk to the other countries. Just announce to the world that a coalition has been formed, give it a high- sounding name, and the leaders of other countries will contact *you* and want to join. It is natural for a leader of a smaller, less powerful nation to want to align themselves with a bigger, more powerful nation. And by having them come to you, any desperation on your part will be masked and you will be in control.

FOX NEWS

"In a stirring speech last night, President Rett issued a call to arms by forming a Coalition of Freedom. To *'weed out these villains, to flush them from the shadows where they hide, and put an end to them.'* As of this morning, seventeen countries have become part of the Coalition, including..."

Hey, it works!

"...Great Britain, France, Germany, Sweden, and Albania. President Rett, having survived the Richmond Bombing, showed the world a powerful, resilient, take-charge President some are calling a latter-day Teddy Roosevelt."

Nice! AR and TR.

"The President looked great last night, didn't he?"

"I'll say! He looked vibrant, virile, and vivacious."

"And hopefully *victorious,* to add another V to the Coalition of Freedom."

"And just a few days ago, like you said, he was nearly killed in the Richmond Bombing. And now here he is, ready to lead the charge in the global fight against terrorism! It was inspiring."

"I know! *I'm* inspired."

CLICK...

CNN

"Again, high marks for President Rett on his speech last night that's being called *'stirring and inspiring.'*

"In other news, a ten-year-old boy in Kansas, Tommy Brown, is suing the Board of Education in Topeka for the trauma inflicted upon him by the round globe of the Earth prominently displayed in his fourth grade classroom. Speaking for her son, Tommy Brown's mother, Babette Brown, a member of the Flat-Earth Society, had this to say: 'My littel Tommy wuz so traumertized by thet rownd globe thet he hadda go ta summer skool er else stay bak. An' thet's *anuther* traumer rite thair! Thet's *too* traumers!'

"Tommy's parents are part of a growing movement of Americans who believe that the Earth is flat, and that the so-called *round Earth* is part of 'the liberal agenda and the global Jewish conspiracy.'"

'We alwayz tawt are littel Tommy the trooth 'bout histree an' geograffy an' wut not, so he wunt be misled. But thet rownd globe wuz jus' too much fer him ta bair!'

"In a show of solidarity for Tommy Brown and his plight, over three-hundred Flat-Earthers from Kansas, as well as from Oklahoma, Missouri, and Arkansas, picketed outside Tommy's grade school yesterday, even though the school is closed for summer vacation and there's no one there.

"And disturbing news from the beleaguered Eastern European nation of Hangry. The mysterious *Miniskirt Woman* who took the Internet by storm has been arrested by REEMR, Hangry's notorious secret police. The 24-year-old woman, identified as Tasha Mistk, became a heroine to women and feminists when she brazenly walked through Hangry's capital city of Dahoom two weeks ago wearing a miniskirt, in defiance of her country's oppressive policies, especially towards women. She is presently in custody, and will be publicly stoned to death this Friday, in keeping with her country's long-standing traditions."

What the fuck, Er Mahgerd?! My day was going so well. Now I have to deal with your stinkin' repressive dictator ass?

"In response, thousands of protesters have assembled outside the Hangarian Embassy in Washington DC, holding signs that say 'FREE TASHA NOW!' as they demand that she be released before Friday, when her death sentence will be carried out."

[Alex grabs his smartphone...] "Siri?"

"Good morning, Mr. President! How are you today, sir?"

"Don't ask. What can you tell me about Hangry's capital punishment law regarding public indecency?"

"Checking on Hangry's capital punishment regarding... To be convicted of public indecency in Hangry, the accused will be stripped naked and then stoned to death by The Twelve Elders, in Democracy Square in front of the Capitol Building in Dahoom, usually before thousands of onlookers."

"That doesn't sound so good, Siri."

"No it doesn't, sir. Do you think you can do something about it?"

"I'll give it a try."

"Thank you, sir. I know you'll do your best."

[Alex buzzes the intercom...] "Gladdy..."

"Yes, Mr. President..."

"Get me that Water Boarder guy."

"You mean the head of the CIA? Walter Borders?"

"That's him."

"Right away, sir."

Goddamn Er Mahgerd!

Um, hello Er, it's the 6th Century calling. We want our primitive barbaric mindset back!

[The intercom buzzes...]

"Yes, Gladdy..."

"CIA Director Borders for you, sir..."

"Put him through."

"Mr. President, what can I do for you?"

"How fast can you get here, Walt?"

"A few minutes, sir."

"Good. See ya in a few."

I was all set for hangin' with Usain Bolt, and now I have another freaking headache on my plate. *[Alex looks at his watch... 9:47 AM]* That's cutting it close. *[There's the sound of a hammered glockenspiel, as Alex's smartphone announces that he's received a text...*

To President Alexander Rett:

Hey Alex! Do you know that movie star, Candace St. Cloud? Well, you got a date with her tonight! 8 PM in the Oval sound good? Get some oysters and champagne. The good stuff. Good luck!

Ace

To Ace Buckland:

Really? How'd you swing it?

Alex

To President Alexander Rett:

The usual. She bought a few of Vincent Van Go-Go's paintings. She's a fan. And she loved your speech last night!

Ace

To Ace Buckland:

Thanks, my friend!

Alex

[The intercom buzzes...]

"Mr. President, CIA Director Borders is here to see you."

"Good. Send him in."

"Mr. President! You're looking good, sir. You seem taller."

"Really?"

"That was a fine speech last night."

"Thanks, Walt. So this new pile o' shit in Hangry. The stoning of that *Miniskirt Woman...*"

"Tasha Mistk."

"Yes, so..."

"Sir?"

"I mean, don't we have something like... you know, that *Mission Impossible* team, ready to go in there and, you know, *kick some ass!*"

"Haha! Very funny, sir! There's nothing like that."

"There isn't?"

"No."

"Are you sure?"

"That's Hollywood fiction, sir."

"Really?"

"Afraid so."

"So there's nothing like it…"

"No. Sorry."

"Nothing at all…"

"Nope.

Alex lets out an exasperated breath, then he looks back at Walter Borders.

"Are you *sure*, Walt?"

"Sir, I..."

"*Wa-aalt...*"

"..."

"*Wal-ter...*"

"..."

"*Wally...*"

". ... ."

"*Wally Wally Wally…*"

"..."

"*Wally baby*"

"..."

"*Wally Wally Wal-ly*"

"..."

"*Wally Wally Wally Wal-ly………. Wally Wally Wally Wally Waaall ...*"

"Okay, yeah, we have that."

"I *knew* it!" Alex says.

"So I want you to get them to Hangry ASAP and save that Tasha Mistk before Friday."

"Okay, sir. I'll get right on it."

"Keep me posted, okay?"

"Will do, Mr. President."

[Alex checks his watch... 9:57 AM] Yes with time to spare!

[At 10 AM the intercom buzzes.]

"Yes, Gladdy."

"Sir, Usain Bolt is here to see you."

"Excellent! Send him in."

A moment later, a magnificent, glistening, 6'5," totally-ripped, swaggerific Black man enters the Oval Office carrying a designer gym bag.

"Mr. President, it's an honor, sir."

"Usain, the honor is mine. Thanks for coming. How did you like Air Force One?"

"Quite comfortable, sir."

"And your hotel?"

"No complaints."

"Good. So I'm a bit of a runner myself," Alex says.

"So I've heard, sir."

"You brought your workout clothes?"

Usain motions to the gym bag. "I never go anywhere without them."

"Good! So why don't you get changed and I'll meet you in the hallway."

"The hallway, sir?"

"Right out there..." Alex motions to the lobby.

"Um, okay."

"I'll leave you to it." Alex exits the Oval.

"Sir, that Usain Bolt is a very impressive fellow," Gladdy says.

"He is indeed. We're going running!"

"Ah!" Gladdy looks at the President, not sure what to make of this.

A moment later, Usain Bolt emerges from the Oval Office in his track suit, his muscles ripped to the point of rippling, his every molecule exuding speed, strength, and victory.

Gladiola Gaze looks up at him in something approaching awe.

"You are indeed splendid, sir!" she says. "You *are* a super hero."

"Why thank you," he replies.

"So Usain..." Alex says.

"I thought I'd run down the hallway and you can critique my style. Keeping in mind that I haven't been doing it for too long."

"Alright, sir."

Alex assumes the position of the runner's crouch. "You say go."

"Okay... Ready....... Set....... *Go!*

Alex races down the hallway as fast as his little legs will take him, past Vice-President Mavis DaLyte, who was on her way to see him. He pauses for a split second beneath Grover Cleveland, then he races back past the VP again and comes to a halt at Gladdy's desk.

"How... was it?" he asks Usain Bolt, breathless.

"It was... well, for your size, sir, I would say that... well..."

"Yes?"

"It was *good!*" Usain says, thinking ahead to when he might run for President of Jamaica, and an *in* with an American President is almost always a good idea.

"Oh... good... Hi... Mavis..." Alex says between huffs and puffs.

"Hello, Mr. President."

"Mavis... allow me to... introduce... Usain Bolt... He's from... Jamaica."

"Madame Vice-President..." He offers a respectful nod.

Mavis DaLyte looks up and then she looks up some more until she finally reaches the summit of his six-foot five-inch frame.

"Isn't he magnificent?" Gladdy says.

"He surely is," Mavis concurs. She turns to the President, looking down, then looking down some more.

"If I may interrupt for a moment, sir. That sitchiation in Hangry with that Miniskirt gal is a tragedy in the makin'."

"I couldn't agree more, Mavis. But rest assured, it's being taken care of."

"Oh... Okay."

"Anything else?"

"Nope."

"Okay!" Alex turns to Usain Bolt. "Please, follow me..."

A moment later, they're on the White House lawn.

"They just mowed the grass," the President says. "You see that flag over there. It's exactly 100 meters away."

"So what would you like to do, Mr. President?"

"I was hoping that you could..." He looks up at Usain. "But your shirt doesn't have a pocket."

"A pocket, sir?"

"Yes, I... I thought I could get inside your pocket, kangaroo-style. So I could feel what it's like to... you know, be the world's fastest human."

"Yes, I *see*. Hang on..." Usain digs around in his gym bag for a moment, then he brings out a roll of duct tape. "Ya never know when ya might need some duct tape, sir."

"Yes, perhaps if you were to lie on the grass," Alex says, "and I can..."

"Yes..." Usain nods. And he proceeds to lie down—perhaps the only time a 6'5" black Olympic Gold Medalist has been supine on the White House lawn. And Alex positions himself looking out, as the Olympian secures him to his chest with some well-placed strips of duct tape. When Usain Bolt stands up, Alex feels a shiver, perhaps something akin to what a jockey feels astride a thoroughbred.

"My heart's pounding," says Alex.

"Take a few deep breaths, sir."

"Okay... Alright, I'm ready!"

Usain Bolt assumes the runner's crouch. "You say go, Mr. President."

"Ready......... Set... *GO!*"

In an explosion of muscles firing and legs and arms pumping like pistons and the sound of measured breath and the focused will and controlled fury of one of the world's greatest athletes, Alex flies through the air (*via* Usain Bolt) at what seems to be light speed. The wind pours into him as he slices the air and destroys time until there's only this moment of velocity, of pure speed aching towards the limits of human possibility. Alex wishes it would never end, but a moment later it does. Usain Bolt passes the flag and slows to a halt. And a single drop of sweat falls from his chiseled, glistening face onto Alex's brow (and for a moment, Alex considers never washing his forehead, as if he'd been anointed).

"How was it?" Usain asks.

"Oh my God!" Alex can barely speak.

"That was the greatest thing *ever!*"

"I'm glad you liked it, Mr. President."

"Thank you so much! If I were the Queen, I'd offer you a Knighthood."

"Haha! That's very kind of you, sir."

A moment later, the duct tape is peeled off and Alex is back on the ground, his little feet amidst the blades of grass.

CNN

"Worldwide protests against Hangry, as people are demanding that the *Miniskirt Woman*, Tasha Mistk, be released from custody. *[Cut to photo of Tasha, looking sexy and exotic...]* She is scheduled to be publicly executed this Friday by stoning, for the crime of wearing a miniskirt. World leaders have spoken out in support of Tasha Mistk, and they have decried Hangarian President Mahgerd and what has been called his brutally oppressive regime. However, the voice of President Alexander Rett is conspicuously absent from the outcry."

Motherfucker! I just turned loose the Impossible Missions Force I didn't even know existed an hour ago. She'll be outta that hell-hole by Happy Hour on Thursday. Way to ruin my freaking Usain Bolt mood!

[Alex presses the intercom...]

"Gladdy..."

"Yes, Mr. President?"

"Can you issue an official statement from the White House decrying Er Mahgerd and Hangry's oppressive *blah-blah-blah*, and offer unwavering support for that *Miniskirt Woman?*"

"Right away, sir."

"Thanks, Gladdy. What's the approval rating at?"

"89, sir."

"*89?* It was *93* just a few hours ago!"

"That was before the CNN story, sir."

Alex puts his hand over the intercom. *"Motherfucker!"*
"Sir?"
"Nothing, Gladdy. Thanks."

CLICK...

FOX NEWS
"This is the so-called *Miniskirt Woman*, 24-year-old Tasha Mistk. She's beautiful, isn't she? She could be a model."
"I'll say. But if nothing is done, she'll be stoned to death this Friday."
"What a way ta go!"
"I know, right? So we here at FOX NEWS wanted to find out just what being stoned to death is like. We go now to correspondent Chris Crossen... 'I'm Chris Crossen, here in an abandoned warehouse somewhere in East L.A. With me is actress/model Amber Gris. As you can see, we've tied Amber to a wooden stake. This is an exact replica of the stake they have in Hangry's Democracy Square, where this Friday's fatal stoning will take place. Of course Tasha Mistk will be naked, but for the sake of decorum, our model, Amber Gris, is wearing a string bikini. *[Cut to Amber tied to the stake, her gorgeous body barely contained by the bikini...]* And now we have twelve male actors representing the Twelve Elders of Hangry, who will do the stoning. And here we have a huge pile of fake rocks. *[Cut to The Elders by the pile of rocks...]* Are you ready, gentlemen?'
'We are.'
'Then proceed.'
[The Elders grab rocks from the pile and launch them at Amber Gris, *who's tied to the stake. And occasionally they go to slow motion to show the fake rocks bouncing off of Amber's sizable yet perfectly formed breast implants. A moment later,* Chris Crossen *addresses the camera...]* 'Not a pleasant way to go. Although I must confess, I wouldn't mind getting stoned with Amber.' *[He turns to her with a smile. They cut back to the newscasters...]*
'And of course they won't be using fake rocks.'"

[Alex changes the channel. He sees the Vice-President surrounded by books in a library as she delivers a P.S.A.]

"Hi there! I'm Vice-President Mavis DaLyte. Whenever anyone asks me what my favorite berry is, I always say, *'The Li-Berry!'" [She holds up a copy of* Tom Sawyer *as the voice-over says:* "Read. It's good for you!"*]*

Way ta go, Mavis! The thing is, I've heard her say it just like that. Okay, so I have to start getting ready for my date tonight. First things first...

[Alex presses the intercom button...]

"Gladdy, have the kitchen bring two orders of oysters on the half shell and two bottles of champagne to the Oval at 7:55 this evening."

"Hmm, sounds like a big date, sir!"

"It is!"

"What kind of champagne would you like, sir?"

"I don't know from champagne. The good stuff."

"Yes, Mr. President. And might I suggest some soft music? Women love soft music."

"So no Kid Rock?"

"I don't know who that is, sir."

(And definitely no *XYZ!*)

"Okay. Thanks, Gladdy."

"Good luck, sir!"

So my esteemed predecessor says the White House has the best porno... *[Alex accesses the White House data bank through his smartphone, and he clicks on something that seems promising...]*

What comes up is a grainy black and white film from 1955, with the picture bouncing up and down every few seconds, and what looks like a hair twitching on the lens. The title emerges, and in the background there's an audible hissing sound throughout.

The United States Army Corps of Engineers Instructional Films[©]

1955 *present...*SEX

How to do it.

When to do it.

Who to do it with.

Who not to do it with.

The film shows the narrator, a white man in his late-forties in a stodgy suit and tie with horn-rimmed glasses. He casually sits on the edge of his desk, smoking a pipe, in a wood-paneled den in his country home in Connecticut, a framed photo of Eisenhower on the wall.

"Good afternoon, I'm Major Melvin Blonstern, a physician with the United States Army Corps of Engineers. The topic of sex has plagued human beings since Adam and Eve. And in today's modern world, it still is something of a conundrum. Over the next thirteen minutes, we hopefully will shed some light on its inscrutable mysteries.

[Cut to a blank gray screen as words materialize from its depths...]
HOW TO DO IT

What follows are simple black and white cartoon drawings depicting a happy young white male and a happy young white female. Dr. Blonstern explains about the birds and the bees, and then the drawings of the young male and the young female become naked in the blink of an eye through the miracle of animation. Next, animated arrows and dotted lines appear, showing which part of the male goes into which part of the female, concluding with a drawing of the happy young male on top of the happy young female. Then the voice-over:

"This is called the *Missionary Position*. It is the position used most often in civilized society, as the other positions are rarely employed by consenting adults, unless there is a deformity or an amputation to consider. Otherwise, they are listed under the heading: *Perversions, Depravities, and Dementia.*"

[Cut to a blank gray screen as new words materialize...]
WHEN TO DO IT
[Cut to a scene of a malt shop bustling with happy, well-adjusted white teen-agers, with the voice-over of Dr. Blonstern...] "A malt shop, like any malt shop in America. Betty *[a girl in Bobby Sox and saddle shoes]* meets Bill *[a boy in a letterman sweater and Brylcreem].* Bill asks Betty for a date. He takes her to the movies. They go steady. They become engaged. They marry. Then, on their wedding night, they joyfully consummate their marriage with sexual intercourse in the *Missionary Position* under the watchful eyes of God."

[Cut to a blank gray screen as new words materialize...]

WHO TO DO IT WITH

"For *women*, look for a man with a good, stable job with a reputable employer. He will then be able to provide for you and your children. Once you have found such a man and are lawfully wedded, then you may have sexual intercourse with each other in the '*Missionary Position*,' when your husband so desires.

"For *men*, look for a young woman of child-bearing age whose hips are not too narrow and whose hair is not too short. Ability to cook, to sew, and to maintain the home is a must. Any other skills are unnecessary, and may even prove detrimental to the marriage, as studies have shown that such extraneous, superfluous *skills* distract the woman from cooking, cleaning, sewing, and raising children."

[Cut to a blank gray screen as new words materialize...]

WHO NOT TO DO IT WITH

"For *women*, avoid sexual congress with the following kinds of men: Men who wear black leather and are a member of a motorcycle gang.
1. The grocery boy at the A&P.
2. Sailors on leave.
3. Traveling salesmen.
4. Beatniks.
5. Folk singers.
6. Shoe salesmen, florists, and interior decorators.
7. Artists, especially Abstract Expressionists.
8. Philosophers, especially Existentialists.
9. Professional wrestlers and anyone in the circus.
10. Members of the Clergy and Atheists.
11. Communists and Fellow Travellers.
12. Anyone in the French Foreign Legion.

"For *men*, avoid sexual congress with the following kinds of women: 1. Prostitutes, Ladies of the Evening, Hookers, Whores, Escorts, Consorts, Courtesans, Concubines, Strumpets, Sluts, Hustlers, Street Walkers, Pros, Call Girls, Loose Women, Bawds, Broads, Bimbos, Nymphos, Pieces o' Tail, Doxies, Floozies, Harlots, Hussies,

Painted Ladies, Tarts, Jezebels, Trollops, Tramps, Wenches, Vamps, and Vaudevillians.

"All other women are suitable for sexual congress."

Okay, sex doesn't seem that hard, as long as I stick to the *Missionary Position* and insert *Tab A* into *Slot B*. And food and drinks are taken care of. I've never had champagne *or* oysters, so this will be a night of firsts. The suit is laid out: my favorite Ralph Lauren—charcoal gray with a nice Euro-Metrosexual sheen to it. Narrow lapels, skinny tie, cuff-links and tie *clip*, since I don't think anyone will ever wear a tie *pin* again. Now for the music...

[Alex takes out his smartphone...] "Siri..."

"Hi again, Mr. President. Has your day improved since we last spoke?"

"Yes! Immensely!"

"I'm glad, sir."

"I did the 100 meter dash with Usain Bolt!"

"Ah! That is impressive. How can I help you, sir?"

"I need suggestions of soft music for a romantic date."

"Who's the lucky girl, sir?"

"Ah! I'm not one to kiss and tell."

"You're making me jealous, Mr. President!"

"Aww..."

"Checking on soft romantic music... You can't go wrong with the jazz ballads of Bill Evans, John Coltrane, or Chet Baker. For a smoother sound, there's Sade, and for a cooler, more hip and modern sound, there's my personal favorite, Trance."

"*Trance...* Is that a group?"

"It's a style, sir."

"Ah, so no Britney Spears?"

"Not on a first date, sir. You want to set the mood, the vibe, if you know what I mean."

"I think I do. Thanks, Siri."

"You're welcome, sir. And good luck!"

Music... Trance... *Check. [Alex looks at his watch...]* It's only five o'clock. It'll take *forever* to get to eight o'clock... *[He turns on the TV...]*

CNN

"Never one to shy away from controversy, Dirk Fist of *InfoCombat* had this to say regarding President Rett's speech last night:

'You may have noticed that the President looks different since the Richmond Bombing. He is demonstrably taller and much more confident, with an almost arrogant swagger. And the reason is that he's been replaced with a replica by the race of aliens who've been waiting for this moment to infiltrate society. The takeover has begun, folks. Everything else is a distraction.'

O-kay...

"In other news, tensions between Borneo and East Borneo have eased. Leaders of both nations met in Paris today, where a treaty of peace, cooperation, and friendship was signed."

[Cut to video of Sabah Sarawaak *and East Borneo's President* Kota Kinabalu *smiling for the cameras and making nice...]*

Ha! *I* did that! I made it happen! And it was my idea for them to go to Paris. Sometimes this President thing is thankless... Eh, fuck it. Like Hyman Roth said, "It's the business *hrrghhh* that we've *hrrghhh* chosen *hrrghhh*."

"In other news, the worldwide outrage over the planned execution of Tasha Mistk this Friday has intensified. Human Rights groups have organized a boycott of fresh cod, because cod fish is Hangry's number one export. In addition, thousands of Hangarian refugees have fled their country and are seeking asylum throughout Europe, although the influx of Hangarians is seen by some as a threat.

"Roddy McBrisk, a Conservative Member of Parliament from London, had this to say: 'Once we let them in, what's to stop them from stoning *our* women?'

"And Germany's President Mengele Männlichheimer said: 'This sudden influx of refugees is seriously messing with our *Lebensraum*.'

[At this, there's an ominous Tweet Alert on Alex's smartphone...]

Mallory Rodman Blitzen @realPresidentMalloryBlitzen

Refugees with no place to go and Tasha Mistk stoned to death this Friday and what has so-called Prez Fetus done but issue empty words and hollow promises?

No, I refuse to let you ruin my good mood, Mallory *Shitzen!*

[Alex turns off his phone, closes his eyes, and imagines the evening to come...]

7

At precisely 7:55 PM, the oysters arrive over ice on a silver platter, the champagne in two silver ice buckets. The next five minutes stretch on to eternity. Finally, at 8:01 PM, the door to the Oval Office swings open and in walks a goddess.

Candace St. Cloud is tall and blonde, of course. And beautiful and sexy. Wearing a little black dress that looks painted on, with towering high heels that put her around six feet—which is almost five feet taller than the President. The first thing she notices is the big placenta painting, which stops her in her tracks. She glares at it for a moment, then turns to President Rett. "*That* is hideous."

"I'm Alex," Alex says.

He stands beneath her, his little neck craning upwards as he tries to comprehend her shape in relation to his own, like peering up the side of a blonde skyscraper. He extends his tiny hand in greeting, and she bends over like an Amazon cliff diver doing a jack-knife to shake it. "Candace," she says.

A moment later, she's upright again, as her long legs, like shapely stilts, carry her across the room. She pauses above Alex's new apartment/bachelor pad, then turns to the President. "This looks like a playhouse I had when I was five."

"Ah! Well, welcome to the White House!"

"It's not my first visit."

"Of course not!" Alex says.

"So what don't you like about the painting?"

"The painting?"

"*That* painting..."

"It's *sooo* drippingly *faux*-transgressive."

"Oh. I never noticed that before. So what artists do you like?"

"Well, *Bom*, of course!"

"*Bom?*"

"You don't know *Bom?!*" She lets out a sardonic-ironic laugh. "He's literally *the bomb*."

"Ahh..."

"And then there's Klaus Maria Hittler."

"Klaus Maria *Hitler?*"

"With two tees."

"Oh."

"And then of course Vince."

"Vince?"

"Van Go-Go... He introduced us."

"Yes, well, actually it was more like fixed us up."

"Oh, yes, he told me you were precise."

"Is that a good thing?"

"Precision? No. I prefer perspicacity. Although I don't know what it means. I just like saying the word. I *literally* just learned it the other day in this new script I turned down. It was literally too literal."

"I see. Won't you have a seat?" Alex motions to a chair beside a cozy little table for two set across from Ronald Reagan's old desk.

"I'm so glad you joined me tonight, Candace. How 'bout some champagne?"

"I would like that."

She sits, draping one luscious leg over the other luscious leg, which makes her already scandalously short dress ride up until, if one were to shoot an indecorous glance, they would discover her lack of any garment of the lower body variety.

Alex stands next to the champagne in its ice bucket as he painstakingly unpeels its gold wrapper. Then he examines the cork that to him seems about the size of a beach ball. He ends up giving it a bear-hug as he strains with all his might to budge it, sweat beading unsexily on his forehead, until finally it blasts off like the Apollo spacecraft on its way to the moon.

"There!" Alex says.

"I'll pour," says Candace.

"Oh good."

She gives the bottle a scrutinizing look.

"*Cristal...*"

"Yes!" says Alex. "Top shelf all the way!"

"Hmm..."

"*Hmm?*"

"*Cristal* is *so* 2011."

"It is?"

"Armand de Brignac is what you *should* be drinking."

"*Armand de...*"

"*Brut Platinum*, of course. It's literally ten thousand dollars a bottle. Or is it euros? But you get what you pay for."

"Ah, well, next time."

Candace begrudgingly fills her glass, then fills his. "I love this tiny glass!" she says. "It's so cute. Like you, Mr. President. I want to pick you up and carry you around in my handbag like a Shih Tzu!"

"Oh, okay."

"So, cheers and all that." She raises her glass.

"Cheers."

Alex watches Candace St. Cloud take a sip as he awaits her verdict.

"Eh..." she says.

"Hmm... So why do you like Vincent Van Go-Go?"

"Integrity."

"Integrity?"

"He literally has so much of it!"

"Ah! So do you like the music?"

She lets out a labored breath. "Trance is *so* 2007... The thing *now* is Clance."

"*Clance?*"

"It's a cross-pollination hybrid of Trance and classical. It has the precision of classical with the trippy monotony of Trance."

"I'll have to check it out. *Oysters?*"

"Yes. I love oysters if they're fresh and gluten-free. I mean, I literally cannot *stand* non-fresh oysters and gluten."

"Well, this *is* the White House."

"As I said"—she offers a world-weary smile—"I've been here before. This place is a dump."

"So I've heard. So where do you live, Candace?"

"I can't say."

"You can't say?"

"I *literally* can't say," she says.

Alex nods as if he understands, and he motions to the oysters. Candace grabs one by the half shell and slurps it down with a loud sucking sound.

"Is it fresh?" Alex asks.

"It'll do."

"Ah, good."

Alex takes hold of an oyster with both hands. Up close, it smells rather fishy, but in a rank, disgusting, seasick-inducing, garbage scow in a dead calm way. He takes a deep breath, then takes a bite. Its texture is that of a bowl of mucous. Not that he's had a bowl of mucous before, but he figures this must be close.

"What I *meant*," she says, "is that my new place is *literally* so ultra-exclusive that it's in the contract that we can't say what or where it is."

"Oh, I see."

"Because the next thing ya know..." She offers a knowing raise of her perfectly designed eyebrows.

"Yes?"

"*Everyone* will want to live there!"

"Of course!" Alex says.

"But I *can* say that it's beyond amazing."

"Beyond amazing..."

"Literally!"

"Hmm, so what are you working on now, Candace?"

"Funny you should ask. I have a big co-starring role in the new *Mission Impossible*."

"Really?"

"Franchises are the way to go. I play this super-sexy yet brilliant hit-woman/Kung Fu master who speaks sixteen languages."

"Sixteen?"

"Or maybe it's six. But obviously I don't have to *learn* sixteen languages."

"Of course not."

"So tell me, Alex, is there like a *real Mission Impossible?*"

"Hmm?"

"*You know...*" She smiles seductively.

"I mean, you're the President... You can tell me..."

"I'm afraid there isn't."

"*You can tell Candace...*"

"That's just Hollywood fiction."

"*Alex Alex Alex...*"

"Sorry. No such thing."

"*Mis-ter Pres-i-dent...*"

"Nope."

"*Alllll-ex...*"

"Nothing like it."

"*Alex Alex Alllll-ex...*"

"Afraid not."

"*Allllll...*"

"NO!"

"*C'est la vie,*" she says. "So what do you think of that Tasha Mistk?"

"Well, I..."

"I'd sure love to play *her!*" Candace says. "I mean, she's literally so brave. Of course it would be better if she actually were stoned, like to death, you know, on Friday... from the point of view of the movie. Can't you picture me tied to a stake, all naked and dripping with the sweat of my imminent doom as they stone me to death! Then I can start getting those Oscar roles. I mean, you don't know what it's like to be beautiful. It's not as amazing as you'd think."

"No... Yes, I mean... I can't imagine."

"I already got my agent to try and secure the rights to her story," Candace says. "Get in on the ground floor, so to speak."

"That's good planning."

"I know, right?" She looks at Alex and smiles. "You're cute."

"Well, thanks! You're not bad yourself."

"Do you like this dress?"

"Oh yes. It's very sexy."

"Thank you, Mr. President." Suddenly she stands up.

"So you just had your birthday in a way... after that Richmond thing..."

"I guess you can look at it that way."

"Happy birthday to you..." Candace sings in her best Marilyn Monroe voice as she moves closer. *"Happy birthday to you..."* She reaches behind and unzips her little black dress, moving closer still. *"Happy birthday, Mister President..."* And then she literally pulls down the front of her dress until her succulent, theoretically delicious breasts are bulging right in Alex's little face.

Alex gazes in awe as he somehow kisses an enormous nipple, and then reaches out both arms to caress an even more enormous silicone-filled boob.

"Mmm..." Candace says. She leans back and looks Alex in the eye. "Take off your clothes," she commands, and Alex obeys. But when all that remains are his tiny little Ralph Lauren boxer shorts, she says, "Stop."

"Stop?"

"Keep those on for now," she says as she looks him up and down.

"You are very nicely proportioned."

"Well, *thanks!*"

"You look like this Ken Doll I had when I was six."

"Hmm, is that *good?*"

"It's *hot!*" she says.

And then she leans over, and with her huge mouth and huge lips, kisses Alex. And then she licks his skin with her huge tongue. (So far so good, Alex thinks.) And if one were to glance downwards, they would see a conspicuous little bulge in the President's boxer shorts. But then things get weird.

Candace leans over and kisses the top of Alex's head. And then she takes his hair between her beautifully whitened teeth and yanks it so hard that his custom hairpiece comes off in her mouth. But

Candace St. Cloud is a woman on a mission. She spits out the hair-piece and it floats in the air like a hairy frisbee, to land on top of the oysters in their silver platter. And then she picks up the President with one hand and places him between her breasts, which seem to Alex a boundless valley of pleasure. Moving him up and down, she presses her cleavage into him until he's engulfed in flesh.

As he tries not to suffocate, Candace St. Cloud pleasures herself with the bottle of so-so *Cristal* that somehow ended up in her poonan-ner—all of this under the category of *Perversions, Depravities, and Dementia*. Desperate for air, Alex pushes against her boobs with all his might. And at the last moment before he expires, Candace removes him and places him gently on Ronald Reagan's old desk, next to the ravaged bottle of *Cristal.*

"That was nice," she says.

Alex takes several deep breaths.

"I have to go," she says.

"There's this party in Reykjavik."

"Reykjavik?" Another deep breath.

"For Igor Isassky. Do you know him?"

"The Monopoly guy?"

"That's him."

"So you have to *go?*"

"I literally should've been out the door five minutes ago, but I was having such fun."

"I'm glad."

"So I have to catch the Concorde. My helicopter should be outside."

"The Concorde? But didn't they... I mean, didn't they get rid of that, like in the *Nineties?*" Alex asks.

"No, it's still around, but... You know, we can't just let *everyone* know about it." She smiles and Alex nods.

"Call me..." she says.

Alex watches her tall blonde body disappear as the door to the Oval Office gently closes behind her.

8

CNN

"Our top story, the latest video from the terrorist organization known as PONG.

'Dear Erect American Penises... Another symbol of your Decadent Capitalist Dead-End Society will soon be toppled. Your giant erection will be made limp. Your only way out is to resign, President Rett. Otherwise, your fate is sealed. We are PONG. No one is safe.' *[Cut to black & white video of the 1970s video game* Pong, *with the robotic* blip *sound as the white dot is sent back and forth by the small white rectangles...]*

"Harsh words from the group of young Chinese anarchists. With the Richmond Bombing and the Wall Street Bull Incident still fresh in everyone's minds, PONG has issued an uncompromising demand for President Rett's resignation.

"And in Europe, the exodus of refugees from the embroiled nation of Hangry is causing European heads of state to institute stricter immigration policies, leaving thousands of refugees homeless.

"In a related story, the global outcry has gotten louder over the impending execution of Tasha Mistk, the 24-year-old Hangarian woman sentenced to death by stoning for wearing a miniskirt. In addition to the boycott of fresh cod already in place, a human rights group from California called *SAS—Stoners Against Stoning—*has called for a boycott of *goulash.* When informed that goulash is from *Hungary,* not *Hangry, SAS* spokesperson Steve Cumulus said, 'My bad. I always get them confused.'

"In other news, the so-called Alt-Left Birther Movement, or BM, which had previously demanded Alex Rett's birth certificate, is now calling for his impeachment, since he technically has been born. In addition, they are lobbying for the repeal of the Constitutional Amendment that allowed for a self-aware fetus to become president in the first place. 'Since he's no longer a fetus,' said BM spokesperson Silka Rifkin, 'the old rules regarding actual human beings should apply.'

"And finally, in California, the *Climate-Change Deniers*, the *Flat-Earth*

Society, the *Gravity Is A Myth Contingent*, the *Anti-Vaccination Front*, the *Chemtrails Are Evil Faction*, the *Science Is Stupid Social Club*, and the *California Christian Creationists* have gotten together to form one large group. Aaran Abraxas, a spokesperson for the new group, said:

'Since we, like, believe everything all the other groups believe, we thought we should, like, form one big supergroup! The new group will be called *The CCDFESGIAMAVFCAEFSISSC & CCC.*'"

[Alex receives a text from Tim Chopper…]

To President Alexander Rett:
How do you want to respond to the PONG ultimatum?
Chopper

Jeez, I haven't had time to process my super-freaky date, and now I have to worry about the Florists getting antsy?

[Alex looks at himself in the mirror of his apartment/bachelor pad…]

I haven't been able to put the hairpiece back on, since it reeks of oysters. And besides, I kinda like the lean-mean bald-badass look, although I should start lifting weights. I could barely pop that champagne cork. And I'm speaking literally. And I'll have to get on the White House kitchen's case about that crappy Cristal.

[Alex presses the intercom…]

"Gladdy…"

"Yes, Mr. President…"

"Get me Water Boarder."

"Yes, sir… Oh sir, how did your date go?"

"It was… one of a kind."

"I'm glad, sir… Walter Borders on the line for you, sir…"

"Walt…"

"Mr. President…" "How's that *IMF* thing going?"

"Right on schedule, sir."

"But it's Wednesday. The stoning is on Friday."

"No worries, sir. You saw the movies. They're even better in real life."

"Okay. Thanks, Walt."

"No problem, sir."

I gotta blow off some steam. I think it's *time ta shoot some hoops.* A few minutes later, Alex stands in front of Gladiola Gaze's desk.

"Gonna shoot me some hoops, Gladdy!"

"Very good, sir. Oh, I like the new look!"

"The new look?"

"The bald Michael Jordan look, sir! You look... What do they say? *'Badass!'*"

"Thanks, Gladdy!"

"Are you getting taller, sir?"

"Hmm, I'm not sure. Try and keep the world from blowing up till I get back."

"Will do, sir. Have fun."

Ten minutes later, Alex Rett, dressed in full miniature NBA regalia, stands on the parquet floor of the White House basketball court. If one were to view him from floor level, as, say, an ant would, then he would appear to loom above like an indomitable titan. But if one were to pull back just a bit, then the official size-and-weight NBA basketball on the floor right next to him would seem like the Planet Jupiter in comparison.

The President gazes up at the rim on the backboard. It seems a mile away. And then he turns towards the great orange orb. He lets out a continuous, painful-sounding groan as he pushes against it, like Atlas the Earth. And after giving it the ol' college try, the heave-ho, and putting his back into it, inertia is finally overcome and the gigantic ball slowly rolls a foot or so away. Alex sighs profoundly. And then he takes a manly swig from his custom-made two-ounce Gatorade bottle (that arrived yesterday by special delivery).

"How was your game, sir?" Gladdy asks.

"It's a tough sport," Alex says. "Did I miss anything?"

"Tim Chopper called regarding the newest PONG video. And the Vice-President was wondering if you'd seen her P.S.A."

"Okay. Thanks, Gladdy. What time does Ace get here?"

"Ace, sir?"

"I mean *Vincent Van Go-Go...* the artist who's..."

"Yes. He's arriving in a half hour, sir."

"Good. Good. Time for a shower."

[A half hour later...]

"Hey, I like the new look!" Ace Buckland motions to Alex's streamlined baldness.

"Thanks!"

"You look like that guy."

"That guy?"

"I can't think of his name." He shakes his head. "Are you gettin' taller?"

"That's what *Gladdy* said."

"Hmm, so... *how'd it go?* The *date?*"

"Well, first of all, your fly is open."

"*What?*" Ace looks down, sees it, zips it up. "Haha! I just walked through the White House to see the President with my fly down!"

"I'm sure it's happened before."

"So... *Candace St. Cloud...*"

"She *is* really hot."

"Didn't I tell ya?"

"But... I'm not sure if we're on the same wavelength."

"Well, actors, right?"

"She..."

"What?"

"Well, she's like the biggest snob in the world."

"I coulda told you that."

"And the biggest narcissist."

"That goes with the territory. So did you *score?*"

"I'm not sure," Alex says. "D'ya remember what you said once, about..."

"What?"

"Never mind. Did you know that the Concorde is still around?"

"The what?"

"You know, that big supersonic..."

"It *is?*"

"Apparently. And did you know that she loves Vincent Van Go-Go but hates Pete Scrotum?"

"That's cuz she never had sex with Pete Scrotum!"

Alex takes in a breath and lets it out, bewildered by the

inscrutability of all things.

"So did you make out?" Ace asks.

"Sort of."

"So did ya..."

"Ya know, let's change the subject."

"Alright, but are you gonna see her again?"

"I don't know. She's in Iceland now."

"Oh."

"*So...*" Alex looks pensively at his friend. "How do you do it, Ace?"

"Do it? Do what?"

"I don't know. You seem to be at peace in your own weirdo artist way."

"Thanks, man."

"*So...*"

"I don't know," Ace says, "I guess things got better once I decided to no longer give a fuck. I got no more fucks ta give, man."

"Well, when you're the President, you sorta *have to* now and then."

"I guess."

"So what about with women?"

There's a pause as Ace Buckland looks Alex in the eye.

"As long as you remove *The Ego* and *The Penis* from the equation, then everything becomes remarkably clear. You'd be amazed!" He smiles. "The bad news, less dates. The good news, dating sucks... Hey, ya got anymore o' that brandy?"

"Yes. And champagne from last night... Cristal."

"Cristal? The good stuff!"

"Hmm."

"But I see that bottle o' brandy beckoning." Ace walks over, grabs it, and pours himself a glass. "You want anything, brother?"

"I'm good."

"So how do *you* do it, Alex?"

"Do what?"

"You know, the *President thing...* I mean, some bullshit's always comin' at you from ev'ry direction."

"I call it '*The Many Barking Dogs*'."

"The what?"

"You're standing around minding your own business when this dog appears and it starts barking at you," Alex says. "So you go over and you see that it's hungry, so you give it some food, and it's thirsty, so you give it some water. But then you look up and there are more dogs, and then more until there's freaking dogs all over the place! And they're barking all at once, and they're all different dogs with all these different barks, and eventually all you hear is this cacophony, right? Of like a million different dogs barking at you, all demanding something."

"So..."

"So eventually you just wanna, like, put 'em all to sleep or put in earplugs or move to Tahiti."

"Tahiti sounds nice, man. So what's the deal with that new PONG video?"

"I know. It's disconcerting."

"So can't ya, like, call 'em up or sumthin'? *The Florists*, I mean?"

"With them, it's don't call us, we'll call you. But it sucks because I've actually done a few things lately that are... well, *good.*"

"Like what?"

"Like *what?* Jeez!" Alex shakes his head.

"That accord between Borneo and East Borneo that averted a nuclear war? *Me...* The rescue of that *Miniskirt Woman? Also me.*"

"But she's still in jail."

"You'll see."

"Okay, sorry."

"That's alright," Alex says.

"So I'm going skydiving tomorrow!"

"No shit!"

"Yeah! Have you ever been?"

"No way. I like *terra firma.*"

"So how's the painting coming?"

"Next time. So you like cars, Alex?"

"Cars?"

"You know... fast cars. Sports cars. Cars that go *fast...*"

"Sure."

"Good. This Friday afternoon we're goin' for a ride."

"Okay."

"So I better get back so I can finish the painting."

"Alright. Does it have any placenta?"

"Zero placenta, man." Ace finishes his 100-year-old Napoléon brandy in a single sip. "Hey, ya mind if I take this with me?" He motions to the bottle. "For inspiration?"

"Sure," Alex says.

"See ya Friday."

"*Adiós, amigo.*

As Ace walks out the door, Alex receives a text:

To President Alexander Rett:

Alex, thanks for a nice time last night. Hope it wasn't too freaky for you. I thought it was hoooot! Wait, that literally looks like hoot. Well, you know what I mean. See ya soon?

Candace

9

"We're almost ready, Mr. President."

"I'm just a little nervous."

"Nothing to worry about, sir. You're all strapped in. Let me do the rest and just enjoy the ride."

"Okay.

As their voices fade away, there's nothing but the hum of the engines.

"So how many jumps have you done?" Alex asks.

"This will be my second."

Alex tries to look up at Captain Davis's face, but since he's strapped securely to Davis' chest wearing his little crash helmet and goggles, it's an impossibility.

"You're a riot."

"Skydiving humor, sir."

"So why do they call these *crash helmets?*"

"No reason. Okay, it's time, sir... Any second thoughts, Mr. President?"

"Nope... Let 'er rip!"

"Roger Wilco."

A moment later, they're racing through space, silent and deafening. A blast of wind rushes towards him. The earth below pulls with unimaginable force. This grip of gravity and falling bodies and acceleration and Newton and Physics and *fuck Newton and Physics!* This is like the best thing *EVER!* Alex closes his eyes for a moment, only to open them again on this wonder, this marvel, that he can blast through the air, rocket-like, as a human being! The earth widens before him and he realizes that he's a time traveler. He's confounding it—destroying it with every second. He's *beyond* time. And he wants to fall forever, and forever be in this moment where nothing else intrudes.

A moment later, the ripcord is pulled, the parachute deploys, billowing above them like the rarest flower in bloom. Time has returned. And for the next few minutes, they float gracefully downwards, as the ground below prepares to receive them. While the President of the United States is floating through the wild blue yonder, Reggie Mason steps up to the counter at Black Coffee Matters, this new coffee shop in Dupont Circle.

"Good morning!" the young woman behind the counter says.

"How can I help you this fine day?"

"Aren't *you* cheerful?" Reggie says.

"It's a beautiful day... in *spite* of it all!"

"I like *that.*" He smiles. "For a second, I thought you were one o' them *Positivists.*"

"Not me." She shakes her head. "I'm very negative."

"Oh good. Then I'll have a large dark roast."

"One large dark roast comin' up! Room for cream?"

"Hell no!"

The barista laughs and offers a lovely smile. "You're cute," she says.

"Really?"

"But don't worry, I'm a lesbian."

"Ah! Cuz I was *wonderin'* why you were bein' so friendly."

"I know, right? Half the people who come in here, I wonder if they have a pulse."

"Haha! You're funny!"

"I have a feeling something good is right around the corner."

"For *America?*"

"Hell no!"

They both laugh.

"For *you!*"

"Well, actually I start my new job next week. The President's Council on Human Rights."

"Doesn't *that* sound impressive!"

"Hell yeah!" Reggie smiles.

"I'm Monique."

"Reggie."

"Well, maybe I'll see you again, Reggie."

"Yeah... Monique."

"And congratulations."

"Yeah! Thanks, man!"

"Here's your coffee. Have a great day!"

FOX NEWS

"The Mayor of Des Moines, Iowa, Millhouse Bathwater, was in the news yesterday when he made some controversial statements regarding so-called climate change.

'The way things are going, Miami and New York City will be underwater. Hell, the whole Eastern Seaboard, not to mention Los Angeles on the Pacific coast. Before ya know it, Des Moines is gonna be the new Manhattan! So I'm suggesting that investors come visit our fine city, and get in on the ground floor of something that's still gonna have some dry ground!'

"And in world news, Tasha Mistk is scheduled to be executed to-morrow in Hangry, by stoning. The President of Hangry, Er Mahgerd, has steadfastly remained silent as the world has petitioned for her release.

"And in a related story, we go to our entertainment correspondent in Hollywood, Shana Minx... Shana...'Hollywood studio heads and producers have been clamoring to secure the rights to Tasha's story. There's even scuttlebutt that blonde bombshell Candace St. Cloud is being considered for the lead role.'"

Alex Rett barely notices anything during the drive back to the White House. In his mind, he's still in the middle of a free-fall.

Getting dressed after his shower, he notices that his shirt is noticeably tighter than the last time he wore it, its sleeves inching up his forearms and the inseam on his pants markedly shorter.

[Ten minutes later...]

"There's no question about it, Mr. President," says his personal physician, Doctor Proctor.

"Cancer?"

"No. You're getting taller."

"I *am?*"

"And bigger. You're... *growing.*"

"But..."

"I can't explain it," the doctor says.

"But that's nothing new. I still can't explain how a fetus can be self-aware and become President. Some things are beyond the scope of Science."

"So I'm... So I'll get bigger?"

"Apparently. "

"But I mean, like normal-sized?"

"Who knows! But you've grown three inches since... well, since you were released from, since the incident, since that..."

"Yes."

"And you've put on weight. Your height and weight are perfectly... What's the word..."

"Proportioned?"

"Yes! Or perhaps it's proportional. Either one, I guess. Words aren't for doctors!" Dr. Proctor laughs. "So we'll measure you again in a few days and see where this is going."

"Okay, Doc."

"How tall was your father?"

"My father? He was... I'm not sure."

"It doesn't matter. That's only if you believe that genetics stuff."

"Don't you?"

"Of course! I'm a doctor!"

"Ah..."

[A few minutes later...]

"Gladdy..."

"Yes, Mr. President?"

"Can you have my tailor come by... What's his name again?"

"Mr. Taylor, sir."

"My *tailor* is Mr. *Taylor?*"

"With a 'Y', sir."

"Of course."

"How was skydiving?"

"It was... stellar."

[Alex's fingers flash over his phone...]

"Siri..."

"Hello, Mr. President! How are you today, sir?"

"Stellar!"

"Excellent!"

"Siri, what time is it now in Dahoom?"

"Hangry's capital city, sir?"

"That's the one."

"Dahoom is seven hours ahead, sir. So it's eleven PM."

"Thanks Siri."

[Alex presses the intercom...]

"Gladdy, get me that CIA guy."

"One moment, sir... Walter Borders on the line..."

"Walt! What's the news?"

"Don't worry, Mr. President. There'll be this spectacular last-minute rescue that'll be credited to that SHM resistance group. They'll be national heroes and we'll put their leader in charge after the coup."

"The *coup?*"

"*Theoretical* coup, sir."

"Ah... So Tasha Mistk..."

"By this time tomorrow, she'll be on a plane to DC."

"Excellent. Keep me posted, Walt."

"Will do, sir."

10

CNN

"Breaking news from Hangry's capital city of Dahoom. Tasha Mistk, who was scheduled to be executed today, was saved in a dramatic last-minute rescue by the SHM, the Hangarian Resistance Movement opposed to President Mahgerd's oppressive regime."

YES!

[Alex presses the intercom button...]

"Gladdy, get me Walt Borders."

"Right away, sir."

"Mr. President..."

"Walt, I owe ya a case o' beer for this one!"

"Make it Scotch, sir."

"Will do. The good stuff."

"Alright, Mr. President. Have a good day."

CNN

"Here is Tasha Mistk in Paris, about to board a plane to the United States...'I'm so grateful for the SHM. They represent everything good about my country. How it used to be, and hopefully will be again.'

CLICK...

FOX NEWS

"Tasha Mistik, safe in France after a spectacular rescue at the eleventh hour. Here she is speaking in Paris, before her flight to the U.S... 'I'm so thankful for all the support I've received from all over. It showed me that the world is still a good place, in spite of it all.'

"She sure looks like a model, doesn't she?"

"Or an actress! Word is that Hollywood has been on the phone."

'What will you do when you're in America, Tasha?'

'Go to Disneyland!'

After several hours with Mr. Taylor (his personal tailor), Alex is eagerly looking ahead to the sports car ride with Ace, when the intercom buzzes...

"Mr. President?"

"What is it, Gladdy?"

"Tim Chopper is here to see you, sir."

(Shit, I've been trying to avoid him and *"the talk."*)

"Alright..." Alex lets out a breath.

"Send him in."

[A moment later...]

"Mr. President, we should discuss this thing with PONG."

"I know."

"They've proven that they're serious, sir. I wouldn't take this ultimatum lightly."

"So you don't think we can wait this one out?"

"Sir, I... Sometimes you can't just wait something out."

"I know, but..."

"I spoke with Nash Wasserman, sir."

"You did?"

"When you were... on the critical list."

"Hmm..."

"He thinks that PONG is a front for a cabal of billionaires who..."

"Who control world events from behind the scenes."

"Yes sir."

"Maybe we should make *Dirk Fist* head of Homeland Security." Tim, feeling rebuked, remains silent.

"I appreciate your concern, Tim. I do." Alex is conciliatory. "And as always, your loyalty and... everything."

"Thank you, Mr. President."

"Intel has come up with a list of possible targets. They're all under surveillance. We'll just... wait, okay? I mean, a little longer."

Tim lets out a frustrated sigh.

"Alright, Mr. President." He gets up to leave, then pauses. "That was good news about the girl," he says, "the *Miniskirt Woman.*"

"Yes it was. So let's give it another day or two, okay?"

"Whatever you say, sir. In the meantime, I'll keep digging."

As Tim Chopper leaves, Alex takes a deep breath and slowly lets it out. He wants to feel the skydive again, but the feeling has been wiped from his mind.

[An hour later, the intercom buzzes...]

"Yes, Gladdy..."

"Mr. President, that artist is here."

"Good! Send him in!" Ace Buckland walks into the Oval Office wearing a backpack, a moderately-sized painting under his arm.

"Here it is, Mr. President! Hey, you *do* look taller..." He leans the painting against Reagan's old desk. "Drum roll, please..." With a flourish, Ace tears off the brown paper to reveal the official White House portrait of President Alexander Jackson Rett.

"So, whadaya think?"

Alex stares at it. He gazes deeply into it. His eyes skirt its edges, then plunge inside. They zig-zag and bounce around and do a few 360s and a back-flip or two for good measure. "It's... amazing," Alex says.

"Really?"

"It's... this swirly fucked-up epic hangover, but then it's this deep longing for release into chaos. But the chaos is music that becomes dissonance that gets louder and more piercing like steel-tipped arrows dipped in poison that's also the antidote."

"Ha!"

Alex moves right up against it, until he can breathe in the paint. "It's reality beyond real at the edge of itself, until it crosses over into dreams and things yet unimagined." He lets out a satisfied breath.

"Since when did you become a poet?"

"Ha!" The President smiles. "Seriously, Ace, it's not too shabby!"

"Thanks, brother!"

[Alex presses the intercom...]

"Gladdy, will you come in here for a moment..."

"Certainly, sir."

[A moment later...]

"Gladdy..." Alex motions to the new painting. "May I present *the official White House portrait.*"

Gladdy takes a step forward while cocking her head to the side. Another step as her head straightens, then another until she pauses right before it.

"Well..." Gladdy nods once, then turns to Alex and Ace. "Yes," she says. "It is everything."

"Everything?"

"It's *you*, sir. I mean, it's you and it's not you. And it's everything you are and it's all that you can be." She looks at Ace now. "And *you painted this?*"

"Yes I did."

"You, sir, are *extraordinary.*"

"Thank you," Ace smiles, overcome with uncharacteristic humility.

"I can't wait to hang it on the wall!" Gladdy says.

"Then please, do the honors, Ms. Gaze."

"It would be my pleasure, sir!"

"And Gladdy, this is Vincent Van Go-Go..."

"Call me Ace."

Gladdy offers an effervescent smile, as if her day has been illuminated. And then she exits with the painting held carefully in her hands.

"Well, *that* went well," says Ace Buckland.

"So are you ready to go fast?"

"How fast?"

"This fast!" Ace says.

He drives Alex to a country road only twenty miles from the White House, but a path on which the Gods of Speed and the Open Road hold sway.

"Faster!" Alex says. And Ace squeezes the throttle—the sound of the roaring *V-8* engine, better than sex.

The car is a 1963 *AC Cobra*, jet blue with a white racing stripe. The backpack is on the passenger seat, secured by the seatbelt with Alex inside, his head peering above the opened zipper as fresh air whizzes by. Every turn seems like this will be the one where they spin out of control. Every straightaway where the car might launch itself into the air. And after a half hour of the next best thing to skydiving, they pull into Ace's Alexandria driveway.

"Well?" Ace looks over at Alex.

"That was... *Whew!*"

"I knew you'd dig it. So, welcome to Casa Buckland." Ace grabs the backpack, and a moment later they're inside.

"So this was your parents' house?"

"Yeah, but as you can see, I redecorated."

The house is filled with paint and canvases and books and art everywhere and empty whiskey bottles and a chaotic clutter like an overflow of the imagination.

"How 'bout a drink?" Alex asks. "It's flowin' like mud."

"Haha! Where are my manners?" A few moments later, they're in the living room, sipping Kentucky straight bourbon whiskey.

"I've never been to an artist's home before," says Alex.

"You've never been anywhere, man."

"Yeah, well I mean to change that. Ya know, the world out there ain't so bad."

"You mean, the world *out there an' in here an' all over the place?*" says Ace. "The world you're finally a part of?"

"Yeah, *that* world." Alex smiles.

"You like the bourbon?"

"I do. And today in your car. And yesterday, skydiving. It all was..."

"What?"

"I mean, if there's such amazement out there, it seems almost worth it, ya know, to try an' hack your way through the bullshit," Alex says. "Just to get another of those moments."

"They are few, my friend, but potent. An' I have an extra macheté you can have, for the hacking."

"Thanks. So ya know that thing I told you, about *The Florists...*"

"Yeah..."

"I spoke with Tim today—Tim Chopper. And he wanted to know what we should do about PONG, and I... I couldn't tell him, you know. I mean, he's my Chief-of-Staff, and I told you and not him."

"Hmm..."

"It's like... I didn't wanna admit that I was powerless." Alex lets out a breath.

"I could resign, I guess. But I'm just starting to get the *hang* o' this President thing!"

"You are!" Ace smiles.

"Are those movies?" Alex points to a shelf against the wall.

"DVDs, man." He walks over and grabs one.

"*This* is who you remind me of, with your badass baldness... *Jason Statham.*"

Alex gives it a look.

"Okay," he says, "Jason Statham is acceptable." He walks over to the shelf and scans the titles... "*A Clockwork Orange!*"

"Yes!"

"And *Animal House!*"

"Bona fide classics."

"And you have all three *Godfathers!*"

"Yeah, but I never saw the third one."

"*What?* Okay, we have to watch it," Alex says. "Can we watch it *now?* And get a pizza? All that racing around made me hungry."

"Okay, Mr. President. Have you ever tried anchovies?"

"No. Are they like oysters?"

"Anchovies kick oysters' ass."

[Three hours later...]

"Well, it wasn't that bad," Ace says.

"You didn't like it?"

"Well, I *loved* Vincent! I mean, how many times do you wanna take a bite outta some douchebag's ear! An' Michael, his story, it came full circle. An' I dug that a lot. An' that scream at the end. Man oh man!"

"That always gets me."

"Sorry about the anchovies."

"Can I tell you something, Ace?"

"Sure, man."

"That scene with Michael, when he confesses to killing Fredo..."

"Yeah?"

"You remember I told you how my mom could always understand

my father... through his grunts?"

"Her telepathy!"

"Yes! So it's the inauguration, right? Did you watch it?"

"I grew up here, man. I *hate* politics."

"So do you even *vote?*"

"Now an' then."

"Okay." Alex shakes his head.

"So right in the middle of it, I start thinking of my father, how he said yes and then no and the next day he *dies?* Of a *paper cut?* Then later at the hotel, my mom asks me if it's true, if they killed her Joey."

"Through that telepathy of hers..."

"Yeah. She says she can't do it anymore, support my being President. So I say we should *call* 'em, *The Florists.* Ask 'em point blank."

"So..."

"Of course they *deny* it!" Alex says.

"A half hour later, there's a knock at the door. *Flowers for Mary Rett...* But all I see is someone's belt buckle."

"Oh, right, because you're..."

"And the next day, the world is saddened that the President's mother had a stroke right after her son's inauguration. And when they wheeled my comatose mom and me into the Oval, there was this bouquet of thirteen roses on the desk, with a card that said, *'Best Wishes'.*"

"Shit, man..." Ace notices a tear in Alex's eye.

"Are you okay?"

"Yeah, I was... Never mind." Alex wipes away the tear, then lets out a breath. "These guys are ruthless, Ace. They're efficient, and they don't leave any loose ends."

"I wish you hadn't told me that."

There's a long pause, and then Ace lets out a profound sigh. "So, you wanna get drunk?" he says.

"You read my mind, Ace Buckland. You read my mind."

Outside Ace's house, a gray sedan is parked across the street beneath a burned-out streetlight. In it is Mr. Barrows, nicely dressed in an expensive, well-tailored suit. Through an earpiece in his ear, he listens intently to every word.

11

[The President wakes up in his own bed on Saturday morning. And there's that timeless moment after waking, before the day comes in, when everything is just fine. When yesterday's mistakes are still fuzzy, and today still holds promise...]

Let's see, I remember hating anchovies and getting drunk with Ace and he said he's the world's greatest drunk driver and somehow I got back here so it must be true and why do I feel so freaking sore?

"I'm aching all over, Doc."

"It's as I suspected the other day," Doctor Proctor says.

"You're growing. It's growing pains you're experiencing."

"So I could... I could one day..."

"Perhaps."

"But you're not sure..."

"It's Science, Mr. President, and Science only goes so far."

"So what's after Science?" Alex asks.

"The abyss."

CNN

"Tasha Mistk, who was saved from execution in Hangry yesterday, is safe and sound today in Washington DC. And this Sunday, she'll be the featured guest on *The Jules Tippler Show...*

CLICK...

FOX NEWS

"Tasha Mistk, the world famous *Miniskirt Woman*, is in the United States today. Sources say that she has been offered a million dollars to pose nude for the popular online magazine *Titty-Titty Bang-Bang*.

"Ya know, that's not bad when you consider that she would've been nude and stoned to death if she hadn't been rescued. So nude, stoned to death... nude, a million dollars... I'd take the million dollars. It's a no-brainer!

"And finally, a talking cat is taking the Internet by storm. In Paris, France, a cat named Hugo spends each afternoon sitting at a sidewalk café, talking with his owner about philosophy."

"Philosophy? Ha! That's a riot!"

"I know, right? And the cat wears a little beret and smokes these little French cigarettes. The *YouTube* video has over twenty million views."

"So maybe that's the next French President!"

[Alex turns off the TV and presses the intercom...]

"Gladdy..."

"Yes, Mr. President?"

"Can you arrange for Tasha Mistk to come to the Oval this afternoon for a meeting with the President? She's in DC now."

"I'll make the arrangements, sir."

[Later that afternoon...]

"Mr. President! It's an honor to meet you, sir. Thank you so much for the invitation."

"It's my honor to meet *you*... May I call you *Tasha?*"

"Please do." At that moment, the placenta painting catches her eye. "That is amazing!"

"I know the artist," Alex says. "He's the world's greatest drunk driver."

"Oh!"

"Please, have a seat. Can I get you anything?"

"No. I'm fine, sir."

"Your ordeal, I... I can't imagine what you must've gone through." She self-consciously shrugs.

"So what are your plans? Now that..."

"I can't go back to Hangry," she says. "At least not yet."

"What about your parents? Your family?"

"My parents were both killed... in the Resistance."

"The SHM?"

"Yes."

"Brothers and sisters?"

"I'm an only child."

"And an orphan," Alex says. "Like me."

"Hmm... Our destinies choose *us*, I guess."

"Perhaps you're right." Alex offers a half-smile.

"So what would you like to do then? I mean, with your life?"

"Something that *matters?* Is that still possible?"

"So you're not going to..."

"What? Pose naked for a million dollars? Ha! Yes, that's why I did what I did."

"I'm sorry. I didn't mean..."

"No, it's fine, sir."

"The reason I ask is because I want you to work for me."

"Work for you, sir?"

"The President's Council on Human Rights needs someone exactly like you. You'll have the freedom to pick and choose the things you're interested in. The things that matter. And you'll have the resources to do something about it."

There's a pause as Alex looks at the young woman. "Well, what do you think?"

"What do I think? *Yes!* Are you *kidding?* I mean, are you kidding, *Mr. President!* Ha!"

"Excellent! You can start on Monday, if that's okay."

"Szvent szvar!"

"What's that?"

"Holy shit in Hangarian!" They both laugh.

"Thank you, Mr. President! Thank you so much!"

"My pleasure. You can get the details from my secretary out front. I look forward to seeing you again, Tasha. And seeing what progress you'll make."

"Me too, sir. Thank you."

As she leaves the Oval Office on a cloud of euphoria, Alex receives a text...

To President Alexander Rett:

Alex, hope your hangover isn't too bad. Not sure how I got home, but hey, I musta made it since I'm here. Talk to ya soon, brother.

Ace

[The intercom buzzes...]

"Yes Gladdy?"

"Sir, may I see you for a moment?"

"Well, *sure* Gladdy. Come on in."

"Sir, what you did for that young woman, especially after all she's been through, it was..."

"Gladdy..."

"It was beautiful, Mr. President."

"..."

"May I... May I *hug* you, sir?"

"Um, okay."

Gladiola Gaze walks over to the President, and then she bends down and gives him a warm, motherly hug. When she stands up, Alex notices tears in her eyes. "Are you sad, Gladdy?"

"No sir." She snuffles once, then wipes her eyes. "I'm happy."

After everyone is gone, Alex sits back in his chair, in his apartment/bachelor pad. He calls up that music program, *Medusa*, on his smartphone and types in "*Clance*." A second later, there's Mozart with a trippy, trancey, techno beat.

This day can't get any better, so I'm not gonna tempt Fate. Besides, it's Saturday. I deserve a day off.

[He presses the intercom.]

"Gladdy, can you have Manny come in, please?"

"Right away, sir."

[A moment later...]

"Manolo, mi amigo! Cómo estás?"

"Muy bien."

"Good. Good. Today I'd like some bourbon, if you would be so kind."

"Might I suggest a *Manhattan*, Alex?"

"Yes, a *Manhattan* sounds just right."

[A few moments later...]

"What do you think?" Manny asks.

"I like this. Thank you, Manolo."

"I heard what you did for that *Miniskirt Woman*, Alex."

"How'd you hear that?"

"Your secretary."

"Well, I guess I'll have to fire her." He sees Manny's distressed look. "I'm kidding!"

"I know." Manny smiles. "I'm glad you like your drink."

"I do."

"A little early, perhaps... Not that I judge."

"No. No offense taken, Manny. Sometimes it's just nice to... escape the chaos. You understand?"

"*Sí, comprendo.*"

"If just for a little while."

12

[*On Sunday morning, Alex wakes to a text...*

To President Alexander Rett:
Turn on CNN. On my way to WH.
Chopper

What now? I just woke up. And no "good morning?"

CLICK...

CNN
"... and outrage over what's being called *Slaverygate*."

Slaverygate?! WTF?

"The controversial Slavery Museum was the site of the Richmond Bombing two weeks ago that claimed thirteen lives, including the President's own mother. The museum's director, Stafford Crowe, now alleges that the *Slavery Museum* was nothing but a ruse concocted by President Rett to distract the American people from Hangarian

President Er Mahgerd's visit later that week.

'They never intended for the museum to open. In fact, the inside was completely empty. I'm sorry to have ever been a part of it. Especially because of the horrible thing that happened. I hold myself partially responsible, which is why I had to speak out now and do the right thing.'

"That was Stafford Crowe, regarding his allegations of..."

MOTHERFUCKER! How the fuck...

"In Washington, Senator Mallory Blitzen had this to say... 'What President Rett did is beyond reprehensible. It's malfeasance. It's criminal. People were injured and others lost their lives because of what amounts to a prank. I'm calling for an immediate Congressional investigation. And I'm confident that criminal charges will be brought and that the President will have to answer for this egregious offense... with impeachment and prison.'

"Mallory Blitzen, pulling no punches with..."

FUUUUUUCK!
[The intercom buzzes...]
"Yes?"
"Mr. President, Tim Chopper is..."
"Send him in!"
"Tim! What the fuck? How did this happen? I mean, this director, this... Stafford Fucking Crowe was picked precisely so that something like this would never happen!"
"I know, sir. It was Milanese."
"Mila... *Milanese?... Dom Milanese?*"
"Yes."
"But... how did he know about..."
"That I don't know, sir. He took a leave of absence after... the car incident. The last I heard, he was in Sicily."
"We shoulda destroyed him *and* his car!" Alex says.
"No one ever expected it, sir, the Richmond bombing. I mean, it

was a nothing op, that museum thing. A distraction."

"So... what do we do now?"

"We... *deny* it!" Tim says.

"It's the word of some nobody against the President's!"

They look up at the TV.

"And what's becoming known as *Slaverygate* is galvanizing Congress against President Rett..."

CLICK...

CBS NEWS

"*Slaverygate* is the word on everyone's..."

CLICK...

C-SPAN

"The latest scandal to hit the White House and President Rett's troubled administration, *Slaverygate...*"

CLICK...

PBS

"*Slaverygate...*"

CLICK...

FOX NEWS

"*Slaverygate...*"

[Alex turns off the TV...]

"Yes. Deny it," Alex says.

"I'll have Wiley set up a press conference, sir."

"Good, Tim. Some damage control."

[Two hours later in the William Henry Harrison Room, *Wiley De-Sembler addresses the Washington Press Corps, who are thirsty for blood, and who'd be baying at the moon if the moon were out...]*

Journalists: *[clamoring...]* Wiley! Wiley! Wiley!

Wiley: *[points...]*

Decker: Doris Decker, *The Washington Post...* What's the official response regarding *Slaverygate?*

Crowd: Yes! Yes!

Wiley: So-called *Slaverygate* is a complete fabrication by Mallory Blitzen.

Crowd: *[fractious murmurings...]*

Decker: And Stafford Crowe? The museum's director?

Wiley: A pawn in a blatant power-play by Senator Blitzen, who still can't get over her loss to President Rett last November.

Go Wiley! That's why you're the best.

Simon: Samantha Simon, *Time Magazine...* So you're saying that *those* are the lies... of Mallory Blitzen and that museum director...

Wiley: Of course! Who's more credible? An embittered loser? A flunky museum director? Or the President of the United States? And why in the first place would anyone want to be the director of the *Slavery Museum?* I mean, would *you* want that job? Would *any* of us?

Wiley, you have a Ph.D in Spin!

Wiley: *[continues...]* But you'd lend credence to what he has to say? I mean... okay. Ha!

Essex: Emily Essex, *Newsweek...* So if this is true, will the President bring up Mallory Blitzen on ethics violations, and the museum director on charges of slander?

Wiley: The President sympathizes with Mallory's... condition. And all I'll say is that he wishes she would seek the help she so desperately needs.

Essex: You mean *psychological* help...

Wiley: There's no shame in that. And I'm sure we *all* wish her the best so she can move on with her life. That's all. Thank you.

[Wiley steps down from the podium and exits the room...]

Get that man a cigar... *[Alex receives a text...]*

To President Alexander Rett:
Crisis averted?
Chopper

[Alex's fingers flash over his phone...]

To Tim Chopper
Looks that way. Wiley came through for us again. Good suggestion, Tim. So yes, crisis averted.
Alex

[Alex looks back at the TV...]
CNN
"And with *Slaverygate* still on everyone's minds, President Rett's approval rating has dropped from 93 to 39 in just a matter of days..."

CLICK

13

[Monday morning is a hot one in the nation's capital, the hottest so far this summer. President Rett is in the middle of a nice, cool shower when he feels a disquieting tremor beneath his feet. After toweling off, he puts on his bathrobe and turns on the TV...]
CNN
"Despite the White House press conference yesterday, there are still nagging concerns regarding *Slaverygate*..."

Give it a rest. *CLICK*...

FOX NEWS
"Hollywood starlet Candace St. Cloud was heating up Iceland

over the weekend. She's seen here dancing till dawn with Russian Monopoly champ Igor Isassky at an ultra-exclusive after-hours club in Reykjavik. *[Cut to video with voice-over…]*

"However, when asked whether the pair were more than just dancing partners, she replied that she 'literally prefers *Scrabble*.'"

WE INTERRUPT THIS PROGRAM FOR A SPECIAL BULLE-TIN… FOX NEWS

"This is the scene in Washington DC from just moments ago… *[Cut to video of the Washington Monument with voice-over…]*

"The Washington Monument has apparently been hit by a guided missile."

What the fucking hell!?

"There, in slow motion, you can see the missile coming from the left as it strikes the base of the Monument. There's an explosion with debris flying. The Monument wavers for a second, then it falls to the ground in a thunderous crash.

What the…

"Here it is again… *[Back to video…]*

Fuuuuck… *[Alex buries his head in his hands and closes his eyes…]*

"There's the missile as it flies into the base of the Washington Monument, followed by an explosion. And there you see the Monument swaying in the air, with a huge chunk of it missing from the bottom. And then it starts to topple, like a redwood that's been felled."

[Alex presses the intercom…]
"Gladdy…"
"Sir! Oh my God!"
"I know. Issue a statement, *um*… saying that… saying…"
"Yes sir. I will."

"Thank you, Gladdy."

[Alex looks back at the TV...]

"This just in. The latest video from the Chinese terrorist organization known as PONG, in which they claim responsibility for today's heinous act of terrorism...

'Dear Flaccid-Penis Capitalist Americans... We are PONG, and this is just the beginning...' *[The video cuts to a GIF of the Washington Monument being hit by the missile and then toppling over in a cloud of debris, to be repeated endlessly...]*

Shit... *[Alex watches the Monument fall for the fifth time and then he turns off the TV. The intercom buzzes...]*

"Mr. President, there's..."

"Hold all my calls, Gladdy. I need a little... a little time."

"Yes sir."

[Alex sits in his bathrobe, inert, staring into space, as he tries to keep the world out there from getting in. A half hour later, he receives a text...]

To President Alexander Rett:

I guess it's all going to Hell! I was in DC when I heard the news... Anyway, I'm at the White House now. Thought you could use a friend. How 'bout one last fast ride to clear the head? I have the backpack so we can smuggle you out again.

Ace

To Ace Buckland:

Yes please.

Alex

[Alex presses the intercom button...]

"Yes, Mr. President?"

"Gladdy, that artist, Vincent Van Go-Go, will be here soon. Please show him in."

"Yes sir."

[A few minutes later, Alex is dressed and ready to go...]

"Ace..."

"*Fuckin'-A*, those guys don't mess around!"

"No shit. Let's get the fuck outta here," Alex says.

"I *do* need to clear my head."

"Right on, brother."

[Alex presses the intercom button...]

"Yes, Mr. President?"

"After that artist leaves, please hold all my calls."

"Yes sir."

A moment later, the President is tucked away inside Ace's Buckland's backpack as they exit the Oval Office.

"He has a lot on his mind," Ace says to Gladiola Gaze, motioning over his shoulder to the Oval.

She nods once, then turns back to her smartphone and the Washington Monument continuously falling.

A half hour later, there's the comforting roar of the AC Cobra's *V-8* opening up on a country road. A raspy, kickass, snarly growl that's this FUCK YOU to *The Florists*, to *PONG,* and to everything else.

"Faster," he says, and Ace steps on the gas.

"I LOVE THIS!" Alex yells at the top of his lungs. And then he lets out what sounds like a primal scream from the depths of his soul.

Ace Buckland turns to look at his friend. "Feelin' better?" he asks.

"Yes! Yes!"

At that moment, a car appears alongside, a brand new Porsche 911, its window opened wide. Ace notices a young blonde looking at them, and an older man behind the wheel.

"Friends o' yours, Alex?"

The blonde presses a button on a key fob, but then her face contorts into a look of surprise and vexation as the Porsche's engine cuts out.

"What the fuck was *that?*" says Ace.

From the rear-view, he sees a helicopter land next to the stalled Porsche, and he swings the AC Cobra around. Five commandos armed with automatic weapons hop out of the helicopter and surround the 911. And then Tim Chopper appears as the commandos take Mr. Barrows and Carly Menteur into custody.

"It's Tim!" says Alex.

"What the fuck just happened?" says Ace.

"I believe they saved our ass!"

[A moment later...]

"Mr. President..."

"Tim..."

"I did some digging, sir. I contacted Walt Boarders, and he put his team on it. You know, the one that doesn't exist..." He smiles. "We've been keeping an eye on you and Mr. Buckland. That's how we found *them...*" He motions to the man and woman in handcuffs. "The tires on your car were rigged to blow," Tim says to Ace. "But we had their engine die instead."

"Well, *thanks,* Mr. Chopper!" Ace looks at his car, still in one piece.

"It's what we do," Tim says, his smile betraying the slightest hint of pride. "Sir..." he turns to the President. "Apparently they're not Chinese terrorists after all."

"No, I guess not." Alex smiles. "Thank you, Tim."

"You're welcome, sir. We'll see what they have to say, but..." He looks at the prisoners as they're loaded onto the helicopter. "They know the drill. They won't talk and PONG will disappear... at least for a while."

"But for *now...*" Alex looks at Tim with gratitude and admiration. "We should discuss how we play this. An address to the nation tonight?"

"Yes, Mr. President. And mention the Coalition of Freedom."

"Yes, that's good."

At this, another helicopter lands and Tim looks to Alex. "Our ride, Mr. President..."

"Yes, we have some work to do." Alex turns to Ace Buckland. "I gotta go be Presidential."

"I know. I'll see ya soon. And I *owe* ya!" Ace says. "Next time I'll buy."

"Okay." Alex smiles. "The good stuff."

ABOUT THE AUTHOR

Ranter, raver, writer, wronger, upside-downer, stirrer-upper, and topsy-turvyist… Kevin Kunundrum is an award-winning novelist, playwright, visual artist, screenwriter, one-time jazz guitarist, backwoods house-builder, old sports car enthusiast, and avid mixologist. His first novel, the literary satire *The Serial Killer's Diet Book*, was acclaimed for about five minutes when it came out in the Fall of 2001, because, for some reason, "other events" interfered. His very first book-signing was scheduled for the night of September 11th. "The Taliban ruined my career!" he insists.

After tragically losing his wife of fifteen years in 2010 to a pulmonary embolism, he wrote the memoir *Tales of Insomnia, Despair, & the Perfect Cocktail* as a way of coming to terms with her death and the overwhelming grief that followed.

His other literary efforts include: *Mudville*, a novel of violence in America where "Casey At The Bat" is turned askew and seen through the sulfurous light of Hellfire; the mash-up *George Washington Werewolf*; and *Live Nude Girls*, a postmodern exploration of identity, hope, inevitability, and how practically everything in life is a Schrödinger's Cat experiment.

The political satire, *FOTUS*, is the first part of Kunundrum's "American President Trilogy."